If Jena knew anything from ̆ ̆ ̆ ̆ ̆ ̆ ̆ ̆ ̆ ̆ this: Everything changed.

SHIFTING DREAMS

Somedays Jena Crowe just can't get a break. Work at her diner never ends, her two boys are bundles of energy, and she's pretty sure her oldest is about to shift into something furry or feathery. Added to that, changes seem to be coming to the tiny town of Cambio Springs, big changes that not everyone in the isolated town of shapeshifters is thrilled about.

Caleb Gilbert was looking for change, and the quiet desert town seemed just the ticket for a more peaceful life. He never counted on violence finding him, nor could he have predicted just how crazy his new life would become.

When murder rocks their small community, Caleb and Jena will have to work together. And when the new Chief of Police isn't put off by any of her usual defenses, Jena may be faced with the most frightening change of all: lowering the defenses around her carefully guarded heart.

Shifting Dreams is the first novel in Cambio Springs, a paranormal romance series from ten-time USA Today bestselling author Elizabeth Hunter.

praise for shifting dreams

[Hunter's] books are different and entertaining and also get a little hot. Well ok, a lot of hot. It has everything I want in a book ...a great mystery that wasn't easy to solve, a romance that took its time building up, and an array of characters that could easily keep this series going for a while.

— I Read Indie Book Blog

4.5 stars! Even better the second time through.

— Rabid Reads

Elizabeth has a talent to take a simple contemporary plot, add a pinch of paranormal and still make us feel like the characters are a bunch of normal people we all can relate to.

— Nocturnal Book Reviews

shifting dreams

A Cambio Springs Mystery

Elizabeth Hunter

To my crazy wonderful family:
I love every last one of you.
We're like the Waltons… only with a lot more wine.
Thank you for always being my soft place to land.

chapter
one

J ena Crowe narrowed her gaze at the old man, whose eyes were twinkling with mischief. The corner of his silver mustache twitched a moment before the air around him began to shimmer like asphalt on an August day.

"Joe Quinn, you better not." She lunged a hand toward him, but only caught the edge of an empty shirt before it fell to the tired, red barstool where Old Quinn's pants had already pooled. An empty straw hat was the last thing to fall to the ground. "Quinn!" Jena darted out from behind the counter.

The bell on the diner door rang, and a scurrying shadow darted toward it. Jena's grandmother almost tripped over the tiny creature as she made her way into the air-conditioning with four pies balanced in her hands.

"Goodness! Was that Joe Quinn?"

Jena ignored her for the moment, leaning down to swipe up the empty hat and charge out the door, her brown eyes locked on an old, red pickup parked under the shade of a Palo Verde tree on the far edge of the parking lot. She raised the hat and shook it in the dusty air.

"Quinn, I'm keeping this hat until you settle your damn bill!"

She saw the telltale shimmer on the far side of the truck; then Old Quinn appeared again, buck naked, sliding into the passenger seat and scooting over to roll down the window. "Aw now, Jena, don't be hard on me. I'll pay you next week. I promise. Throw an old man his pants, will you?"

"Not on your life. I hope the highway patrol gives you a ticket on the way home!"

Jena spun around and pulled the door closed to seal in the precious cool air. The temperature in the Mojave Desert was already in the 90s at breakfast time, and the radio said it would reach a sizzling 120 at the height of the day. She brushed the damp brown hair off her forehead and stomped behind the counter, reaching under the cash register for the hammer.

"That old snake," she muttered as she searched a drawer for a nail.

Devin Moon looked up from his coffee. "I always thought his natural form looked more like a horny toad than a snake."

"Shut up, Dev." She glanced up with a scowl. "And can't you arrest him for driving naked or something?"

"I probably could…" Dev glanced down at the sheriff's star on the front of his shirt. "But I just got my eggs." He went back to sipping his coffee and glancing at the messages on his phone.

"Why is there a pile of clothes here?" Jena's grandmother, Alma Crowe, had set the pies on the counter and unboxed them. "Did Joe shift at the counter?"

"Yup." Jena finally found a nail. "Right after I handed him his check."

"He still hasn't paid that tab? Sometimes I think that man has forgotten any manners his mother tried to teach him. Shifting at the counter and running out on his check. Does he have any sense?"

"Nope." Jena raised a hand and aimed the nail right through the front brim of Old Quinn's favorite hat. With a sharp tap, it was nailed up behind the register, right next to his nephew's favorite Jimmy Hendrix T-shirt. "Typical Quinns," she muttered, eyeing the T-shirt that had hung there since Sean Quinn had abandoned it—and the town —shortly after high school graduation.

Jena turned to the diner that was still half-full from the breakfast crowd. "The hat's mine until he pays his bill. Someone want to toss those clothes out to the parking lot?"

She saw Dev snicker from the corner of her eye as he sent a text to someone. Alma opened up the pie rack and slid her latest creations in. And the youngest Campbell boy, who was busing tables for her until he left for college in the fall, quietly picked up the pile of clothes and took them somewhere out of her sight.

The boy's grandfather, Ben Campbell, lifted an eyebrow and stared at the hat. "Remind me to pay my tab later, Jena."

"I'm not worried about you, Mr. Campbell." The worst of her anger taken out on the unsuspecting hat, Jena leaned over and refilled Ben's coffee. "I doubt you've run from a debt in your entire life."

He winked at her before turning his attention to Jena's grandmother. "Now Alma, what did you bring to spoil my lunch today?"

The familiar chatter of her regulars began again, and Jena put the coffee pot back to start the iced tea brewing for the day. Alma and Ben Campbell started debating the best fruit pie for autumn. Missy Marquez, heavily pregnant, coaxed her four-year-old into another bite of eggs. Robert and John McCann glanced around and debated in low voices about what sounded like plans for a new house. Jena wondered who might be moving back to town while she wiped counters, filled glasses, and took orders.

When Jena had moved back to the Springs after her husband passed three years before, the last thing she had expected was to be running the family diner full time. Cooking at it? Sure. After all, she was a trained chef and this was the only restaurant in town besides The Cave, her friend Ollie's roadside bar that sat on the edge of the highway. She expected to be cooking, but not running the place. Unfortunately, a year after she'd moved back, Tom and Cathy Crowe decided to answer the call of the road in their old Airstream and Jena had to take over. Now, her parents came back every few months for a quick visit while Jena ran the place and took care of the two boys she and Lowell had produced.

Was it the life she had planned for? No. But then, if Jena knew anything from growing up in a town full of shapeshifters, it was this: Everything changed.

Dev finally glanced up from his phone. His mouth curled in amusement as he looked at the old hat hanging on the wall. "Remind me not to piss you off. God knows what you'd nail up for everyone to see."

"Since you don't actually live here, Deputy Moon, that's a tough call. But I'm gonna say those red silk boxers I saw hanging off of Mary Lindsay's line would be the first thing."

"Is that so?" She might have been imagining it, but she thought a red tinge colored Dev's high cheekbones. It was hard to tell. Unlike Jena, who was only part Native American and still burned in the intense desert sun, Dev was full-blooded. His dark skin, black eyes, and lazy grin had charmed half the female population of Cambio Springs, including one of Jena's best friends. But then, Dev had charm to spare, even though he knew better than to try it on her.

She said, "I think Ted's coming in for lunch today. You sticking around?"

"And risk pissing off that wildcat? Nope. But I might go to The Cave tonight."

"Off duty?"

"Uh-huh. You working?"

"Sure am." She heard the cook ring the bell and slide two *huevos rancheros* over the pass. Jena picked them up and slid them in front of two old farmers talking about football at the end of the counter. "Ollie asked me to help out this whole week. Tracey's on vacation with Jim and the boys."

"I'll see you there. What are you doing with the boys if you're working all week? Your parents in town?"

"No. Christy's still home from college." Christy McCann was her late husband's youngest sister and her boy's favorite aunt. "She's hanging out this week while I'm working."

The free babysitting would only last a few more weeks. It was August, and though the boys' school had just started, the state colleges hadn't. Jena would take advantage of the extra hand family provided as long as she could. After all, it was the reason she'd moved back.

"Hey, Jena," Missy called. "Can I just get a to-go box for this plate?" Jena glanced up at the tired young mother and the preschooler with the stubborn lower lip.

"Sure thing." She carried a Styrofoam box over to the booth. "You better be nice to your mama, Chelsea."

"Thanks so much." Missy began shoveling food into the carton.

"No biggie. You feeling okay?"

A wan smile touched the woman's face. The mayor's wife was working on number four. Jena had no idea how she did it. Her two boys ran her ragged.

"I'll manage. My mom's coming over in the afternoons now."

Thank goodness for family. Jena patted Missy's shoulder and ducked back behind the counter. Her boy's aunt. Jena's grandmother. Missy's huge clan. It was a close-knit community, the one place their kind didn't have to hide.

Tucked into an isolated canyon in the middle of the Mojave Desert, miles away from the state highway that the tourists drove, was the little town of Cambio Springs. It was an isolated town, made of the descendants of seven families who had made their way west over a hundred years before. Seven families that discovered something very unusual about the mineral springs that gave the town its name.

Dev stood and walked to the counter. "Well, I'm outta here, Jen. Did you see that Alex was back in town?"

"Really?" Jena looked up from the ketchup containers she was filling and walked over to the cash register. "Have you seen him?"

"Just saw his Lexus out at Willow's." Alex McCann was one of her late husband's many cousins and one of her closest friends in high school. He'd moved, like so many of the younger people, when he went to college. Still, as the oldest McCann of his generation, she suspected he'd be back sooner or later.

"At Willow's, huh?" She gave Dev a sly smile. Willow McCann,

Alex's sister, was one of the few girls Dev hadn't bagged, and not for lack of trying. "He's probably just out for a visit."

"He still doing the real estate thing in L.A.?"

"As far as I know. There's some kind of town meeting tomorrow night. His dad probably asked him to show up."

Dev lowered his voice and glanced at Missy, who was married to the town's young mayor. "Anything I need to be there for?"

Jena shrugged. Monthly town meetings were a tradition in the Springs, and the oldest members of the seven families made up the council. It was an archaic kind of government, but when you were running a town full of various shapeshifters, normal rules of city government didn't always apply. Sure, they elected the mayor… but he pretty much did whatever the elders asked him to do.

Alma Crowe, Jena's grandmother and a member of the town council, poked into Dev and Jena's conversation. "Nothing the tribes need to be concerned about."

"You know we're always available, Alma."

She leaned down to kiss his handsome cheek. "I know. You're a good friend for asking."

The various tribes along the Colorado River had known about Cambio Springs for ages. But sharing a history of wanting to be left alone, they'd tacitly helped to keep the Springs a secret. And it really wasn't that hard. What did the outside world care about a dusty desert town in the middle of nowhere? If you weren't a resident or a friend of one, you were sure to receive a cold shoulder. Visitors, if they happened to come around, didn't stay long.

Jena's voice dropped so Missy couldn't overhear her. "It's probably just Matt pushing another plan to create jobs since the airfield shut down."

Dev said, "It would be nice if one of them worked."

The military air base that had provided half the town with jobs had shut down in the latest round of federal budget cuts, and more and more families had to move away. Moving away meant hiding. Though Jena and the rest of the town could shift at will, some of the myths were true. Come the full moon, the urge to change was almost over-whelming. Except for the oldest and strongest of them, full moons meant feathers, fur, or scales. That meant that families who moved were forced to keep secrets. And as someone who had lived "away," Jena knew just how hard that was.

"It'll all work out," Alma reassured them. "It always does."

Dev paid his bill, still glancing at Old Joe Quinn's hat hanging on the wall behind her, and whistled as he made his way out the door. The continuous hum of conversation flowed around her as Jena went about her tasks for the day. Old men argued. Mothers fed boisterous children. Silverware clattered, the kitchen bell rang, and Jena Crowe saw it all.

SHE HEARD THE DOOR SLAM JUST AS SHE SLIPPED OFF HER shoes.

"We're home, Mom!"

Aaron, her youngest and most cheerful, thundered like a small elephant down the hall. He was the picture of her late husband, Lowell. His sandy brown hair was mussed from his bike helmet, and his shirt was sweaty. The small town school was only a few blocks from the house she'd taken over from her mom and dad, but a few blocks was enough to drench an eight-year-old in sweat in 115-degree heat.

"Is Low home, too?" she asked, wondering why she only heard one child. But then, Low Jr. was almost twelve and in the full swing of human and shifter hormones.

Aaron nodded as he gave her a quick, sweaty hug. It was a good thing she hadn't showered from the diner yet. The Blackbird Diner closed at 3:00, which meant she got home from work right about the time the boys came home from school. Usually, her evenings would be devoted to homework, more cooking, and wrangling two active broth-ers, but since Ollie had asked her to help out at The Cave, her evenings had become more hectic.

Jena finally heard the door to Low's room close.

Not a word of greeting to her. Jena frowned. It was typical recently. With shifter kids, who usually had their first change in puberty, adolescence took on a whole new hairy, feathery, or scaly dimension. Low was coming up on his change; she could feel it. Or, it was just wishful thinking, because for the small percentage of kids who didn't shift, a far harsher fate awaited them.

"Aaron, homework out on the kitchen table. I'll make you a snack as soon as I get out of the shower." She walked down the hall to Low's door, which was closed. She gave a quick knock and heard shuffling inside.

"What?"

Her eyebrows lifted at the haughty tone. Jena cleared her throat and knocked again, a little louder. Finally, Low came to the door.

"What was that?" she asked.

He had the manners to look embarrassed. "Sorry, I thought you were Bear. He's been bugging me all day."

"You shouldn't be rude to either of us. Do you have homework?"

"Finished it in study hall. I just have a book report to do."

"Anything interesting happen today?"

Low shrugged.

"What does that mean?" Why did her son have to be so much like… her? Jena frowned. He was, too. From the dark hair and olive skin to the sullen expression. Her mother had enjoyed that one. Jena knew she hadn't been the easiest teenager, so it was fair. Rotten, but fair.

Low gave a tortured sigh. "Kevin shifted last night. He wasn't in school today."

"He did?" Her face broke into a grin. Kevin Smith was her friend Allie's oldest son and she knew Allie had been worried sick. He was older than Low by a year and his shift was beginning to seem uncertain. Allie and Joe had been a wreck about it. "What did he—?"

"Fox, like his mom."

"Aww." She melted. Allie would love that. She'd married another canine shifter, so her kids would always be furry, but it was nice when a child's natural form took after one of his parents. In time, Kevin would be able to shift into any canid he focused on, but his natural form, his first shift, would always be his most comfortable. It was hard to explain, but then, Jena rarely shifted out of her natural form.

Low still had a sullen expression on his face. "I'm never going to shift."

Ignoring the flutter of fear in her heart, Jena patted her son's shoulder and reassured him. "Yes, you will. Just be patient."

"Dad didn't."

She swallowed the lump in her throat. "That doesn't mean it will happen to you, Low. You know how rare that is."

Rare it may have been, but for the descendants of the seven families who *didn't* shift, life was short. Heart attack. Premature stroke. Lowell Sr., Jena's childhood sweetheart, had been lucky to make it to his late twenties before a mysterious brain cancer had cut his life short, leaving Jena with two small boys and an aching hollow in her heart that still echoed on the loneliest nights.

Low just shrugged his thin shoulders and grabbed a book out of his backpack. "I'll help Aaron with his homework. I know you have to get ready."

"Thanks, kiddo."

"Is Aunt Christy coming for dinner?"

"Yep. She'll be here around five."

"Cool."

Low walked down the hall. Jena called out to him. "Low?" He turned. "I know she lets you stay up late, and I'm okay with it for you, but make sure Bear's getting enough sleep, okay? You're his big brother."

He rolled his eyes. "I know, Mom."

"Good kid. I'm gonna get clean. Then I'll come out and get you guys a snack."

"Thanks."

HOURS LATER, AFTER A RUSHED DINNER, JENA WAS PRIMPED and ready for another night of work at the bar. Her long runner's legs were encased in skintight jeans that showed off a trim figure. She'd put on a halter-top her other best friend had convinced her to buy on a girls' weekend in Palm Springs. It was snug in all the right places and even gave the illusion that Jena had breasts, which hadn't really been true since the last time she'd breast-fed, but then, illusion was everything when it came to good tips.

Plus, it was just fun to get out every now and then. She never minded helping Oliver Campbell run his family's old roadhouse on the edge of town. The Cave was an institution and drew some of the best business in the desert. It was also the unofficial boundary of the Springs' territory. Few outsiders ever got past Ollie. They were welcome to the cold drinks and the good music, but if you weren't one of the regulars from the Springs, the Tribes, or one of the motorcycle clubs that made The Cave their home, then don't linger. And don't get too familiar with the staff.

But please, tip your waitress, because Mama needs to buy two growing boys shoes before their toes poke out of the old ones.

Jena did all right. The diner was a steady business and she didn't need much to get by. The house was family property and didn't have a mortgage. Her car was paid for. But keeping up with everything two kids needed was still a challenge some months. And that was another reason Jena dolled up and headed out to Ollie's. A few good tips wouldn't hurt the bank account.

She pulled into the back and could hear the band warming up. Despite the isolated location, The Cave had become known for some of the best music in the desert. Rock, blues, old-fashioned country. If you were an independent musician looking for a gig, then The Cave was the place to play. Ollie paid the bands decent, but the money wasn't really the draw. Saying you'd survived the tough-as-nails crowd at The Cave without bottles being thrown at you was the real prize. More than one famous musician or group had a picture on the wall that led to the bathrooms.

Not behind the bar, though. Nothing was behind the bar besides beer, liquor bottles, and the hulking form of Ollie Campbell.

"Hey, honey." Jena slipped into Ollie's office and put her purse on the bookcase behind his desk. Ollie's office was very much like the man himself. Solid furniture, an eclectic mix of decor, and quiet, soundproofed walls.

"How was your day, Jen?"

He had a pencil in his mouth and he was chewing on it. He'd been doing that since the year before when he stopped smoking.

"It was fine. You gotta stop that, Ollie. You're going to ruin your teeth."

He chuckled. "Doubtful. You know what these teeth tear up on a regular basis?"

"I'm not talking Bear Ollie. I'm talking Regular Ollie and you *will* ruin your teeth if you keep doing that. Try some gum."

"Yes, Mom."

She whacked the back of his head. "Shut up, you're two months older than me."

He just gave her a quiet smile. Quiet smile. Quiet man. If you didn't know him, Ollie Campbell might seem like a hard case. He was well over six feet tall, had dark curly hair, trimmed short, and a full beard that hid his dimples. Black and grey tattoo work decorated most of his suntanned arms and a lot of his back.

And Ollie was a giant teddy bear.

"Hey, did you hear Kevin shifted? Fox, just like Allie. Low told me he wasn't in school today."

Ollie's face softened at the mention of Allie. But then, it always had. Ever since they were kids.

"Good." He nodded. "That's real good. She was worried about that. I'm sure Joe's relieved, too."

"Yep." Ignoring the sorrowful tinge to his eyes, Jena fluffed her hair and put her hands on her hips. "How do I look, boss?"

He whistled. "If you weren't like my sister, I'd hit on you. Between the band tonight and those jeans, we should both make out pretty good."

"Good to know."

Ollie rose from his desk and ushered her down the hall. "Hey, did Old Joe Quinn really run out of the diner buck-naked today?"

"He shifted and ran when I handed him the bill. His favorite hat's nailed behind the cash register."

Ollie chuckled and shook his head as they walked down the hall and into the bar that was growing louder by the minute.

"He won't forget that one."

"Neither will I."

chapter two

The music was good. Loud, but good. The beer was cold, and Caleb Gilbert was just a little drunk. Not too much, but if he was going to make it back to his hotel in Indio that night, he'd better switch to coffee. Which was too bad, because the brunette behind the bar who'd been serving his drinks had grown a little more flirtatious with every beer. Or maybe that was wishful thinking.

The band on the stage was better than he'd expected. The hard rock with a bluesy edge was just what he'd been looking for when he'd been out the night before. The hotel bar didn't have much to offer, but the boys who'd been bragging about playing The Cave had invited him to come catch their show the next night. When he'd heard the name "Cambio Springs," Caleb knew he couldn't pass it up.

"Another beer?" The brunette was smiling at him and he gave her his most charming, crooked grin. He hadn't shaved that morning. Hadn't thought he'd be trying to impress anyone, but then Caleb knew his looks weren't what drove most women away after a few months. Looks had never been the problem. So he cocked his head at the waitress and rubbed a hand over the stubble on his jaw, then back through the curling black hair on his neck.

"I'd love one. Love to keep running up my tab for you, too, but I gotta drive back to Indio tonight. How about some coffee?"

"On the house." She smiled. "And aren't you responsible?"

"Pathologically."

She raised her eyebrows at him before sliding away to grab a mug for coffee. She'd been drinking, too, but only a couple all night. And she bantered back and forth with the scary guy behind the bar with no hint of fear. He'd been listening to the band and watching her all night. It was the best entertainment he'd had in months.

She was damn cute. Tall and lean. Long, sexy legs and nice hips that begged for grabbing. She was no girl, but then, he wasn't exactly a kid, either. Caleb Gilbert had more than a few miles on him. Over five hundred according to the odometer he'd reset when he left Albuquerque. Taking the job as a police chief in the Mojave Desert wasn't what he'd planned on, but plans change, especially when life and family got messy.

The brunette came back after arguing with a surlier customer down the bar. That had lasted all of about two seconds before the giant bartender—the owner, if he was guessing—stepped in. The woman put a cup of steaming coffee in front of him. Despite the fact that it wasn't beer, it did smell fantastic.

"Cream or sugar?"

"Just black, thanks. Who is he?" Caleb nodded at the big guy. "Owner?"

"Ollie? Yeah, his family's had this place for years."

"And who are you?"

She smiled and he blinked a little. Her smile was gorgeous. It made her eyes light up. Dark eyes. More than cute. When she smiled, she was beautiful. "I'm Jena."

"I'm Caleb. So, is Ollie your boyfriend? He seems pretty protective."

"Ollie?" She laughed. "No. No boyfriend. Ollie's like a brother. A big, snarling one if I want him to be."

"Is that right? No boyfriend, huh? That's hard to imagine."

"It wouldn't be if you knew me." She smiled again, and he let himself get his hopes up, just for a minute.

Caleb glanced at her ring finger. No ring, not even the shadow of one. She hadn't slipped it off for work. Not that he'd blame her if she did. A pretty, single girl was bound to get more tips with a crowd like this. The music kept pounding and he saw her head bobbing along.

"You like the music?" he yelled.

She shook her head. "Yeah, but that's not really what you want to ask me."

He raised an eyebrow. "It's not?"

"Nope." She leaned a little closer over the bar.

"What did I want to ask you?"

"If I want to dance." Her dark eyes were lit up with mischief.

He glanced at the owner, who was watching them—no, *him*—with suspicion. "I'd love to dance if your boss wouldn't mind."

"He won't. I haven't taken a break all night."

"Then dance with me, Jena."

"You didn't ask, Caleb."

Oh, he liked the way she said his name. Caleb stood and held out a hand. "Won't you let me have this dance, Jena?"

"I thought you'd never ask."

Jena untied her apron and stepped out from behind the bar, pointing to an imaginary watch on her wrist and mouthing "fifteen" at her boss while Caleb held out a hand.

The band had just switched to something more mellow. He pulled her toward the dance floor where several other couples were already swaying and took her in his arms, placing one hand at her waist. Just right. He liked the curve of her hip under his rough hand. It felt... nice. Comfortable and hot at the same time. She was tall for a woman, five nine at least, and he barely had to look down at her to meet her eyes, which was nice for someone over six feet.

"So, you're from Indio?" she asked.

"No." He wasn't sure he wanted to talk, but then, she was quick, too. And that was even nicer than the feel of her hand in his. Caleb liked smart women. The flirting was so much more fun.

"Aren't you the talkative one?"

He gave her a sly grin. "Sometimes."

Jena shook her head. "I bet you barely have to talk to the girls with that smile, cowboy."

"Why 'cowboy?'"

"Boots and attitude. You can always tell a man by his boots. You're not an office kind of guy. I can tell. I'd even bet you've got a hat hanging around somewhere."

He nodded. "You could say that."

"So, just passing through?"

"You could say that, too." At least for tonight. "And I left my hat in the car. My mom would skin me alive if I wore it inside." She'd skin him alive for a lot of things lately.

"Good. I've had a tempestuous relationship with hats today."

"Now that's a statement that begs a story."

She shrugged and leaned a little closer. "Maybe, but it's not one I feel like telling tonight."

Caleb pulled her a little closer. "What do you feel like doing tonight?" No way in the world could he be that lucky.

A slow smile spread over Jena's face. "Dancing."

"We're already doing that."

"And maybe kissing a cute cowboy who's passing through."

Well, well. He wasn't going to complain about that. Caleb looked around the bar. "Hold on. Let me see if I can find one for you."

Jena laughed and pulled him away from the dance floor. The band had switched to something loud and pounding as the crowd rose to its feet. Caleb followed her as she pulled him down a corridor, teasing his hands along the sliver of skin at her waist as she pushed him past the restrooms and out the back door.

He was laughing. She was laughing. Then suddenly, she put her hands over her face and shook her head. "What am I doing?" she groaned. "I don't do this kind of thing."

But she was still smiling, so Caleb grabbed her hands away from her face and pulled her in front of him, leaning against the back wall of the bar as the half-moon shone down on them.

"Hey," he said. "There's no kind of thing. No pressure. You're fun, Jena, and I don't expect anything. Dancing with you was the highlight of the night. And the band was getting kind of loud. If we just hang out here and talk, that's fine by me." He really did want to kiss her, though. He'd bet a month of the meager police chief's salary he'd agreed to that she was a great kisser.

She was shaking her head. "I'm being silly."

"So keep being silly." He drew her closer, looping a finger through the waistband of those ought-to-be-illegal jeans. He spread his legs and leaned back until they were almost eye-to-eye. "Kiss a lonely cowboy."

Jena started to smile. "You don't have a hat."

"It's all about the boots, remember?" He slowly drew her in. Her eyes weren't telling him to stop. Neither were her hands, which had come to rest on his shoulders. "Boots and attitude?"

She nodded, tilting her face up to his. "You got it."

"Yeah. I do." He took one finger and lifted her chin, angling his lips down over hers.

Sweet and hot. He almost groaned at the taste. She'd been drinking a raspberry wheat beer, and the flavor still lingered on her lips. They were soft and met his eagerly. He heard a low purr in her throat and pulled her closer; then it was all her.

She curled into him, her hands moving from his shoulders, down his chest, then around his waist. She hugged him tight and Caleb forced his hands to rest on the small of her back. His fingers teased under the waistband of her jeans, but that was as far as he'd let himself go. It was enough.

Jena was on fire. Kissing and nipping at his lips as he dove deeper into one of the hottest kisses he'd had... ever. Her mouth opened to his and their tongues danced together to the harder rhythm that pounded out the walls of the old roadhouse.

When was the last time he'd let himself enjoy a kiss like this? Jena tugged at his hair and he stopped thinking, losing himself in the feel of her hands digging into his back, her thighs resting against his, and her lips doing incredible things to his mouth.

She pulled back and her teeth nipped at the stubble along his chin. Suddenly, he was glad he hadn't shaved. She seemed to like the feel of the rough skin against hers. He felt her hand trail from his neck, along his collarbone, and up to his jaw, where she rubbed her fingers against his chin and made that damn purring sound again. If he had his phone out, he'd record it; it was so sexy.

"You're just passing through, right?" she whispered in his ear.

Should he tell her? The responsible part of him said yes, but then she might stop kissing him.

Caleb murmured, "Something like that." Then he dove back in.

MATT MARQUEZ WAS EXACTLY WHAT CALEB HAD EXPECTED from a small town mayor. He was friendly in an "aw-shucks" kind of way. He had a starched polo shirt and a pair of khakis from JC Penney. His secretary was old enough to be his mother and he had a picture of a beautiful blonde with three small girls displayed prominently on his desk.

Mayor Matt saw Caleb examining the photograph with bleary eyes. "My wife, Missy. And our three girls. We're having a boy next month."

Matt and Missy? Caleb cleared his throat. "Congratulations."

"Are you? Married, I mean. You didn't mention…"

Caleb shook his head, pushing down the instinctive bitterness. "Divorced. No kids." And hadn't that been the sticking point? "It was years ago. We were young."

Matt nodded. "Missy and I were high school sweethearts. It's a small town."

Well, that much had been obvious on the drive in. After a late morning filled with very distracting dreams about a certain brunette, he'd driven up from Indio for his meeting with the mayor of Cambio Springs. After the meeting, he was being introduced at some kind of town hall meeting that night. It seemed unusual to him, but then, he had little experience with small-town police procedures. He wasn't even sure where he was going to be working. Caleb had yet to see a police station anywhere near Main Street.

"I'd just like to thank you again for taking this job." Matt was smiling nervously. "Honestly, someone with your credentials—"

"It's nothing. Really. I was looking for a change."

"Still..." Matt laughed. "I mean, state police commendations. Special task force experience..." Matt frowned. "Can I ask why you wanted to leave Albuquerque for a small town in the middle of the desert?"

Caleb let the stony expression he'd perfected over twelve years of police work slide over his face. "I told you. I was looking for a change."

Matt, seeing that the subject was off limits, quickly backtracked. "Well, we're lucky to have you! The most likely crimes you'll see around here are the occasional vandalism charge and drunk driving."

"And domestics, of course. In my experience, those are everywhere."

That brought Matt up short. "Well... there's some of that, of course, but it's pretty rare. We're a small town and most people look out for each other. Pretty close families."

"That's good." Caleb narrowed his eyes at the squirming man. "Mayor Marquez—"

"Please, call me Matt. Everyone does." The young mayor was a little disappointed by that, if Caleb had to guess.

"Matt, why did the city council decide to hire a police chief? Honestly, it sounds like the sheriff's department was doing a good job taking care of the stuff you needed done."

"Well"—Matt nodded nervously—"the sheriff's department is excellent, of course. But I believe some changes are coming to the community that will make it beneficial to have our own *independent* police force."

"Changes, huh?"

"Not anything I can talk about right now. And you'll meet the council tonight when I announce your hiring."

Caleb blinked. "Wait. The city council doesn't even know you hired me?" He leaned forward. "What do you mean? Who approved the funds for my salary?"

"I did." Matt smiled. "I have... discretionary funds in the budget to cover it. Please don't worry about being paid, Chief Gilbert."

He wasn't worried about the money. He really didn't need it, but the idea of being thrown into the deep end of unfamiliar small-town politics irked him. "I don't want to be seen as an intruder here."

"You will be." Matt shrugged helplessly. "There's no avoiding that, I'm afraid. Like I said, this is a very small town. An old town with old families and there's no one we could have brought in that wouldn't feel like an outsider, at least for a while."

"Why not hire from within, then? Surely there were people who might have some connection—"

"I didn't want a connection," Matt said firmly. "The town needs fresh blood. We need new perspective. People need to be more accepting of change and part of the change is you, Chief. I hope it doesn't scare you off, but eventually, everyone will adapt." Another campaign-worthy grin crossed the young man's face. "It's a very friendly place, once everyone gets to know you. I promise."

"Right." Somehow, Caleb had a feeling this was going to be far harder than the mayor hoped. "Right."

AFTER AN ABBREVIATED TOUR OF CAMBIO SPRINGS' SMALL downtown and a trip out to the "station house," which was really an abandoned building between the town and The Cave, Caleb and Mayor Matt pulled into the parking lot of a small building with a cross on top.

"A church?" he asked. "You have your town meetings at a church?"

"Non-denominational," Matt explained. "More of a chapel, really. We're not big enough to have many houses of worship, so it kind of rotates. The Catholics have a week, then the Baptists. We just take turns."

Caleb nodded. It was unusual, but admirable, in a way. "Well, good for you. And everyone will be here?"

"I'm sure they will. Town meetings tend to be very well attended."

There sure were plenty of cars in the parking lot, more than one he recognized from The Cave the night before. Was one of them Jena's? He'd finally left the bar after another ten minutes of making out and still another hour chatting at the bar and wanting to get her alone again. She was fantastic. Caleb had been looking for signs of her everywhere they went that day, but so far, no luck.

Plus, he had a sneaking suspicion she wasn't going to be thrilled to see him.

As he mounted the steps, he looked up. An old cross hung over the doors and Caleb sent up a quick plea that, somehow, he'd see Jena again. And that the first crime he investigated in his new job wouldn't be an assault on him for lying to her. He hadn't really lied.

Exactly.

Matt opened the doors and the blessed air-conditioning poured out. The two men stepped into the small foyer and Caleb blinked as his eyes adjusted to the light. The first thing he really saw was a beautiful stained-glass window at the front of the church with a lion lying next to a lamb. The next thing he saw was a room full of people. And very near the front, just to the left of the aisle, was the flushed face and furious eyes of the beautiful woman he'd been kissing the night before.

Caleb grinned and caught her eye. What do you know? Heaven was smiling on him after all.

chapter
three

Jena's eyes widened for a second before she spun around and tried to slouch down as far as she could in the hard church pews.

"God hates me," she muttered.

Allie frowned down at her. "What are you doing? And I'm pretty sure you're not supposed to talk about how God hates you when you're in church."

Ted was craning her neck to stare at the handsome stranger. "Who is he? He's hot. Hot men never come to the Springs. Is he lost?"

Allie said, "Alex is hot. Weren't you just talking about how good he looks since the last time—"

"Shuuuut up, Allie, his mother is sitting right across the aisle from you. And technically, Alex doesn't live in the Springs anymore."

"Shut up, both of you," Jena hissed. "That lying asshole!"

"Jena, language!" Allie said, motioning around them to the normally comforting walls of Cambio Springs' only house of worship. "And what did Alex lie about? Have you talked to him since he's been here? Joe said he only got in yesterday. Did he come into the diner?"

"Not talking about Alex."

Jena could almost feel Ted's eyes boring into the side of her head as she tried to slouch farther down in the seat. It was fairly difficult considering how tall she was. She'd never wished for Allie's petite figure more.

The small church buzzed with the normal chatter that usually preceded Elder meetings, though slightly quieter and more guarded since a stranger was present. It wasn't unheard of for someone to visit a meeting. Outsiders could stay for the first part. Then they were politely escorted out so the real meeting could begin.

The seven oldest members of the original town families sat up in the front of the church at a table that had been set up. The two McCanns, Jena's Grandmother Crowe, Old Mr. Campbell and Old Joe Quinn. Despite his dubious reputation and propensity to run out on his diner tab, he was still the oldest member of the reptiles, and some traditions did not change. Paula Leon was also there sitting next to Ted's Grandpa Vasquez.

Most of the elders were just that, old. Shifters who lived a normal life and stayed in the Springs got around one hundred and twenty years of robust health, not that an outsider could tell by looking at them. Jena's grandmother didn't look a day over seventy. It was the way of things. Her grandfather had died almost thirty years before, but he was from away and Jena didn't remember him. The rest of the people in attendance were mostly shifters. Most spouses and other residents weren't required to be there.

In Cambio Springs, you were born a shifter, you married one, or you occupied one of the truly rare "friend who could keep a secret" spots. And most shifters married outside the town, which was a good idea if you wanted to avoid that pesky inbreeding problem.

Hey, honey, do you love me? Let's get married and move to the desert so our children can turn into coyotes and grow up among their peers. It'll be fun!

No wonder so many people stayed single.

"Jena..." Ted began. "Why are you trying to do an impression of Norman Quinn?" Norman's natural form was a desert tortoise. Needless to say, getting stuffed in a locker by the McCann boys happened on a regular basis.

"Shut up. Does he look like he's staying for the meeting? God hates me."

Allie said, "Why do you keep saying that? And he's taking a seat in the back row, so yeah, it looks like he's staying."

"Why are you...?" Ted's laser beam eyes narrowed, then widened in excitement. "Oh! He's the Hot Cowboy, isn't he?"

Jena slapped her hand over Ted's mouth. "Shut. Up."

"The amazing kisser?" Allie whispered, leaning closer to Jena. "You said he was from Indio."

"Obviously," Jena said through gritted teeth, "I was somewhat misled about that."

"Oh." Allie's blue eyes narrowed and her bow mouth tried its best to look severe. "He is an ass—*suming* person." She changed course when Ted's mother, Lena Vasquez, glared at her from the first row. "To... *assume* that you would not find out about him... not being from Indio."

Ted snorted as Jena pulled her hand away. "Nice save, Allie. Awkward, but nice."

Jena said, "At least she didn't announce my embarrassing make-out session to the whole town, like some people."

"I don't remember you describing it as embarrassing." Ted shifted so she could look over her shoulder again. "'Mind-numbing.' 'Fantastic.' Allie, I missing anything?"

"Something about him doing more with his lips than most men could do with their—"

"Why am I friends with either of you?" Jena hissed again. "Shut up. My grandmother is already looking at me."

Ted murmured, "He's way hotter than you said, Jen."

Ted's mother glanced back and lifted a curious eyebrow. "You know the visitor, *mija*?"

"No," Jena said.

"Yes," Allie said at the same time. "He came into The Cave when Jena was working last night. They were—"

"Flirting," Jena interrupted. "You know... just flirting. Kinda."

Ted smirked. "Is that what they're calling it now?"

"Don't tease your friend, Teodora. And all three of you girls turn around and stop giggling. The meeting is about to start. Jena, we'll find out why your new friend is here soon enough."

Kill me now. Ted's mom knew, which meant all the cat clan would soon know. Lena's mother would tell her Grandma Crowe. Then word would trickle down to the Quinns...

"Shit."

Ted muffled a laugh and Jena elbowed her. Allie was blushing a little, still embarrassed to be corrected, even at age thirty-two.

Soon enough, Robert McCann, Alex's father and the unofficial head of the council, opened up the meeting with a short prayer and the Pledge of Allegiance. "Now, I'd like to give the floor to Mayor Matt," Robert said. "He's got a visitor tonight that he'd like to introduce. Matt?"

Poor Matt, Jena thought for the thousandth time. In another life, he'd probably have a great future in politics. He was bright and charming. He tried to promote progress in a way that Cambio Springs desperately needed and just as desperately resisted. He had a beautiful, supportive wife and family. Matt Marquez could have gone far.

Unfortunately for his political future, he didn't have another life; he had one where he turned into a bobcat every few weeks and had to contend with the female-dominated cat clan who populated much of the Springs. Matt Marquez was a cat shifter from the Leon family who had married into the Vasquez clan, knowing full well he would never escape the town once he did. The cats, like the wolves, rarely wandered far.

"Hey, folks!" Matt stood and walked to the front with a confident step. "There are some exciting things going on. As many of you know, since the base closed down, we've been applying for a lot of federal money to get some more development in town and create jobs."

Matt paused, but you could have heard a pin drop, so he continued. "Well, I'm happy to say that a lot of those grants are coming through! And one of the things they're funding is our own police station." A few quiet rumblings started among the Quinns in the back of the room and Jena's senses came alive with tension.

This was not good.

Matt was still talking. "While we've been making do with the sheriff's office, our own dedicated police force is something we've needed for a long time."

Ollie's deep voice may have been quiet, but it carried throughout the room. "For what?"

Matt looked irritated. "Well… for a lot of reasons. It's better in an emergency if we have our own—"

Ted interrupted this time. "What emergencies? Between me and the volunteer fire fighters, we have most of the regular stuff covered."

Matt held up his hands and nodded. "Ted, I agree. For medical emergencies and any kind of rescue work, you and the fire department do an amazing job. We're lucky to have you. But in other cases, the sheriff's office—"

"There a crime spree happening we don't know about?" someone— Jena thought it was one of the Quinns—piped up from the back.

"I don't know. Why don't you ask your brother?" another voice answered. Scattered laughter spread across the room. Jena glanced back at Caleb-who-was-not-just-passing-through. He had an amused expression on his face and was watching the room with measuring eyes.

"Aren't you responsible?"

"Pathologically."

He was a cop. He was *their* cop.

Jena died a little inside. Shit. There was a reason she didn't date. She didn't have time and she didn't particularly want her personal life spread around any more than it was already. Everyone in the room had known her since she was born. She was Lowell's widow. Low Jr. and Aaron's mom. Tom and Cathy Crowe's daughter. Max and Beverly's beloved daughter-in-law. The owner of the Blackbird Diner. A responsible, hard-working, single mother.

And she wasn't known as a woman who fooled around with strange men at The Cave.

"Stupid, stupid, stupid."

One lonely night. One irresistible grin. Jena had given in to a passing impulse and was now, no doubt, going to be thrown into the deep end of the Cambio Springs' gossip pool.

Matt was trying to regain the attention of the church. "Everyone, I know that this is going to be a change, but—"

"What about Dev?" Ollie asked in his attention-commanding voice. "Dev's in the sheriff's department, and he's always made the Springs a priority if we need anything. I still don't understand why we're wasting the money on some cop from who-knows-where."

Jena glanced around. No one was arguing with Ollie. They rarely did. When the quiet man offered his opinion, people listened and they generally did what he said. Just then, she saw Alex McCann rise to his feet.

If Cambio Springs had a golden child, it was Alex McCann. Oldest son of the oldest son, Alex was the descendant of the elder McCann brother, one of the two Confederate veterans who had come west with a mismatched group of families to the isolated springs in the middle of the Mojave Desert. The McCanns became the wolves and other canine shifters. If her husband Lowell had shifted and survived, he would have given his loyalty to Alex. If either of her sons shifted into a wolf— which they had a fifty percent chance of doing—they would belong to the McCanns. The wolves were the unofficial alphas of Cambio Springs and, other than the cats—who had no loyalty to anyone but themselves —they led and others followed. Alex was the heir apparent.

And he was also one of her closest friends. He may have lived away for now, but everyone knew he would end up back in the Springs. It was his town.

Alex walked up to the table, leaning casually against the podium set off to the side.

"Hey, everyone. Hope you're all doing okay tonight. Thanks for coming out. I know this meeting was kind of last minute."

Jena could see the expression around Matt's eyes tighten. He wasn't pleased, but he wasn't going to say anything, either.

Matt said, "Thanks for stepping up, Alex. Maybe you could explain a little better—"

"You know, folks, I think this is a good move."

Alex was being deceptively casual. He was putting on the easygoing charm that made him such a successful real estate investor in Southern California. When Alex McCann wanted to get his way, he didn't try to convince you. He just explained things in such a way that you came to the decision all by yourself.

"I think things in the Springs are changing for the better. We're going to be having some investment coming in soon. Some new challenges come along with that. It's just my opinion, but I think Matt's made a good decision here."

"What kind of changes?" Ollie asked.

Jena saw the two old friends exchange some wordless conversation before Ollie's shoulders relaxed a bit, and he settled in his seat.

Alex continued. "And I think the mayor's done a hell of a job picking a new chief of police. Caleb Gilbert—Caleb, do you mind coming up?"

Alex lifted a hand and Jena stiffened when Caleb-who-was-kind-of-a-liar walked up to the front of the church. If possible, he was even better looking in full light. The previous night at The Cave, she'd been attracted to his smile first. He had a gorgeous full mouth that kept lifting at the corner, like he was amused by a private joke. She knew she'd never seen him before, but something about him seemed familiar. He had angled features that hinted at some Native American blood, a mess of wavy brown hair, and eyes that were almost black in the low light of the bar. But it was his mouth, those unexpectedly full lips curved up with mischief, that had dragged her attention back to him over and over again as she worked. She saw him peeking at her from the corner of his eye as he walked toward the front.

"Nice ass," Ted whispered.

"Nice boots," Allie said. "No wonder you—"

"Please, shut up."

Actually, on second thought, Caleb-with-the-*superb*-ass-and-boots didn't walk. He swaggered. Jena narrowed her eyes. Yep, that was definitely a swagger. A cocky one. One that said, "I'm going to blow your mind with my kisses, then hang around for another hour looking tempting." Okay, maybe it only said that to her. Jena peeked at her two best friends, one of whom was married and the other who claimed no man would ever live up to her exacting standards. Two sets of eyes followed Caleb intently.

Never mind, apparently the swagger was a universal language.

She was an idiot for thinking she could have one crazy night without consequences. It may have been just a kiss—or a few—but Jena Crowe was not the kind that usually gave in to temptation that way. It was one thing when he was a cute guy passing through town that she'd likely never see again. Someone who lived in the Springs? No way. She was just going to have to pretend the new chief of police didn't exist.

And really—her shoulders slumped a little—Caleb-who-really-was-an-amazing-kisser would move into town, take one look at the myriad family, community, and professional obligations heaped on Jena's shoulders and back away quickly. It would be more like a fast jog than a swagger, if she had to guess.

Matt took over. "Everyone, I'd like you to meet Caleb Gilbert, former decorated detective of the Albuquerque police department. Caleb here was on several very prestigious task forces before he decided to make a move to California. We're very lucky to have him. He was instrumental in—"

"Good evening." Caleb stepped in front of both Matt and Alex, easily drawing the attention of the curious crowd. "I'm pretty positive your mayor and Mr. McCann will paint me in a far better light than I deserve." Caleb offered a friendly grin to the crowded church. "The simple fact of the matter is I'm really looking forward to making this my home. I lived in the city for years and... well, I never really got used to it to tell the truth. I'm from a small town myself."

That would explain the boots and the attitude, Jena thought. In her experience, men who carried themselves like Caleb Gilbert hadn't grown up in the cushioned comfort of air-conditioning and smooth roads. The holes in his jeans weren't put there by the manufacturer.

"Anyway, I'm sure I'll have a lot to learn about all of you, and I'm looking forward to that. I've been informed that Jeremy McCann here" —Caleb nodded to one of Alex's cousins near the front— "is going to be my deputy, and I'm looking forward to working with him."

Well, that part made sense. Jeremy and his wife were expecting their first child. He'd been living near San Bernardino and working in the police department there, but McCanns always moved back to the Springs when they had kids.

"Anyway, I don't want to draw this out. I have a lot of work to do, organizing everything from the ground up, but, like I said, I'm looking forward to it." Then Caleb grinned. His eyes deliberately sought hers and locked, just for a second, before they continued on their friendly journey. "I'll go ahead and let you all talk behind my back now." That drew a low laugh from the crowd. "And I'll be on my way. Deputy McCann and I should have the station open early next week if any of you want to stop by. Consider the door open to anyone who's curious." Then Caleb tipped his head in a fashion his mother would approve of and turned to shake Matt and Alex's hands.

His new deputy rose and met him at the back of the room before the two walked out into the night. Silence blanketed the church. Jena could hear some shuffling papers and feet, but not a single person spoke.

Ted mumbled, "Wait for it…"

Outside, the engine in Jeremy's truck started. Low voices drifted in the wind. One door slammed. Then another. The sound of spitting gravel hit the night air and a few moments later, the telltale retreat of the old Dodge could be heard by everyone in the church.

The silence was broken by Elder Gabe Vasquez glaring down at Matt and Alex. His voice boomed through the silent desert night.

"Will someone please explain to me what the heck just happened?"

chapter
four

As Caleb drove away from the church with his new deputy, he cracked open the window to let the creosote air flow into the pickup truck. It was monsoon season in the desert and a quick intense burst of rain had come during the meeting he'd just left. He didn't know quite what he had stepped into, taking the chief's position in this odd desert enclave, but he knew one thing: he wasn't bored. And that was a good thing, because a bored Caleb Gilbert wasn't fun to be around.

Jeremy McCann drove the truck over the rutted gravel road that led toward the old concrete block building that would be their station, once they cleaned it up. Caleb decided he liked the quiet man already. He had the lean, confident look of a man who could handle himself in a fight and the intelligent eyes of a born cop who'd try to avoid the conflict in the first place. Yes, he liked the idea of Jeremy backing him up. The young deputy had worked for four years for the San Bernardino County Sheriff's department, but was moving back to his childhood home. A young cop who would appreciate Caleb's experience and a local who would set the rest of the town at ease. Jeremy McCann might just be the saving grace of this tangled mess Mayor Matt had dumped him in.

"So," Caleb finally said, "think they're talking about me yet?"

A smile lifted the corner of the young man's mouth. "The question is are they *still* talking about you? Or have they moved on to Alex's latest scheme?"

"Alex McCann has a scheme?"

Jeremy chuckled. "My cousin always has a scheme."

Caleb narrowed his eyes. "Just what percentage of this town are you related to, McCann?"

"Call me Jeremy. Really, there's too many McCanns around to call me by my last name. And the answer to your question is... probably a quarter, though a lot of that is distant. All the McCanns claim relation one way or another. And then, over the years there's been people move in and move out. The main families you have to know in the Springs are the McCanns, the Campbells, the Vasquezes, the Crowes, the Leons, and—the ones you'll meet the most—the Quinns. That's the seven families who founded the town."

Caleb's instincts buzzed for the second time that night. The first had been when he'd set eyes on Jena. There had been a second, just as she'd turned and he caught the angle of her jaw, that the woman was familiar on a gut level. He'd known her, or at least recognized her from a long time ago. If he were still in Albuquerque, he'd think she shopped at the same market or took the same route he did on the way to work. Then the moment passed, and she was just the pretty woman he'd had the distinct pleasure of flirting with the night before.

"Seven families, huh?"

"Spread out and diluted now. Lots of new families have come in over the years. Most tend to go away, then come back after we get married and have kids. It's kind of a hard place to pull away from completely, if you know what I mean."

"I know exactly what you mean."

He'd watched her. Watched her try to avoid him. Watched her friends needling her quietly, knowing it meant she'd talked about him. He liked the idea. He liked the idea a lot. And it was a small town; no doubt he'd run into her again.

"What family does Jena belong to?" Caleb asked.

She'd belong to one. After she'd overcome her initial embarrassment, the woman had watched him with the rooted confidence of an insider as he'd spoken to the assembly. Caleb was careful to play up his small town credentials, which were entirely genuine, if very much in the past. You didn't get much smaller than a town in the checkerboard of Northwest New Mexico. He'd escaped his grandmother's home on the Navajo reservation as a teenager, but if someone mentioned the word "home," the dusty town was still what sprang to mind.

"Jena? Jena Crowe?" Jeremy's eyebrows raised in amusement. "Where did you meet... Oh, you went to The Cave last night, right? She's helping Ollie out this week."

Caleb shook his head. "I forgot how creepy it is, knowing everyone's business like it's your own."

Jeremy chuckled. "Jena's a few years older than me, but she's one of Alex's best friends. And she runs the diner. Everyone knows Jena."

"Jena Crowe." He liked the sound of it.

"Technically, she might be a McCann, but I don't think she ever changed her name when she got married."

His head whipped toward Jeremy's. "She's married?"

"Widowed."

The instant of relief was taken over by a weight in his chest. She was too young for that.

Jeremy continued. "She goes by Crowe now. A lot of girls from the Springs don't change their names to begin with. The Crowes own the Blackbird Diner on Main Street. Her grandmother is one of the council members who runs things."

"Ah." Not just an insider, but an important one. Interesting. "The diner, huh?"

"Yeah. She's..." Jeremy chuckled. "Good luck with that one."

Well, things just got more and more interesting. "I like a challenge."

"You'll get one."

"Claws?"

Jeremy grinned. "Talons."

THEY PULLED INTO THE GRAVEL PARKING LOT IN FRONT OF the old building. Jeremy flipped on the truck's light rack, which flooded the front of the building. An enormous owl was perched on the porch railing, as if waiting for them. It gave an eerie blink, then flapped its enormous wings and soared into the night. Caleb heard Jeremy muttering under his breath.

"What's that?"

"Nothin'. The place will be good once we get it cleaned up. Let me make sure the lights are working." He took a flashlight from the door pocket and clicked it on; then he ambled around the side of the old building surrounded by cactus, scrub brush, and hairy-looking yucca plants that looked like they needed a shave. Jeremy walked back around after a few minutes and waved to him; then he opened the door and flipped on the lights of the old building, flooding it with the cool, buzzing glow of old fluorescents. Caleb got out, the wet gravel crunching beneath his feet.

"What did you say this was? The building, I mean?" He stepped through the door. It was dusty and cluttered, but not as bad as he'd imagined. It needed paint, but the old block walls were in good shape and would stay cool during the worst of the heat. It was a solid building. He nodded in satisfaction. He'd worked in worse.

Jeremy was already tossing empty boxes into a corner. "It was a sheriff's station for a while. Maybe... thirty or forty years ago? But then, there wasn't really enough money to keep it running, and not enough reason, either."

"I'm still not quite sure why the town hired me." He joined Jeremy, moving old boxes to one corner while he kicked a mummified rat toward the open door. "It sounds like there's not much crime."

"I don't think there is. I'm not asking too many questions, to be honest. I'm just glad I'm not going to have to commute to Barstow with a new baby at home."

Caleb felt guilty. He may not have had a life, but Jeremy had a nice wife at home whom he spoke about in glowing language. She was five months pregnant.

"You don't have to help me do this. I'm still gonna drive back to Indio tonight and I don't want to—"

"It's no big deal." The young deputy shrugged his narrow shoulders. "Brenda's staying with her mom in Hesperia for the week while I get our house set up here, so there ain't nothing waiting at home for me except beer and reruns on the TV."

Caleb looked around the dusty office and grinned. "That doesn't sound bad, actually."

Jeremy laughed. "No, it doesn't. But this has got to be done, and it'll be easier to do it now, when it's not so hot."

"Speaking of that..." The building was stifling, so Caleb walked over to the windows and tried to pry them open. One moved. The other was stuck. But the two on the other side of the building opened and created a nice cross breeze, clearing out the dead air and filling the station with the earthy scent of rain and creosote.

Caleb took a deep breath. Much better.

"Now, I think..." Jeremy began fiddling with some old keys at the back door. "This part of the building was added on. There are a couple holding cells back here that..." One of the keys finally worked and the metal door opened with a screech. "Nice! Come take a look, Chief."

"Call me Caleb."

"Eh... I'd better call you Chief. You're going to have a hard enough time as it is with these folks."

"Why does that not surprise me?" Caleb walked through the door and into what felt a lot like a walk-in refrigerator. It wasn't quite that cold, but almost. Despite the stuffy air, the room felt refreshing. He ran his hands along the smooth walls around him. "Is this...?"

"Adobe. The old kind." Jeremy smiled and looked around. "This must have been a house at one point. Look how small the rooms are. They turned it into cells. Clever. The walls are thick. The windows are small."

Caleb nodded. The rooms were dark, but the flashlight showed two rooms, one of which was split into two cells with thick old bars and the other, which he supposed they could use for a break room or an interview room, should the need arise. "I can tell you one thing. When it's one hundred and twenty degrees out there, the prisoners are going to be nice and comfortable."

They both laughed, but Caleb knew it was true. His childhood room at his grandmother's house had been in the old adobe part of the house. With clay walls over a foot thick, the old construction kept cool air in better than any modern insulation. And in the winter, a heated adobe room stayed nice and cozy.

"Why did we stop makin' houses out of this stuff?" Jeremy mused.

"Hell if I know. Took too long to build. Too expensive, I guess."

"A lot of the older houses in the Springs still have parts that're adobe. The families that built 'em still own them, so they've stayed in good shape."

Caleb narrowed his eyes and walked back in the front office. There it was again. That instinct sparking. Something about this town was… off. Not quite right. There was no other way to explain it. Things weren't as they seemed. But he had no idea what it was that was different. Had no idea why he even felt that way. Shaking his head and diving into another pile of old boxes, he focused on the task at hand.

He had a lot of work to do before he had time for idle speculation.

CALEB DREAMED THAT NIGHT. SOFT, DRONING SONGS THAT floated over a dark desert. Sparks catching fire and the smell of burning sage. He ran. Bare feet slapping in the dust, leaping over dry brush and small ravines. Running from someone.

Something.

Then four paws touched the ground and the smell of the desert sharpened.

The moon was full and vivid over his head as he ran.

The old songs drifted. Twisting in the night air. Filling his mind with the old stories. Dark fears and warnings.

Cold clung to him.

A shadow crossed the moon over his head. He lifted his nose and caught the scent in the air.

Prey.

No, not prey.

Something else.

Something…

The song grew louder.

Louder.

He ran faster.

It was chasing him.

The singing broke off and all he heard was the wind whistling past the red canyon walls. The hawk's scream pierced the night air, and Caleb woke with a choked gasp, sweating in the chill of the air-conditioned hotel room.

chapter
five

It had been ten minutes since Jeremy and the new Cambio Springs Chief of Police had left, and the church was still awash in angry voices.

"—just blindside us like this, when we ought to—"

"This should have been a community decision, Matt. Why wasn't there some kind of vote or—"

"If we really need this, then why don't we just have Jeremy do it? Other than the fact that he's a McCann and all—"

"—no sense. No sense at all bringing some outsider in. What was he thinkin'?"

Jena sighed and leaned closer to Ted. "This isn't going to end well."

"What is Alex up to?" her friend muttered. "This has Alex all over it. What does he think he's doing?"

Allie leaned over. "Have you talked to him since he's been back?"

Jena said, "Allie, Ted and Alex meeting up either ends with shouts the whole damn town can hear, or no talking at all, if you know what I mean."

Ted curled her lip. "Shut up, cop-kisser."

"Hey!" She looked around. Luckily, no one was paying attention to them. "Will you keep your voice down?"

"No one's eavesdropping on us, *chica*. Oh…" Ted narrowed her eyes. "There he is. Sneaky bastard, what are you up to?"

Jena's eyes shot to the front of the room, where Matt was trying to answer questions piled on top of questions. The meeting was quickly spiraling out of control, until Alex McCann stood up and held his hand in front of Mayor Matt.

"Matt, be quiet and let me handle this."

Jena winced internally at the slap. *That was stupid, Alex.* Her eyes shot to Missy, who was sitting a few seats down in the row in front of them. Missy looked tense and even more pregnant than when Jena had seen her yesterday. She caught the slight snarl at Alex's slight of her mate. Matt may have not been an alpha to the wolves, but the cats were highly territorial and very, *very* proud. Matt was one of theirs. Two of Missy's sisters leaned forward, but Missy reached out to calm them, and they relaxed.

Alex ignored the harsh reactions of the cat clan and lifted his voice.

"All of you, quiet!" It wasn't instantaneous, but the room slowly settled down. "Now, you've got questions and we've got answers. But none of them are going to get asked or answered unless you all calm down. First, I'd like to ask any of the Elders if they have a question for me right now."

Nicely played.

The Elders usually stayed out of any town debate, but in the end, they were the ones who voted. And any vote had to be unanimous, or it didn't pass. If a single building permit was held up because one of the elders' sister-in-law had a sentimental attachment to the land someone wanted to build on, then it didn't pass. And there were no hard feelings allowed. That was the way it was, and when it was your turn to object, you'd get the same consideration.

Did feathers, fur, and scales get ruffled? Yes, but the traditions of the Springs held. Unanimous, or not at all.

Gabe Vasquez was the one who spoke up. "Alex, what is this all about? There hasn't been any unusual crime. There hasn't been any need for this in the past. Why on earth did you and Matt—I'm assuming that's what happened here—take it upon yourselves to hire a police chief we didn't need with funds we don't have?"

Jena's grandmother, Alma Crowe, added, "The town is struggling as it is. We can barely make our budget. The roads are all in awful shape, the school budget is shrinking, and we're going to have to cut the library hours back to practically nothing if that grant doesn't come through."

Alex started nodding halfway through. "I know. I know this seems foolish, but what Matt said is right. One of the grants that did come through was to hire more police officers. Now, we didn't have any to begin with, but this does provide a few jobs and a more secure environment. The sheriff's department is fine and the ones around here are very... understanding. But this is our own department. Staffed by one of our own—"

"And a complete stranger!" Steve Quinn piped up from the back. "Who is this guy?"

"He's a decorated police detective. He was planning on early retirement, from what I could find out, but he agreed to a change of pace. He's the best."

Jena said, "If he's the best, and he's an outsider, how the heck do you think we're going to keep him in the dark about... everything? We're all pretty good about hiding—even the kids—but he's going to be living here. And he's a detective. That's not a good combination from where I'm sitting."

A low hum of agreement started up at her words and she could tell Alex was annoyed, but she wasn't going to hold her tongue, not when it came to her kids' safety. And, as far as she was concerned, that's what it boiled down to. She'd come back to the Springs so her kids wouldn't have to hide who or what they were. It was the safe place. The *only* safe place. And Alex had just invited an outsider to live there.

Allie said, "This isn't like when someone gets married away and brings back a husband or wife, Alex. Outsiders that marry in are family. They already know about us, and we trust them. This guy has no connection to any of us. He has no reason to keep our secrets."

"And he's not some drunk at The Cave who I can pass off to the sheriffs and convince them that he drank too much," Ollie added. "This guy's a cop. If he says something's up, they're going to believe him."

Jena could tell Alex was annoyed with them, but it was too damn bad. She and Ollie, Ted, Allie, and Alex were some of the oldest cousins in their generation. If nothing tragic happened, some or all of them would be sitting in the elders' seats where their grandparents sat now. It was their job to watch out for the town, and Jena couldn't help but feel a little betrayed that Alex hadn't talked this over with them before he did it.

"The police chief has to happen!" Jena could see Alex's eyes start a faint golden glow and she knew he was angry. "We have to have an outsider here. Someone who can be neutral and settle things. Every single person in this town has loyalty to a clan that's above our loyalty to the town. That's perfectly natural, but we need someone like Caleb Gilbert around, and if that means we all have to be a little more careful, then that's what we're going to do."

"But why?" Ted finally spoke. "What are you not telling us, Alex? What's going on?"

A calculating glint came to Alex McCann's eye. "I have an idea. One that might just save this town, but you're going to have to trust me."

JENA'S MOUTH WAS HANGING OPEN. FLIES COULD HAVE made it their home. Set down rugs, hung curtains, and everything.

Ted was the first to speak after Alex's bombshell. "You want to build a *what*?"

"A hotel. Really more like a resort."

"A resort?"

"Very exclusive. Very expensive. Cambio Springs has seven of the most unusual natural springs—"

"They *define* unusual, Alex," someone said from the back of the church. "We can't let outsiders near the fresh spring."

"I'm not talking about the fresh spring. Of *course* we're not talking about that one. I'm talking about the other hot springs. The caves. The mud alone—people pay boatloads of money to go to these spas that surround hot springs for their health benefits. Our springs are no different. The water has been tested safe. We all use them. What I'm proposing is to build a small, very exclusive, hotel and spa that will take advantage of what we have here already. We can do spa treatments, but also offer hikes and classes. Art classes. Yoga. All that stuff. A hotel and spa like that will create jobs. Jobs we desperately need."

"So we're going to have tourists running all over town all the time? Do we really want that to happen?"

Alex was nodding. "I know. I know. But depending on how things work out, we may only be open part of the year. We'll see."

"Which part?" Ollie grunted.

"Winter. Palm Springs is a tourist trap. People want something new. A quiet place. A destination that's not too far from L.A. and Vegas, but just far enough. I'm talking about creating something very unique and very private. Where people—people with a lot of money—are going to be willing to pay big bucks for a few nights or a few weeks. I know this can work."

Allie's dad, Scott Smith, was an outsider who had married a McCann years ago. Allie's mom had died when she was young, but Scott remained, raising his small brood of canine shapeshifters among his wife's people and becoming a fixture in the community where he ran the farm supply store. "Alex," he said, "that's all well and good, but this is a farming town. We don't know anything about running hotels. What you're talking about would take loads of experienced employees."

Alex nodded at Scott. "Exactly. *Employees*. Let me ask you, how many of you have lost jobs since the base closed?"

No one raised a hand. No one wanted to admit the shame of being unemployed, but they didn't have to. A heavy silence fell over the room.

"This town *has* to change. We have to be open to this. What else do we have?" Alex looked around and Jena could see the fierce concern in his eyes. Say what you wanted about Alex McCann, but he loved Cambio Springs. "We have to do this, or the town is going to die. Farming can only expand so much. The Cave brings in outside dollars, but that's only one business. The monthly market is great, but it's been drawing fewer and fewer people every year." He took a deep breath. "We depended on the base for most of our jobs, and it's gone. It's not coming back. This hotel… I know there are dangers, but we need this."

The church fell silent. Jena looked around. She could see the people were considering Alex's arguments. She was, too.

Finally, Ollie spoke again. "Who's paying for all this? Something like this would take a lot of money, Alex."

"I am," Alex said.

"And if it fails?"

"Then I'm out a whole hell of a lot of money. But at least I'll have tried."

Jena and the rest of the town could see the grim resolve on Alex's face.

She asked, "How exclusive?"

"We'll get big enough so the town has enough, then no more. I promise. I don't want this to become a tourist town. We'll have one resort. One season. That keeps it exclusive enough to charge the big bucks and still retain the allure. I'll be marketing it to the Southern California crowd. Entertainment people. Music people." Alex nodded toward Ollie. "You can help with that one, don't lie."

Ollie shrugged as if he didn't have signed pictures of music royalty hanging next to the men's bathroom door.

Ted asked, "How many jobs are we talking about here?"

"Initially, there's the construction. That's going to take a while. Other people who want to work at the spa or hotel will have time to get training. Internships. Stuff like that. Matt says there are grants for that kind of thing available for those who don't have the money. They can go to schools in Indio, Barstow, Palm Desert. There will be options."

Matt finally stepped forward, relieved to be back in the spotlight. "There already are. And once I can show that some meaningful business is coming into town, I can apply for grants to revitalize our downtown area. Rich people like to shop. That means boutiques and cafes."

"And restaurants." Alex caught Jena's eye. "I want at least one very nice restaurant at the spa, and I know exactly the person to be the chef."

Jena tried to stay pragmatic, but a flutter of excitement leapt in her belly. A restaurant? A real one?

"Restaurants, shops, hosts for the hotel, spa personnel, maids, janitors, gardeners, security, maintenance on the hot springs and the facilities. Wilderness tours and hikes. I'm talking about the whole desert, clean air, red canyons, and open skies experience, guys. This is not going to be something that only benefits a few. I wouldn't invest this much money unless I thought it was going to change the town for the better. Ted, you'd be able to expand the clinic. Make it a real medical center. That will create jobs, too. Nurses. Support staff."

Lena Vasquez spoke from her seat in the front row. "This is still a very dangerous thing. This will change the town in ways we can't foresee."

Alex nodded. "I know it will. But, Lena, how many children do you see coming into your kindergarten class come August?" Alex looked around the room. "Hm? More and more young people are going away for school or work, and *they're not coming back* because there's nothing here. More and more people are having to raise their children among strangers. In places where they'd be considered freaks." He slowly shook his head. "Not if I can help it. This town needs to stay alive. And if we have the resources to do it, then we need to, even if there are costs."

Another, more thoughtful silence fell over the church.

"It's true," Lena finally said. She was the principal of the small school in town. The school that was slowly shrinking. "I know of seven young families in our clan alone that want to come back, but can't because there is no work here."

Alex nodded. Steve Quinn said, "If this would create work... well, even if things change, we'd have some kind of control over it, right, Alex? Instead of people having to live away."

"That's what I'm aiming for."

Jena said, "It'll be hardest on the kids. They're going to have to be more careful. And things like shifting out in public"—she glared at Old Quinn where he sat at the council table—"will have to stop. There's no way we're going to be able to hide if people keep doing stuff like that. They'll think we're putting drugs in the water."

A voice said from the back, "Hey, that might draw an entirely different crowd!"

Old Quinn just shrugged his shoulders and laughed. "I guess we can all live with a few changes if it means a better town for everyone. I don't relish the idea of anyone in my clan not feeling like they can call this place home."

"Where you gonna build it?" Scott Smith asked.

"The land closest to the hot springs is my parents' property and Joe Quinn's. But I'll pay everyone fairly for their portion." Old Quinn sat up a bit straighter when he heard that and a general murmur of agreement came from the back corner of the room where his clan sat. "And since the springs themselves are community property, I plan on paying the town a yearly percentage for the use of them. That's going to allow the council to do things like repair the roads, fix up the school, open the library more hours, stuff like that."

"And what if outsiders catch wind of this? What if some come looking to build more?" Allie asked.

Robert McCann, Alex's father, spoke up from his seat at the Elders' table. "This council approves all building permits in Cambio Springs. Always has. Always will. That's not gonna change. No one builds here without our permission."

Lowell's Grandfather John sat next to Robert. He said, "And

Willow's the only water witch who can find wells around here. If Willow doesn't cooperate, no one's going to be able to build outside the city limits, either."

Willow McCann, Alex's cousin, nodded from her perch in the front corner of the room. She was a quiet woman, an artist who matched her name and sent her work out to galleries all over the Southwest. Willow McCann was also the lone water witch in the Springs. Each generation of McCanns bred one witch who could sniff out water with pinpoint accuracy when no other, more modern methods, seemed to work. Grandpa John was right. If Willow didn't cooperate when someone needed a well, one wasn't going to be dug.

"Okay then." Alex let out a long breath. "I'm sure there are other questions we didn't get to. Detail-type stuff. Things are going to come up and we'll deal with them, but does everyone here feel like they have enough information for an initial vote to get the ball rolling?" He looked around the room, then turned to the Elders' table. "Elders, do you have any other questions for me? Will you vote to allow me the permits to clear the land for a hotel and spa here in Cambio Springs?"

One by one, the elders looked at each other, all of them either shrugging or nodding their heads, indicating they were ready for a vote. Jena took a deep breath. She could feel Ted and Allie on either side of her, both tense and waiting.

Robert McCann, steel-haired and handsome, even in his late sixties, spoke first. "Robert McCann, descended of Robert McCann, first of the wolves, votes yes on this matter."

His great-uncle sat next to him. Lowell's grandfather, white-haired and over one hundred and ten years old, was still unbent by age. "John McCann, grandson of Andrew McCann, second of the wolves, votes yes on this matter."

Old Joe Quinn—who still didn't have his favorite hat—said, "Joseph Quinn, descended of Rory Quinn, first and only snake, votes yes on this matter."

Ben Campbell, Ollie's grandfather, spoke next. "Benjamin Campbell, descended of William Allen, first and only bear, abstains from voting on this matter." A quiet murmur filled the room, and Ben continued, "Understand this. I cannot bring myself to approve of anything that will invite outsiders into the Springs. The Allens and the Campbells have guarded the gates to this town for over one hundred years, but we cannot guard against outsiders that you invite in. At the same time, I will not stand in the way of progress others feel is necessary. We are a small clan and do not have as many to take care of. I understand both sides of the argument, so at this time, I will abstain."

The murmur died down and Jena glanced over at Ollie. She could tell he wasn't pleased, but she wasn't sure exactly why. Did he wish his grandfather had voted no, outright? If he had, the whole vote would have stopped. Tension began to build in the room. The cats were next, and the cat clans defined unpredictable. Would they defy the wolves out of spite? Or would they consider this plan as much Matt's as Alex's and vote for it?

In the front of the room, Gabe Vasquez, Ted's grandfather said in his slight accent, "Gabriel Vasquez, descended of Gabriel Vasquez, second of the cats, votes yes in this matter."

Paula Leon spoke next. "Paula Leon, descended of Reina Vasquez de Leon, first of the cats, gladly votes yes in this matter."

Well, that answered that. For the cats, loyalty to the mayor and their clan trumped natural suspicion of outsiders.

The last to speak was Jena's grandmother, Alma. A tiny woman, her voice still carried over the church. "This isn't an easy vote. I think..." Her voice dropped. "I think we need more time to think about this." Jena could hear the collected gasp around the room. This was unexpected. Her grandmother was usually one of the most progressive on the council. "Alma Crowe, descended of Thomas Crowe, first and only in flight, votes no on this matter."

chapter
six

I t had been a week and a half of cleaning, hauling, and more cleaning, but Caleb looked around the small police station with pride. It was rough, but efficient. Two desks sat in opposite corners of the room, with a divider of bookcases sectioning off a portion of the room for the "Chief's office." Jeremy's desk sat with a good view of the parking lot and a small receptionist's desk sat near the door. They still hadn't hired an actual receptionist, but they had the budget for someone and Jeremy claimed he "knew someone" who would be good.

He had quickly learned that whatever he might need, Deputy Jeremy McCann was pretty sure to "know someone" who could get it. And chances were good that it was a relative.

Caleb had been sleeping on a cot in one of the back cells—which really did stay the coolest throughout the day—and showering over at Jeremy's when he got the chance. But Jeremy's wife was officially moving in the next day and Caleb had taken enough borrowed showers.

"Jeremy?" he called out from behind a bookcase where he was examining some old mining maps of the area.

"Yeah, Chief?"

"I need a place to live."

He heard the young man chuckle. "You mean you don't want to use

Brenda's soap when she moves in? It's real pretty. You'll smell fresh as a rose."

Caleb smothered a smile. "Unless you want your first investigation to be the inside an outhouse, you're gonna 'know someone' with a place to rent. Doesn't have to be big. In fact, I prefer small. But I want it in town."

Jeremy poked his head around the bookcases. "How small?"

"It can be a glorified tent, for all I care, as long as it has plumbing. And air-conditioning."

Wait for it...

"Yeah." Jeremy sounded amused. "I definitely know someone."

CALEB HAD PUT OFF VISITING THE BLACKBIRD DINER ever since he heard who owned it. It wasn't an easy temptation to resist, but he was still in preliminary investigations about Jena Crowe and didn't want to jump the gun. He'd gathered a short collection of facts about the attractive brunette, none of which made her any less appealing.

She was a trained chef—had studied in Seattle, in fact—but ran a diner her family owned. She was thirty-one and had been widowed for three years. Had two boys—Caleb figured she must have had the oldest almost right out of high school—who attended the elementary school in town and were McCanns. In fact, most of the information he'd mined was from Jeremy who was a second or third or who-knows-what kind of cousin to Jena's late husband, who sounded like he'd been a decent guy.

Caleb pulled his dusty truck into the parking lot, looking for shade, but not expecting any. He hopped out of the late model Ford and stepped onto the small porch that lined the front of the diner. It was just after eleven on a Friday, so there was a small early lunch crowd he could see through the windows, but not too many people.

That was good. If Jena Crowe was going to bare her rumored talons, he'd prefer as small an audience as possible.

Kicking the dust off his boots, he opened the door and relaxed into the cool rush of air that enveloped him. A few curious glances turned his way, but Caleb's eyes were glued to the figure leaning over the counter at the far end of the room. She was laughing at something an old man was saying and her eyes were lit up. That gorgeous smile that transformed her face was in evidence, and he noticed one of her legs kicked up behind her in a girlish pose.

Damn, she was cute.

Then Caleb noticed that all eyes had turned to him. He tipped the edge of his hat at the two older women sitting at a booth eyeing him before he walked to the counter and sat on a deserted stool just to the right of the cash register. Caleb set his hat on the stool beside him and ran a quick hand through unruly black hair. He glanced back down the counter to see Jena's narrowed eyes watching him.

No claws... yet.

"You need a haircut, young man."

He shot a crooked smile to the older woman behind the counter. She was taking out what looked like a blueberry pie from the case.

"Yes, ma'am, I do. Know where I could get that taken care of?"

She had a cap of silver hair and dark brown eyes that twinkled the same way Jena's had when they'd been flirting at the bar. She must have been in her seventies or eighties, but Caleb would've bet when she was young, she'd been a hell of a good-looking woman.

"Well, there's Patsy's place on Main Street if you want it to look nice. Unfortunately, you have testosterone, so you're stuck with Manny."

"That doesn't sound promising."

The woman chuckled while she sliced the pie. "Manny's place is the only proper barber shop in town. He learned one cut back in 1964 and became an expert. Unfortunately, he never really branched out."

"Ah."

"So it'll be clean, short, and look like every other man that sits in his chair."

Caleb couldn't hold back the laugh. "I'll keep that in mind."

She winked at him. "But I'm told he does give a very nice shave, if you're looking for that."

"Thank you, Mrs...."

"Crowe. I'm Alma Crowe, dear. Grandmother of that pretty young thing you've been looking at from the corner of your eye."

"You're also on the town council. I remember you."

"Humph." She huffed a little. "I'm currently the most popular member, as a matter of fact."

So, sarcasm ran in the family. Good to know. There was definitely a story there. His interest piqued, he said, "Popularity isn't everything, is it?"

Her brown eyes glittered with amusement. "That's a very good attitude for you to have, young man. Especially in your situation."

"Call me Caleb, please. And what situation is that?" Four or five theories popped into his mind, but he was curious what Alma was thinking.

She examined him thoughtfully, her dark eyes taking stock of him in a way that reminded Caleb of his own grandmother. "You're in for an interesting season of life, Chief Gilbert. But I think you might just be the right man for the job, after all."

Now, what the hell did that mean? And why did this seemingly harmless old woman suddenly set off every instinctive alarm he'd honed in the past fifteen years?

"Hey, Grandma, can you take that pie to Mr. Campbell?" Caleb's eyes darted to the right to see Jena approaching. He quickly shook off the sense of foreboding that had enveloped him under Alma's inspection and turned his attention to Jena. Her long legs were encased in a pair of worn jeans and a simple apron covered up a green shirt the color of dusty cactus. Her dark hair was pulled back into a ponytail and her expression was calm and carefully blank.

Caleb turned his most charming grin on her as Alma walked away.

Then he and Jena were the only two people in a room that buzzed with slowly growing chatter.

"Jena Crowe."

"Caleb Not-just-passing-through."

She was quick. He liked that. "Please, feel free to call me Chief Not-just-passing-through. I strive for professionalism."

"What can I get for you?"

He raised an eyebrow and Jena rolled her eyes.

"To drink, Chief."

"Iced tea if you have it."

"Of course." She turned to grab a glass from the counter behind her, filling it with ice and black tea before she set it down in front of him. "So... you live here now." It wasn't a question.

"I do."

She was being awfully quiet. Gone was the bold woman at The Cave with her flirting eyes and quick smile. New Jena was all caution and suspicion. If he had to guess, she was a woman who strived for as much privacy as a very small town would allow. He could see curious eyes turn toward them, but a quick glance from her made them look away.

"You sure didn't mention that the night we met at The Cave."

"Well..." He took a sip of his tea. "I didn't live here then."

She leaned over the counter. "Is that considered an evasive answer, Chief Gilbert?"

The corner of his mouth turned up. "Am I a suspect?"

She straightened and Caleb very pointedly did not look at the soft curve of her hip that was right at his eye level. Nope, didn't look at that at all.

"Suspect?" She shook her head and poured herself her own glass of tea. "You could call it that."

"Jena..." He drew out her name with pleasure, liking the sound of it in his mouth. He glanced around and lowered his voice. "I'm not sure what you think about me, but you should know I'm not a gossip."

Her cheeks reddened slightly, but he kept talking. "I'm not a loud mouth and—as a habit—I listen more than I talk. So what you and me—"

"There is no 'you and me.'"

He smothered the short burst of disappointment and plowed forward. "What you and me are or aren't or might be is none of anyone's business but our own."

She finally gave a quiet laugh. "Oh, Chief Gilbert. It's been a while since you've lived in a small town, hasn't it?"

Caleb grimaced. She wasn't making this easy. But then, if Caleb Gilbert had learned early on, the good things—the really good ones—didn't come easy. Jena was focused on a very short past, and he was far more interested in the future. Diversionary tactics were necessary.

He glanced behind her at the hat hanging on the wall. "You have a tempestuous relationship with hats."

She snickered and a flicker of the woman he'd met two weeks ago peeked out. "I told you. And I see that you've left yours well out of reach. That's probably a smart thing."

"Don't touch my hat, woman."

"Ha!" She smiled and turned to grab her order pad from the counter behind her. "Men and their hats."

"This is police property. I'd have to arrest you."

Now why did that make her cock her eyebrow like that? He bit back the evil smile that wanted to come out.

"What can I get you, Chief?"

"Call me Caleb."

She didn't say anything, just looked at him expectantly. He smiled. "How about a burger, medium-rare, with everything, and the keys to one of those fixed up Airstreams that sit out at the back of your property?"

Her jaw dropped. "Wh-what?"

"Well…" His smile grew. He liked catching her off balance. He'd have to do it again. "I asked my new deputy if he knew anyone with a small place to rent. Amazingly, the rental market in Cambio Springs isn't booming, but he assured me that you have two great trailers out behind your place that you manage for your folks." He shifted a little closer to her. "You came highly recommended."

"You want to rent one of my mom's trailers?"

"They're empty, right?"

"Um… yes." She was scribbling furiously on the pad. Probably telling the cook to poison him.

"And you manage them for your folks?"

"They're my mom's project mostly. They're old, but she fixed them up inside and they're really nice. Full hookups and—why am I telling you this?" She was blinking rapidly and her mouth twisted in annoyance. "You're not going to rent one of my mom's trailers."

"Why not?" He looked at her innocently. "Feel free to run a background check, Jena. I'm a very upstanding citizen."

"Because…"

He waited. She'd rent one to him, if for no other reason than to *not* rent one would appear suspicious. Jeremy had said both of the trailers were rented out occasionally to friends and family of residents who were in town for a long visit, but Jena's mom had been complaining that she could use a regular tenant.

"Because, I…"

He leaned toward her. The color was high in her cheeks and he could almost feel the waves of annoyance pouring off her. It made him want to poke at her all the more. He was an irritating bastard sometimes. "You… what?"

She was stuck. Her teeth were clenched, but she finally said, "I'll get you a rental application."

The grin took over his face. "Much appreciated."

The gritted teeth remained. "And when were you looking to move in?"

"Oh, as soon as possible."

"Of course you were." She cleared her throat pulled her shoulders back. All business. "Would you like fries or coleslaw with your burger, Chief Gilbert?"

"Is the coleslaw homemade?"

"I make it fresh every morning."

"Then I'd love to get a taste."

There were those gritted teeth again. What do you know? She was cute when she was pissed off, too. "Fantastic."

He heard the bell jingle as she spun around to give his order to the cook. A tall man wearing a uniform sat one stool down from him and held out a hand. "You must be Caleb Gilbert. Saw the truck outside. Devin Moon. Sheriff's department."

"Deputy Moon." Caleb held out a hand, set at ease by the familiar presence of law enforcement. He'd been told that Devin Moon was the deputy who handled most of the occasional problems that cropped up in the Springs. Jeremy had spoken to the man on the phone more than once and Caleb could tell the two were friendly. "Nice to finally meet you. I've heard good things."

"Thanks." The other man's eyes took a quick assessment, then looked away. "I've heard... interesting things."

Someone had been on the phone with Albuquerque. "Oh?"

"All good." Devin offered him a slow nod. "Very impressive record, Chief Gilbert. You have quite the reputation in New Mexico."

"Thanks, but I'm happy to be in a smaller town now."

Devin shrugged a shoulder. "Hard to imagine you won't get bored."

Just then, Jena stalked past, grabbed his cup, refilled it, and nodded at Devin.

"Hey, Dev. The usual?"

"Yep."

"Coming right up."

Caleb tried to catch her eye. She finally looked at him sideways and he winked. He bit back a laugh and smiled when she sneered. "Thank you, Jena."

"Your burger is almost ready."

"Can't wait." It was probably wrong how appealing he found her when she was irritated.

Devin glanced between Jena and Caleb, whose eyes were glued to the backside of the curt woman. Caleb heard a low chuckle.

"Never mind," Devin said. "Maybe you won't be bored, after all."

CALEB WAS HALFWAY THROUGH A REALLY EXCELLENT BURGER after inhaling Jena's coleslaw. The woman could definitely cook. And give orders. And run a very tight ship. None of these qualities were making her any less attractive. When he met her, he'd been looking for a fun distraction, but he didn't usually think about distractions quite this much.

It was a little worrisome, but he tried not to think about it.

He liked the diner. It had a relaxed atmosphere that fit the town. Eccentric, with a mix of traditional diner food and more exotic specials. He liked the burger, but was starting to regret not trying the *carne asada* tacos that Devin had ordered. The smell of earthy spices mingled with the aroma of frying beef and potatoes.

Caleb was talking shop with Devin when a small tornado entered the place. It whirled and clattered, throwing a cloud of dust, backpack, and bike helmet as it spun onto the seat between Devin and Caleb.

"Hey, Uncle Dev!" The whirlwind settled into a small boy that Caleb would put around six or seven years old. Bright green eyes looked up at him and a quick, friendly smile lit up the boy's face. "Hi! Are you the new policeman?"

Caleb decided he liked the small whirlwind. "I am." He held out a hand for the boy to shake. "Caleb Gilbert."

Jena broke in. "And you can call him Chief Gilbert, Bear." Jena bent over the counter and kissed the boy's forehead. So this was one of her boys? He looked nothing like her. Must have looked like the dad. "Want a snack? And where's Low?"

"Out talking with Kevin about... stuff."

A look passed between Devin and Jena. A silent conversation that Caleb had no part of. Interesting.

Devin rose from the bench. "I'll go check on 'em. Bear, guard my seat."

"Okay!" The small boy settled onto Devin's stool, sneaking glances at Caleb when he thought he wasn't looking. Finally, Caleb broke the silence. "Bear? Is that your name?"

"No. My name's really Aaron. But when I was a baby, Mom called me Aar-Bear. Now they just call me Bear." He giggled. "Even though I won't turn into one or anything."

"Well, I guess not." Caleb laughed. "But it's still a cool nickname. What grade are you in?"

"Second. I'm in Mrs. Strickle's class."

"So you're... seven?"

Aaron's eyes lit up. "Yeah! Do you have any kids?"

"Nope. But I have a lot of cousins who do."

"That's cool."

Jena slid a plate of cut apples and cheese slices in front of Aaron before she rushed away. The diner was in the middle of the lunch rush. She was barking orders into the kitchen and sadly, had no time to be irritated with him.

Suddenly, a thought occurred and he turned back to Aaron. "Hey, shouldn't you be in school? I don't want to have to arrest you for truancy when we just met."

Aaron giggled and bit into an apple. "Nope. Half days on Fridays."

"Well, that's pretty cool."

"I know. Mom has to work, so we hang out here. Or sometimes Low watches me at home."

Was it sneaky or just friendly to talk to the kid of a woman you were interested in? He wasn't exactly grilling the little guy. He was just curious. "How old is Low?"

"He's almost twelve. Is that your hat?" The boy talked with his mouth full, but Caleb could still understand him. He glanced over at the simple straw Stetson that lay on the stool next to him.

"Yep. That's mine."

"That's a cool hat."

"Thanks. Keeps the sun off."

Elizabeth Hunter

Aaron glanced down the counter at his mother and leaned toward Caleb. "You better make sure you pay for your lunch."

Caleb's eyes darted between Aaron and an old hat nailed up on the wall behind the cash register. Suddenly, one mystery seemed a little more clear. Tempestuous relationship with hats, huh? He nodded at Aaron. "I'll keep that in mind. Thanks for the tip."

He heard the bell to the door chiming in the background, but his eyes were locked on the kid, who was staring at him with an odd expression. Aaron narrowed his green eyes and tilted his head to the side.

Caleb said, "Bear?"

A tentative hand reached over to his arm and Caleb could feel the warm palm resting on his forearm as Aaron continued to stare. Just then, a sweet smile crossed the boy's face. "You're like us."

For a second, a strange instinct tickled the back of his mind, as if there was something Caleb had forgotten that he was on the verge of remembering. "What do you—?"

"Come on, Bear." Another hand pulled Aaron's arm away and Caleb looked over his shoulder, annoyed to have been interrupted. "We need to go home. Now."

This was definitely Jena's other son. The dark suspicious eyes that watched him with intelligent caution. The thick, dark hair and angled planes of a face that was distinctly boyish, but familiar, nonetheless.

Caleb held out a hand. "Hi, I'm Chief Gilbert."

The older boy—who must have been Low, the eleven-year-old—ignored his hand and nodded. "I know. Come on, Bear. Dev's going to take us home."

Caleb hadn't even noticed Devin standing behind the boys. The deputy called out to Jena, "Is that cool, Jena? I can drop them off on my way out."

Jena smiled as she slid two plates over the pass. "Thanks, Dev. Appreciate it. Low, you have your key?"

"Yeah, Mom."

"I'll call Nana McCann to check on you in a little while."

❄ 58 ❄

Low gave a distinctly adolescent sigh. "It's fine, Mom."

There was a moment then, a quick, heated moment with mother and son staring at each other across the room. A tumbleweed might have rolled between the booths. The tension held for a moment before a slight flush crossed the older boy's cheeks and he said, "I'll make sure to look for her."

Jena said, "Good. Make sure you guys do any homework for the weekend before I get home. You can ask Nana for help if you need it."

"Okay."

Jena crooked a finger at the boy and he walked behind the counter. She bent down, whispered in his ear, and Low's face flushed with pleasure.

"Promise?" he said.

"Promise. Now go take care of your brother. I'll see you a little later."

She was tough, but not harsh. The affection in the boys' faces was clear and she watched them with an expression that reminded him a little of his cousin Stephanie, who was a single mom of three back in Albuquerque. Steph and her kids were one of the few reasons he'd had a hard time leaving, but he knew she understood.

Low and Aaron rushed out the door followed by Devin, already talking on the phone. Caleb turned back to Jena, who was filling three drink orders. "You're a good mom."

The corner of her mouth turned up. "Get that from a five-minute conversation, Chief?"

"Didn't even take that long. I'm a trained investigator."

"Ha!" Jena passed the drinks to a girl who was serving the booths and took the ticket she handed her and passed it to the cook. "I'm a busy mom, that's for sure."

"Two boys will do that."

"You have any kids?"

"No. My ex didn't want any. I have a lot of cousins though, and most of them do."

"Hmm." She started refilling ketchup bottles.

"Jena?"

"Yes?"

He leaned forward, pushing his empty plate to the side. He'd drawn out his lunch as long as he could, but he had to get back to the station. "You're pretty busy, huh?"

She smirked. "That's not what you really want to ask me."

"No?"

"Nope."

He caught her eye and the woman actually stopped rushing around for a minute. "Go out to dinner with me," he said.

She took a deep breath, held it, then let it out slowly. "Where, exactly? Here? It's the only restaurant in town."

"Get a drink with me at The Cave."

"Where I work at night?"

"Every night?"

She sighed. "Caleb…"

"I like the way you say my name," he said in a low voice. He could see her bite the corner of her lip. "I like the way you run your place and the way you talk to your boys. I like the way you kiss—"

She slapped a hand over his mouth and glanced around the diner. He didn't care who heard them. He grinned beneath her hand and tried to nip at her fingers, tasting a bit of ketchup.

"Ugh!" She turned and went to wash her hands at the sink behind the counter. "Boys."

"Go out with me."

"I'm not going out with you. There's a reason I don't date."

"Never?"

"Never. I'm busy. I've got too many responsibilities and not enough time for the life I have. I may like the way you look, Chief Gilbert—"

"You like my boots, too. Don't lie."

She rolled her eyes. "I don't date."

"So I'm going to have to settle for week after week of flirtatious lunches with my new landlady?" He stood and grabbed his wallet from his back pocket, peeling off a few bills before he set them on the counter and reached for his hat.

Her eyebrows furrowed together. "You're not coming in here every day, are you?"

Caleb cocked his head. "I'm thinking about it."

"Don't."

"Why not? That was some great coleslaw."

Her mouth gaped open for a moment before she snapped it shut. "You're..."

"Handsome? Witty? Ruggedly appealing?"

The cook rang a bell. "Order up!"

Jena grabbed two plates before she walked out from behind the cash register. "I was going to say irritating."

He stepped in front of her so she had to pause. Jena looked up at him with a scowl, but Caleb only smiled. "I'm also persistent, Jena Crowe. And I like a challenge."

"Get out of my way, Chief Not-just-passing-through. Or I'll dump this Coke down your pants, and I know for a fact you don't have your own shower."

"I'm trying to rent yours." He slipped his hat on, tipping it at her before he walked to the door. "See you later, Jena." He slipped out the door before she could say anything. He did love getting in the last word, and he had a feeling it wouldn't happen too often with the woman.

Caleb walked to his truck with a spring in his step, nodding and smiling at the curious residents he passed. It may have been small, dusty, and in the middle of nowhere, but Cambio Springs was looking better all the time.

chapter
seven

J ena peered into the glare of the late morning sun that hit her when she stepped out the church doors. Aaron darted around her, already racing toward the punch and donuts with one of Allie's boys.

"Bear, you watch where you're going!"

Low sauntered behind her, clumsily flirting with the new girl in his class. Her family had just moved back to the Springs. Jena suspected the girl's mother, who was part of the cat clans, knew her daughter faced her first change soon. Jena smiled toward the uneasy father, who was already shaking hands with Reverend Bullock and being invited for coffee by Ted's father after church.

Her grandmother bumped her shoulder. "Come over for coffee with the boys."

"Okay. I've got everyone coming over for dinner later, but coffee sounds good."

"And I've got a pie cooling with the last of the peaches."

"Now that sounds *really* good."

She saw Aaron run up to Caleb Gilbert, who was leaning against his truck in the parking lot, talking to Jeremy and his wife, Brenda. The man said something to her youngest, then winked, sending Aaron and his friend into peals of laughter before they ran away. Caleb looked up, caught her eye, and winked at her, too. Jena pretended not to see him, but it was hard to ignore the persistent man. He'd been coming into the diner almost every day and it was getting harder and harder to dismiss him. He was smart with a teasing sense of humor that quickly made him friends with her regular lunch crowd. He and Mr. Campbell debated which of Alma's pies was the best. He always took the time to say hello to Missy and ask how she was feeling. He tipped the busboy way more than he should have and talked football scores with Devin.

And he flirted with her. Relentlessly. Jena couldn't help but be flattered. It wasn't like any of the other men in town—most of whom she had known since preschool—ever paid her attention like that. For the first time in years, Jena felt like someone was looking at her. He wasn't looking at Lowell's widow, or Aaron and Low's mom. Caleb looked at *her*.

"That one has the subtlety of a bear after honey," Alma said.

"I know."

"I approve."

Jena turned to Alma; she could already feel her cheeks heating up. "You what?"

Her grandmother only pinched her arm and walked to her car. "See you at the house!" Then the old woman sauntered past Caleb's truck, stopping to chat with Brenda and garnering a hat tip from Caleb before she got into her old Jeep and took off into the desert.

Jena was distracted by another tug on her arm. It was Alex.

"I've been here for two weeks, Jen. Two weeks of coffee and pie and no answers." Alex patted his trim stomach. "I'm jogging twice as much every morning and I still have no idea why she objects to the resort."

"If you're asking me if I know, you're out of luck. She hasn't told me. What do you all talk about when she's feeding you pie?"

Alex sighed. "Who's growing what and what's in season. State water allocations and the federal riverbank restoration project. Who's having babies and who's moving out of town. Who's moving into town. Where your parents are traveling this month. How my grandmother's knee is... The woman can chat for hours about anything and everything except the resort that has the potential to pull this town from the edge of poverty."

Jena tried not to smile. Alma didn't chitchat needlessly. Never had. So whatever Alex's frustrations, her grandmother had a reason for dragging out their discussions.

"Will you just ask her? Please?" He pulled off his sunglasses and gave her his best puppy dog eyes. "I'm begging. I've got a dozen balls all set to roll on this, but I have to get her approval. Once she's sold on it, everything can start and people can actually work again. At least mention that to her?"

Jena shrugged. "I'll talk to her, but no guarantees. You know how she is."

"I know." He dropped a kiss on her cheek. "You're a doll." He started toward his car before he turned back. "Hey, dinner at six, right?"

"Yep. Bring whatever you want to drink. Allie and I got the rest."

"See you then." Alex turned and nodded at Caleb, who was watching the exchange carefully. Then Alex reached over and punched Jeremy in his arm before he pretended to grab a laughing Brenda. Jena laughed, watching the cousins play-fight before they waved good-bye. She caught Caleb glancing at her before she heard Low.

"Mom? We going to Grandma's or what?"

ALMA CROWE, LIKE ALL THE CROWE WOMEN, HAD RAISED her children in the family home in town, near to the church, the school, and their neighbors until the next generation had been born. Then she and Jena's grandfather had built a small home out in the desert butted up to a sheer wall of sandstone that glowed red in the morning sun and shaded the old house in the afternoons. It wasn't an easy place to find, but then Crowes tended to like their solitude.

Jena pulled her Subaru into the graveled drive in front of the house; the boys were already on the way out of the car.

"Mom, we're going to the Cliff House!"

"Okay. I'll call when it's time for pie."

The boys whooped and hollered as they clambered up the rocks. The "cliff house" was a narrow sliver of cave cut into the rock face who-knows-how-many years before. It might have been one of the numerous shelters for the desert dwellers who had fled, leaving petroglyphs and pottery shards, or it might have been naturally made. For Jena and her sons, it served the purpose of a childhood fort. Cambio Springs didn't have much in the way of tree houses, but the Cliff House was even more special.

She climbed onto the small porch, which was hung with dusty blinds to keep out the sun, and into her grandmother's house. Alma must have just turned on the air-conditioner that hung in the window, because the house was still warm.

"Grandma?"

"Back in the kitchen, Jena."

She set her purse down and walked back to her grandmother's pride and joy. The kitchen was immaculate, the one indulgence in an otherwise simple house. Alma Crowe had been baking pies long before Jena had been born and her recipes were famous. When she and her husband had started the Blackbird Diner, it had been a pie house, serving Alma's famous pies for breakfast and lunch. Her grandmother still had every recipe, though she only made dessert pies for Jena on a regular basis and only rarely made her breakfast pies.

"Hey." She sat down at the long table that ran through the middle of the room.

"The boys at the Cliff House?"

"Yep."

"Good. Talk to me about that handsome sheriff."

"He's not a sheriff. He's a police chief."

Alma said, "He could be a Fed for all I care. He's finally turned your head, which is more than I can say for any other man in the last three years."

"He hasn't turned my head." Jena tried not to think about Lowell. "I don't have time for that stuff."

Alma patted her shoulder as she moved to the small pie safe that stood in the corner of the room. "You should make time. It's not good for you to be alone. And you don't see your face when he comes in the diner. You light up."

"I do not." Did she?

Her grandmother smiled. "It wouldn't be obvious to anyone but me. It's nice. You haven't looked like that in a while. You need to get out."

"I don't have time for—"

"You're not an old woman," Alma said. "You're entitled to a little happiness for yourself. Lowell wouldn't have wanted you to be alone."

He hadn't. Her late husband had told her himself. Jena said, "You been talking to Mom again?"

"Always." Alma set the pie down on the table before she settled down next to Jena. "My favorite thing about my son is his wife. I let him know that on a regular basis."

Jena thought about the two grubby boys climbing on rocks. "I just hope my daughters-in-law like me as much as Mom likes you."

"That's the curse of having boys. Sucking up to your daughters-in-law becomes a full-time occupation," Alma said. "I'm joking, Jen. Your mom and I were just talking yesterday—they're in Wyoming, of all places—and I may have mentioned that there was a handsome new man in town. She was curious, that's all."

"Grandma!" she squeaked. "Why would you do that?"

"I can see the writing on the wall..." Alma gazed out the window. "I'm mystical like that." Then she turned to smile at her granddaughter. "I'm glad he's persistent. You need someone to bother you into a little fun."

Deciding a subject change was in order, Jena asked, "Speaking of persistent, Alex is starting to bug me."

"Starting to bug me, too. That boy can put away food. Don't know how he stays so skinny."

She shook her head. "Then why do you keep inviting him over and not talking about the hotel?"

Alma chuckled and stood, walking to the counter to pull out two mugs and pour the coffee. "Alex McCann is a good boy. He's also a very smart one."

"Yep, and he really does think this resort is a good idea for the Springs. He's sinking a lot of his own money into it with no guarantee of success, just because he thinks it's the right thing for the future."

"I'd like to point out," she said as she sat down, "that I didn't say 'no.' I said, 'not yet.'"

"Tell me the difference from your perspective."

Alma sipped her coffee. Black. Always strong and black. Jena poured a dollop of cream in hers.

"He's smart and dedicated to the Springs," she said. "But he's young. And he's been living away. I'm probably going to give him my approval. But the more he has to justify it to me, the more thought he puts into it, and the more pieces of everyday news he has to absorb, the better the project's going to be."

So that was the reason behind the chitchat. "You think he's out of touch."

"I *know* he is." She stood again to grab four plates and a sharp knife. "He's been living in L.A. for over ten years. He needs to be thinking where the water is going to come from to use in this hotel. People on vacation like taking long showers."

"We've never been short on water. Not really. Despite what we tell outsiders."

"I know that, but it's still something to be mindful of. He needs to think about who's going to be around. How is this going to affect the children in town if they have to mind their every word? He doesn't have kids yet because he and Ted keep dancing around each other, but he will someday. He needs to think about how this is going to affect the farmers in town. Is dust going to become an issue with his pretty hotel landscaping? He'd be building right along the Smith's farm. And how are hotel guests going to react to tractors outside their windows instead of pretty desert views? All this stuff is going to affect the decisions he makes at the very beginning, so there's no need to rush into this."

"There are people out of work, Grandma." Jena spoke quietly. She respected her grandmother, but she saw Alex's side of the argument, too. "There are things in motion to get people jobs again. Give people some hope. At least give Alex a sign that he's not spinning his wheels on this."

Alma started cutting the peach pie and the sweet scent wafted up and into Jena's nose. As if called by the dinner bell, she heard the boys scrambling on the back porch, no doubt sweaty and tired from climbing on the rocks.

"Hands. Wash. Now." She pointed toward the sink as they burst through the door.

"Yes, Mom," they said in chorus.

Alma started serving. Jena said, "At least let him know you're giving it some thought, Grandma."

"I'll think about it. Now, how many slices of pie do my boys want?"

"I AM GOING TO WIN HER OVER ON THIS," ALEX SAID AS HE and Ollie tended the grill and Jena put another salad on the table. "Alma Crowe is going to think I'm the best thing that ever happened to this town by the time I'm done convincing her."

The sun had slipped behind the mesa, so the evening was starting to cool off. Allie had turned on the sprinklers when she and Joe had turned up with their four kids, so six shrieks of excited laughter rang from the backyard while dinner was put on the table. They were eating on the back porch, which was screened in so they could have the kitchen open to the backyard.

"Is Dev coming over?" Ted asked, and Jena saw Alex shoot her a glare.

"I don't know. I invited him, but he said he might have to work a shift for someone today."

"How about the cute police chief?" her friend teased.

Alex muttered, "Are you making passes at every single man in town now, Ted?"

Ted curled her lip and threw a dinner roll at him. It fell to the ground where Ollie's mastiff, Murtry, immediately scooped it up and trotted away. Jena peeked out the kitchen window to see Allie's three-year-old daughter, Loralie, hop on his back. The dog turned, gave the small girl's face a giant lick, then ambled toward the sprinklers with the baby clinging on.

"The chief of police is already pestering me every lunch rush and living behind my house." Jena glanced out back where she could see a sweaty, shirtless Caleb unloading another box into the 34-foot Airstream trailer at the back of her property that was now his home. If she noticed the lean muscles that glistened in the afternoon heat, well... that just meant she was observant, didn't it?

She hadn't even done a background check, just called Jeremy, who assured her the chief seemed pretty tidy for a bachelor and not likely to run out on the rent. Her mother had been thrilled. "He doesn't need to be intruding on our Sunday dinners, too."

"He's more than welcome," Allie said as she pulled a casserole from the oven. "There's plenty of food."

Ted said, "Ah, but, Allie, that would defeat Jena's purpose in playing hard-to-get."

Jena rolled her eyes. "Why is no one listening to me? I'm not playing hard to get. I'm playing... not-gettable."

"I don't think that's a thing," Alex said.

"It should be."

Ollie's low voice boomed from his station by the grill. "Can we talk about something other than Jena's love life? I feel my hair starting to braid itself."

"Let's talk about Alex's failed hotel idea," Ted said.

"It's not failed." Alex's glare reached across the table. Ted just smiled sweetly at him. "I told you, Grandma Crowe will be putty in my hands. I'll get it passed by the council."

"I hope so," Allie's husband, Joe, said. "Sure would be nice not to have to work in that piss-poor excuse for a farm supply store anymore."

Jena bit her tongue and looked away from Allie's embarrassed face. That "piss-poor excuse" for a store that Allie's father owned was the only thing keeping food on the table since Joe had lost his job as an electrician at the base. In Jena's experience, some men took to unemployment with the pragmatic attitude that "this, too, shall pass" and went on about their lives. Joe wasn't one of those men, and the strain on her friend's face was becoming more and more evident as the months went by.

"Seems like any honest work that takes care of your family is good work to me," Ollie said quietly.

Joe glared at Ollie. "I'm going out for a smoke. Allie, watch the kids?"

"Sure thing." He slammed the screen door as Allie watched him go. "He and my dad were fighting about hours last week."

Jena saw Ollie and Alex both roll their eyes behind Allie's back before they turned back to the meat on the grill.

"Of course," Ted said soothingly. "It's fine. Hey, Allie, don't the kids need a check-up? Seems like I haven't seen them in ages. And I should check Kevin out since he's shifted. Just make sure everything's okay on that end." Few people in town were as educated as Ted. She was an M.D. who also took as many online veterinary courses and seminars as possible. Just par for the course when half your patients turned into something furry or scaly a few times a month.

"I... uh—"

"Just bring them in, *mamá*," Ted said under her breath. "I'm not gonna charge my best friend."

"It's only until we get back on our feet. Then I'm paying you back."

"Of course. And Jena?"

"Yes, Doctor. I'll call the office tomorrow and make appointments for the boys."

"You're due for your annual, too. Both of you."

"Whoa! No," Alex said, holding up a spatula like a shield. "We're not talking about that stuff in front of the guys, okay? We have to draw a line somewhere."

"You boys have been getting your prostates checked regularly, right?" Ted gave them a wicked grin. "You're not in your twenties anymore. I'll give you the family rate."

Alex made a disgusted sound as Ollie silently backed around the corner of the house and disappeared.

"Ted, you do know how to clear a room."

"Don't get me started about colon health."

Allie said, "Okay, *I'm* drawing the line on that one. Are we almost ready to eat?"

"Meat is... done." Alex put it on the platter Jena set out. "Give it about ten minutes to rest and I'll slice it." He nabbed a chip from a bowl as he walked past before he opened another beer and made his way to the backyard to watch the kids with Ollie.

"It's so nice having him back," Allie said. "Do you think he'll stay?"

Ted snorted. "Not likely."

"Has anyone talked to Willow lately? Maybe she knows." Allie asked.

Jena shook her head. "She's been at that art convention in Boulder this month. I haven't seen her."

"Neither have I," Ted said. "Now, Jena, since the boys left us alone, let's talk about the delicious man who now lives within grabbing distance."

"Can we not?" She sat down and sipped a can of soda.

Allie sat next to her. "He's so cute! And he's really interested. I can tell."

"The whole town can tell," Ted said. "He's totally hot, Jen. You should go for it."

"He's asked me out a couple of times."

Allie and Ted exchanged an incredulous look. "Why haven't you said yes?"

She shrugged. "Too busy. And I don't feel like hiding who I am."

Allie gave her a sympathetic look. "Well, I can understand that."

Ted said, "Who knows, maybe he'd be okay with you having feathers."

"And talons," Jena said. "And wings. Yeah, I'm imagining that conversation right now. It ends with me being that crazy chick he kissed one night."

Ted shook her head. "He's going to find out eventually. He's not an idiot."

"We just have to be careful," Allie said. "It's probably good practice for when the resort comes anyway."

"Do you guys want it?" Jena asked. "I still haven't decided to be honest."

Ted said, "I'm on the fence too, but leaning to yes. There are a hell of a lot of people out of work. The Springs can't survive without something new coming in. And if the town doesn't survive..."

She didn't have to finish her sentence. Every shifter from the Springs knew it was unique. This was the place the water flowed. This was home.

Allie glanced at her husband, brooding in the corner of the yard. "I do. If Joe doesn't find something soon, I... I just don't know."

An awkward silence descended between the three of them. Jena knew that Allie and Joe had problems, but her friend tended to put the happiest face on any situation, and she hated to rock the boat.

Finally, Ted said, "I don't know why Alex thought he could pull off hiring a detective from away, though. He should have just had Jeremy—"

"Shhh!" Allie hissed. "*Someone* is coming over."

Caleb strode toward the house. His hat was perched on his head and his chest was bare. His jeans rode low on his hips and Jena could see sweat dripping down the V muscles that framed his abdomen.

"Those are some seriously impressive *transverse abdominis* muscles he's got going on there," Ted muttered.

"I'm not sure what that means, but... wow," Allie said. "Jena, you're officially crazy."

Just then, Caleb looked up and shot her that grin that made him so damn irresistible. Jena melted a little, Allie sighed, and Ted said, "You know, if you're really not interested—"

"Shut up and back off, Ted. Don't even think about it." Jena didn't know what made the words pour out of her mouth. She still wasn't sure what to do with him, but Caleb Gilbert was hers. She'd figure it out later. At the moment, she was transfixed by... man. Hat, dirty jeans, and man. Who was walking right toward her. With no shirt.

A small groan left her mouth. "He's not playing fair." Ted and Allie laughed. "And you two are no help."

"Give up and go for it, Jen," Allie said. "I shudder to think how long it's been."

Ted added, "Think about your health."

She cleared her throat as Caleb approached and tried to look disinterested. "Fine. I'll think about it."

"Hey there," Allie called out, raising a hand to wave at Caleb. "So you're the new neighbor?"

He leaned against the split rail fence and nodded. "Yes, ma'am. I don't think we've officially met."

Allie grinned. "Allie McCann. I'm Jena's best friend. My dad owns the feed store here in town. That's my husband Joe over there." Allie pointed to Joe, who looked like he had cooled off and was playing with the kids in the grass. Joe gave a friendly wave. "And most of the short ones running around are mine, too."

"Ah." Caleb nodded and waved back at Joe. "You're a busy girl. Nice to meet you, Allie. I think I met your husband the other day. Needed some rope, and he helped me out."

"What did he need the rope for?" Ted muttered under her breath. Jena elbowed her. Hard.

Caleb must have caught it. "And you must be Dr. Vasquez."

"You can call her Teodora," Jena said. "She likes that."

Ted scowled. "Or Ted. Please."

"Or 'pain-in-the-ass,'" Allie added, shooting Caleb a bright smile. "She does prostate exams."

Caleb opened his mouth, but nothing came out. "I... have nothing to say to that. Dr. Ted, nice to meet you."

Ted laughed and said, "Likewise, Chief Not-just-passing-through."

"I see my reputation precedes me."

Ted shot Jena an evil grin. "In so many ways..."

Caleb smiled back before giving Jena a scorching once-over. She cleared her throat and tried to ignore the flush in her cheeks. "Is there something I can help you with, Chief?"

"I can think of a few things."

"With the trailer?" Jena tried not to smile. He knew he was pushing her buttons. If her face was as red as it felt, he had to.

Luckily, Caleb had mercy and asked, "I'm having trouble with the AC. Think you can take a look? I'm not real familiar with—"

"We'll check it out." Jena heard Alex interrupt as he and Ollie walked around the corner. "Alex McCann." He held his hand out and Caleb shook it.

"Nice to meet you. But I don't want to bother your dinner—"

"No bother." Ollie said. "Ollie Campbell. And Jena's family. Besides, I helped her mom fix up those things. I'm happy to help."

"We both are." Alex slapped Caleb on his shoulder and started toward the trailer. "Give us a chance to get acquainted with the new chief."

Caleb paused, then gave the two men a nod. "Thanks for the help." Then he turned back to Jena and the girls and tipped his hat. "Ladies, enjoy your dinner."

"We will," Ted said. "Enjoy your... air-conditioning."

"I definitely will." He took off his hat to wipe the sweat that had collected in the desert heat. "This town is way hotter than I expected." Then he caught Jena's eye again before he turned to walk away.

She tried not to laugh. What was she doing? He was smart, funny, not put off by her kids or her job. Despite her initial reservations, his swagger hadn't turned into a run. Caleb Gilbert was turning into someone she looked forward to seeing every day. Even her own mind was rebelling against her; she kept flashing back to that amazing mouth.

"You know," Jena mused as the three men walked away, "if Ollie gets the AC fixed, he might put a shirt on again."

Ted took a sip of her beer, her eyes following her friend's. "You can always break it if you have to."

Allie said, "Think the boys will scare him off?"

Jena made herself a mental deal. If Alex and Ollie couldn't make Caleb back off, then she'd give him a chance. Maybe. "If Caleb can't handle Alex and Ollie getting alpha male protective over me, then he doesn't need to ask me out in the first place, does he?"

"I guess not," Ted said.

Jena watched the three men walk toward the silver trailer. "Definitely not."

chapter
eight

S o, these were Jena's bodyguards. Unlike his earlier concerns at the church service that morning, he wasn't getting any romantic vibes between Jena and either of her two friends. Still, she hadn't hesitated throwing him to the wolves instead of checking the air-conditioner herself. By the look in her eyes as she had examined his deliberately bare chest, he had a feeling she might have given him a replay of their first meeting if she had.

Caleb had a wry smile on his face as he crossed the scrub, leading the two men to his trailer. The AC was the only problem with the place, which had proven to be exactly what he was looking for. The proximity to his current distraction was only an added benefit. Jena's house sat on a couple of acres that stretched back from Spring Street and butted up against the red cliffs of the canyon. Caleb's trailer and one other sat at the back of the property, within shouting distance of Jena's place, but with enough privacy not to be intrusive. From his front yard, he could see the fabled natural springs that gave the town their name, surrounded by a park with some trails and picnic areas. One of these days, he needed to go jogging again. Then maybe he'd sleep better.

"This place working out for you?" the big one, Ollie, asked. He was the owner of the bar and he looked like a cross between a farmer and one of the bikers that frequented his place.

"It's working great. Perfect size."

The other one, Alex, said, "Just you, then? No wife? Girlfriend? Kids?"

Caleb crossed his arms and grinned. "Sorry. Don't swing your way, Alex. But I have a cousin you might be interested in. We look a lot alike."

Ollie laughed and tried to cover it up behind a hand. Alex just looked pissed.

"You know why I'm asking, smartass."

"I get it." He nodded and reached down to right a chair that had tipped over in the dry breeze before he pulled on the T-shirt that had fallen to the ground. "You're looking out for Jena. Nothing wrong with that. I know I'm new in town, but I also know that you did a very thorough background check on me, Mr. McCann, so how about you back off the personal questions you already know the answers to, huh?"

He dusted off his hands as he heard a low sound. Caleb turned and frowned. Did this city boy with the pressed pants and nice shoes actually just... *growl* at him? Who the hell did that?

Alex was curling his lip until Ollie grunted and nudged his shoulder. Caleb liked the big guy. He had the easy confidence of a man who would use violence, but preferred to be left alone. The city boy was a bit of a hothead, if he had to take a guess. Used to getting his way, that was for sure. He wondered if the man had ever set his sights on Jena. He doubted it.

Ollie broke the silence. "Chief, why don't you let me take a look at the AC. Cathy—that's Jena's mom—is great at fixing these things up. She's a hell of a carpenter, but she skimps sometimes on the electrical. I should be able to tell what's going on with it."

Caleb nodded and let the big man into the trailer while Alex paced outside.

The 34-foot Airstream would have been a pain to haul down the road, but it made the perfect apartment. Small and efficient, deep cabinets lined the curved walls, holding the books Caleb hadn't been able to part with back in Albuquerque and the rest of his belongings. The low ceiling just skimmed Caleb's six feet. Ollie had to duck.

"Let's take a look. Is it turned on?"

"Yep."

Ollie frowned. "And not even a hum."

As he walked back to check the breaker box, Caleb tossed a few dishes in the sink. He didn't eat here much, but it was enough. The fridge and freezer were new and the old sink had been replaced by a deeper, full-sized model. The whole trailer had a spare, desert style with a feminine touch, but not in a fussy way.

"I think it's just the breaker. The rest of the electrical's working?"

"Yep. And the plumbing's fine. The AC's the only problem."

Ollie knelt down, fiddling with something in the bedroom. "This place working for you? It's small for a permanent place."

"Yeah, it's good. Enough space for my stuff."

"You travel light."

"I left a lot of stuff back in New Mexico."

"That's good." Ollie stood and brushed off his hands. "Opposite of me. I need to go through my house and get rid of shit."

"Oh?"

He shrugged. "It's a huge old family place, you know? Lots of stuff and just me."

"Really?" Caleb frowned. Despite his rough appearance, Ollie seemed like the more settled type.

"Yep, just me," he said. "I think the fuse is blown, so it's probably no big deal. Go talk to Allie's dad in the morning. He'll have something."

"The farm supply store?"

"He's got a little of everything. Can you make it without AC till tomorrow?"

"I'll have to." It wasn't ideal, but he had fans. Plus, the desert cooled off at night. "I'll keep the windows open."

Ollie's mouth twitched under his beard. "Just keep the doors closed and your stuff pulled in. Full moon in a few nights, there'll be lots of animals out."

"Yeah?"

"Yeah…" There was that smile again. "We get a bit of everything out here. It's the springs."

Water in the desert. Well, that made sense. "I was going to ask, there any good hunting around here?"

The sudden darkness in the man's eyes actually had Caleb taking a step back. "We don't hunt around here."

He blinked. "What? Never?"

"Never. Anyone catches you… Just don't, Chief. It's not a good idea."

And the weirdness was back. Caleb shrugged. "Not even birds, huh? I was on a dove hunt not far from here a while back, and… What?"

Ollie had started laughing under his breath. "Especially not birds. Take my word on this one. You do *not* want to be shooting at birds around here."

"I'll keep that in mind." He opened the fridge, which was still nice and chilly. "Want a beer?"

"Wouldn't turn one down."

Caleb handed him a bottle, which he quickly twisted open.

"Your friend out there want one? He seemed like he could cool down a bit."

"Eh, don't mind Alex. He's on edge right now. But he'll never turn down a beer."

Caleb grabbed another and the two men made their way outside. The sun had started to tilt toward the horizon and the sky had turned pink.

"Alex? Beer?"

"Yeah, thanks." Alex reached out, took the cold bottle, and lifted it. "And sorry about prying. It's a habit."

"Understood. Privacy's a habit for me."

Alex grinned. "You're in the Springs now. You can kiss privacy good-bye."

He grunted and took a drink. "I hear you want to build a hotel out here."

Alex looked at him from the corner of his eye as the three men stared off into the distance. "I *will* build a hotel out here. It's just a matter of time. It'll be the talk of the desert. Very high-end."

"It true that Jena's grandma is the one holding it up?" He drained half the bottle. Damn, it was hot outside. The sun couldn't set fast enough.

"Alma's got some concerns, but nothing I can't work around. I expect the town council to approve it by next month."

"That will certainly make things more exciting around here. More people, tourists coming in and out."

Ollie said, "Better business."

"Like you're hurting for it," Alex said.

The man shrugged. "People like to drink."

Just then, Ollie's attention was caught by movement on the edge of Jena's house. It looked like Jena's friend Allie and her husband were having an argument. Caleb glanced to see where the kids were, but they were all gathered at the large table on the edge of Jena's yard, well out of the way of the arguing couple.

Damn domestic calls. At least the kids weren't around, though he could tell by Jena and Ted's body language that the tension was palpable.

Caleb was two seconds from starting toward them when Joe's voice lifted, carried on the breeze that continued to blow.

"—don't even know why I bother with you!"

An honest-to-goodness snarl erupted from Ollie's throat and he started toward Jena's place, but Joe had already hopped in the car and taken off, the dust spinning out behind him and covering his wife. Caleb could see Ted rushing to her friend as Jena corralled the kids into the house.

"Ollie!" Alex yelled at his friend. "Don't."

Caleb looked between the two men, conscious of some layers of history he wasn't seeing between the group of friends. Ollie halted as he watched Joe's car drive away from the house. Then his shoulders slumped a little. "I'm just going to check on Allie and the kids."

"Ollie—"

"Not another word, Alex." His voice was low, but it carried. Then Ollie continued walking, and Caleb heard Alex sigh.

"So…" Caleb said. "That's obviously complicated. Do I need to worry about the two of them?"

"Joe and Allie or Joe and Ollie?"

"Ha! Allie and…" He trailed off when he caught the unamused expression in Alex's eyes. "I'm talking about Joe and Allie. I'm gonna trust your friend's smart enough to not get in the middle of that."

Alex smirked. "Chief Gilbert, he's been in the middle of that for years. But don't worry about Joe. He's nothing but talk. Everyone's edgy this week."

"Oh?"

Alex opened his mouth, then closed it before he mumbled, "Just something in the air."

There was that weird feeling at the back of his mind again, like he was supposed to remember something and couldn't quite grab it. "Okay, but tell your friend that I noticed him, and he'd better calm down. If I get even a hint of something criminal, I'm not a good ol' boy about it."

"I know." Alex tossed his empty bottle into the trashcan by the door. "You're a boy scout. That's part of the reason I hired you."

"I thought the city hired me," Caleb called as Alex walked away.

The man's only response was an arrogant laugh.

DEPUTY MCCANN WAS EDGY. THE USUALLY CALM MAN WAS practically jumping out of his chair as they sat in the afternoon heat and killed time at the station. Caleb was studying maps of the area again. There were a ton of them for the surrounding desert. Old maps from mining companies, newer maps from various sources. Tribal maps. But there was startlingly little detail about the area immediately surrounding the Springs.

Caleb frowned as Jeremy shuffled the papers in front of him. Then the man started tapping his foot.

He took a slow breath.

Do not kill the deputy, Caleb Gilbert. Do not kill the man.

Maiming... maybe.

If I just took off that right foot, he wouldn't be able to tap—

Jeremy's chair suddenly scraped across the floor as he stood. Caleb could hear the gravel crunch in the driveway and he leaned around the divider, looking for who had pulled in.

Hot damn, it was Jena and her boys.

The little tornado named Aaron—or Bear—was the first through the door.

"Hey, Cousin Jeremy! Where's the jail part? Can I see? Mom said she needed to talk to you, so we could come too, 'cause I wanted to see where the people get locked up. Hey, Chief Gilbert! Do you still like your little house? I told everyone at school that a policeman lives with us, but then Mrs. Strickle said that probably you didn't live *with* us but just behind our house and her ears got really red! What makes people get red ears?"

Caleb couldn't contain his smile. "Maybe she had chili peppers for lunch."

Aaron decided this was the most hilarious thing in the world. He laughed his little head off, then proceeded to touch every single item of interest on Caleb's desk, from the chunk of petrified rock to the wobbly hula girl the boys in Albuquerque had given him as an early retirement present. Caleb blinked in astonishment. How did Jena live with all that energy?

Aaron continued chattering in the background as Jena and her older son slumped through the door. Well, Older Son slumped.

Man, did he look like his mom. He had high cheekbones and a mop of dark brown hair that fell into his eyes. The boy was twelve? Thirteen? However old he was, the girls probably fell over themselves to catch his attention, but Low carried himself with the familiar world-weariness perfected by most adolescents. Caleb smiled and ignored him, turning his attention to Jena.

"Hey all," she said as she pulled off her sunglasses. She didn't wear anything fancy, just an old pair of black aviators that looked a little scratched up. Her hair was pulled into a ponytail and the wind had whipped it around so that pieces fell around her face. She looked perfect. And just like Jeremy, she seemed on edge. Aaron was bouncing around the room, even Low, as nonchalant as he tried to be, radiated concealed tension.

What the hell was going on in this town? Maybe the wind out here did make you a little crazy after a while. It had been blowing steady for days.

"Hey, Jena, what's up?" Jeremy asked. "The boys just want to take a look at the station?"

"They've been asking for a while—well, Bear has—but I had a question for you, if you have a minute."

Jeremy looked over to Caleb. "Chief, you mind?"

"Naw." He swung his legs out from under his desk and stood. Aaron immediately came to his side and pulled on his arm. "Why don't I take shorty here back to see the cells? Low, you want to come, too?"

The older boy shrugged, but Jena nudged his shoulder. "Go help with your brother. Make sure he doesn't break anything."

He gave a small sigh and stood. Caleb led the two boys back to the conference room where Aaron quickly fell on the donuts.

"Bear, not too many," Low warned.

Caleb waved a hand. "It's all right."

"No, it's not. Mom'll get pissed if he gets all wound up."

"You mean this isn't wound up already?"

"Nope. Normal Bear."

Aaron limited himself to one donut as Caleb showed him around and answered his questions.

Did bad guys really get put into handcuffs? Usually.

Would Caleb let Bear handcuff him? Definitely not.

Where was his gun? In the holster at his waist.

And the really big guns?

He was relentless. And fun, Caleb had to admit that. Open, friendly. The complete opposite of his older brother.

"So…" Caleb started. "You're in fifth grade?"

"Sixth."

"Ah." Aaron climbed in the cell and crawled up the bed, clutching the edge of the small window until he could peer out. "Wow, he's like a monkey."

"You should see him on the jungle gym at school."

"There's just one school in town, right?"

"Yeah, it's too small here to have more than one. Even the high school kids are on the same campus."

"Huh." Silence again. "What's your favorite class?"

"Lunch. And you don't have to do this, you know." Low looked through the hair in his eyes, glancing up into Caleb's face. The boy would be tall. Probably taller than Caleb, though he looked a little on the rangy side.

"Do what?"

"Act all friendly with me because you like my mom. I can tell. Everyone can tell."

Caleb smiled. "That obvious?"

"That obnoxious. She doesn't like it."

He lifted an eyebrow. "Oh really?"

Low's chin lifted up. "Yeah, really. She doesn't have time for people like you."

"What kind of people are those?" Caleb clamped down on his temper. It was no use letting the boy get the reaction he wanted. For a minute, Low seemed at a loss to explain himself.

"Just… people who—who aren't from around here. That's all."

Caleb shrugged. He had a feeling this was more Low's wishful thinking than anything else. "Well, I'm here now."

An angry light flared in Low's eyes, and for a minute, the boy looked so much like his mother that he caught his breath. "Just leave her alone, all right?"

Aaron bounced over. "Leave who alone?"

Low shoved his brother in front of him and headed toward the front of the building. "No one, Bear. You see enough of the police station?" The boy's voice had softened as he spoke to his brother.

How long had his father been gone? Three years? Four? Important years for a boy. Years that he'd been, whether Jena realized it or not, the small man of the house. A small man who didn't appreciate Caleb cutting in on his territory, as he saw it. It was something to think about. As he came through the door from the back, Jena's low voice reached his ears.

"—I just know she's new in town. I don't want to impose."

Jeremy seemed to be reassuring her. "It's fine, Jena. Call her. I can almost guarantee it won't be a—"

"I wouldn't even ask, but... well, you know."

"It's fine. She gets it. Really, she does. And she really likes the boys. Just call her."

Jena grabbed him in a quick hug. "Thanks." She pulled away and turned to look for the boys. "Hey, Bear! Was it cool?"

"Totally cool, Mom. You gotta go look. There's, like, this window, but it doesn't have bars or anything. It has funny glass. And a cell—that has bars—and donuts!"

Jena laughed. "I'll go take a peek."

"Cousin Jeremy, can I see the big guns?"

Caleb grinned as the barrage of questions focused on his deputy. Then he turned to Jena, motioning toward the door. "May I?"

A glint came to her eye. Caleb liked that glint. A lot. "You may."

Something was different. He tried not to get his hopes up, but the nerves that had made Jeremy so jumpy all day seemed to be different coming off Jena. Caleb could feel the tension start to curl in his belly as he followed her in back, taking care to shut the door behind him.

Jena looked around. "This is an old building. Adobe?"

Elizabeth Hunter

"Mm-hmm." He watched her peek in the conference room, then the cells. She turned to him and grinned. "Did you really sleep back here before I rented you the trailer?"

Caleb leaned against a wall. "I did. It wasn't as bad as it looks. Very quiet."

She leaned against the opposite wall. "Pretty kinky, Chief. Sleeping in a jail cell."

"Is that an invitation?" He let his eyes run up and down, smiling when she began to laugh.

"You're shameless."

"I am. Persistent, too."

"I've noticed." The energy coming off her was palpable. She felt like a live wire, even from across the room.

"Why won't you go out with me?"

"Maybe you're not asking the right questions."

"Is that so?"

She shrugged. "You'll figure it out. So, the boys liked it back here? Bear has been asking for days."

"He's a live one. No wonder your legs are so sexy, running after that kid."

Jena smiled. "He does keep me on my toes. It doesn't bother you that I have kids?"

"No. I like kids. They're fun and more honest than adults."

"Yes, they are."

He forced himself to lean against the wall. The urge to kiss her was almost overwhelming. He wanted to touch her. Wanted to run his fingers along her skin.

Jena asked, "You don't have any? Kids, I mean."

"My ex didn't want any."

She paused. "That's too bad."

"I thought so. But then, that's part of the reason we're not together anymore."

"What are the other reasons?"

Caleb narrowed his eyes. "I don't know. That's more of a... third date, deep conversation over coffee kind of talk, Jena."

"Oh really?" She looked amused, but with an unmistakable edge of hunger in her eyes.

"Yep, definitely third date material."

He had to touch her. Caleb pulled away from the wall and walked toward her slowly. If she wanted to leave, she could. But she didn't move. Not even a muscle. The dry air sparked as he approached. He saw Jena take a deep breath as he leaned toward her. She smelled like dust and roses. A slight tang of salt from the sweat of the day. He licked his lips and saw her watching his tongue as it darted out.

"Will you go out with me?"

He could almost feel her heartbeat. It lay right under her skin, pulsing into the charged air around her.

She whispered, "Maybe."

"Will you kiss me?"

"Yes."

Caleb bent toward her, feeling her rapid breath against his lips. This was beyond fun now. There was something about her. Some puzzle begging to be solved. He leaned in a fraction of an inch. Another. Ducked in to flick his tongue against her full, lower lip, then he pulled back.

It worked.

Jena leaned forward, her body moving into his like a magnet. She pressed against him. Then her hands gripped his waistband and swung him around so his back was against the wall and she pressed her lips to his in a long, hard kiss. He kept his hands flat against the cold adobe walls to keep from grabbing her and focused on her mouth.

Hot. Sweet. *Better*. It was better than he remembered, the taste of her now flavored by the woman he was beginning to know.

Caleb's mind was whirling when Jena pulled back, nipping at his lower lip with her teeth before she leaned in and whispered in his ear.

"That was one of the right questions."

HIS DREAMS WERE FRANTIC, BUT NOT FOR THE REASON Caleb would have hoped.

He was running again, chased by some shadow that panted on the desert wind. He ran naked over dry washes and gullies, his legs torn by the claws of the tumbleweeds that dotted the barren landscape. A shadow passed overhead. A low growl before a cat screamed in the night.

Where was he running?

The old songs floated on the wind. A memory of his uncle's frown and his grandmother's laugh.

Who was singing?

And who was chasing him?

Caleb was breathing hard and drenched when he sat up in bed. The full moon shone across his pillow, its bright glare lighting up the bedroom. In the distance he heard what sounded like wolves, and a coyote yipped close by. A rustling sound crept into the trailer from some small creature outside.

Caleb blinked and looked at the clock by the bed.

3:00 a.m.

The wind whistled over his head. The desert was alive. So alive. He blinked the sleep from his eyes and stood, walking to the small bathroom to splash water on his face. The moon was so bright, he didn't even need to turn on the lights to move around, and though he knew he was in the middle of town, Caleb had the creeping feeling that he was completely and utterly alone.

His phone rang, startling him so that he banged his knee on the doorjamb as he walked. It was on the table in the kitchen. The screen lit up with his deputy's name across the top.

Why was McCann calling at three in the morning?

Just then, he felt it. The familiar rush of adrenaline absent for so many months he'd actually stopped counting. It cleared the sleep from his eyes and brought his senses to a razor's edge in an instant. It pumped through his veins as he reached for the phone. He didn't need more sleep. He didn't need food or drink or company.

He only needed this.

Caleb spoke in a low, steady voice. "Detective Gilbert."

"Chief?"

That's right. Chief, not detective. Where was he?

Desert. Supposed to be quiet. But it wasn't quiet. No place was quiet. The coyotes yipped closer and the memory of old songs rose in the back of his mind.

"Yeah, it's me. What's up?"

"I need you out at the Crowe place."

"What?" He yelled it, immediately reaching for the gun that rested in the small cabinet over the fridge.

"Not Jena, man!"

"What the hell is going on, McCann? Make it quick."

He could hear the young man take a shaky breath. "It's Alma Crowe, Chief. Something attacked her. She's dead."

chapter nine

N ot real. *Not real not real not real.*

But it was all so glaringly real. The minutes—sometimes hours—after she came out of a moon shift always put her on edge anyway. Her vision, achingly acute when in her hawk form, still caught every nuance. Light was brighter. Colors more vivid.

The splayed form of her grandmother. Naked. Ready for a flight with her granddaughter.

"We haven't gone flying in months, Jena. See if you can find someone to watch the boys so we can go together next moon."

The claw marks that had slashed along her torso, warped and no longer recognizable as feline.

But they had been, she was almost sure of it. Her keen avian eyes caught that. Her grandmother, like all shifters, reverted to her human form upon death, but Alma had been trying to flee. She had been naked, near a kitchen window. If the old woman had been able to fully shift—

She hadn't. Whatever had caught her grabbed her out of the air, piercing the elegant barn owl's heart and tearing across her abdomen until she bled out.

That was how Jena found her. Pools of blood leaking out of her grandmother. There was so much blood. Would it bleed through the carpet? The floorboards? Down into the sand underneath the house?

The hawk had flown to the window, seen her grandmother's body, and screamed in rage. Then Jena had panicked and flown to John McCann's old place. Lowell's grandfather was the oldest of their pack and he and his wife would be watching the children of those who had to shift. It was one of the responsibilities of older shifters and non-changing husbands and wives.

"Jena? Why are you here? You're shaking out of your skin, girl. Is something wrong? Where are the boys?"

"It—it's Alma... Dead, Grandpa John. She's—"

"What?"

"Someone killed her. I think it was one of us."

"Corinne, stay with the children! I'm going for Jeremy."

She'd been naked and trying to remain human when he shifted. The old grey wolf leapt off the front porch and took into the night. By the time John's wife, Corinne, came out with a blanket to cover her, Jena had shifted to a hawk again.

"Jena, wait!"

She couldn't. Couldn't leave her grandmother out in the desert all alone. Her wings beat against the night sky, soaring up and over the houses. Past the lights of the town and into the barren land that Alma had adored.

How long would it take Jeremy to shift back to his human form? He was young, and wolves were notoriously bad at repressing a change on moon nights. He'd be able to do it, but it wouldn't be easy.

Moon nights were usually times for celebration. Their animals were let out to roam and non-shifters watched the younger children, often gathering in family groups and letting the children have slumber parties and game nights to fill the evening. Jeremy's wife, Brenda, was new in town and still shy around many of his family, so she'd been happy to watch the boys for Jena while the single mother flew with her grandmother. Usually, Alma would gather the boys and go stay at John and Corinne's house, talking with old friends, playing cards, and letting the children stay up way too late with their wolf cousins.

Jena shifted back when she landed on Alma's porch, then walked inside and found an old shift dress of her grandmother's that just barely fit. She grabbed the shotgun from over the door before she went back to sit on the porch. She resisted the urge to cover up her grandmother, knowing Ted would need to see her.

See her like that?

She choked back the tears and kept watch for Jeremy's truck. Would Jeremy be able to find Ted? Ted was better at coming out of a shift, but she'd have to be tracked down. Would one of the cat elders track her down and let her know?

One of the cats...

Jena gritted her teeth, the anger clearing her eyes as she started.

Her eyes.

She let out a harsh breath and stood. Her eyes were better than anyone else's. She could see things, especially right after a shift, that human eyes never would. Colors were more vivid to her, and she picked up and recorded visual information with an almost photographic memory.

She needed to go back inside.

Slowly, she stood and pulled the groaning screen door open, then paused, listening again for any movement. The only sound was the clock over the mantle, ticking.

It had been a wedding present from her grandfather, the wild railroad worker who had fallen in love with the girl who worked at the diner near the tracks. Alma had been stunning when she was young, a petite brunette with the high cheekbones of her Cherokee blood and a secret that she had entrusted to the eager boy who pursued her. The boy who loved her for sixty-seven years until the heart attack took him. Jena barely remembered him, but he'd had a long life for an outsider. Ninety years. His wife had longer, as all shifters did, but Alma had expected that.

Jena blinked back another round of tears as she stepped toward the kitchen. Many of the older shifters could live to one hundred ten years or more in robust health. They never got sick. Never a failed heart or a cancer diagnosis. Her grandmother, at almost one hundred years, had looked like a woman in her early eighties. Now she looked like a mangled doll.

She was naked, lying in a pool of dark blood. Both arms were spread, reaching out as if she was just about to fly from the room. Her body was angled toward a large open window, where the dusty night breeze still flipped the curtains into the house. Her legs were bunched under her, bent as they would be when she first went into her shift.

Was she human or owl when she was killed? From the position of the body, Jena was guessing owl. She'd fallen, then shifted back to her human form. Jena couldn't—couldn't look at the deep gashes that marred Alma's torso. She tried, but every time, the urge to vomit almost drove her from the room. So she dug her teeth into her lower lip and forced herself to look around the kitchen.

There were pies cooling on the counter. One in a box, as if ready for a guest to take home. For Jena? Maybe. How had Alma's attacker gotten inside the house? She walked to the back porch, carefully stepping around the body to push the door open. There were scratches at the bottom that looked new. Small, not a mountain lion. Bobcat, maybe? Lynx? She didn't know enough. Maybe Ted would. There was something different about the claw marks, but she couldn't think what. Her brain felt scrambled. She took one last mental picture, then went back inside.

The blood. The sight of it hit her again, and her stomach churned. There was so much blood. Alma's eyes were wide open in shock. Jena couldn't help herself. She reached down and closed them. Then she crumbled to the ground, her back against the cupboard doors her grandfather had carved.

"Are you with him now, Grandma?" she whispered as the tears poured down her face. "Please be with him. Don't linger like Lowell did. Please. Go to Grandpa. I'll be okay."

Alma was silent, her body only a shell of the vital woman she had

Elizabeth Hunter

been. Other than the warped gashes across her abdomen, she looked curiously unharmed. There were no scratches or bruises that Jena could see. But her sun-darkened skin was pale and bloodless. Her lips more blue by the minute. Jena pulled up her knees, laid her forehead on them, and sobbed.

Jeremy and Ted found her like that, curled on the ground, shaking and aching to return to the safety of her hawk form.

"Jena, why are you in here?" Ted sounded like she was on the verge of tears. "Come on. Come out on the porch with me."

"I can't!" she cried. "I can't."

"Jena." Jeremy's voice was soft and firm. "Let me take care of her now. You go with Ted. I need to get a scent profile. Then I'm gonna have to call Chief Gilbert. I need you out of here, Jena. Your scent is too strong."

"You're not just saying that?"

"No, hon." Jeremy knelt down and helped Ted get Jena to her feet. "You'll help her more if you're out of here."

She nodded and let them lead her out to the porch. It was better, better for Alma that way.

"Do you need to go back inside?" she asked Ted.

"No. It'll be easier for Jeremy to scent if I'm not in there. Just having your smell and mine clouding the area is going to make it difficult enough."

Just like Jena's vision still wore the strength of her hawk form, Jeremy's body still wore the strengths of his wolf. He was one of the smaller wolves in the pack, but smart and quick, according to Alex. He had quickly moved up the complicated wolf hierarchy that no one truly understood outside the McCanns. His sense of smell could be a definite advantage in finding out who had killed Alma.

Ted continued. "I'll be able to examine the body—I mean... examine her later. And she's probably going to have to go somewhere else, Jen. Another... lab. I don't have the facilities here."

Just the thought choked her again. Ted pulled her into her arms.

"Oh, Jena," she sniffed. "I'm so damn sorry. I don't know what to say. I can't believe it."

"We were gonna go flying. We hadn't been out together in months. If we'd just stuck with our routine, then she wouldn't have even been here."

"I know."

The weariness was starting to hit. "Why didn't we just stick with routine?"

"This isn't your fault, Jen. Only one person is at fault for this, and we're going to find him."

"Okay." For some reason, she didn't doubt it. "Someone we know, Ted. One of our neighbors. Could it have been an animal attack?"

"I don't know."

"Maybe it was random." She knew she was rambling. "Or—or an accident?"

"Jena—"

Ted broke off when the front door opened. Jeremy was looking ragged around the edges, obviously feeling the effects of forcing himself to remain human, but his voice was still calm and soothing. His eyes were steady and confident.

"Ted, you can come in now. I've got as much as I'm gonna get. Now, Jena, I'm gonna have to call the chief. You understand that, right?"

She nodded. "Right."

"Which means you better think of a good reason you were out at your grandma's house in the middle of the night on a Tuesday. Ted drove your car over here, so you won't have to explain that. Think up a reason Alma wasn't wearing anything." Jeremy looked like he was at a loss. "I... I wish I had a suggestion, but you'll probably—"

"I'll think of something."

Ted got up to retrieve her case from the pickup truck, and Jeremy knelt down next to Jena on the porch steps. "I know we gotta keep him in the dark about a lot, but try to give him as much information as you can without revealing anything you can't. He's good, Jena. I've seen his record. Murder cases. Drug rings. Gang stuff. He knows his stuff. If anyone can find who did this…"

"Did you get anything from the scents?"

"I did. But don't worry about that now. I want to let Ted get her stuff and the chief get his before we start putting all this together."

"I saw some things, too."

"Figured you might have, but we'll talk about it later. Right now, I'm gonna make that call, okay?"

She nodded. There was no delaying it. She wanted to see Caleb again, but she didn't want him to question her. For once, she wanted to be held by someone who felt stronger. Someone she could depend on. She wanted to cry and rail and know that *someone* was aching because she was hurt. Something told her Caleb Gilbert might just be strong enough, but that wasn't why he was coming. Jena took a deep breath, pulling the raw grief inside. She only hoped the man was as good at his job as Jeremy seemed to think, because there was a hell of a lot they weren't going to tell him.

chapter
ten

W hy had he thought it would be easier?

As Caleb drove out to Alma's house, following the cryptic directions Jeremy had given him, he steeled himself to deal with seeing the body of the lively old woman who had served him pie and teased him about her granddaughter. The same granddaughter who had found her dead body a matter of hours ago.

"Why were you out there, Jena? Why did it have to be you?"

Unlike the city, here there was no one to call. No backup or disinterested detective.

'I know the victim. Put someone else on it.'

'I'm involved with her granddaughter. Find someone else.'

There was no "someone else" anymore.

Caleb realized something as he pulled into the gravel in front of Alma's house. While the city may have been impersonal at times, it had sheltered him with anonymity. In Cambio Springs, there was no shelter. He would know every victim along with their families and friends. He'd deal with the aftermath of violence long after the case had closed. He hadn't thought about that part. He'd looked forward to the expectation of easy days and no midnight calls.

Now, as he looked at Jena's slumped shoulders on the porch—her devastated eyes, her shaking body—he didn't want to question her. He wanted to hold her. In some ways, this was going to be the hardest case he'd ever solve. But he would solve it. Caleb may have had a bad track record of taking care of the living, but the dead were a different matter.

He closed his eyes, took a deep breath, and focused. Then he opened them and looked at the house with new eyes.

Jena had found her grandmother before dawn on a Wednesday morning. Why was she here? Had Alma called expecting trouble or was this related to the cryptic conversation he'd overheard her having with Jeremy?

"—I just know she's new in town. I don't want to impose."

"It's fine, Jena. Call her. I can almost guarantee it won't be a—"

"I wouldn't even ask, but... well, you know."

"It's fine. She gets it. Really, she does. And she really likes the boys. Just call her."

He would bet Brenda McCann was at Jena's house that very moment. And Jeremy was already here, which meant Jena had called him first. Not all that unexpected. Despite their growing friendship, he was still the unfamiliar element in this town. Well, that and murder. Caleb had looked at the sheriff's records. The last homicide in Cambio Springs had been fifteen years before, when a man had shot his wife in a domestic dispute. It had been tragic, but a clear crime of passion. The husband had been sitting on the porch when the deputies had come, weeping and near suicide over his actions.

From what little Jeremy had told him when he called, this was something altogether different.

"Not sure, Chief. Looks like an animal attack. It may be that, but it's inside. It's possible something wandered into the house, since she does live out in the middle of nowhere. It's a weird one."

Alma Crowe was no dummy. She wasn't likely to let an animal in her house in the middle of the night. What was really going on here?

Caleb opened the door and stepped out. Jena, wearing an odd dress, was sitting on the porch steps with Jeremy. Not her dress. He could see that immediately. Had she gotten blood on her clothes and wanted to change? It wouldn't be the first time he'd encountered it with witnesses. Blood was a primal reminder that something had gone terribly wrong. Most people avoided it. The sight of it. The smell. Caleb tucked the information into the back of his mind and looked around the house.

The scene. Not the house, the *scene*.

Jeremy's pickup was pulled up front. Jena's car around the side. A kitchen door? Family and close friends would use the kitchen door. He couldn't see Alma's car, but it might have been in the detached garage he could see behind the house. Were they going somewhere? Was Jena supposed to drive? He approached the two cautiously. Jeremy was speaking in a low voice, and Jena kept nodding mechanically. Her eyes were red from tears, but her skin was pale and drawn. She was a hundred victims he'd seen before. She was the only victim ever.

Caleb wanted to hold her.

He pushed the urge back and nodded as Jeremy looked at him.

"Chief."

"Deputy. Jena." He kneeled down on the lowest porch step so he was even with her. Jena lifted swollen eyes to his and he couldn't help himself. He reached out and tucked a piece of hair behind her ear, brushing a finger over her cheek. It was hot, like she'd been crying for a long time. He saw her eyes start to well again, so he pulled back. "I'm sorry," he said in a soft voice. "I'm so sorry, Jena. I'll help her now. Do you understand?" She nodded and closed her eyes. Then she took a deep breath and started to speak.

"I was coming out here—"

"Let me..." He interrupted gently. "Let me go look first. It'll just take a few minutes. I'll be back. Jeremy, you picked up Ted, right? Is she in there?"

It hadn't surprised him to learn that Teodora Vasquez, only doctor in Cambio Springs, was the coroner as well. But unlike some coroners in small towns, he had a feeling Ted would take this job just as seriously as setting bones or giving exams. That said, it was a quiet town and this was probably her first violent death.

"Yeah, she's in there."

"I'll go back. Wait with Jena?"

Jeremy nodded while Caleb rose and walked up the steps. He paused a moment before he entered the house, wishing he'd had time to visit before its owner became a murder victim. He quickly shoved the thought to the back of his mind and opened the door.

It was the same everywhere. The metallic scent that sometimes hit him at scenes. Death had many scents, but this time, it was the over-whelming smell of blood that drifted to him. He followed the quiet sound of Ted's voice that led him to the kitchen. She was taking notes into a small voice recorder. All the expected stats as she measured and sampled. The myriad familiar tasks that a forensic examiner performed as she cared for the remains and collected evidence. It wasn't quite as exciting as the television shows made it out to be, but the evidence was important, nonetheless.

Ted glanced at him once, but kept speaking her notes into the recorder as she crouched next to the body. Caleb could tell from her actions that she'd done this before. She paused and switched her recorder off before she stood up and met his professional stare. She was devastated, but hiding it well. She also anticipated his question.

"I worked for a few years in L.A., but no, it's not the same."

"It never is when it's someone you know."

"You ever had a victim you've known?"

"That I investigated? No. Not like this." Created? That was a different story.

"We could call Dev."

He tried to not be insulted. "He knew Alma better than I do. It'd be harder for him to be objective."

"Yeah, but he's not trying to get into her granddaughter's... Never mind. You'll be fine."

Caleb's eyes narrowed at the dig. He'd once been Albuquerque's top detective, but he didn't feel like justifying himself to her.

"First impressions, Dr. Vasquez?"

Ted straightened and turned on her professional face, despite the exhaustion and grief in her eyes.

"Body temperature suggests death around two in the morning. Cause? Well... as you can see, that's both obvious and odd."

For the first time, Caleb truly turned his eyes on the body.

Not Alma. Just a body.

A body that had succumbed to massive blood loss from the gashes ripped across her chest and abdomen. It was as if a giant claw had swiped from shoulder to hip, tearing into everything it met. Deep. There were three... Or four? One claw mark was shallower. It was an injury that looked like it had come from a giant paw.

"That looks like an animal attack."

"I know."

What had a paw that big? Caleb squinted and moved closer. He looked around the room, immaculate save for the blood spray. What could have made that kind of wound?

"You get bears around here?"

She stuttered. "Bears?"

"Yeah."

"Um... some. But none that Alma was going to risk around her china cabinet."

"You're right. She'd never let a bear in." He glanced at the kitchen door. He'd examine it later, but there were no obvious signs of break-in.

"She knew him. Let him in."

"Him?" Ted's voice sounded weird. "This looks like an animal to me."

"Would she have let an animal into the house?"

Animal? Human? The wound looked animal; the scene looked human. There were a few signs of struggle, but nothing extensive enough to have been put there by an animal big enough to make those wounds. There was blood splatter on the walls and over the floor, but not as much as he would have expected considering the size of the slash marks.

"She was moving when she was killed," he murmured. "Trying to get away."

"It looks like it."

There was that itching at the back of his mind again. Something about this scene...

It was wrong. Just wrong. His instincts screamed it. There was an element missing. A blind spot he couldn't angle his eyes into. A lens out of focus. He blinked as he looked at the body again.

"She's naked."

Ted looked nervous and glanced away. Embarrassed by the sight of her friend's grandmother or something else?

He muttered, "Why was she naked?"

Ted cleared her throat. "Maybe she sleeps in the buff. Been known to do it myself on occasion."

"No evidence of clothes?" Had the killer undressed her?

"Not that I've seen. And no cloth in the wounds that I can see. You might ask Jeremy."

"No... her body doesn't look like he undressed her after death." If he had, there would have been smears on the skin, evidence that someone had forced limp arms through cloth. The angles of her body would have been unnatural and bent. The victim had fallen on her side, but it looked like she'd been left alone to bleed out without being further molested.

Caleb walked around the body, measuring, taking it all in, and locking it in his memory. "She wasn't sleeping. Jena was coming over and she was expected." He glanced around. Where was the laundry room? There, over by the kitchen door. It was possible that the old woman had been on her way to get clothes from the dryer. When he'd lived in the big empty house in New Mexico, he'd done the same, wandered to the laundry room after a shower to get a favorite shirt or pair of jeans.

"Tell me about the cause of death."

She sighed. "Here's where we get obvious and odd at the same time. The wounds, obviously, are what killed her. They're deep, almost three inches, and clean. Something strong. Cut over her ribs starting at the shoulder and then into her gut. She bled out. I'd say animal, but the wounds are... too clean. That's the odd part."

"Not like an animal attack."

She shook her head. "Not like any I've seen. I stitched up Steve Quinn last August when he got into a scuffle with a mountain lion. The wounds were similar, but not like this. These are... Well, you can see."

Ted crouched down, careful not to disturb anything. He squatted next to her and his eyes immediately went wide when he saw the slashes. "What the hell..."

The slices were raw and bloody, but just as Ted said, clean. Like an animal, but too smooth. The flesh looked like it had curved into the valley the weapon had left, distorting the edges of the skin. Even— impossible to think—healing partially.

"There's no way," he said under his breath. "No way." Alma Crowe would have been dead in minutes. There was no way her body would have been able to heal, even a little bit. It was impossible. There had to be another explanation.

"Not an animal, unless it's something we haven't seen before."

He turned his head to her. "And you're sure you've never seen anything like this before?"

The flinch was so minute that even he barely caught it. "Nope. New to me, too."

She was lying. Why was she lying? He tucked the information away to examine later.

"Right. You going to send the body to San Bernardino?"

She nodded quickly. "I don't have the facilities to handle this here."

"Do what you have to."

He made quick work of examining the rest of the scene, hoping that he wasn't letting some vital piece of information slip his observation because he was distracted. He was leaning outside the kitchen door an hour later, gathering his thoughts.

Who had Alma trusted enough to let in before dawn?

Why was she naked?

What had made those wounds?

It wasn't an animal; that was for sure. The scene was too clean. An animal wouldn't have attacked like that, then left the body alone.

Knives? How would the tracks between slashes remain so even if it was a knife? She'd been alive when the blades had gone through her flesh. His mind rebelled at the implication, but Caleb forced his way through it. No mercy had been granted Alma Crowe, and if she'd suffered the terror of having her life taken by a monster who would carve an old woman up over and over again, then she deserved to have someone relive the experience with her, even if it was just in his imagination.

Had she been drugged somehow? He'd wait for the toxicology report, but the position of the body implied flight. Then there was that blood spray. So small. So contained. Not as if a grown woman had struggled at all. More as if…

A child. That's what it had reminded him of. The blood spray matched a small victim, the blood pooling on the floor a larger victim.

The tickling at the back of his mind grew irritating. Ted was lying. And Caleb was putting off talking to Jena.

He sighed and walked around the house to the front porch, glancing down to make sure that there was no blood on his clothes. Then he glanced at Jena's car pulled up the side of the house and frowned. Caleb turned the corner just as the light was peeking over the horizon. Jena was still waiting outside the house that her grandmother had been murdered in, sitting next to Jeremy, staring out into the slowly lightening day. His arms ached to scoop her up, put her in his truck and drive far, far away from here. Far enough away that she would forget her sadness and laugh again. But Caleb knew better than anyone how useless running was.

He came up to the porch and nodded at Jeremy. "Ted needs to take some pictures. She may need your help."

"Sure thing, Chief. Jena?"

The woman gave a slight nod and leaned away from him, then turned and rested her back against the porch railing to face Caleb.

"Hey."

Her voice was hoarse when she answered. "Hey."

"How you holding up?"

"How am I supposed to hold up?"

He knew better than anyone there was no answer to that. "Someone staying with the boys?"

She blinked back tears. "Yeah, I called Ollie. He came over and took them out to his place."

"Good." He paused. "Jena—"

"I came out here at two thirty or so. I know it probably sounds weird, but Grandma liked to go use the mud pools by the springs. There's two that you can soak in. She claimed it was good for her health. Kept her young and all that. So every now and then, when the moon was bright, I'd take her to the canyon and we'd go. She liked going at night. That's why I was here so late."

Too smooth. She'd practiced that one a few times.

Caleb pulled out his notebook. Then he sat down across from her and propped one knee up on the steps, quickly running through the standard questions about when she'd arrived: What had she done? Had she touched the body at all? Did she notice anyone suspicious hanging around? She answered just as quickly, as if she knew what he was going to ask and was expecting it. He closed his notebook and looked at her.

"So she was expecting you."

"Yes."

"But she wasn't wearing clothes. Not even a sign of them at the scene."

Her eyes glinted in surprise, then anger, as if she was irritated that he'd gone off script. "She probably hadn't put on her robe yet. You don't wear clothes in the mud pool."

Lying. Every inch of his gut told him. That itching in the back of his mind begged to be scratched. Why the hell was she lying to him?

"And you weren't wearing clothes when you came."

That surprised her. She looked up, alarm coloring her features for only a moment before she answered.

"I had borrowed this old dress from her. I was returning it. Do you think I killed my grandmother or something?"

"No, I don't." He didn't just think it. He knew it. Knew the woman sitting across from him—who had obviously adored Alma—could never have killed the woman. He knew Jena was devastated. And it killed him to have to question her when he wanted to be comforting her. "I don't think you would ever hurt your grandmother."

"I thought this was an animal attack."

"It might be."

"Then why all the questions, Caleb?"

Caleb, not "Chief." He sighed. "Jena, I'm trying to get an idea about what happened tonight. There are a lot of things that don't add up. And your dress is only one of them. I'm trying to figure out who would've known that Alma and you were going out tonight. Who might have known that she'd even be awake at that hour. Who she would have let in wearing nothing at all. There was no sign of a break in, so—"

"There were scratches by the kitchen door. Did you see them?" Her voice was raised in challenge.

"Scratches?"

"Yes. Fresh ones down at the base of the door and the threshold. It was obviously an animal."

"I'll take another look. But something about this doesn't seem like an animal attack to me." She looked away. That tickle became a thorny, spiky burr, boring into his skull. She was hiding something too. He let out a frustrated puff of air and shook his head, muttering, "This damn town."

"I guess old women never got killed in Albuquerque, huh?"

He managed not to glare at her, conscious of the terrible shock she'd been through. "Yeah, Jena. People get killed in Albuquerque. Old women, children, all sorts. And I've worked a lot of murder scenes, all over the place. So when I say something about this whole thing seems wrong to me, I'm not talking about the fact that someone or something killed Alma. I'm talking about the fact that everyone—you, Ted, even Jeremy—is lying to me and I can't tell why or about what."

She seethed in quiet fury. "I want to go home."

"Fine. I'll have more questions for you later, but I'll take you home."

"I have my own car, thanks."

"You don't need to be driving right now."

He stood and held out a hand; she ignored it and stood on her feet, walking toward the side of the house.

"I need to get my car home."

"Why don't you just leave it for Ted? Driver's seat is already scooted up for her height anyway."

She froze, but didn't turn around.

"I imagine the keys are in her purse, because I don't see yours around anywhere. Big leather thing, the boys' school pictures hanging off the strap." He stepped closer. "You don't go anywhere without that purse. But it's not here, is it?"

She was shaking. Nerves? Anger? "I'm not talking to you anymore."

He let out a breath. "Fine. I'm still driving you home. You really shouldn't be behind a wheel."

"Fine."

Jena walked to the car, opened the door, and got in. She was silent the whole way home.

HE SPENT ALL DAY FILLING OUT PAPERWORK. TED AND Jeremy waited at the house for the ambulance that would take the body down to San Bernardino and the sheriff-coroner's office there. He sifted through Jeremy's report and filled out his own. On the surface, it looked like Alma had died of an animal attack, as bizarre as it seemed. There were no other signs of struggle or break-in. No theft. No damage to her body other than the four unusual claw marks. But the scene didn't have the random feel of an animal attacking.

Maybe someone around here bred those crazy giant cats that some people liked to keep. He'd run across a few of them when he was in Narcotics. Sometimes dealers liked to keep them around isolated factories or farms. And he had seen how the damn things could be trained to attack. That was at least one idea that might make sense when not much else did.

In the city, he'd be questioning neighbors and relatives, but Alma's only relative was Jena, and she lived out in the middle of nowhere.

The only motive he could think of was Alma's objection to this planned resort of Alex McCann's. He remembered the man's determination when they'd spoken the week before.

"I will build a hotel out here. It's just a matter of time."

Alex had motive to get rid of Alma. And he was a hothead.

How many people's jobs were being held up by the old woman's objection to the resort? He'd noticed the groups of men hanging out at the farm supply and the diner. There were a lot of men out of work. Men who would probably be employed in construction if the resort were built.

Caleb sighed, suddenly realizing he had a few more suspects than he'd originally thought.

He was about to fall over by the time he made it back to his trailer. Jena's house was dark. He wondered if she and the boys were staying at Ollie's for a little while. The man had seemed like a solid guy and he treated Jena like a little sister, so the idea of her being over there made him feel a little better.

He wondered if her parents would be back in town soon. His heart absolutely ached for those two boys. He'd seen them with their great-grandmother at church. They'd already lost their dad. How much loss could one little family take? Though he'd been trying to stay emotionally detached as much as he could, in that moment, he knew if Alma's murderer stood in front of him, Caleb would kill him with his bare hands.

He ate a little and tried to settle down, but he couldn't relax. Details from the crime scene kept running around his brain. The waning moon was up when he left the bedroom, tied on his running shoes, and started out the door.

Caleb ran up the street in front of Jena's house, past the park and the springs that were fenced off. He ran farther up the canyon, his eyes adjusting to the darkness and the moonlight, his heart falling into a steady rhythm as he ran out his energy. He followed the floor of the canyon past the springs, up and into the rocks. Jogged through the numerous fingers that branched off and turned him around. It was almost like a maze in there. Only the sound of the springs kept him centered when he got turned around. Finally, he turned and headed back. The worst of his tension had burned off, and he was exhausted again.

When he got to Springs Park, he slowed and began walking. The desert air should've been cool against his skin, but that night, it pressed on him. The moon reflected off the largest of the pools scattered over the park.

Seven springs fed from underneath the desert floor, people in town said. Three were large and fed into one pond in the center of the park. They said the children swam there in the winter, enjoying the warm temperatures even when snow fell. Three more dotted the back of the canyon. Smaller and more scattered, one was more like a mud pit and the others he could see steaming, even at night. Hot. Far hotter than the large springs and more laden with minerals.

His heart began to even out as the wind picked up. Caleb's eyes climbed to the few petroglyphs carved into the black desert varnish that marked the canyon walls. Luckily, no one had marred the perfection of their outlines. Familiar figures beckoned him closer. Spirals and whorls. Animal figures. The hunchbacked flute player whose song whispered to him on the wind. Kokopelli. He wondered if it was rain he smelled.

Caleb blinked and looked around. He could hear singing. Old songs he'd heard as a child at his grandmother's feet. He must have been truly exhausted, because he could have sworn he heard Mary Yazzie's voice and his Uncle Raymond's low laugh. The smell of a bonfire and fry bread. He shook his head to clear it. No one would know the old songs here. The wind gusted again, and a black slash in the rocks beckoned him from the corner of his eye.

Seven springs… He saw six. Where was the seventh?

The old songs rose on the breeze and Caleb turned toward them. His feet moved of their own volition as he approached the black void in the canyon wall. It was a cave cut into the rocks. As he drew closer, he heard a shuffling in the bushes and a silver animal darted in front of him.

He was *Mah-ih*, "he-who-roams-about" to his grandmother's people. The large coyote paused in the path, then turned and looked at Caleb. His pelt was silver in the moonlight, his ears large and tilted toward him. Caleb walked toward the animal, but it didn't bolt. The coyote walked a little farther down the path, then paused to look at him again. Caleb followed.

The animal darted under a fence that Caleb hopped over. Then there was another path, this one not marked by gravel or concrete.

It twisted over the rocks and through the brush, leading him toward the void. The coyote ran up the path, darting forward before he paused and turned, waiting for Caleb to follow. He felt the wind at the back of his legs and pressed on. The moon hid behind the canyon walls as he made his way into the darkness. Pulling a flashlight from his pocket, he switched it on and looked around as he entered the cave.

There were small alcoves carved into the walls with candles, matches, and one pair of abandoned sandals that looked like they belonged to a teenage girl. A hideout? Drinking spot? He looked around. There was no trash or graffiti. If this was a place the kids gathered to misbehave, he saw no evidence of it. He could hear running water coming from somewhere. This must have been the location of the seventh spring.

He saw the silver body of the coyote at the edge of his light and he turned the flashlight toward him. It was definitely the oddest coyote he'd ever met. They were shy animals for the most part, happy to avoid humans and keep to themselves. But this one...

The animal put his head down, lapping at the rocks. No, not the rocks. Caleb moved closer. A sandstone pillar, two or three feet wide, rose up from the floor of the cave. It was only three feet tall or so and a large basin had been cut into the top, forming a pool of clear water that spilled over the edge and into a small rivulet that ran into the darkness. It was the small stream of water that the coyote was drinking. It must have been fresh.

Maybe it was exhaustion combined with an hour-long jog. Maybe it was the strange mood that the wind and the scent of blood and the memories of his grandmother had worked on him, but Caleb Gilbert strode to the pillar, stuck his face in the cool water, and drank as if his life depended on it. Deep gulp after deep gulp, he drank the spring water like mother's milk as the wind whistled outside and the night birds sang. It was the sweetest water he had ever tasted.

And when he was full, he walked back to his trailer and fell into the deepest, most peaceful sleep he'd ever had.

chapter
eleven

Two nights later, Jena heard the knock on the door. She'd just put the boys down to bed and was drinking a cold beer, exhausted after another day of condolences. She tensed at first, then, recognizing the distinctive heavy step, stood and ran to the door, pulling it open.

"Daddy," she cried before flinging herself into her father's arms.

"I'm here, honey." He held her and rocked back and forth for a moment before he cleared his throat. "Better get inside. The boys asleep?"

She sniffed and wiped at her eyes. "Just put them to bed."

He moved into the front room, his presence immediately taking it over. Thomas Crowe was built like a rock, six feet tall with shoulders broad as the canyon. The Cherokee blood of his ancestors was strong in his face, which was dark with grief and anger.

"I landed at Max and Beverly's an hour ago," he said in a hoarse voice.

Her father's natural form was a raven, not half as fast as Jena's hawk. "You must have flown for hours."

"We were in Colorado. Your mom's driving back with the trailer right now."

He sat in the old recliner that had been his chair for as long as Jena could remember. She walked to the kitchen, calling out, "Are you hungry?"

"I will be in about an hour, but for right now, one of those beers looks good."

"Got it." She grabbed one from the fridge and walked back to the living room.

Her father was staring at a picture of the family over the mantle. They had taken it last Christmas and Tom had an arm around his tiny mother. He had his father's size, but looked just like a Crowe. According to Alma, he was the picture of his namesake, the ancestor who had seen the vision of the canyon from thousands of miles away, guiding the wanderers into the desert where they had found an oasis. The original Thomas Crowe's natural form had been a raven, too, the very first avian shapeshifter in the Springs.

"You were in the air when I called Mom, weren't you?" She handed him the beer and sat on the couch.

Tom blinked, as if just waking up. "She came to me. I thought it was a dream at first. Haven't seen a spirit in so long. I left right after she did. Max filled me in on the details when I flew in. It's... not real yet."

Like a few others in their family, Tom and Jena could sometimes see the spirits of those who had passed. Usually only family members or close friends. Jena hadn't seen one until the boys' dad had passed away and Lowell had kept her company on the drive back home to the desert.

"She tell you anything?" Her voice cracked.

His black eyes glittered. "Nothing about who killed her. Who was it, Jen?"

She tried to clear her throat, but her voice still croaked. "Don't know yet. I think it was a cat. I'm pretty sure, but Jeremy—"

"The McCann boy?"

She nodded. "He's working with the new police chief."

"This is the outsider that Alex brought in?" Jena nodded and her father let out a disgusted sound. "What the hell was that boy thinking?

That man isn't going to be able to figure out a damn thing without knowing the whole truth. And he can't know that. He's not family."

Jena shrugged and wiped her eyes. "I'm sure Alex wasn't expecting the man to have to solve a murder the first month he was here."

"This is the guy living in one of Mom's trailers?"

"He seems like a decent guy, but..."

Tom leaned forward, tension hovering in the air around him. "But what?"

Her father was almost seventy years old, but like most shapeshifters, looked about twenty years younger. She wouldn't bet against him in a fight. Not in a hot minute.

"Nothing. It's nothing, Dad."

"He giving you problems? I won't put up with it, Jena."

"It's nothing like that. It's just... He's a good detective." Her voice cracked again. "He knows we're hiding something. And he's persistent. I don't think he's going to give up on this case until—"

"What's the official word? You ask Ted?"

"She's encouraging the examiner at the county to list it as an animal attack, even though it's unusual."

Tom frowned. "What's unusual about it? It was an animal attack. We just know it was murder, too."

"She was shifting, Dad. It was the full moon, and she was shifting when he killed her."

He frowned. "So?"

"The cat—or whoever it was—caught her mid shift. At least that's what Ted thinks. She's never seen it before either, but the wounds..." Jena blinked back tears when the image of Alma's mutilated body flashed to her mind. "The wounds were... stretched. The edges twisted, so it looks almost like they healed partially. That's what's giving the medical examiner fits. It looks like an animal attack, but not a normal animal. And the claw marks grew when she turned human again, so they don't look like a cat at all. They look as big as a bear or something."

Tom settled back in his chair, pain evident in his eyes. When he finally spoke again, there was a tremor in his voice. "Let them classify it however they like. They'll give up when there's not an easy answer. That's the way ordinary humans work. They can blame it on a *chupacabra* for all I care. Just make sure Ted knows they leave her body alone."

"Dad—"

"They leave her alone, Jena. As much as possible. The last thing any of us need is some doctor digging into our medical history."

Their bodies were normal, for the most part. But any researcher studying the town would quickly find it unusual to have a small town where none of the children ever had broken limbs or got sick. Most of the old people lived remarkably long with no chronic illnesses, and everyone healed exceptionally fast. Ted had done a few studies of her own and Jena knew the results hadn't been shared with anyone.

"I'll talk to Ted's mother in the morning. I'm sure the cats understand the seriousness of the situation. And since you're fairly sure it was one of them—"

"I'm sure. I don't know who, but it was a cat's claws. It wasn't just the claw marks on the body, but there were marks at the back door."

"He scratched to get in?"

She nodded. "And Grandma let him in. So she knew him."

"Or her." Tom raised an eyebrow at her. "Don't ever underestimate a female cat. As a rule, they're far more vicious than the males. I've learned that by experience."

"Fine. Or her." Jena took another drink, then leaned back into the couch and closed her eyes. "It was too soon," she whispered.

Her father moved next to her and put an arm around her shoulders. "I know."

"I know she was old, but…"

"We take our elders for granted." Tom squeezed her shoulder. His voice was rough with grief. "We get to keep them for so long, we start to take for granted they'll always be there."

"I'm really angry, Dad. Someone stole her from us. From the boys."

"I know." He swallowed. "I'm angry, too. This is going to be dealt with, Jena. It doesn't matter what the police do. We'll deal with this our way."

"People around here are really good at keeping secrets."

He nudged her shoulder. "And others are good at seeing what's hidden."

"Are you and Mom going to stay for a while?" Like many of her father's generation, Cathy and Thomas Crowe had taken to wandering during their retirement. Older shapeshifters had raised their children, taken care of their responsibilities to the Springs, and mastered their shifting abilities. It was easier for them to blend in, so many in their sixties and seventies took to traveling until their elders passed away and new responsibilities were thrust upon them. The Crowes were a small clan, and her father was the oldest now.

"We'll figure it out, honey. Don't worry about it."

"When's Mom going to be here?"

"A couple days at most. She's been on that headset thing on her phone the whole trip, if I guess right. She'll take care of the memorial and the church stuff. You take care of you and the boys."

"Can you help at the diner for a while?"

"Course." He squeezed her arm and Jena leaned into his shoulder. "Whatever you need, Jen."

THE NEXT DAY, TOM WAS BEHIND THE GRILL AND JENA WAS wiping down counters when Caleb came in. He tipped his Stetson before sitting down and setting it on the seat next to him.

"Jena, a word?"

It was just after eleven o'clock, but there were a few patrons in the diner. She had the urge to run to him and away from him at the same time. "I'm pretty busy right now."

"You're gonna have to give me some answers eventually."

She kept looking at the counter. "Am I a suspect?"

"Of course not."

"Then I don't have to talk to you."

She could see him grit his teeth. Part of her was annoyed by the perceptive officer, but the other part...

Well, she kind of loved him for it. It probably would have been easier for him to believe what the county believed. After all, Jena knew the truth. Most normal humans saw what they wanted and dismissed anything that seemed out of the ordinary. But Caleb hadn't. He'd seen the outrage done to her grandmother and was determined that Alma Crowe would have justice.

Blinking back tears, she said, "I can't talk about it, Caleb."

He leaned forward, his eyes boring into hers. "Do you know who did it?"

"No, I don't. I promise."

"But you know more than you're telling me, don't you?"

"Caleb, I—"

Tom's voice broke into their quiet conversation. "Something I can get for you, Chief?"

Caleb drew back and examined the older man before he held out his hand. Tom took it. "Mr. Crowe?"

"That's me."

"I'm very sorry about your mother, sir. I'm focusing all my energy on solving her case."

Tom glanced between Jena and Caleb. "Didn't the coroner decide it was an animal attack? It's tragic, but—"

"The county," Caleb interrupted, "is still determining cause of death, but my investigation is ongoing."

Tom picked up a bar towel and started polishing glasses. Jena could tell that every eye in the diner was glued to the two men. Old Mr. Campbell. Mayor Matt, picking up lunch for Missy, who was home with the new baby. Allie's dad and one of the Quinns.

Tom said, "Doesn't sound like there's much for the police to investigate. If there's anything to find..." Tom glanced around the diner. "We'll find it. We take care of our own, Chief Gilbert. You can be sure of that."

His smile was polite, but Jena could see the anger burn in Caleb's eyes. "Well, no disrespect intended—I know she was your mother—but she was part of this town, and that makes her mine, too. She served me pie and invited me for coffee that I never got to join her for. That makes her mine." Then Caleb looked into Jena's eyes for a minute before he glanced over his shoulder at the rest of the diner he could see watching him. "And Alma Crowe was murdered by someone she knew. In this town. Under my watch." He stood up from the bar and slipped on his hat. "And that, Mr. Crowe, makes her most definitely mine. Have a nice day, Jena." He tipped the edge of his hat toward her, then strode out of the diner.

Tom and Jena watched him walk to his truck, slamming the door before he backed out and headed back in the direction of the station.

"He seems like a good man," Tom murmured, picking up another glass as Jena blinked back tears. "But he's just a man."

BY THE TIME JENA'S MOTHER ARRIVED THE NEXT DAY, THE memorial at the church had already been planned. The flowers were ordered, the minister secured. Cathy Crowe, in her typically organized fashion, had arranged the entire event on her phone while pulling a 28-foot trailer over the Rocky Mountains. Sometimes, Jena was intimidated by her mother. Today, as she sat in the full church, listening to others sing the praises of the grandmother she had loved, she was just relieved.

Aaron, despite being a very mature seven years old, perched on her lap. Low sat between Tom and Jena. Cathy sat to her right, her hand resting gently in her youngest grandson's as she sniffed her own quiet tears for the mother-in-law who had been closer to her than her own mother.

Jena barely managed to keep from crying when she stood at the front of the church and read her grandmother's favorite verse from the book of Isaiah. "'Even the youths shall faint and be weary, and the young men shall utterly fall,'" she read to the crowded church. "'But they that wait upon the Lord shall renew their strength; they shall mount up with wings as eagles; they shall run and not be weary; and they shall walk, and not faint.'"

But after the service, after the lunch at the family home where Jena had been raised—the same home where Alma had raised her own children—she hid in the back yard, sitting on a small bench as she cried. Allie and Ted found her there.

"Oh, Jena," Allie said, sitting next to Jena and pulling her into her arms. "I'm so sorry. I don't even know how you're dealing with this."

"I can't—" She hiccupped. "I can't handle this again. First Lowell and now Grandma. The boys..."

Ted murmured, "Jena—"

"They're devastated all over again. This was supposed to be the safe place. Alma wasn't supposed to die right now. She wasn't supposed to die like this!" The sobs took over, days of being stoic finally catching up with her. Part of her wanted to be alone. The other was grateful for Allie's comforting arms and Ted's protective stance as she stood over them.

"It's okay," Allie murmured, stroking her hair as she calmed. "The boys will get through this. You'll get through this. Your parents are here. Your friends—"

"I am so angry."

"Good," Ted said. "You should be angry. This is fucked up."

"Ted!" Allie said.

"What?" Her friend looked furious. "It is. Alma Crowe was an elder in this community. Elders are supposed to be sacred. No one should have touched her. She should've been safe in her own home, and someone *murdered* her, Allie. Possibly one of my own people, which pisses me off even more."

Jena sat up straighter. "We're gonna find out who did this."

"Damn straight, we are."

Allie looked worried. "Guys, we're not police. We can't just—"

"The police can't do anything, Allie. Get your head out of your ass!" Ted said.

Allie stood up and snarled in her friend's face. "You watch yourself, Teodora Vasquez. You can go off like a hothead, but some of us have children to protect. And don't think your outrage means you miss Alma any more than we do."

"The children in this town aren't going to be safe until this animal is dead. If he could do this to an old woman, then no one is safe."

"Girls," Jena said in a quiet voice as she stood, "calm down." She looked between them, the lion and the fox shivering under the surface of their skin. "We're going to find out who did this." She looked at Ted. "And we're going to be quiet." Then Allie. "And smart. No one else is going to get hurt. But Ted's right. The police can't do anything. Caleb's only working with half a brain because he's not a shifter, and Jeremy has to work with Caleb, so he can't investigate the way he wants."

"He can give us information, though."

"Yeah, he can. And he will. We'll get Alex in on this if we have to. He's Jeremy's alpha and he'll tell him anything."

"I can poke around the cats," Ted said. "Since I agree with you that it's one of us. Unfortunately, there are a lot of cats."

Jena grimaced. It was true. Cats had big families and tended to stay in the Springs. Probably a third of the population was some kind of cat or another.

Allie said, "I don't know what I can help with. You're welcome to my nose, I guess. And if you need someone fast…"

"Thanks, Allie."

"Just give me some notice. Seems like Joe's gone more than he's home lately, so I have to make sure someone can watch the kids."

Ted asked, "Where's he going all the time?"

Allie shrugged and looked like she wanted to change the subject, so Jena said, "And I'll watch. I already noticed something that the police can't do much with. There were fresh scratch marks at the bottom of Alma's door."

Ted's ears perked. "Lion?" There weren't very many full mountain lions in the springs. Not ones in their natural form, anyway. And on full moons, anything but your natural form was almost impossible to pull off.

She shook her head. "I'm not sure, but I don't think so. It was a medium cat. Bobcat, I'd guess."

"Shit." Ted's head fell back. "There are a ton of bobcats in this town. Scads of them. They're like rats on moon nights."

Allie mused, "But they eat the rats, so that's kind of nice."

"Way to look on the bright side, Allie."

"I try."

Just then, Jena noticed Caleb pulling up to the trailer in his truck. He'd been at the memorial earlier, but she had no idea where he'd gone after. He looked grim when he got out. And... sad. His usual swagger wasn't in evidence; his hat was pulled low and Jena saw him lean against his truck, looking down the canyon toward the springs, his body a long black stripe in the setting sun.

Ted and Allie noticed him too.

"I admire his dedication. And he's really good at his job. I can tell," Ted said. "But he's got to stop digging. He's like a dog with a bone about this, and he's going to end up learning too much."

Allie sucked in a breath. "He can't. If he finds out—"

"Whoever did this doesn't want an outsider on his trail." Jena's heart plummeted. "If Caleb keeps digging, there could be more than one murder victim in Cambio Springs."

The breeze shifted then, sweeping down the canyon and lifting the dust around the trailer, making it swirl and twist toward them. Jena closed her eyes and held a hand over her nose to keep the grit out, but she heard Allie next to her making a strange noise. "Allie?"

The vixen was leaning forward, her eyes lit up, completely focused on the man near the trailer. A high whine, inaudible to human ears, caused Ted to wince.

"What the hell, Allie?"

"He's different," she hissed. "His scent has changed."

Jena frowned. "I thought you said human scent changed all the time?"

"No." She walked closer, lifting her head in the breeze, inhaling the wind. "He doesn't smell right. Not like a normal human."

Ted and Jena exchanged a worried look. "Allie, what are you talking about? What does he smell like?"

"Like the water," she whispered. "He smells like the water."

chapter twelve

The week after Alma Crowe was murdered, Caleb walked into the Blackbird Diner in a foul mood. Despite his wishes, the county coroner had officially ruled Alma's death an animal attack. Since Caleb had no concrete evidence to the contrary, he was forced to accept the ruling, but he knew he wasn't getting the whole story. And when even the relatives of the deceased seemed determined to obstruct his investigation, there wasn't much he could do.

Officially.

He was hungry and tired. Hungry for answers and tired of the endless, vague dreams that had plagued him for over a week. He hardly remembered most of them, but every morning he woke with a vague sense of unease that there was something he had forgotten. The combination of frustration, exhaustion, and nagging worry combined to put him in a foul mood that he knew grated on anyone he came in contact with.

Obviously, he needed to see Jena.

When he walked in, he could see the object of his continuing frustration arguing with her father in the back. It was early for lunch, so the diner was mostly deserted. He was just about to head for the counter when he heard a small voice to his right.

"Hi, Chief Caleb."

It was Aaron. The boy looked a little pale and droopy sitting in the big booth alone.

"Hey. What are you doing out of school?"

"I wasn't feeling good." He didn't look good either. His face was drawn and pale. The normally exuberant energy nowhere in sight.

"You got a cold or something?"

Aaron only shrugged. Caleb had to wonder whether the sickness was more a reaction to the grief of losing a beloved great-grandmother. He sat down across from him. "Want to join me for lunch? I hate eating alone." Actually, he preferred it, but since the offer seemed to boost the small boy's spirits, he was happy he'd made it.

"Yeah, thanks!" A smile crossed his face. "I like the meatloaf sandwich. Have you tried it?"

"Nope. I usually have a burger."

"You should try the meatloaf."

"I will."

Aaron fell silent and sipped at the Sprite in front of him. Caleb could hear Jena and her dad still muttering in the back, but he couldn't make out what they were saying.

"How are you doing?" Caleb asked.

Aaron shrugged again. "You're more like us now. Mom can't tell yet."

The memory of their first meeting came to his mind. "What do you mean by that?" Was he talking about being more at home in the Springs? For some reason, Caleb didn't think that was it. "You said that before. The first time we met."

"I dunno." Yeah, he did. But the little boy was as good at keeping secrets as the rest of the damn town. "Does it feel like home yet?"

Caleb hesitated, but finally said, "I like it here."

He was surprised by how true it felt. Despite his current frustration, Caleb had an ease about him he hadn't felt since he'd left his grandmother's home when he was twelve and moved to the city.

"It's like when you find the right pair of shoes."

That brought a smile to Caleb's face. "Yeah, I think I know what you mean."

"Grandma's house was like that. It was always the right place. But Mom says we shouldn't go back."

Caleb wondered if he could talk to Jena about that. He hadn't had a ton of experience with victims, but he knew enough to know that Jena probably had post-traumatic stress from finding Alma the way she had. It was a stress the boys didn't share, however, and keeping them from their grandmother's house, with all its good memories, would probably do more harm than good.

"I think you'll be able to go back someday. Your mom's just sad right now."

"Like when we lost Dad. I don't remember much. Just that she was really sad."

"Yeah." His heart actually ached. "Probably something like that."

In a quick moment, Aaron slipped under the table and crawled up next to Caleb. "I miss my grandma."

"I do, too." He tried to relax with the little boy sitting next to him. It was surprisingly easy to do. "She was a great lady."

Aaron looked up at him seriously. "I don't know why she had to die."

Every ounce of frustration drained out of him, and a low burning determination filled its place. He looked into Aaron's clear, green eyes and said, "I don't know yet, either. But I promise you, I'll find out."

The boy held his gaze for a few more minutes. Caleb heard the bell on the door chime, but he ignored it. Ignored everything except the testing gaze of the seven-year-old boy next to him. His heart swelled and grew, taking in the small child's trust and holding it like the precious thing it was.

I promise you, Bear. I will find out who killed your grandmother. The county and this town be damned. I will find the answers. For you.

Finally, Aaron nodded and rested his small head on Caleb's shoulder. "Okay."

"Okay."

And for the first time in months, Caleb Gilbert felt a hint of peace.

The man and the boy sat quietly for a few more minutes until there was a knock on the window. Caleb looked up; it was Low and an older woman with a familiar smile. They walked through the door and the woman took in Caleb and Aaron sitting together, the boy's head still resting against his shoulder. Caleb wouldn't have shrugged him off for the world.

"Hi," she said.

"Hello. You must be Jena's mom."

"Cathy Crowe." The woman held out her hand and Caleb shook it. "You feeling any better, Bear?"

"Yeah." Caleb felt him nod. "I do now. Did you get popsicles?"

"Uh-huh. I put them in the freezer at home, then decided Low and I would join you for lunch."

Low was glaring at Caleb, but he ignored it. The older boy was suspicious and protective of the people he loved. Caleb could respect that, but he wasn't about to move Aaron if Aaron didn't want to be moved.

"Chief Caleb is going to try Mom's meatloaf sandwich."

Cathy and Low slid into the booth across from them. "That's a good one. I usually eat the roast beef." She smiled at Caleb. "Low here's a burger man."

Aaron picked up his head. "Just like you, Chief Caleb."

Caleb had a feeling the association didn't sit well with the older boy. "I like lots of stuff," he said sullenly.

"Aaron, do you mind if we join you?" Cathy asked. "Or is this a guy thing?"

"No..." Then Aaron looked up at Caleb. "Is it a guy thing?"

Feeling playful after the heaviness of the morning, Caleb smiled. "Bear, you should always make time for a beautiful woman."

Low let out a disgusted sound, but Cathy only laughed. "Don't make him too much of a charmer, Chief. He already has the little girls following him."

"Please, call me Caleb. It's really nice to meet you. I love my trailer."

Apparently, that was exactly the right thing to say, because Cathy launched into a lively conversation about the joy and satisfaction of restoring Airstreams. Caleb had trouble keeping up. The woman was a firecracker and obviously shared the same keen intelligence as her daughter. Soon, she had Caleb and both boys laughing along with her as she told stories about life on the road. Jena came out, took their orders, then left with a raised eyebrow pointed in his direction. He just smiled, pleased to see the little flush rise in her cheeks.

The four were interrupted by the somewhat manic figure of Mayor Matt just as they were finishing up their lunch.

"Cathy!" he said with a broad smile. "So good to see you." Then his smile fell. "Well... not under the circumstances, of course. I'm so sorry about Alma. Such a tragic accident."

Suddenly, the lively mood of the table fell flat. Aaron squirmed next to him, and Caleb looked at Cathy.

She smiled at the man graciously. "Thank you, Matt. How are Missy and the baby?"

"Great!" The man's mood lightened again. "So happy he's finally here. She delivered just a few days after... well after. She was getting a bit testy being overdue."

"That's to be expected. Not a fun time to be pregnant with all the heat." It may have been fall, but the days were still steaming. "I heard she delivered at home?"

"Her sisters were there. Her other deliveries with the girls were so easy, she wanted to try it at home. She said it would be more relaxing."

"More and more girls are doing that these days. And one of her sisters is a nurse, right?"

"Yep. So, are you and Tom staying for a while?"

"We're not sure how long we're staying." She glanced at Caleb, then back at Matt. "Lots of things to take care of with the extended family."

Extended family? Caleb frowned. How big a family did they have? He seemed to recall Jena mentioning she was an only child.

"Of course." Matt nodded. "It's just, there's a council meeting next week, and I was wondering if Tom would be taking Alma's place on the—"

"Not really the time to be talking about that kind of thing, is it?" Cathy's voice was sharp, and she glanced at Caleb. "And you'd have to ask Tom about any of the town business. Not my area."

Well, that had cooled off the conversation considerably. Matt looked crestfallen and took a step back. Cathy had shut him down quickly, and Caleb wondered why. Did Cathy want to avoid talking about Alma in front of the boys? Or want to avoid talking about the town council in front of Caleb? The archaic form of city government Matt had described to him started to seem more and more odd the longer he was here.

As far as Caleb could tell, there were no elected leaders in the city except Mayor Matt. The town council controlled every decision and consisted of the oldest members of the seven families that had settled Cambio Springs. Where did that leave the families who had moved in since? Why did they agree to it? Caleb wasn't even sure it was strictly legal, but he had no idea what the laws were regarding that kind of thing.

Matt made some excuse, then left to go pick up an order at the counter. Cathy looked at the boys, then at Caleb.

"Who wants a piece of pie?"

HE WAS DREAMING AGAIN.

This time he wasn't running; he was stalking. He felt the cool metal of the rifle on his fingers, his right hand resting comfortably on the stock. He moved quietly through the brush as the silver coyote slinked next to him.

What was he hunting? He followed the game trail past the springs and farther into the canyon until he heard it. The high whine of the pup echoed through the canyon a moment before he heard the cat scream. He moved faster and the coyote trailed him, jumping over dry gullies and dodging the shadows of cottonwoods that filled the moonlit night with soft puffs drifting in the breeze. The pup yipped again, this time in terror.

It was on him. The slinking form of the bobcat crouched over the small pup in the rocks. Where was the mother? The coyote growled next to him as he raised the rifle. He sighted in the moonlight and squeezed the trigger, hitting the predator in the neck with one shot. The wolf puppy scurried off as he approached the animal, but when he drew closer, he realized it wasn't the bobcat.

The black eye of the silver coyote stared up at him before his mouth pulled up in a bloody grin.

You did the right thing.

No! He screamed in his head. *I didn't want to shoot you.*

You did the right thing.

He kneeled down and stared at the blood soaking into the sand. *I didn't want to shoot you.*

You did what you had to do. I was going to kill him.

You weren't supposed to be here.

The coyote blinked. *I forgive you.*

But I don't forgive myself. He reached out and touched the animal's silver fur, soaked with blood at the neck.

They forgive you.

"No," he whispered. "They hate me."

They hate me more. Forgive yourself, Caleb.

His heart was pounding.

No—

Caleb blinked awake. The light from the half moon was glowing through the window and someone was pounding on the door of the trailer. He brushed his hand over his face and sat up.

Who was pounding on his door in the middle of the night?

He moved toward the pounding, still halfway dreaming. Was he still in the canyon? Had he fallen asleep there and this was a dream?

He pushed open the door to see Jena standing there. She was wearing the same shirt she'd worn the first time he saw her. The one that made her boobs look really great. And her hair was all tangled over her shoulders. He blinked again.

Still dreaming. But this was a way better dream.

She stood with her hands on her hips in the moonlight.

Caleb gave her a sleepy grin. "Gotta love that attitude."

Then she frowned. "What?"

He stepped toward her, not hesitating a moment before he closed on her lips.

Oh… this was better than his other dreams about her. She stood stock-still for a moment until his tongue teased the crease of her mouth, then she opened for him and made that sexy noise in the back of her throat. Mmm, Dream Jena was so much more accommodating than Real Jena.

She tasted like lime and sugar. He wrapped his arms around her, pressing her skin into his bare chest. She needed less clothes. He wanted to feel all of her.

"Why are you wearing clothes?" he murmured against her lips, nipping at her bottom lip as she pulled back with a gasp.

"What?"

Caleb pulled her back for another kiss, but she pushed him. He ducked to the side and sucked her earlobe between his lips. "Mmm, take off your shirt, honey. I want to feel your skin."

She slapped a hand on his bare chest. "Oh my—what is wrong with you?"

That was kind of weird. Slaps usually didn't sting in dreams. He pulled her hips into his and pressed them together, murmuring into her neck, "Trust me, nothing is wrong with me that you can't cure."

Jena pinched his earlobe. Hard. Ouch.

Oooouch. He pulled his head back and she slapped him. More ouch.

"What do you think you're doing, Caleb Gilbert?"

He blinked again. Then rubbed his eyes. Oh…

"You're not Dream Jena."

Her eyes widened. "Dream Jena?"

"I thought I was dreaming. Wait—what time is it?"

"One in the morning. I was helping Ollie out at the bar tonight."

"Wearing that?" He frowned. "That's my special shirt."

She sputtered. "You—you're special…" She pinched his ear again.

"Ow!"

"Wake up, you idiot!" Then she seemed to notice the very evident tent in his pajama pants. "And get that situation under control."

"Want to help me out with it?" He slapped a hand over her mouth before she could curse at him. "Sorry. Sleeping. No filter." She bit his finger. "Ow! Stop hitting and biting me. Unless… you're into that. I mean, it's not usually my thing, but I could—"

"You need to stop talking right now, before I kick you in the nuts and never speak to you again."

He raised two hands to rub his face. "Man, you're mean when I just wake up."

She stood glaring at him as he blinked and slapped his cheeks. Strangely, Mad Jena did little to calm down the problem down south she kept glancing at every few seconds. He smothered a smile. Maybe it wasn't such a problem after all.

"Okay," he said after a couple deep breaths and a few more bracing slaps. The night air was crisp and he wasn't wearing a shirt, which woke him up more than anything. "Why are you pounding on my door at one in the morning? Unless you do want to help me out with that situation you were referring to, in which case, we should go inside. I'm not much of an exhibitionist, and I'm pretty sure your kids could see us from the house."

"You are such an asshole."

"Duly noted. You're pounding on my door in the middle of the night. Why?"

"What were you saying to Aaron at the diner today?"

He frowned. "What?"

"Before you started charming my mother with your polite-as-shit cute cowboy routine, what were you and Aaron talking about?"

He smiled. "Your mom likes me, doesn't she?"

Jena pulled at her hair, obviously frustrated. "Caleb!"

"There are so many better ways you could be shouting my name right now."

She held up a furious finger at him. She was practically vibrating with anger. "You cannot blame that on the sleep at this point. I will slap you."

Jena moved toward him and Caleb ducked to the side, slipped behind her, and pulled her back into his chest, wrapping a long arm around her waist as he pulled them back to lean against the cool aluminum siding of the trailer. Then he ducked down and whispered in her ear, "Can't slap me now, can you?"

She was still tense, but he felt her move into him, ever so slightly, and he smiled. Curious Jena was even better than Dream Jena.

"Let me go."

"Why are you mad? I was just talking to him. He was sad about Alma." He paused and leaned his chin down to rest on her shoulder. "I was just trying to help. I'm sorry if I upset you. He's a great kid, and I hated to see him so down."

Her shoulders relaxed a little, and he rested his cheek against her neck. "He said you're going to find out why she died."

"I am." He let his nose run along the shell of her ear. She smelled like the bar, but underneath? All Jena. He took a deep breath and felt her shiver.

She put her hands over his where they lay at her waist, but she didn't pull them away. "You have to stop investigating this. It was an animal attack."

"I believe you. It was also murder." He brushed his lips against her temple. "I know it, and you know it. I'm not sure how it all fits together, but—"

"Caleb—"

"I can't let it go," he whispered, tightening his arms around her.

"She deserves more than that, and you know it. Why won't you help me?"

Jena stilled for a moment, then slowly pried his hands away from her waist. He let her. She stepped away as he leaned against the side of the trailer, watching her. She didn't look mad at him anymore. She looked upset, maybe even a little scared. Caleb wanted to rage at whatever unseen thing had put that look on her face.

"You've got to stop. Let it be, Caleb."

"You know I won't."

Her mouth firmed and a sad resolve came into her eyes. "Then you better stay away from my kids. I won't have them hurt because of you."

His instincts pricked. "Why would they get hurt because of me?"

Jena opened her mouth, then closed it.

"Why, Jena?"

She shook her head and started backing away. "Just stay away from them. And me."

chapter
thirteen

Saturday night, Jena and Allie tucked their kids into the den at Jena's house for a mass sleepover while the grown-ups had a meeting. Tom and Cathy had gone to meet with the other elders about who would take over Alma's seat on the council; so Jena, Ted, Allie, Alex, Ollie, and Devin sat around the table behind the house, Jena checking carefully to see if there was any movement from Caleb's trailer. It was completely dark.

Was he out? Where would he go?

"Who's working The Cave tonight, Ollie?" she asked.

"My cousin Sandra said she could watch it. She's a pretty good bartender and the band I scheduled for tonight had a breakdown outside of Vegas, so it shouldn't be too busy."

"Sandra?" The tall, statuesque brunette from Palm Springs was stunning. And had great hair. *Hopefully, it's a bad hair night.*

"Why are you talking about Sandra's hair?" Ted gave her a funny look.

Oops, must have said that aloud.

"What? No reason." She looked around the table. "Anyone need another drink before we start?"

Alex waved a hand. "Sit down, Jena. We all know where the beer is. Let's talk."

"Fine." She looked around at her closest friends. "So we all know Alma was murdered. The question is, who was it? There's no way the police can solve this because they can't know the real story, but between the six of us, we should be able to narrow it down. Devin?"

The deputy looked up. "Yeah?"

"You want to help us out any, Mr. Deputy Sheriff?"

"Uh… Jen, the only dead people I've ever investigated ended up being killed over a woman or drugs, so I'm not sure how much help I'm gonna be."

Ollie said, "I think it's fairly safe to assume that neither of those motives is going to match Alma's case."

"Well," Jena said, "what motives would? Are we all assuming this has something to do with the resort vote?" She saw Alex pale and quickly added, "It's not your fault."

"Yeah…" He frowned. "But it kind of is. I wish I'd never even—"

"Suggested something that could benefit the town tremendously?" Ted asked. "This had nothing to do with you, Alex. It had something to do with a killer not getting their way and thinking getting rid of Alma would help them. This is not your fault."

For some reason, Jena knew Alex needed to hear it from someone other than her. She was grateful Ted had spoken up. "She's right. The only one to blame for this is whoever killed Alma."

Alex still looked guilty, but his expression steeled, and he nodded.

"Getting back to what Ollie was saying," Allie said, "what would be the motive?"

Jena shrugged. "It's like Ted said. They thought it was going to help them somehow. And if their goal was to get the resort built, it probably worked. My dad and I have talked about it. He thinks it's worth the risk of exposure to save the jobs. I'm pretty sure he'll vote yes."

"So whoever killed Alma is getting what they want," Devin said. "Who would have benefited the most from this resort?"

Alex raised a hand. "Me."

SITTING AT HIS DESK, CALEB STARED AT THE WHITEBOARD he'd started. He didn't have much else to do on Saturday night since he didn't feel like going down to The Cave alone. A little voice in the back of his head told him that he probably wouldn't have to leave alone, but he shoved it aside. He was still fixated on Jena and didn't want to bother with anyone else. It was an unusual feeling, but he was getting more and more comfortable with it as the weeks passed.

Jena. The damn woman turned him inside out and left him wanting more even when she was mean to him. And she was royally pissed that he wouldn't back down about Alma's death. She hadn't spoken to him since the night at his trailer.

So Caleb's hot weekend night consisted of staring at the murder board he'd started for the woman no one would admit had been murdered. The first name that hit him was Alex McCann.

McCann had motive, for sure, but something struck Caleb as not quite right about that theory. For one, he was obviously close to Jena. Family, almost. McCann was unlikely to kill a woman who had fed him cookies as a child. Of course, he could have ordered it done. He had the money for it and the motive. On the other hand, he didn't really have all that much to lose if the resort didn't happen. He could always move back to L.A. and continue his real estate business, which was—from all accounts—very successful.

Although… he was a hothead who was used to getting his way.

No, that didn't seem to fit, either.

Maybe that was Caleb's hang-up with the man as a suspect. He was *too* hotheaded. He'd lose his temper with Alma, but commit a murder so careful that he'd covered any evidence of it even being a murder in the first place? He didn't think McCann thought that way. Caleb would check his alibi, but McCann wasn't high on the list.

ALEX CONTINUED. "I OBVIOUSLY DIDN'T KILL HER, BUT let's face it. I had the most to gain."

Ted spoke up. "Not really. You had the most to lose, too, since you were putting up the money. If this doesn't work, you can just go back to your life in L.A."

Alex shrugged. "I've told my dad I'm moving back anyway. I'm done with L.A."

"You are?" Ted looked surprised.

"The whole pack knows. Theoretically, one of them could have tried to pin it on me, but I don't see why."

"I thought it was a cat. We think it could be one of the wolves?" Allie looked uncomfortable with the idea of the pack being involved. Though she was a fox and didn't belong to the pack in the strictest sense, all the canines had family connections.

"We're fairly sure it's a cat," Alex said. "Jeremy said the strongest scent at the site was definitely feline, but there were others, too. Alma wasn't a hermit. She had lots of visitors. Jeremy scented lizard. Bird, obviously. Canine. Bear. Cat was just the strongest scent."

CALEB MOVED TO THE NEXT PERSON WHO HAD CAUGHT HIS attention. Good old Mayor Matt.

Something about the overly friendly man bothered him and it wasn't just the abundance of aftershave. No, Matt was shifty. More, he was frustrated by a sense of his own unachieved greatness. He had the appearance of power, but none of the real deal, and Caleb could tell it was eating at the man. This resort was something he'd worked on with McCann, and it represented a concrete contribution to the town. It was the Big Deal. The legacy that everyone would point to if things went right. If that greatness were held up by one old woman...

Well, that could be mighty frustrating.

Could Matt have planned something this carefully? Caleb had an easier time believing it than he did with Alex McCann. Matt was a politician and, by nature, untrustworthy. In Caleb's experience, they had a deft hand at saying one thing and meaning another. And politicians were especially good at justifying their actions if they thought it was for the "greater good." Even if it was a small corner of the world, it was Mayor Matt's corner, and he had yet to make his mark.

Ego, Caleb had learned, was more of a motivator than most people realized.

"So we're not sure it's a cat?" Ollie asked. "What else—?"

"There were claw marks, Alex. Fresh claw marks at the back door. I saw them. That's a hard coincidence to dismiss."

Alex held his hands up toward Jena. "I know, and I'm not saying we dismiss them, but…"

"There are other things with claws," Ted said.

"Like what?"

"Birds." Devin looked uncomfortable even saying it. "I mean…"

"Someone in my family?" Jena was incredulous. "Our clan is pretty small, Devin. And most of them don't even live here."

He shrugged. "I'm just throwing it out there."

"What about canines?" Allie added. "A desert fox or a coyote—"

"They were too narrow for canine claws," Jena said. "Too sharp."

"Lizards," Ollie said in a low voice. Everyone turned to him. "Hey, there are lots of lizards that have claws and some of them are pretty damn big. Ever seen a Komodo dragon?"

"Have you ever seen a Komodo dragon?" Ted stared at him. "Who around here has a Komodo dragon as their natural form? Gila monster, maybe, but dragon?"

"Any shifter with skill can turn into any species with enough practice," Ollie said. "Even if a rattlesnake was your natural form, you can still shift into a lizard. I saw Sean shift into a Gila monster once to scare Sarah Ryan."

Allie murmured, "The things high school boys do…"

Alex said, "He's right. It could be a lizard."

Jena held up a hand. "One, it would have to be something big enough to take down a full-grown owl. Alma was not small in her natural form, and I doubt she would have shifted to anything else if she was panicking. Two, we're talking about a moon night. Shifting into another species is possible most of the time, but on a moon night?" She paused. "Come on! Have you guys ever even tried it?"

Devin raised a hand. "Okay, non-shifter here, but aren't the old people good at doing that?" Everyone stared at him and he started to squirm. "I'm just saying, isn't that skill supposed to come with age? Maybe one of the elders could shift into something like a Komodo dragon if they tried."

One of the elders? Jena's stomach dropped even thinking about the possibility.

CALEB STARED AT THE PICTURE OF OLD JOE QUINN. DAMN. He liked the old guy. Really liked him, despite the innate criminal vibe he got off the man. But if he was considering suspects, Old Quinn had to be on the list.

He'd heard the man himself, railing to anyone who would listen at the farm supply store about that "damn old bird" who was going to ruin his family. The Quinns owned the land adjacent to the McCann's and Caleb knew Alex had already spoken to Old Quinn about buying the property. The Quinn family was big, and from what Caleb could tell, kind of broke, too. Most of them lived on the edge of the town. A few seemed to be pretty successful, but a lot of them made up the unemployed masses that had been laid off with the recent base closures. Joe Quinn was the head of a whole clan of unemployed, borderline shady people, who had the opportunity to make a lot of money before the possibility was snatched from under his nose.

But was he smart enough to plan a murder?

Damn it, he was. The old man had a mind like a steel trap. More than that, he had the type of scheming smarts that effective criminals and shady lawyers seemed to share. Caleb grimaced. If he had to pick one man in Cambio Springs who could plan a criminal operation, Joe Quinn would be it.

His shoulders slumped, Caleb decided that it was time to go home.

THE NEXT DAY DIDN'T IMPROVE MUCH WHEN ALEX MCCANN stormed out of the police station, ranting about "good-for-nothing outsiders who need a damn hobby."

Caleb turned to Jeremy, who was eyeing him with caution. "What?" Caleb bit out. "I asked him for his alibi and he acts like it's a federal offense. He's an asshole."

His deputy shrugged. "I think it's more the implication that he murdered one of his best friend's relatives. You know, the one who fed him cookies when he was little and let him sleep over at her house?"

He threw up his hands in frustration. "Everyone in this damn town is related! Or friends with someone who's related. Or... married to someone who's friends with someone who once volunteered at the library with Alma on Saturdays, so they couldn't *possibly* have done it!"

"Uh, Chief..."

He stomped back to his desk, steaming. "If we're going to find out the truth, then you're going to have to deal with the fact that someone you know—are possibly related to—and probably like, was involved in Alma Crowe's murder."

Jeremy was utterly silent. Caleb finally turned around. He'd expected Jeremy to be angry. Or frustrated. Maybe even a little amused at his outburst. But he wasn't.

He had the same look that Jena had the other night. Worried. Scared. Not of him, *for* him.

"Chief," he said softly. "I think you're a hell of a cop. I like you, and I really admire your determination on this. But you've got to let this go. This was an animal attack. Can't you realize that?"

Caleb's anger got the better of him and he stormed over to Jeremy, shoving the younger man up against the wall and pinning him with his glare.

"It was not an accident. I'm going to get to the bottom of this. And I am going to find out why the hell everyone who's supposed to be helping me is lying to my face!"

He let go of Jeremy's shoulder, grabbed his keys, and strode out to his truck.

JENA FROWNED WHEN SHE HEARD THE POUNDING ON THE door. She looked at the clock. The boys weren't due home for another hour and the diner had been slow, so her dad had told her to go home and catch up on the housework she'd been griping about. She was drying dishes and frowning at the clock when the hard knock came again.

"Who is it?" she called as she walked to the door.

"It's Caleb."

Well, didn't he sound like he was in a fine mood? Jena curled her lip. She'd been avoiding him since the awkward—okay, it was kind of hot—night by his trailer. She should have been mad at him, and the fact that she wasn't mad bothered her more than his stolen kisses did.

She threw open the door. "Why are you pounding on my door?"

He looked ready to punch something. "I'm exhausted. And frustrated. And that damn air-conditioner is broken again, and all I want to do is take a nap without my face melting. Is that too much to ask?"

She narrowed her eyes. "Get off my porch if you're going to talk to me that way, Caleb Gilbert. You're out of line."

He took three steps back, pulled at the back of his neck, then let out a frustrated "Argh!"

Jena nodded at the old shed she and her dad had been meaning to tear down. It was infested with spiders, and the boards were half rotted out. "See that shed?"

Caleb glanced over his shoulder, then back at her. "Yeah."

"Go kick the shit out of it, then come back and talk to me like a human."

His eyes lit up. "Really?"

"Gonna tear it down anyway."

He strode over the shed and drove a fist straight through the siding. Jena blinked. He was even madder than she'd thought. Then he started kicking. Caleb punched and kicked the side of that shed until half of it was lying in a heap. Then he pulled off his sweat-soaked shirt and went at it again. Jena was going to look away in disgust at his blatant display of temper.

Any minute now...

A good ten minutes later, he came back to the porch, sweaty, dusty, and with bloody knuckles.

"Thanks for tearing down the shed. Feeling better?"

She dropped the dishtowel she was holding when he bent down, grabbed her face between dirty hands, and kissed her.

Oh, so he was *that* kind of frustrated, too.

Heat shot straight through her. It was a ferocious kiss, wild with hunger that had her clutching on to his sweaty shoulders just to stay standing. Then, just as abruptly, he let go and Jena had to put one hand on the doorjamb to make sure she didn't fall over.

Caleb panted. "I feel a little better now. Can you call your father about the air-conditioner?"

"Yeah." She cleared her throat. "I can do that."

His eyes looked past her. "You're cleaning your house?"

"Yes."

"You done vacuuming?"

"Huh? Yeah, I'm done with the—"

"I'm gonna fall asleep on your couch now. If I get it dirty, I'll have it cleaned, okay?"

Without asking, he toed off his boots at the door, strode into the living room, and collapsed on the sofa. As Jena turned around, she saw him take a deep breath and his eyes flickered closed. She picked up the dishtowel and quietly closed the door.

"All right, then."

She stared at the incredibly attractive, half-naked man who was already snoring and decided that ice water was a good idea.

For her.

JENA HAD FINISHED CLEANING THE KITCHEN AND WAS quietly folding laundry in the bedroom when she heard the boys come home from school. She started toward the living room to warn them not to make too much noise and wake up Caleb. Though judging from the rhythmic snoring, she guessed the man might sleep through a herd of elephants. She still couldn't believe he'd just showed up and fallen asleep on her couch. Just then, the snoring stopped and Jena heard Aaron.

"Hey, Uncle Alex! Why are you sleeping on the couch?"

Jena stopped dead in her tracks. *Uncle Alex?*

She ran into the living room to see Alex sitting up from the couch wearing Caleb's jeans. Then the shirt she'd been holding dropped to the floor and her heart went into overdrive when she saw him sit up. Alex? No... Caleb? No. What. The—

The man with Alex's face spoke in Caleb's hoarse voice, "Oh, hey Bear."

Low dropped his backpack, his mouth gaping open. Aaron wrinkled up his little forehead in confusion. Jena looked at the man sitting on her couch, watching them all with bleary eyes.

"What's going on?" He blinked and rubbed his eyes as the skin on his face rippled. "Sorry, I think I may be getting sick."

Caleb. No, Alex. The eyes were Caleb, but the mouth was... He was changing before her eyes, his fair skin turning darker along with his hair. The angle of his jaw shifted and Jena gasped.

He spoke again in Caleb's voice. "Jena?"

"Wh—what are you?" She moved in front of the boys, shoving them both behind her.

Alex—no Caleb—no whatever-he-was spoke again. "Jena? What's wrong?" His eyes searched the room for the threat until he glanced at the mirror that hung in the entryway. Then the black eyes widened, he bolted up, and his hands went to his face in confusion. "What the hell?"

Jena backed farther away, herding the children behind her, but Aaron popped his head out from the side and said, "See, Mom! I told you he was like us!"

Then Caleb's face drained white as a sheet, and he fainted dead away.

chapter
fourteen

What was he sleeping on? Whatever it was, he'd have to—

"Caleb?"

Who was that? It sounded like Jena.

"Caleb?"

If he had gotten lucky and couldn't remember it—

"It looks like he's waking up."

Uh... Bear?

"Low, run and get a washcloth."

"Can I help, Mom?"

"No, just stay back."

Caleb's eyes flickered open. There was a ceiling fan and Jena's face. She was so beautiful when she smiled. But she wasn't smiling. Her face was...

Her face.

His face.

"Shit!" He sat bolt upright, hitting his head on the coffee table by the couch. "Fuck!"

Jena slapped his shoulder. "Hey! Watch the language."

Caleb looked around the room. Aaron was there, grinning at him as he sat on the ground. "You owe me a dollar. That was two bad words, Chief Caleb. And you said a couple before you passed out, too." The boy ran down the hall just as Low came back in the room with a cool washcloth that Jena pressed to Caleb's forehead.

His face! He jerked away from her and touched his face, but it felt normal. His stomach, however, felt like it wanted to turn itself inside out.

"It was a dream," he panted. "Just a crazy dream. Must have been—"

Low interrupted. "If you're talking about your face getting all wonky and turning into our Uncle Alex, then it wasn't a dream."

"Fuck!" The nausea rolled through him.

"Will you stop?" Jena yelled.

He heard the rattle of coins and a half-full Mason jar was waved in front of his face.

"That's another one!" Aaron crowed.

"Bear, put the jar down." Low grabbed his arm and pulled his brother away as Caleb stumbled to his feet.

"What the hell?" He patted his face and looked in the mirror. "What happened to me?"

Jena finally spoke again, the wet washcloth dangling from her fingers. "I don't know, but will you stop with the language around my boys, please?"

He spun and glared at her. "My FACE looked like someone else's, Jena! I'm not too concerned about my language at the moment!"

"Well, learn some manners in my house, Caleb Gilbert!"

Aaron slowly slid the Mason jar on the coffee table. "I'm just gonna leave that out for now…"

"My face, Jena. What the hell happened to my face?"

"You don't know?"

"Of course I don't know!" His eyes popped open. "It's this crazy-ass town, isn't it?"

"Don't blame this on my town!" She was livid.

"Uh… Mom," Low said. "He probably should blame it on the town. I mean, it turns us into animals, so—"

"Into what?" Caleb stared at the boy. "Into *animals*?"

Low had a smug look on his face. "Wolves, cats, snakes, birds."

Aaron piped up. "Uncle Ollie turns into a bear!"

Caleb felt lightheaded. "You're all crazy."

"But you turned into another person," Aaron said. "That was way cool. I told you, Mom."

"Aaron, be quiet," Jena snapped. "Caleb, did you drink from any of the springs?"

He just kept looking between the three of them. Jena looked irritated, but mostly concerned. Low wore that little smug smile on his face, like Caleb was an idiot who'd been left out of an inside joke. Aaron... the little boy looked up at him with frank admiration and pure delight.

They seemed like such a nice little family. "Too bad you're all batshit nuts."

Jena scowled and Aaron said, "I am going to make so much money today."

"Will you get your mouth under—?"

He strode over to her and slapped a hand over her mouth before he turned to the boys. "Bear, how about I just buy you a car when you turn sixteen? That sounding all right to you?"

Low piped up. "I want one, too."

"Lose the attitude and I'll think about it."

Jena pried his hand from her mouth. "You jerk! Stop manhandling me! Now, did you drink from any of the springs or not?"

"No one turns into animals." He shook his head and stepped back. The faint nausea had worsened, and his stomach turned. "I'm gonna be sick."

"Caleb?"

"You're all crazy, and I'm gonna be sick."

"Hey!"

He stumbled toward the door, feeling dazed. "Have to get out of here. Crazy people in this house. I had to fall for the crazy girl, didn't I?"

"We're not crazy," Low said. "And we may turn into animals, but that thing you did with your face was way weird."

Caleb shook his head and put his hand on the doorknob. "I'm not weird. You're weird. No one turns into animals. No one turns into other people…"

Just then, Caleb caught his reflection in the hall mirror. He sighed in relief and closed his eyes. It was a dream, just a crazy dream. Just like he'd been dreaming about beating the shit out of Alex McCann right before he woke—

"Mom, he's doing it again."

"Oh hell."

His eyes popped open and he looked in the mirror. A faint shimmer, like the heat off the desert road, rippled over his face. His hair lengthened and lightened…

"Oh shit."

Not a dream.

He bolted for the door, flinging it open just as he emptied his stomach on the porch.

CALEB DUMPED ANOTHER BUCKET OF WATER OUT BEFORE HE grabbed the old broom and swept it over the side. "Sorry about the puke."

Jena shrugged. "Someone puking is probably the most normal part of this day so far. At least I'm not the one cleaning it up."

He fell silent while he worked. *Sweep.* Ignore Jena's stare. *Fill the bucket.* Ignore the fact his face had changed shape before his eyes. *Scrub.* Did he have a brain tumor? *Wash.* Did everyone have brain tumors? *Sweep some more.*

"Do you really turn into an animal?" he asked quietly.

"Uh…" She watched him cautiously. "Yep. You gonna puke again?"

He blinked and shook his head. "I don't think so. Tell the truth. Is this some weird joke you pull on new people in town?"

"Nope."

Somehow, he knew she was telling the truth. That tickle in the back of his mind—the one that had bothered him since that first night at the town meeting—sighed in relief as if to say, "Of course! So that's what's seemed off. You moved to a whole town full of people who turn into animals." There was no explanation for this. It couldn't be real... except for the fact that he knew it was.

"It's not a joke, Caleb. I'm sorry."

"It's the water in the springs?"

"Just the fresh spring," she said quietly.

"The fresh spring?" He finally finished and leaned against the porch railing across from her. He could see the boys peeking through the windows, but they stayed away from the door. "That's... it's the one in the cave, isn't it? I drank... I'd been jogging in the canyon. I saw the coyote drinking, so I figured it was safe. I was in such a weird mood..."

It had been more than a mood, he realized. The coyote had led him there. Coyote was the trickster god. He should've known. The superstitions of his grandmother reared up and he fought the instinctive cringe. He didn't believe in that stuff. He didn't. If he did, then what just happened to him was more horrible than he could imagine.

"It's the water, isn't it?" he said. "That's what caused all this. The water turns you into animals. It turned me into... something else. Everyone in town?"

"Everyone descended directly from the founders. There were seven families at first. Two brothers, the McCanns, both former Confederate soldiers. Poor. Trying to protect their homes. There was one Native in their company. A Cherokee who served as a scout."

"Your ancestor?" He knew she had some native blood.

She nodded and continued. "They went west. Their town in the mountains had burned, and Thomas Crowe had a vision about a raven flying over an oasis in the middle of the desert. Far away from everyone. A safe place. They gathered more people as they traveled. A free black man who ran off some thieves attacking their camp, William

Allen. A pickpocket who Thomas saved from drowning in the Mississippi, Rory Quinn."

He thought about sneaky Old Quinn. "That explains so much."

Jena smiled. "There was a rancher and his sister in Texas. Gabriel Vasquez and Reina Vasquez de Leon. She was widowed and he was broke, but they had animals and equipment. They wanted a fresh start, too."

"Seven families."

Jena nodded again. "They found their way here. Thomas could only take them so far, but the younger McCann brother, Andrew, he was able to sense the water. He led them to the springs. There was only one with drinkable water. It was in a cave, but Andrew told them where to dig."

He was drawn in, the low sound of her voice hypnotic as she told the story of this strange place. A humming filled his blood, the same electricity he remembered from the sings his uncle did when he was a boy. "They found the fresh spring."

"Yes," she said. "All of them drank it. They hollowed out a basin in the rocks and used it like a well. It tasted great."

"It still does."

"Yes, it does." She paused. "They had been living in the bottom of the canyon for months before anyone noticed anything."

"Who noticed?"

"Thomas. His journals say he'd been having strange dreams. Then, one day, he woke up and... he wasn't. That's what he wrote. He had turned into a raven in his sleep just like in his dream. It always happens first in your sleep, like your mind has to be unconscious to turn the key that first time."

"You?" he asked. "What do you...?"

Could he ask that? Was it too personal? She hesitated a moment.

"A hawk," she said. "But I can turn into any bird I want to if I concentrate hard enough. All the Crowes turn into different birds."

"Jeremy warned me you had talons." He shook his head and swallowed the lump in his throat. "The boys? Are they...?"

She blinked back tears. "Not yet. Their dad never shifted when he was younger. That's why Lowell died young. But he was a McCann. He should have been a wolf. Most of the McCanns are. The boys could be either when they shift. Bird or wolf."

Caleb forced his mind to bend around it. "This isn't real, Jena."

He saw her blink away tears. "It's terribly real, but I'm sorry you got pulled into it."

Caleb shook his head, the rational part of him still trying to wake up.

"What were you dreaming about?"

He looked up, surprised. "What?"

"Earlier. When you... changed."

He closed his eyes and let out a rueful laugh. "I was dreaming about beating the shit out of Alex McCann because he wouldn't give me an alibi the night Alma was killed. It was a pretty satisfying dream until I woke up."

"You turned into him. You were dreaming about him and you turned into him."

"I guess so."

"By the way, Alex couldn't give you an alibi, but he was with Jeremy and the rest of his pack the night Alma was killed. It was a full moon that night."

"And you and Alma... you weren't going to the mud pool, I guess."

She shook her head.

"Flying?" She'd said all her family turned into birds.

Jena nodded.

"That's why you weren't wearing clothes. You'd flown out there."

She whispered, "We didn't get to fly much together. She usually watched the boys for me."

All the mismatched puzzle pieces seemed to fall into place. And that, more than anything else, confirmed that Caleb's reality was no longer what it had been. What was it that Sherlock Holmes said? Rule out every other option and whatever crazy shit was left over had to be right. Or something like that.

"The problem is, Caleb, you're not like us." Jena said. "No one is going to know what to do with you. Outsiders never drink from the spring. They usually never find it. But even people that marry in don't seem to be affected when they drink. Trust me, more than a few have tried. And no one I've ever heard of has turned into a people-shifter."

"Is that a technical term?"

She ignored him and rose. "I'm going to call my dad and Devin."

"Devin Moon, the sheriff's deputy? He knows?"

"All the tribes along the river know," she muttered as she walked in the house. The boys were sitting on the couch, watching television like it was any other afternoon. Caleb supposed that for them, the idea of people shifting into other people wasn't really all that big a stretch. "And Devin's dad is an elder."

"And you trust him? Trust them?"

"The Tribes don't want outside attention any more than we do, except at the casino. And Devin may play the good ol' boy, but he's way smarter than he looks."

They walked inside, and while Jena went to the kitchen to call, Caleb sat on the couch next to Aaron, who immediately scooted over to his side. Low glanced at him, but the normal glare was gone and the boy was examining him with new eyes. Apparently, being a cop who liked his mom was suspect, but a weird-ass supernatural creature who could transform his face accorded Caleb some respect.

Teenagers.

DEVIN WATCHED HIM WITH A PURPOSEFULLY BLANK STARE while Jena explained to him and her dad what had happened. Tom perched next to the boys on the couch, Jena was pacing, and Caleb and Devin both leaned against opposite walls in the crowded living room. Caleb was watching Jena as she flitted around the room. He was intensely curious what she looked like in hawk form. Was she just a normal hawk? Bigger? Did she hunt? Could she lay an egg if she wanted to? Then he blinked. Somehow, he knew asking that one was a bad idea.

"So" —Devin interrupted— "what you're saying is he's like you guys?"

"Um, no! We turn into animals. He's actually turning into other people, Dev."

Caleb's scowled. "Can I ask why you're acting like what I'm doing is so much weirder than you getting feathers every few weeks?"

"Animal shifting is completely natural."

Dev muttered, "Not really."

"Besides, I—" She looked at her dad. "We... Well, it's just normal for us. But turning into another person—"

"Seems like it would be slightly more complicated," Tom interjected. "I mean, when we're animals, we're still us. We still think like humans, for the most part, though we can't talk. Did you... I mean, did your mind feel any different? Did you realize you had changed?"

"Only when I saw my reflection. Though, admittedly, Alex and I are roughly the same height and build. If I turned into someone smaller—"

"Turn into Mom!" Aaron said.

"No," Caleb and Jena said together. It was too weird to even think about. He'd try to cop a feel on... himself. He shuddered.

Caleb saw Devin's eyes narrow. "Try shifting into me."

"Are you sure?" he asked.

Devin shrugged. "I'm shorter than you, but not too much. I'm about the same build, but a little thicker in the shoulders. We're close enough that you'd probably feel it, but not too much."

He glanced at Jena, but she only gave him a confused shrug.

"Okay," he said. "I'll try. I have no idea whether I can do it again."

Low asked, "What were you thinking about earlier? When you started to shift before you puked?"

Thanks for the reminder, kid. "I was just remembering Alex's face. My face when I saw it in the mirror. Just that."

"Well," Tom said, "try that." He stood and took a protective stance in front of the boys and Jena.

Caleb took a deep breath, stared into Devin's eyes for a few minutes, then closed his own. He let the picture of Devin's face float in the front of his mind. "Anything?"

"Nope."

He kept his eyes closed. What would it feel like to be Devin Moon? Why did he hide his intelligence behind a facade? What did he really think about the people he claimed to be protecting? Why did he do that thing with his thumb and his front tooth? He delved into the mind of the man across from him...

"Whoa... Mom, are you seeing—"

"Shhh."

Devin was Native. What tribe? The Colorado River Indian Tribes had four or five tribes, if he remembered right. Navajo? No, Caleb would be able to tell. Hopi? Mohave? Was his family traditional? Did he grow up on the reservation?

He'd chosen to be a cop. But not a homicide detective like Caleb. Did working with the dead carry the same cultural taboo for Devin's people as it did for Caleb's? Was his family proud of him?

"Mom?"

"Oh my..."

Did his grandmother hate him? Disown him? Turn away from him as if he was dead? The nausea was back.

"Caleb, open your eyes if you can."

"I can't," he rasped. "Not... not yet." He could feel his body had shifted. His jeans were a little tighter. The t-shirt he'd put on stretched across his shoulders and the muscles in his arms bulged strangely. He knew his body had changed, but the idea of opening his eyes and seeing the evidence in the mirror terrified him.

"Caleb." Jena was in front of him. But it wasn't him. "It's okay. It's still you."

"I changed, didn't I?"

"Uh-huh." Her voice was low and calm. "You look just like Dev. But you know what?"

"What?" He could barely hear his own voice.

"Your voice is still the same. And the face you're making right now? It's totally Caleb. You're still you."

"Jena!" He held out his hands, grasping for her. She took them, enfolded them in front of her, and pressed them to her chest.

"I'm still me when I'm a hawk. And you're still you. You're just borrowing a different skin for a little while."

He let his eyes open and locked onto hers. The angle was wrong. They were closer, but they weren't looking at him in horror or revulsion.

"Okay?" she asked.

"Yeah."

"Gonna puke?"

Caleb heard Tom's voice from across the room, but he didn't look. "The nausea must be the same for him as it is for us. Chief, don't worry about that. We get the nausea too, the first few times. It gets better as you adjust to the sensation of shifting. Nothing to worry about."

Jena still had her eyes locked on him. "Think you can look?"

"Do I have to?"

"It's pretty amazing. I'm not gonna lie. Except for the voice, you're Dev's twin."

Caleb finally let his eyes leave Jena's. He looked up, avoiding the mirror, and looked for Devin Moon. The other man was plastered against the opposite wall, staring at Caleb with a combination of awe and revulsion.

"Witch," Devin hissed.

Caleb shook his head. "No."

"*Clizyati*," Dev added. "You're not right."

He felt the sick twist in his stomach at the old words. "You're not Navajo. You don't know what you're talking about."

"I know enough."

Jena looked between the two men in confusion. "Dev? What's going on?"

"How many years did you work with the dead, Caleb?"

Old guilt ate at him. "Shut up."

"How many taboos did you break? What kind of evil did you let inside your soul?"

His temper spiked and he felt his body shift. He grew taller. Leaner. The familiar clench as his hand curled into a fist.

"You don't know what the hell you're talking about."

Jena said, "I don't know what you're talking about, either. Will someone explain what's going on? Dev, are you speaking Navajo? I thought you were Mohave."

"Does your family know? Or are you dead to them, skinwalker?"

"Skinwalker?" He could feel Jena try to pull away. "I thought—"

Devin continued. "I may be Mohave, but you think I'm gonna live next to a town of shapeshifters and not do my research? I know what you are, Caleb Gilbert. Tom, get the kids out of here."

Caleb heard both the boys protest before Jena turned to them. "Out! Now!"

He dropped her hands as if they burned. "You think I'd try to hurt your kids?"

Jena's eyes swam with remorse and confusion. "I don't know what's going on. What's he talking about?"

"You think I'm evil now?" He didn't know what he looked like on the outside, but inside, his bruised heart ached. He'd thought that it had been kicked beyond all feeling at that point, but what do you know? He was wrong.

Tom didn't say a word, just took the protesting boys out through the back door. Taking them away from Caleb. Away from the taboo-breaker. The unclean one. The killer.

Tears came to Jena's eyes. "I don't know what to think."

Devin spoke again as soon as he heard the back door slam. "I know your legends. There's only one way for a Navajo to wear the skin of another human, and it's very, very dark magic. Which member of your family did you kill?"

chapter
fifteen

J ena's mouth gaped in horror. Caleb stepped back, looking like
he'd been punched in the face.

"It's... it's not like that. I don't know what's going on, but it's
not that." He turned to her. "Jena? You don't believe...?"

Her mind flew in a thousand different directions. He couldn't. He
didn't. He was a good man; she knew that. But she'd heard the stories,
too.

Caleb stared at her for a few more minutes, then a cold mask slid
over his features. He walked to the door, then stopped and turned a
little, staring at the ground.

"Mr. Charles Yazzie Singer was killed by gunfire during a raid coordinated by federal and local police who were executing arrest warrants
in a coordinated operation in the greater Albuquerque metro area. Mr.
Singer was killed while attempting to fire on officers in the East Side
Narcotic Team led by Detective Caleb Yazzie Gilbert. Detective Gilbert
was commended for his actions during the raid."

Then he opened the door, stepped out, and shut it quietly
behind him.

Jena couldn't breathe. *Yazzie*. Same middle name. Cousin? Brother?
Jena sank onto the couch, tears rolling down her face. Devin was
quietly banging his head against the wall.

Elizabeth Hunter

"Damn, damn, damn, I should have known." Devin shook his head. "Stupid superstitions. I remember that raid, and I didn't put it together. It was all over the news. Even national. He'd been the one to coordinate the local teams with the feds. Hero cop and he takes early retirement. I should have known there was more to the story."

"I should have known, too." She swallowed the lump in her throat. "I feel horrible. He thinks I don't trust him, Dev. Thinks I thought he'd hurt the boys. I know he wouldn't. I'd never put his shifting together with the Navajo myths. But then I heard that word, and—"

"Don't blame yourself. Skinwalkers make for some seriously messed up stories."

Like Devin, Jena had acquainted herself with most of the local beliefs from the Native tribes around them. There were lots of shapeshifter stories, few of them were anything but sinister, especially in Navajo beliefs. Skinwalkers were black magic witches that perverted the natural harmony of life. They killed and cursed to get power. Broke traditional beliefs in a quest to trick and manipulate the people around them. They were said to be able to shift into any animal they wanted. The most evil among them, by killing a relative, were able to wear the skin of human beings themselves.

For anyone raised Navajo, the practice of shifting into an animal or anything else was considered black magic. Jena didn't know the specifics, doubted anyone outside the tribe did, but it wasn't good.

But those were just legends. Weren't they?

"The dead," she heard Devin say. "He must have touched the dead so many times…"

Dead bodies were a serious taboo for traditional Navajo.

"He worked in homicide before he went into Narcotics," Devin said. "His family must have loved that. He told you much about them?"

"No. He doesn't talk about the past. I think he grew up in Albu-querque. How bad would it have been for him?"

Devin shrugged. "Depends on how traditional his family was, but it could have been bad."

And yet, he'd stood for those who'd been killed and couldn't speak. Jena hung her head.

"I wonder if that's why he switched to narcotics," Devin said. "To appease his family."

"And then he had to kill a family member?"

Devin slumped down next to her. "No wonder he wanted to leave New Mexico."

"Then he comes out here and gets caught up in our craziness. A town full of shapeshifters. A murder. And now the poor guy's turning into your ugly self."

"Hey." He nudged her shoulder, but Jena knew he wasn't really annoyed. "You need to go talk to him."

"He probably hates me. And he has every reason to."

"Did you see his face, Jena? He doesn't hate anyone but himself."

Could your heart actually hurt? Jena's did. "He's probably sick from shifting, too."

"You got anything to help that?"

She shrugged. "Ginger tea helps a little when you first shift."

"Go. Take him some and apologize for doubting him. I'll go track down your dad and talk to Caleb later. I owe him an apology, too."

"He's going to be mad."

"Then he'll be mad, Jena. He has a right to be. We still have to apologize."

She sighed. "You're right."

JENA STEPPED OUT OF THE DOOR A HALF AN HOUR LATER holding a thermos of ginger tea. Her dad was walking back from Caleb's trailer.

"Got the AC working again."

She groaned. "I completely forgot about that."

"Well, there was a bit of excitement. Your mom's gonna have to buckle down and get a new one for that unit. The old one's shot. The boys are with her, by the way."

"Okay."

"You bringing him some tea?"

"Yep."

"That'll help." Tom looked off toward the trailer. "Poor kid. Hell of a thing to stumble into. It's a lot to deal with."

"We all manage."

"Yeah…" Tom was thoughtful. "But we've got family and clans and friends we've known our whole life here. He doesn't have any of that. Not really. And he's not really like any of us, either. I don't envy the man."

"Did Dev explain about the skinwalker thing?"

Tom shrugged. "A little. Said the guy had to kill his cousin or something in a police raid."

"That's what it sounds like."

"That's horrible. As for the rest of the superstitions?" Tom frowned, then looked away. "I don't figure any legend tells the whole truth about anything, you know? It's superstition. We're more than the stories they tell about us, aren't we, Jena?"

She blinked away tears and nodded. "Yeah, we are."

Tom slapped his work gloves on his leg a few more times, then started back for the trailer parked on the far side of the property. "We'll keep the boys for a while. I'll tell Cathy to figure on fixing them dinner. Go help your friend."

It was as good as an endorsement as Thomas Crowe was ever going to give to a man who liked his daughter. "Thanks, Dad."

He nodded and Jena continued toward Caleb's place. The blinds were all drawn, though she could hear some quiet music coming from inside. She tapped on the door, then stepped back, letting him decide whether he wanted to speak to her again.

After a few minutes, he opened the door. He was in a pair of sweatpants and nothing else.

"Hey," she said.

"Hey."

"I… uh, I came to apologize."

He didn't say anything. She almost wanted him to yell. It would have been better than his quiet condemnation.

"I would never in a million years hurt a child. Any child. But especially yours."

She brushed a tear that escaped down her cheek. "I know that. I *know* that. I was scared. And I didn't know what to think. I reacted poorly when you were probably just as scared. And then Dev accused you of… you know. And I know there must be an explanation—not that you owe one to me, or anything—but I know there must be one. And it was… it was surprise and shock. And I'm so sorry." She bit her lip and forced herself to look into his dark eyes. "I'm sorry, Caleb. Not my finest hour."

His face had transformed from grim condemnation into something that looked almost amused. "That's okay. When you first told me you turned into a bird, I wanted to ask if you could lay an egg."

Jena blinked. "A—an egg? Are you asking that just to piss me off?"

"Maybe. Can you?"

She huffed and pushed her way into the trailer. "Oh, for heaven's sake."

Caleb was smiling, almost back to his normally affable self. "It's a reasonable question."

"That I'm not gonna justify with a response. Drink your tea." She put the thermos on the counter.

He examined it. "What is it?"

"Ginger tea." She patted his stomach. Oh holy… abs. Jena cleared her throat and pulled her hand away. "It'll help with the nausea. My dad's right. We get the same reaction when we shift back to our human form. At least at first. It'll pass, but the tea helps."

"When did you shift the first time?" Despite his deliberately upbeat demeanor, he still looked a bit green around the edges. And tired. Jena was glad her father had gotten the AC fixed.

"Twelve. Pretty average. For shifter kids it tends to come right before puberty."

"So my voice is going to change again?" he asked. "Thanks for the warning."

"And don't forget that strange hair in odd places."

He took a mug from the cupboard and paused. "That takes on a whole new meaning when you're talking about werewolves."

"Uh..." She shook her head. "Don't call them werewolves. They hate that. We're not monsters or half-animals or anything. We look just like regular animals. Birds look like birds. Wolves look like wolves. About half the pack in the Springs is Timberwolves and half Mexican grey in their natural form."

"Natural form?" He poured some tea into a cup.

"It's the first animal we shift to. It's what will always be easiest. For me, it was a hawk. My dad is a raven."

"Alma?" He watched her reaction carefully.

"A barn owl." She smiled.

"Beautiful bird."

"Yep. She was."

"Big?"

Jena nodded. "Almost two feet tall. She was on the big side for a female. Great flyer. Excellent hunter."

"Right." She saw Caleb shake his head. "Right. She was a barn owl when she was attacked. Of course. That's why the blood pattern..." He blinked and looked at her. "Sorry. This probably isn't the best time to ask, but does this mean you all are finished lying to me about this murder?"

He was already thinking about that? Jena decided to be relieved. "Yes. It was only ever because you weren't supposed to know about the shifting. It wasn't that I didn't trust you."

"Nice to hear. So, Alma was an animal when she was attacked." He nodded. "And it must have been another shifter in animal form..."

"Yes. That's why Ted thinks the wounds are so warped. The claw marks were probably from a bobcat, but they grew bigger when she died."

"They grew as she did." Caleb was stretching his hands out, trying to picture it in his mind. "So she turned into a human when she died?" He paused to sip the tea before he sat down across from her in the small banquet. "Does everyone?"

"Turn back to human when we die? Yes. We're humans first and finally. We only take on animal form when we want to and at the full moon."

"You *have* to change during the full moon?" He narrowed his eyes. "Alma was murdered on the full moon. It was so bright that night it woke me up. But you were human when I came to the house. So was Jeremy. Ted? She a shifter, too?"

"Mountain lion."

"That's not terribly surprising."

"And I changed back, but it was hard. The only other time I could resist the change was sometimes when I was living away from the Springs, and when I was pregnant with the boys."

"No shifting for pregnant moms, huh?"

She shook her head. "It'd cause miscarriage. No idea why. But the first symptom of pregnancy for female shifters is an aversion to the shifting instinct. I felt it before I ever knew I was pregnant with either boy."

"You just don't want to?"

"No." She shook her head. How to explain? "You *want* to, you just know you can't. It's very frustrating. By the time we deliver babies around here, we're pretty bitchy."

His mouth turned up at the corner. "Duly noted. I'll have to look over all the files again. Talk to Ted and Jeremy..." He paused, took another sip of tea. "You probably don't want to hear all this, though."

"I'll help with whatever I can. She was my grandmother."

He nodded, watching her with an odd expression she couldn't decipher. "The boys' dad... you said he didn't shift?"

The old wound ached, just a little. "It happens every now and then.

It's not common. If a child doesn't shift, they always die young. Heart attack. Cancer. Stroke."

"Their dad?"

"Brain cancer." She kept blinking to suppress the tears. "Only took about five months."

"Damn. But you knew? When you married him, you knew he was going to die young."

Jena gave him a rueful laugh. "We both did. Tried to deny it. We ran away. Don't know what we were thinking, but then, Lowell always hated it here, anyway. Hated being the only one of his cousins who was different. So we left. And in the back of my mind, I thought... maybe it would work. Maybe if we left the Springs, it wouldn't get him. That we'd have more time."

"How old was he?"

"Twenty-eight."

"Wow. And you had two kids."

She nodded. "He worried, but I knew... even if he was gone, I wanted to have a part of him. I was young, crazy in love. I was a baby myself when I had Low. Most of the women in my family wait until their thirties to have kids. I was barely out of high school."

Caleb fell silent, sipping his tea again. "I'm glad you did." His voice was hoarse. "They're great kids, Jena. You're lucky."

"Not many would say that."

"Then they'd be wrong."

He was thinking about his family again. She could tell. Jena rose, took him by the hand, and led him back to the bedroom. "Don't think you're getting lucky, cowboy. You look ready to fall over. Just lay down for a nap."

He sighed and let her lead him. "I'm exhausted. I don't ever remember being exhausted like this before, not even in the middle of an investigation."

"That's normal, too."

"You gonna tuck me in?"

She stifled the grin. Opportunistic, determined idiot. "You gonna behave?"

"Define 'behave.'"

She chuckled and pushed him back on the bed, but he grabbed her hand and she tumbled after him.

"Hey!"

"Just lay down with me." His voice was already sleepy. "I want to hold on to something right now."

Her heart fluttered. "Anything? I can get a teddy bear from the house."

Caleb nosed down into the curve of her neck. "You, Jena. I want to hold on to you."

"Oh." Flutters turned in to a warm melted twist in her stomach. She'd known he wanted her, but this... It felt like more than just wanting. "You're pretty cuddly for a badass police officer."

"Can I make a joke about going undercover right now or will you hit me?"

She couldn't stop the laugh. "You're shameless."

"I know." He sighed and nestled her into his body. Her back was to his chest and he had one leg thrown over hers. One long arm draped over her waist and his hand rested on her stomach. His other arm bunched under the pillow and tilted their heads together so his face was buried in her hair.

"So you're a snuggler."

"I'm a very modern man. In touch with my feelings and all that shit. Plus, you smell really good."

"I think you're getting in touch with more than your feelings there, Chief."

He gave her hip an affectionate pat. "Shhh. Let the tired skinwalker sleep."

She shivered at his words and he tensed.

"I'm sorry. I shouldn't have said that."

"It's just the name," she whispered quickly. "It's not you. You're you, Caleb. And... that's who I care about."

His hand gripped her thigh a little harder, and she turned to look at him. As soon as their eyes met, he gave her the softest, sweetest smile she'd ever seen. "You fit, Jena Crowe," he whispered. "Like the right pair of shoes."

Then, he leaned over and kissed her. Soft and sweet, he kept kissing her until she felt his lashes flutter against her cheeks and his eyes closed. Then she tucked her head into the hollow of his shoulder and fell asleep.

THE SUN HAD SET AND THE SKY SHONE WITH BRILLIANT reds and golds when she woke up. Caleb was sitting up in bed with her head resting against his thigh and his hand was playing with the ends of her hair as he stared out the window. As soon as he saw she was awake, he began speaking in a low voice.

"Charlie was my cousin. But... it's not the same for Navajos. Not traditional ones like my grandmother, anyway. My mom was kind of the black sheep, getting knocked up by an Anglo guy, but the rest of her family, they were real traditional. When my dad took off, we went to live with them. I don't remember anywhere else. My mom's older sister was like another mother to me. Her husband, my Uncle Raymond, was like a father. And Charlie was their oldest son. We were about the same age. More brothers than cousins."

She wondered if he had ever told this story to anyone. He looked raw. Exposed in a way that she never would have expected. "What happened?"

"I shot him. It was at a drug raid in the city."

"Why was he there?"

"It's a long story."

"I have time."

His hands stopped combing through her hair and he looked her in the eye. "You said you didn't. Said you didn't have time to date me. To get to know me."

She had, hadn't she? But it was an excuse. Just a way of locking away that part of herself she'd buried with Lowell when he died. And was that what he'd wanted for her?

"Then I'll make time," she whispered.

She'd say it again a hundred times if she could see him smile like that. He was a little boy who'd just been given the perfect present. The young man who won the baseball game. But then his smile fell.

"Are you sure?"

"Yes."

He took a deep breath. "It happened when we were kids. Charlie's little sister Beth was playing away from the house. Don't know exactly where, maybe over by the sheep corrals. But she disappeared. It probably seems horrible to you, but we didn't notice for a while. She was always wandering off and it wasn't like anywhere else. We all just assumed she was safe."

"But she wasn't." Jena's heart filled with dread.

"No. We noticed by dinnertime, and they found her body the next day out in the desert. No one would tell any of us what happened to her. To this day, I don't know. I don't even know if my uncle does."

"What did the police say?"

"Nothing." She frowned and he continued. "You can't touch a dead body, Jena. You can't be in the same room with it or touch anything that touches it. If someone dies in a house, you leave the house and never return to it. You burn it, sometimes. My Uncle Raymond brought her body into the house and we left. We weren't allowed to see her. They dug the grave and buried her, and when the tribal police came by, they said she was killed by a coyote. My uncle knew them, so they accepted it. They burned the house. They built a new one that she'd never been in before. And Charlie and I never knew what happened."

"How old were you?"

"About Low's age. And I hated them for lying to the cops. Because I could tell they were lying. But they had buried the evidence. Burned the house. Would never tell anyone where they'd found her body. And I hated them for it. In my gut, I knew it wasn't a natural death, but

Beth had no justice. So when my mom remarried and left for the city, I went with her, even though my grandmother and my aunt and uncle and Charlie begged me to stay."

"And you became a police officer. Who had to touch dead bodies as part of your duties."

"My own personal rebellion. I about puked the first time I had to guard a scene. Just an old man who'd died from a heart attack, but I had to stand in the same room with him for hours while they did everything. I thought I was going to pass out. I went home and show-ered until the water was freezing cold. Rubbed my skin raw."

"But you conquered it."

"I did." He heaved a giant sigh and pulled her up to sit next to him. "I did. And the longer I did it, the more evil my grandmother said I'd become. She's not the most rational person anymore. Part of it was old age, but part of her… she really thinks that. No one understood. Except maybe Charlie. But he'd gotten so messed up by then it was pretty bad."

"Drugs?"

Caleb nodded. "Drugs. Drinking. Stealing. Vandalism. He never hurt anyone that I knew of until…"

"He pointed a gun at you."

"At my men," he whispered. "At the men I'd sent in. Fellow officers. Guys just trying to get home to their families. I *saw* him. I knew it was him. I didn't even know he'd been working for them."

"You couldn't have known."

"I shot him the minute he lifted a gun in their direction." His voice was hollow. "I could see the look on his face. He wanted to die, and I shot him."

Jena sniffed and buried her face in Caleb's neck. "I'm so sorry."

"They hate me. All my mother's family. Well, maybe not my cousin Steph. She's not so superstitious."

"Are you sure they really hate you?" Jena had a feeling that Devin was right. The person who hated Caleb Gilbert the most was Caleb, not his family.

"They won't have anything to do with me. I'm the one who touched dead bodies and refuses the sings that would bring him back in harmony." He paused, frowning. "It's not that I don't respect their beliefs, it's just that, if I agree to do the ceremonies, it's like I'm agreeing that the work I was doing—solving crimes, standing up for the dead—was wrong somehow. And I refuse to believe that. I've made my peace with it. It doesn't matter what they think. Not really. I have my mom and stepdad, who are both pretty great. A half-sister, but she's a lot younger. Mostly, it's just me."

"I think…" What did she think? He was so much more than who she'd thought he was. Darker? Yes, a lot more dark corners. But he still managed to smile. Still managed to make a little boy laugh and stand as a witness for an old woman when no one else would back him up. "I think you're an amazing man, Caleb Gilbert. And I'm proud to know you. And call you a friend."

"Hmm. Just a friend?"

She knew she was blushing. "For now."

A slow smile spread over his face. "A friend you kiss. I'm making progress."

Jena rolled her eyes and tried to scoot away from him. "I have to get home, Caleb. It's late."

"Stay. I promise I'll behave."

"Behave how?"

He grinned. "Caught that one, did you?"

"Uh-huh." She scooted away again and he let her. "I don't want to be gone when my boys wake up in the morning."

He sighed and rolled off the bed. "Okay." They walked out the door and down the steps. Caleb placed a hand around her waist, holding on to her even as she walked away. "Hey, Jena."

She turned. "Yeah?"

"Thanks. For listening." He bent down. Slowly inching his way toward her lips. "For the tea." A soft brush against her lips that brought a flush to her cheeks and started her blood humming. "For explaining about all the crazy shifter stuff. For making the time."

She melted against him. "You're—"

He cut her off with his mouth. Jena sighed and wrapped her arms around his waist. Oh, he was gonna eat her alive and she'd die happy. Caleb pushed her lips open and curled his tongue around hers. Turning and twisting her inside out as his hands ran down her back, over her hips, and down to cup her backside and push her flush into him.

It wasn't like the sweet, slow kisses they'd shared before sleeping. Caleb's lips were a scorching brand on her skin. Claiming. Marking. She pulled away with a gasp.

"Caleb!"

He grabbed her hair at the nape of her neck, running his hand through it and tilting her head back to press his lips to her neck. He pulled and bit at the skin, snaking his tongue up until his lips tugged at her earlobe and his teeth gave a little nip.

"Oh," she breathed out. "Stop. I have to—"

"Go," he panted. "I know. I just wanted to make sure you realized something."

"Yeah?"

He pulled back and reached a hand down to give her bottom a quick pat. He grinned when she yelped. "I can be patient, but I'm not finished with you by a long shot."

"You—"

"Night!" He lifted a hand to wave toward the house. "Hi there, Cathy!"

Jena whirled around to see absolutely no one in the yard. Then the door slammed and she could hear Caleb laughing his ass off inside. She turned and stomped toward the house.

"Stupid, idiotic male."

She was in so much trouble.

chapter
sixteen

A week later, Caleb was making faces in the mirror. Literally. He'd discovered through trial and error that thinking about other people and concentrating on getting in their mind would transform his face and body at will. He still had the feeling his body was changing in the night during sleep. Most mornings, he ached as if he'd been lifting weights after sitting for way too long. The nausea that went with it seemed to be under control—or better, at least. The weirdness of being able to change faces? Well, that was going to linger a little longer, if he had to guess.

Ted came by and Caleb reluctantly agreed to a short physical, just to check that his body was as normal as possible. He was impressed with the woman's professionalism. She also appeared completely nonplussed about the fact that he turned into other people. Score one for the good doctor. Jena's other friend, Allie, also came by bearing a pot of soup and two frozen casseroles that took up most of his small freezer and promised to keep him from total starvation. If he didn't like Jena so much already, he might have fallen for her just for her friends.

After three days of hiding in his trailer, Caleb decided if he was going to join the weird supernatural world of Cambio Springs, where people turned into wolves, lizards, birds, and bears, he wasn't going to be the only one who couldn't control his abilities. If he was going to be cursed with some weird shapeshifter thing from drinking the damn spring water, he might as well get good at it. He couldn't stand doing things half-assed.

He tried to approach it from a professional standpoint. It wasn't really all that much different than getting inside the head of a suspect to understand their motivations. Only, this time, he actually *became* the person he was trying to understand. The first few times, he upchucked every time he looked in his mirror and saw a different face. Then he shifted back and the nausea struck again. He'd probably lost a good five pounds over the week from not being able to keep anything down. But eventually, he'd gotten a handle on the nausea. And the shifting seemed to happen with less effort. By the end of the week... well, really weird and creepy was turning into more than a little cool.

There was a hard knock at the door. Caleb looked away from the mirror and felt his face tilt back toward the familiar before he went to answer it. Other than Jena—who had come by to give him more tea—and her two friends, he'd been a bit of a hermit. He'd talked to Jeremy on the phone, but—predictably—nothing was happening at the station, so the time off didn't seem like a big deal.

When he opened the door, Tom was standing next to a giant box with Ollie at his back.

"Hey. New AC came in for your trailer. You mind?"

"Not at all." He'd been dying without the cool air. Caleb stepped aside and let the two men in. The trailer, once comfortably snug, suddenly seemed claustrophobic with the presence of the two burly men. Ollie gave him a nod as he stood to the side and let Tom examine the unit.

"Chief."

"Hey, Ollie. How's it going?"

"It's going. Not much happening. Fall's always kind of dead at the bar." Ollie was staring at him with a detached kind of curiosity. Caleb started to get annoyed. He began to search his mind for what he knew about the man.

Tough, but quiet. He was a bear. Loyal. Family-oriented. Fierce when provoked…

He felt his face slip into the mirror image of the man across from him. His sweatpants and T-shirt bulged as he shot up six inches in height.

"Want a beer?" he said in a slightly deeper voice.

"Holy shit!" Ollie jerked back so hard he slammed his head on the ceiling. "Holy—I didn't really believe them! What the—?"

"Watch your language." He nodded toward the Mason jar on the counter. "Jena made me start a swear jar."

He heard Tom snort as he poked around the air-conditioner mounted in the center of the kitchen. "Ollie boy, one of us is going to have to get up on the roof to get this done. The thing's just—are you even listening to me?"

"Nope, Tom. Still kinda watching the weird guy who just turned into me. Caleb, I'm gonna say yes to that beer now."

He let his body relax back into itself and reached for the fridge, pulling out three longnecks to hand to the other men and opening one for himself. "Hey, at least I stay human. A bear? Really?"

Ollie shrugged massive shoulders. "Is it really all that surprising?"

Caleb looked at the six-and-a-half-foot giant of a man with broad shoulders, curly dark hair, and deceptively calm expression. "Now that I think about it, not really." He took another drink and turned to Tom. "Can I help?"

"You're probably the lightest of us, so you can crawl up on the roof and get the top half of this thing. We brought a ladder."

"Can't you just fly up there?"

"If I wanted to show my naked ass to you two when I shifted back, then sure." He slapped Caleb's shoulder. Fairly hard. "But since I feel like keeping my clothes on, you can do it, Chief. Make you appreciate that nice cool air a little bit more."

Three hours and a half a Mason jar full of quarters later, the three men sat outside the Airstream in folding chairs, drinking more beer and staring at their handiwork. The new air-conditioner filled the early evening sky with a pleasant hum that filled Caleb's ears with the promise of cool afternoons for months to come.

"Thanks, Tom. Tell Cathy thanks, too."

"It's no problem. Feel bad you've been stuck in there with it cutting out every couple hours."

He shrugged. "I lived. And Ollie, thanks for the help, bear-man."

"No problem... people-man." He frowned. "That one doesn't really roll off the tongue, does it?"

Tom said, "You could just call him a skinwalker."

Caleb shivered. "Please don't. I know Devin probably doesn't know this, but that term is horrible. Skinwalkers are black magic witches that curse and maim and do all kinds of horrible things. They're legends, of course. It's just superstition—"

"Except when it isn't." Ollie nodded at him.

"Yeah... I have no idea how all this happened. My grandmother would say that all the bad shit I've done has finally caught up with me."

Ollie frowned. "What? Like the thing with your cousin?"

Caleb tried not to cringe. Of course the news about Charlie would have spread all over the town within a short time.

As if reading his mind, Ollie said, "It's not all over. Devin just told Alex and me what happened and included that part as a demonstration of his bone-headedness. Don't worry. It's no one's business but yours. But is that what you're talking about? Because I gotta say, man, that's a hell of a thing, but it doesn't sound like it was anything you could have helped."

"Agreed," Tom grunted. "And any family that's going to hold you responsible for your cousin's actions is... Well, I'm sure they're grieving, but there's no excuse for it, in my opinion."

Caleb sat silent, stunned by the unexpected loyalty of these two men who barely knew him. "I... uh"—he cleared his throat— "it's more than all that. It's complicated. There's a lot of superstitions and complicated taboos about all sorts of things where I grew up. Lots of good stuff too, but being a homicide detective violated a lot of cultural taboos from their standpoint. So even though my mom and stepdad raised me—"

"Hard to leave behind how you grew up." Tom gave him a brisk nod. "Understood."

"Well," Ollie finished his beer. "I gotta get back to the bar. Caleb, thanks for the beer. You coming to Sunday dinner at Jena's?"

"Yeah, she invited me."

"See you there, then." He nodded at Jena's dad. "Tom, see you around."

"See ya, Ollie."

Ollie lumbered off and got into the truck with the old AC unit thrown into the bed along with all the junk and packaging from the new one.

"He has a dumpster behind the bar he can put all that stuff in," Tom said casually. "So, you going to Jena's on Sunday?"

He nodded, suddenly realizing that Tom might have an opinion about… things. Things having to do with his daughter. He liked the man, really did. But his interest in Jena Crowe wasn't something he wanted to talk about with her father. Nor was it something he was going to change his mind about if he disapproved.

"Listen, Tom, I really like Jena—"

"I hoped for years that she and Ollie would get together, you know? Love that boy like he was my own. And after Lowell passed… Well, it seemed like the natural thing. They'd always been such good friends." Tom took another drink of beer as Caleb tensed. "But that's all they ever were. More like a big brother to her. And he's got his heart set on something he can't have, so that's fairly hopeless."

Allie. Caleb had seen it weeks ago. The man was pining for a married woman. Nothing good could ever come of that. "Well… I know they're close, but—"

"You seem to… brighten her up," Tom said quietly. "She's happier when she comes back from seeing you. More irritated, too, but then I suppose I do the same to her mother at times." He grinned for a second. "She's a serious girl, Caleb. She's got a lot of responsibilities and two boys who depend on her."

"I know that. I do."

He could feel the other man's stare. "Be careful, Caleb Gilbert."

"Tom, if you're worried about their safety, I can tell you I'll do everything in my power to make them safe. I know there's a killer out there, and I'm not foolish enough to believe I can catch him on my own. I know Jena agreed to help me, but I will make sure she and the boys—"

"Be careful," Tom interrupted. "With *her*. She's not as tough as she looks."

And Caleb suddenly understood they were talking about more than Jena's safety. "I understand, sir."

Tom nodded and stood, ambling toward the path that would lead him back to the big trailer he and Cathy shared. Suddenly, he turned. "Caleb?"

"Yeah?"

"The elders are going to want to speak with you. They're going to have to know who you are and that you know about us."

He nodded, trying not to let the tension show in his face. "Anything I should be worried about?"

Tom shrugged. "I don't think so. We all have secrets. And so do you now. We respect that. It's our water that made you change. So, that makes you one of us. Even if you're not exactly the same. You're still a shifter."

A strange warmth filled him. A kind of acceptance he hadn't felt since he was twelve years old. "So, no problem?"

"I don't think so." Tom smiled. "We take care of our own." Then the old man looked toward Jena's house. "Remember that."

Message received, old man. Don't mess around with Thomas Crowe's daughter without carefully considering the consequences.

"I'll remember."

TWO DAYS LATER, HE WAS BACK AT WORK. THIS TIME, JEREMY was the one taking some time off, since Brenda hadn't been feeling well, and they needed to get some work done on the house. Considering the young deputy had covered for him during the previous week, Caleb could hardly complain. He was sure glad the weekend was coming up. Maybe some drunks would cause problems down at The Cave. He could use the distraction.

He was paging through Ted's notes about Alma's remains—the real ones, not the ones she'd shown him before—when he heard the door open. He peeked around the divider to see Low walking in, looking around the empty room.

"Hey."

The boy's eyes found his. "Hey."

"You looking for Jeremy? He's home today. Brenda needed some help."

"No." Low looked around curiously. "I want to know about my grandma's case."

Caleb nodded. Part of him was tempted to call Jena and ask how much he should tell the boy. The other part remembered how he'd felt when Beth had been killed. The condescending looks from the grown-ups. The useless sympathy. The rage at the unknown. "Go ahead and sit down." He nodded toward the chair across from his desk.

"Okay."

"What do you want to know?" The boy froze, apparently surprised that Caleb was asking.

"Just... about how she died, I guess. And why."

He nodded and kept his eyes locked on Low. "You realize that anything I share with you has to stay between us, right? If I give you details about the investigation, they absolutely must stay between the two of us. No telling your friends. Not even your brother. He's too young."

The boy went from stunned to awestruck in a heartbeat, and he nodded. "Yes, sir."

Caleb looked down at the file in his hands. Too thin. He was hoping

Elizabeth Hunter

that picking the brain of all of Jena's friends at the dinner on Sunday was going to help fill it out a little. But until then…

"I can't tell you everything, but I can tell you that your grandmother was getting ready to go out flying with your mom that night. You knew that, right?"

Low nodded and Caleb continued. "She let someone in who attacked and killed her. Probably someone in animal form. Someone who knew she was going to be at her house. She usually watched you guys on moon nights, right?"

"Yeah, but…" The boy squirmed.

"But what?"

"I told some people." He saw tears come to corners of Low's eyes. "That she was going out with Mom. I'm sorry."

Now the tears made sense. "Low, you had no way of knowing—"

"I was mad about not getting to go to my cousins' house that night. Grandma usually took us over there and it's always really fun."

"You couldn't have known. It's not your fault." Caleb paused as Low cleared his throat. "It might help the investigation if you remember who you told, though. Do you?"

"I was complaining at school. About them being selfish and going out flying while we had to stay home with Cousin Jeremy's wife because she doesn't know everyone yet and didn't want to take us to Grandpa Max's." Caleb saw Low blink away more tears. "Like, everyone in my class probably heard. Lots of people. So all their moms probably know. Mrs. Marquez even told me I shouldn't talk out of turn about my grandma."

He didn't have to elaborate. In a small town, everyone would have known quickly that Alma wouldn't be following her usual pattern and taking her grandkids to the McCanns. Not a big deal… unless you were someone wanting to get rid of Alma Crowe. Caleb's mind finally caught up with one detail Low had mentioned.

"Wait… Mrs. Marquez? The mayor's wife?"

"Yeah. Her daughter's in my class."

So Mayor Matt knew that Alma would be meeting Jena. Another

※ 178 ※

point against the friendly man. But then, like Low had said, the information was probably common knowledge to anyone who was listening.

"Thank you for telling me." Caleb spoke in a steady voice, trying to reassure the upset boy. "I appreciate your honesty. What you told me is really helpful to the investigation."

He brightened immediately. "It is?"

Caleb nodded. "Yes. And I know that you know none of this was your fault in any way. The only person to blame is the person who killed Alma."

He sniffed. "That's what Mom said."

"She's a smart woman."

Low sat silent in his chair for a few more minutes. "You like her a lot."

Oh, so they'd switched to *that* conversation. Caleb suddenly felt as uncomfortable as the boy. "Um... yeah, I do."

Low stared out the window, avoiding his eyes. "She's really pretty, you know?"

"I know."

"There was a guy. He was from away, but he was one of Ollie's cousins. He was doing repairs to the kitchen at the diner for her. Putting in some new stuff. He liked her, too."

Oh did he now? "Oh yeah?"

"But he went away. I mean, his job got finished and he left. And I could tell Mom was kind of sad, but not really. She didn't *really* like him. Not like she likes you."

Relief flooded Caleb. He had no idea why. It wasn't as if the guy was still around vying for her affections or anything. And that, Caleb suddenly realized, was the point. He looked at Low. "Well... I like it here. I don't really see moving away anytime soon."

The boy watched him carefully. "But you will someday?"

Would he? Suddenly, the weight of his answer made Caleb want to squirm. What was this boy asking? What exactly was he committing himself to? Sure, he liked Jena Crowe, maybe more than any other woman he'd met. Including his ex-wife. But he hadn't even taken the woman on a proper date yet. He'd told her secrets that he'd kept hidden for years, then they'd never brought it up again. A few stolen kisses when she slipped away from her responsibilities wasn't exactly enough to commit the rest of his life to. In all honesty, he had no idea whether the woman was really that interested in him or whether she just felt responsible for him since her town had turned him into shapeshifter.

And Low was still watching him. More suspicious than ever.

"No one can predict the future," Caleb finally said. Then a thought occurred to him and he smiled ruefully. "But I guess I don't know many other towns where I would fit in anymore. You all might be stuck with me since I'm just as weird as you are now."

Low smiled at the joke, but it was tight and nervous. Nothing like Aaron's open acceptance. And Caleb knew he didn't deserve the boy's acceptance. Low was old enough to realize something his younger brother didn't. Sometimes, whether they wanted to or not, people left.

By the time Sunday dinner rolled around, Caleb was tight and needy. He wanted to get Jena by herself. Didn't want to spend the whole night with a bunch of her friends and family. Didn't want to talk about Alma's murder, even if he knew it was what he needed to do. He'd only seen her in passing a few times since he'd been back to work. She was too busy to stop by the trailer, or she was avoiding him. Avoiding the hard edges and shadows of his life. Avoiding the inevitable souring of a relationship that had never really gotten off the ground.

"Hey!" She opened the door with a bright smile that immediately flooded him with relief. But the tension still sat in his belly.

"Hey." He bent down to kiss her and she ducked her cheek to the side, blushing a little as a couple of kids he didn't recognize ran through the room.

"Sorry," she whispered. "There's just a lot of people here and..."

He gave her a sharp nod, then ducked down to her ear. "Where's your bedroom?"

Caleb could see the desire spark in her eyes. "Down the hall," she murmured. "Second door on the left."

The house was a babble of voices. Allie and Ted joking in the kitchen. Various kids screaming and laughing outside. Some male voices from the backyard. Caleb pulled Jena by the hand and led her down the hall decorated in children's pictures and family photographs. He shoved the door to her room open and pulled her inside. The shades were already drawn to keep out the afternoon heat. The pretty, feminine room was dark and cool.

He spun around and cornered Jena, pushing her up against a wall as his mouth crashed down on hers. He angled his knee between her legs until she was straddling him, then he pulled her closer, cupping her backside as he swallowed the moan that left her throat.

"Caleb!" Her voice was a high keen. "We can't—"

He cut her off with another kiss. He needed… he just *needed*. Her. Her skin. His hand crept around her neck, clutching at the warm soft skin at the nape. Her curves. His other hand grabbed a handful of her hip as he pressed his knee against the heat between her legs. Her heat.

"I want you, Jena. So much," he groaned, pulling away from her lips for a moment when she lifted a leg, wrapping it around his waist. Her hands clutched at his shoulders, pulling him closer. She was just as frantic as he was, panting his name in soft breaths against his ear. They would fit perfectly, he thought as he kissed her neck. She was made for him. Everything about her. "You're driving me out of my mind."

Jena's skin was flushed a deep red and burning up when he kissed her again. He wanted to forget about everyone else, lay her down on that soft, unexpectedly frilly, bedspread and dive into her. Until there was nothing else but him and her and push and pull and wanting and—

"Moooom!" Aaron's voice called down the hall.

Damn.

Jena pulled back, her head hitting the wall before he could catch it.

He lifted a hand to soothe where it had hit, brushing her hair away from her face and kissing her temple. She took a couple of deep breaths and set both feet on the floor. He gave her a little room... not much, though. He didn't particularly want to let her get away.

"Yeah, Bear?"

"Where's the juice boxes?"

She rolled her eyes. "In the blue ice chest where they always are."

"Oh." He paused. "Why are you in your room? Uncle Alex was looking for you. And is Chief Caleb coming?"

"Not likely," he whispered, making Jena stifle a laugh.

"We—I'll be out in a minute. Tell Uncle Alex to put the tri-tip on, okay?"

"Okay!" He heard the little boy's feet stomping down the hall.

"Not likely?" she whispered, trying to look severe. The smile fighting to get out killed the effect.

"Someday?" He kissed her neck. "Hopefully?" Then he gave the hollow behind her ear a little lick and whispered, "Don't pretend you don't want me, Jena."

Her face burned. "Wanting? Sure. Acting?" Her face fell a little. "Entirely more complicated."

He put both hands on her waist and spun them around so he was leaning against the wall with her standing between his legs. They were eye to eye when he spoke.

"I missed you."

She sighed. "I'm sorry. It's been a busy couple of days and—"

"I missed you," he said again, pulling her face to his for a soft kiss. "Not just this. I missed seeing your face. And making you laugh. Did you miss me?"

She looked embarrassed and tried to pull away. "Caleb, I..."

"Simple question." But an important one. Was he too strange to her now? She'd had a few days to think. Over a week for the reality of it to sink in. Maybe, like his grandmother's people, she would find him grotesque now. Unnatural.

Jena finally looked up at him and she nodded. "I missed you, too."

The tension that had wrapped around his heart eased a little. "Good."

"But we need to get out there."

He wiggled his hips between the cradle of her thighs. "I beg to differ."

"Hold your horses, cowboy. I've got a lot of hungry people to feed."

Did he have to let that one pass? He sighed and stood up, mentally willing away the tightness in his pants. "Fine. Later?"

"Later we have to talk about the case."

"After that?"

She opened the door. "You're relentless."

"I warned you about that, didn't I?" Then Caleb squeezed her hand and left her in the hall to walk into the riot of noise coming from the kitchen.

chapter
seventeen

J ena watched him as she cooked, sneaking glances in his direction as she put together a salad, heated macaroni and cheese, and tossed instructions at the various small children acting as her minions. Caleb had grabbed a beer and gone to sit by Ollie and Alex at the barbecue, looking as comfortable as if he'd been coming to her Sunday dinners for years.

It was a tradition she'd started when she moved back, wishing to reconnect with her oldest friends and needing the comfort of those who had loved and known Lowell. Over the years, it had become tradition. Everyone brought something to eat and their favorite drink. You didn't call or plan. If you were there, you were there. But most Sundays, Jena's friends were there. Willow was the only one who was still absent, deciding to stay in Colorado for the rest of the month at an artists' retreat she'd been invited to.

"Jena!" Ted called from the back, carrying Allie's youngest, Loralai under her arm. "Where's Allie?"

"I think she's on the phone."

"*Donde esta su esposo?*" Ted asked, switching to Spanish so the baby couldn't understand her question about Allie's absent husband.

Jena shrugged. Joe and Allie were obviously having problems, but her usually cheerful friend was reluctant to talk about them. Joe had always been temperamental. And Allie had always made excuses. He'd moved to the Springs as a teenager, a reluctant addition to the community his parents forced him to accept as his own. By the time he'd shifted to a coyote at age thirteen, Joe seemed to have accepted life in the small town, but Jena had always sensed restlessness in him.

Ted muttered something uncomplimentary about Joe's mother under her breath, but the baby only giggled. She was Allie's surprise baby, eighteen months old and a handful of energy. Within seconds, she had taken off into the backyard again, where she crawled onto Caleb's lap with no introduction and proceeded to babble something that made the man laugh. Jena watched him. He'd mentioned that he had lots of little cousins in the family, and he was obviously at ease with the kids running around. But that picture…

"It's enough to trigger spontaneous ovulation," Ted said with a sigh. "Cute man, cute baby, and the smell of barbecue in the air."

"You're an odd one, Ted."

"No, I'm just hungry."

Jena smothered a grin. "Alex is right out there. I'm sure he'd be able to—"

"Don't finish that sentence and expect me to still like you, Jena Crowe."

Jena bit her lip and continued watching the scene in the back as she cut the cornbread Ollie had brought. "He says he's moving back to town."

"Trust me. He's said that before. Plenty of times." Ted turned her head bitterly. "He always goes back to the city."

"Maybe—"

"Maybe we should talk about the hot cowboy, your oddly wrinkled shirt, and the look of frustration he was wearing when he arrived."

"Shut up, Ted." She flushed bright red.

Her friend gave her a smug smile. "Admittedly, the people-shifting thing is a little weird, but at least it means he'll stick around."

"Yes, just what I've always wanted. 'Hey, baby, since we're both freaks of nature and I'm stuck in this town, let's get together!' It's a love story for the ages."

"Please, he was hot for you before he turned into a freak of nature. Now, you can just be freaks together. Plus, he's smart, and... he genuinely seems like a good guy."

Jena piled the cornbread onto a plate and turned to grab the macaroni out of the oven. "I'm not saying he's not a good guy. I'm just saying he's..."

"What?" Ted looked confused. "I'm not sure why you're holding back here, Jen. He's a good man who you're obviously attracted to and he's completely into you. Even the guys like him, and that's saying a lot."

She shrugged. "He had family problems in New Mexico, and... he left. He had people he loved and cared about there—lots of them—and he took off when things got hard. I'm not saying that sometimes you don't need a fresh start. I understand that more than anyone. But it's not just me I'm worried about. I don't want the boys getting attached to someone who might just leave. Bear already thinks he walks on water."

She glanced up to see Caleb surrounded by the kids, who were mobbing the new person. Loralie had planted herself on Caleb's lap, Aaron had grabbed his hat and he and Austin, Allie's seven-year-old, were charging around the yard making their fingers into pistols. Even Low was standing nearby with Allie's two older boys, trying to act cool and gulping down sodas as they watched the three grown men by the fire.

"You fit, Jena Crowe. Like the right pair of shoes."

He fit, too.

For now.

"You're right," Ted said. "There's nothing tying him here. Not really. But maybe he's looking for a reason to stay. You can't live your life waiting for people to leave you, Jen." Ted bumped her shoulder as she took a pile of plates out to the table in back. "Not every man is Lowell, and not every relationship has a set expiration date."

Jena blinked back an unexpected tear before she saw Caleb look up and meet her eyes through the window. He frowned when he saw her expression, but she just smiled and turned back to the stove.

HOURS LATER, AFTER FOOD HAD BEEN EATEN, THE KIDS HAD been tucked away, and the leftovers packed up, Jena still couldn't shake the melancholy. And Caleb wasn't helping. He'd seemed to sink into a sullen mood as soon as the kids left the room. Joe still hadn't shown up and Allie wouldn't say why, but Devin had come round for dessert and coffee and stayed to chat about the case.

"Now that Caleb can get all the information," Alex said, "I'm hoping we can make some headway."

"The cats are still ignoring my dad," Jena said. "He's asked them for weeks now to help with the investigation, but…"

"There hasn't really been one," Ollie said. "My granddad has mentioned it more than once. He's disgusted with them all. The Elders meet, everyone talks about how tragic it is and how dangerous to have someone out there who could do something like this, but no one is really taking charge. At one point, Gabe Vasquez asked Granddad why *he* hadn't guarded Alma, because the Campbells and Allens are supposed to guard the Springs."

"That's ridiculous," Allie piped up. "It's not like you can control what we do ourselves! You all guard the town from outsiders, not our own people."

Ollie flushed with embarrassment. "I'm sure it was just spoken in anger, Allie."

"And Grandpa Gabe is a total blowhard," Ted said. "Aunt Paula will rein him in. I'll let my mom know. I apologize, Ollie."

"Not your fault."

"Still," Alex butted in, "if we're going to find out which cat or cats did it, we need Gabe and Paula's help."

Elizabeth Hunter

"Why are you so sure it's a cat?" Caleb finally spoke. "Fill me in on your reasons."

Ted answered, "The claw marks, mostly."

"Been meaning to ask about those. Mountain lion?"

"Bobcat, most likely."

He glanced around. "There a lot of those around here?"

Ollie said, "It's the most common cat in the Springs. Mountain lions are less common. House cats crop up occasionally. But bobcats, lynxes, they're the most common."

"So there's a lot of them." He frowned. "Do they hunt in packs?"

"No," Ted answered. "Definitely not. Mated pairs, if both are shifters, but usually we hunt alone."

Caleb nodded again. "So alibis become a problem."

"Wolves are pack animals," Alex said. "We're highly social and tend to shift together and hunt together on moon nights. That's why Jeremy can alibi me and we can vouch for most all the wolves."

"And me!" Allie added. "I ran into the pack when I was running from one of the lions."

"Which one?" Ollie rumbled.

"Aw, don't worry." She bumped his shoulder with hers. "This fox is way too fast for them."

"They do that again, you run to my den," Ollie growled. "Not one of them is going to go into that cave if they know what's good for them."

"Thanks, big guy." Allie said as Ollie blushed. "But I'll be fine."

Caleb held up a hand. "So, all the wolves are alibied, right, Alex?" The other man nodded. "But the cats are pretty much untraceable because they don't shift together, so we have to look at other ways of eliminating cat suspects." He frowned. "No one has mentioned the reptiles."

Jena said, "To be honest, this time of year they're not very active on moon nights. It gets chilly remember? And they're cold-blooded. Most of the Quinns just find a nice warm den and curl up during the winter moons. They like shifting, do it more than anyone else, probably, but only during sunny days."

Caleb looked around. "I'm noticing a distinct lack of scales in this group." He grinned. "Not a fan of the fangs?"

Devin gave a low laugh, but everyone else was silent.

"Sean left," Allie said quietly. "He got out of town a long time ago and never came back."

"He e-mails," Ted said. "He's a journalist."

Jena couldn't help the sharp pang of loss. Sean Quinn had made the seventh of their group of friends in high school. Eight if you counted Joe. It had always been Jena, Ted, and Allie. Lowell, Ollie, Alex, and Sean had rounded them out. The last time she'd seen Sean was when he came to visit Lowell in the hospital in Portland. It was one of the last visits that her husband had been lucid for. She hadn't spoken to her friend since.

Caleb must have noticed the sad look on her face because he was staring at her. Jena cleared her throat and spoke up. "Besides the injuries, there's also the claw marks on the back door. They look like bobcat, or Ollie has suggested a large lizard."

Caleb looked at Ollie. "How large a lizard are we talking about?"

"Hey, I just threw it out there. Komodo dragons are big suckers. They can take down a bird, saw it on Animal Planet."

Everyone laughed a little, lightening the tension. Jena said, "And they have pretty nasty claws. I suppose it could've been a large lizard. I'd have to see some claw marks up close, though."

Caleb asked, "Would they be able to move fast on a cold night? I'm thinking they'd have to move pretty fast to catch an owl in flight."

Jena nodded. "An older one could. They're the most powerful. Our human bodies eventually slow down, but our shifter bodies only get stronger as we age."

"So, it could be Old Quinn," Caleb muttered.

Jena looked around in alarm. "Old Quinn?"

Caleb said, "I like him, but I can't consider that. He could've done it. You said the older reptiles are powerful—"

"He's the most powerful," Devin said. "If any of the Quinns could shift out of their natural form on a moon night and attack quickly, it would be him. Don't let the good ole boy act fool you."

"Oh, I can tell that. He's smart. And motive? What do you all think?" Caleb looked around the back yard.

"The money," Allie said quietly. "He wouldn't care for himself, but his family is hurting right now. The resort that Alma was voting against would provide a lot of jobs."

Caleb nodded as if Allie had confirmed his own thinking. "So Old Quinn could be our killer."

Jena shook her head. "What are you all saying?" She looked around at her friends incredulously. "Quinn? Joe Quinn turned into a Komodo dragon and killed Alma? They may have had their problems over the years—"

"They fought like cats and dogs half the time," Ted said.

"And the other half they didn't talk to each other at all," Alex added. "I'm not saying it *is* him, Jena, just that it could be."

"Well, what about the cats?" she asked. "They're the most likely suspects, but we're not talking about them."

Caleb asked, "Is Matt Marquez a cat?"

Everyone stopped and turned to Ted.

"Yes," she said. "A bobcat. His wife, Missy, and he are both members of the Vasquez clan. My clan. Though Matt is originally from the Leons."

"So, when you all marry, you join the wife's clan?"

"Just the cats," Alex said. "Wolves are different."

"And Missy is the one who just had the baby?"

Everyone nodded in response.

"So Mayor Matt and his wife are bobcats."

"No, just Matt," Ted said. "Missy's a lion like me."

"Hmm," Caleb seemed to consider that, even pulling out a notebook from his shirt pocket to jot something down.

"And Matt was just as invested in the hotel plan as Alex was," Jena said. "But we know Alex didn't kill Alma."

Caleb nodded. "I'll tell you guys, when I made up my list, I had three people on it that stuck out. Alex McCann, Matt Marquez, and Joe Quinn."

Alex muttered, "Well, you know I didn't do it."

"True." Caleb nodded again. "So that leaves me two suspects that I can see. Which one do we take on first?"

"Old Quinn," Jena said immediately. "I don't think there's any way he could've murdered Alma, so let's eliminate him as a suspect."

Caleb's smile turned up at the corner. "Anyone want to act as my deputy? I'm a bit short-handed with Jeremy out. None of you are reptiles, but I have a feeling it'd go easier with someone around he's known longer than me."

Alex said, "Joe and I had words the other day. Probably don't want to take me."

"Not me," Ted said. "He gets nervous around doctors. Any doctor."

"I'll go," Jena said reluctantly. "And I'll even give him his hat back if he talks to us."

Caleb looked at her and, for the first time that night, gave her a full, mischievous grin. "Well, if that won't get him to talk, nothing will."

THE NEXT DAY, HE SHOWED UP AT THE DINER JUST AS THEY were closing. It was three o'clock and Jena had already arranged a sleepover for the boys with Allie and Joe, not knowing how late they'd be questioning Joe Quinn. Jena pulled the nail out of Quinn's hat before she grabbed a sandwich her dad had stuffed into a box.

"What's that?" Caleb asked, looking at the box as they walked to his truck.

"A BLT and a big pile of coleslaw. They're his favorites and he hasn't been into the diner since I took his hat. Bribery works."

Caleb smiled and glanced at the hat. "That is one ugly hat."

"It's his favorite. Alma always said the man had no sense."

She fell silent, nervous about the whole plan. What on earth did she think she was going to find? Joe Quinn hiding in his villain's lair, washing bloody claws and gloating about killing one of his oldest friends? More likely, the man would never speak to her again for even suggesting it. As much as the old snake annoyed her, Jena didn't want to get on his bad side. Besides that, he'd raised Sean. She could never forget that. Suddenly, Jena was irritated with the whole situation.

They drove in silence out toward Quinn's house in the hills. It was just a few miles from Alma's as the crow would fly.

"What has you so serious?"

She shrugged, her irritation mounting with every bump in the road. "I could ask you the same thing."

"Why?"

She shook her head. He'd shown up at her door the previous afternoon and practically eaten her alive within minutes. Then, when it was time to leave the night before, he'd brushed a quick kiss over her cheek before he hightailed it to his trailer.

"It's nothing. Forget it."

"No." He pulled over a little outside of town. "Something's eating at you. If you don't want to go with me, I'll go by myself."

She flushed bright red. "It's not that."

"Then what is it?"

"I just…" She huffed. "I think this is a waste of time."

"If he didn't do it, then we eliminate him from the suspect pool. Either way, it's not a waste of time."

"Fine."

"Fine." He was silent after that. She could see his irritation mirrored her own.

She squirmed. "I don't know what you want from me."

His eyebrows shot up. "Really? I thought I'd made that pretty clear."

"I don't do that, remember?" The anger started to build, and it felt good. "I'm not some roll in the hay that's looking for a good time and—"

"What on earth gave you the impression that's what I'm looking for?"

"—and you... you're not what I expected, and—and you act like you want me one minute, and then I feel like you brush me off the next and—"

"And I feel the same damn way!"

She finally looked at him. He was fuming. His teeth were set on edge and his hands gripped the wheel so hard his knuckles turned white.

"I feel the same way, Jena," he said in a low voice. "I feel like there's some sort of test I need to pass, but I have no idea what the rules are. And I don't even know if you want me to pass or if you're just..."

"Just what?"

"Jerking me around." He shook his head and pulled the truck back on the road. "And the thing is I can't even blame you. I'm not the most reliable person in the world. Hell, that's probably why my ex never wanted kids with me. I get obsessed with my cases, and I'm always looking for the thing that's going to go wrong and mess up the stuff that's going right."

"Why?"

"Why?" He glanced at her, then back at the road. "Because... because things change like *that*." He snapped his fingers. "People lie. And the things you thought you could rely on disappear, or you find out they were never what they claimed to be in the first place."

It hit her like a punch in the gut, and she leaned back in her seat, staring at the harsh desert landscape they bumped past.

"I'm sorry I lied to you."

"It's not..." He shook his head. "I understand why you did. Why everyone did. It's not you I'm talking about."

"Yeah, it is."

"I didn't mean it to be." He paused before he muttered, "I was thinking about New Mexico."

She considered his profile, tracing the worry lines that marked his eyes, the corners of his mouth. He felt responsible for her grandmother and he hadn't even known her that long. How much more would that kind of worry translate to a beloved cousin who was ruining his life? The men under his command? How would it feel to have to choose between them in a split second?

"And aren't you responsible?"

"Pathologically."

"You're a good man, Caleb Gilbert. And they were wrong to blame you," she said softly. "I don't care if it's my place to say it or not, but it was a shitty thing to do. I don't care what their beliefs were. That was not your fault. And I'm sorry I'm not... I don't know. Better at this, I guess. If it makes you feel better, it's my problem, not yours."

"Jena..." He stared out the windshield, but his hands relaxed slightly. "Let's just focus on Joe Quinn, all right?"

She knew there was more to say, but she nodded and let him lead. "Okay, let's talk about Quinn."

"He's a lizard."

"Yes. His natural form is horned toad."

Caleb frowned. "I would have thought snake."

"Nope. Sean's a rattlesnake, though. Old Quinn is his great-uncle. He raised him."

"No kids of his own?"

"Nope. He never married."

"Is that unusual?"

Jena shrugged. She'd never really thought about it. There were plenty of people her age that didn't marry for various reasons, but her grandmother's generation?

"I guess it is sort of unusual. I never really thought about it before. He was just Sean's uncle. Kinda sketchy, but in a funny way. The kind of old man that the phrase 'Don't take any wooden nickels' was invented for."

Caleb chuckled. "Got it. So what's the biggest thing you've ever seen him shift into?"

"A giant iguana, which is actually pretty big. He only did it to scare us once when Sean snuck in late. Lowell and I drove him home and

Old Quinn was waiting in the kitchen, hissing. We all about peed our pants."

Caleb burst into laughter, and so did Jena. "I can imagine!" he said. "Okay, no I can't. Damn, Jena. I don't want it to be him. This is just a formality, right?"

She wiped her eyes, still snickering a little. "I think so. Honestly, I can't imagine Joe Quinn shifting into anything quite that…"

Jena trailed off as they turned the corner and pulled up to the clapboard house that rested under a stand of cottonwoods. An old truck sat parked in front with a giant lizard resting on its hood, its tail so long it practically dragged on the ground. The lizard was lying in the sun, but it turned and hissed at them, baring a forked tongue that tested the dusty air as they parked.

"Just a formality, right?" Caleb stopped the truck, blinking as the radio switched off.

"You've got to be kidding me."

Just then, the air around the lizard shimmered and stretched, and the scaly black dragon turned into a wizened old man sitting buck naked on the hood of his truck. Jena pushed open the door and stepped out.

"Oh hey, Jena!" Quinn waved, completely undisturbed by his own nudity. "Guess where Sean is right now? *Indonesia.* He sent me this picture of a Komodo dragon and bet me I couldn't shift into one. Can you take a picture for me? I been practicing for weeks."

Jena just shook her head. "Son of a bitch."

The old man brightened. "Did you bring my hat?"

chapter
eighteen

"Y ou'd be here about Alma, then." Old Quinn shoveled the coleslaw that Jena brought him into his mouth. The elderly man was tall, stooped a little with age, but his eyes were still keen and his voice did not waver. Thankfully, he'd put on some clothes. "I heard you was one of us now, Chief."

"Something like that." Caleb tipped back in his chair, looking around the old house. They sat in the kitchen while Jena looked outside, searching for any tracks that matched the ones she'd seen at Alma's house.

"Do you want my alibi?" For some reason, this amused Old Quinn and he snorted.

"Pretty much."

"Don't have one. It was cold that night. I tucked into my natural form and found a nice little niche in the rocks that was still warm. Took a nice nap and woke up the next day."

For Old Quinn's sake, Caleb hoped Jena didn't find any tracks outside.

"That's it?" he asked.

"That's it. No one saw me. No one came by." Quinn grinned. "The scaly sort tend to keep to themselves on moon nights."

"So no one can verify…" Caleb crossed his arms and sighed. "Well, shit."

Quinn cackled. "You know I didn't kill anyone."

"I have a hard time believing you killed Alma. Not so sure you've never killed *anyone*."

The quick glint in the old man's eye told Caleb he'd hit a nerve. "I'm innocent as a baby."

"And a good liar, too," Jena said from the door. Caleb turned and smiled at her.

"Anything?"

She shrugged. "I'm still looking. Checked the front. Now I'm gonna go out in the back. Just wanted a glass of water." She reached for the cupboard just to the right of the sink and grabbed a Mason jar. Caleb wondered if she was even aware how easily she moved around the house. It seemed as familiar to Jena as her own kitchen. He turned back to Quinn and saw him watching her. The old man looked… soft. Kind in a way that Caleb hadn't seen before. As soon as Jena spun around, the look was gone and Jena headed toward the door.

"I'll be back. Keep grilling him. If he doesn't answer your questions, he doesn't get his hat."

The screen door slammed behind her and Quinn said, "She's a live one. You ain't never gonna be bored."

"She's not mine to deal with."

Quinn cocked his head. "Ain't she now?"

Caleb ignored the old man, taking in the surprisingly clean kitchen. It obviously belonged to a man, no cheerful towels or trinkets lined the counters or decorated the window, but it was tidy and boasted a gem of an old stove that looked almost new, despite the sixty years it had probably sat in the old place. It reminded him of Alma's kitchen, in a strange way, down to the beautifully finished old cabinet that sat against the far wall, its distinctive pierced panels glowing in the afternoon sun.

Caleb blinked when he realized what it was. A pie safe?

Quinn was finishing his sandwich when Caleb stood and walked toward it. He saw the old man pause, watching him as he ran a hand down one long, smooth corner.

"This is beautiful. Did you make it?" It looked handmade. No factory would put the detail into the corners like that, rounding them in such a way that the edges wouldn't catch on a trailing apron or towel, while still curving in an eye-catching flourish.

"Eh... yeah, I made it. Do a bit of woodworking as a hobby."

"Design it yourself? My stepfather was a woodworker. This is really nice." He opened one door with an intricately pierced tin panel fronting it. Despite the age of the old cupboard, it was spotless, as if it had never been used.

"I... uh, I copied a design I saw once."

Caleb looked over his shoulder and smiled. "Wouldn't have taken you for a baker."

Quinn shrugged. Caleb ran a hand along the top of the cabinet. The wood had been sanded to perfection, the finish burnished to a soft, natural gold.

"When did you build it?" It must have taken hours. Hours and hours of work for a piece of furniture never used, never dirtied, sitting ready for an owner who would never see it.

Quinn's voice was hoarse when he answered. "Almost thirty years ago."

Caleb turned and pretended not to notice the sheen in the old man's eyes as he looked at the old cupboard. Old Quinn blinked and cleared his throat when he heard Jena's footsteps coming up the porch. It swung open and Caleb smiled at her.

"Hey," she said.

"Hey back. We can go."

She looked surprised. "Are you sure? I've checked most of the grounds, but I was going to look around the house, see if—"

"It's fine, Jena. We can go."

She frowned for a minute, looking at the back of Old Quinn's grey head. "Does he get his hat back?"

Quinn cackled, and Caleb grinned. "Yeah, he gets it back."

Jena turned and grabbed it from the bench on the front porch, then stepped back in, plopping the battered old hat on the man's head. "You still owe me on your tab, Quinn."

Caleb saw him smile. "I'll pay you next week, Jena. Didn't I tell you?"

She shook her head. "That's what you always tell me." Then she turned and headed out the door.

Quinn caught Caleb's eye and nodded. Caleb nodded back and headed out the door, taking one last look over his shoulder at Alma's pie safe.

He caught up with Jena at the truck.

"So, what did he say? Did he have an alibi?"

"Nope." He shook his head and opened her door. "Didn't need one."

She hopped in. "What do you mean? Can we really rule him out if we can't—"

"Joe Quinn did not murder your grandmother, Jena." He leaned in quickly and kissed her cheek. "He was in love with her."

"Wow."

He glanced at her from the corner of his eye as he drove. "You keep saying that."

"I mean… wow. Thirty years."

Caleb shrugged. "Or more. He might have had feelings for your grandmother longer than that. It could be why he never got married."

"Imagine loving someone for that long and never telling them."

"It's hard to imagine."

"I wonder if he did tell her." She was staring out the window. "I kinda doubt it."

"And that is one mystery we will never solve."

"I guess not," she murmured. The car fell silent as they bumped over the rocky hills. "I wonder if I would've loved Lowell that long."

He tried to mask the shock on his face. Was she talking about her dead husband?

Did he want her to?

It was hard competing with a ghost, but that's what Caleb felt like he was doing at times. Then what she had said struck him.

"Why would you even wonder? You grew up together, right? You married him. You loved him."

She shrugged. "Yeah. I don't know. I wonder sometimes. I don't think we... I always knew we didn't have long."

It was harder to imagine than any unrequited love. It took a strong and determined woman to build a life with a man, knowing that he was going to die young and leave her with the challenges of raising two children alone.

"I don't know how you did it," he said. "That would be harder than anything, I think. To lose someone you loved like that. And to know you were going to lose them."

"It was hard. But then it wasn't. It was just the way it was. He had his moments, but overall, Lowell wasn't bitter about it. And he probably got away with a lot of shit because of it, too." She laughed. "I never really said no to him. Not that he took advantage or anything. He was a good guy. But there were things he did that annoyed the shit out of me." She laughed again and shook her head. "And I didn't say a word. It seemed petty when I knew I wouldn't have him for long, you know?"

"No." Caleb stared at the dark road in front of them. The sun had gone down and the cool air was rising with the moon. He cracked open a window and sniffed damp creosote from a sudden shower that had hit that afternoon. "I love that smell," he muttered. "I can sympathize, Jena, but I can't really relate. My ex and I didn't even make it five years."

"Why?"

It was such a big question with such a boring response. "You know what it says on the divorce papers? Irreconcilable differences? That was us. Really and truly. We never cheated on each other. There was no abuse. I think she even loved me, in a way, but..."

She angled her shoulders toward him. "What?"

He smiled. "I was a fixer-upper to her. She liked the idea of the rugged detective with the complicated family, but then she wanted to 'fix' me. Make me into someone more like her."

"What was she like?"

He hadn't talked about Leila in ages. They'd split up before the mess with Charlie happened, though the divorce hadn't been finalized. She even made noises about getting back together when it all happened. The cynical part of him wondered if she was more willing to be with him since she'd no longer have to deal with his family.

"She was very driven. Ambitious. She was an assistant district attorney. Very smart. Passionate about her work." He paused. "That was the thing that brought us together. We really got that about each other, which was cool. But she hated my family. Wanted me to like cocktail parties and wine and plays and shit like that. And when I didn't 'civilize' for her, she got irritated. Like, if I really loved her, I'd like all the things she liked, too."

He heard Jena laugh and he turned with a smile, relieved she hadn't been put off by him talking about his past. "What are you laughing at? You like wine."

"But you don't." She shook her head. "You know, there's a saying the old women in the Springs have."

"Oh? What's that?"

"You don't bring home a wolf and wake up with a bear."

He paused. Was there some kind of shapeshifter humor he wasn't getting?

Jena must have sensed his confusion. "People are the animal they are. We may change, but not that much. You love someone for who they are, or you don't love them. That's all."

That's all.

Caleb turned to her, slowing the car until he stopped. She sat in his truck with a smile on her face, watching him with curious eyes.

Elizabeth Hunter

This woman. This incredible, strong woman. Smart, confident. She knew who she was in a way that Caleb had always envied. She'd loved and lost, was still grieving her grandmother, but helping Caleb investigate her death, no matter how painful it was. Kind enough to give an old man back his hat, knowing he'd probably never pay her the money he owed. She wasn't just beautiful; she was good.

I'm falling in love with you. Do you know?

He whispered, "Come here."

Caleb tried not to let the fear show on his face when he leaned toward her, cupped her cheek in his hand, and pulled her into a gentle kiss. It reminded him of the kisses they'd shared in the trailer when he was sick from shifting the first time. Not hungry and wanting, just *there*. In that moment, kissing Jena was the perfect place to be. He pulled away after a few minutes. Her eyes were still closed, her mouth still pursed. He smiled and touched her chin.

"Hey," he whispered. "Does going to question a suspect count as a date?"

She smiled and her eyes fluttered open. "Nope. Sorry."

"Damn. So I'm still not dating you?"

She suddenly looked embarrassed. "You've given it way more effort than anyone else."

"Anyone?" Even the wonderful Lowell?

"Anyone." She blushed and sat back in her seat. "And we should probably—"

The shot rang out, shattering the window and piercing the seat between them where Caleb had been leaning only seconds before.

Jena gasped and pulled back, the safety glass shattering and falling in one chunk onto her lap. Caleb cursed and immediately rammed the truck into gear, gunning the engine so the dust flew behind them. "Hold on!"

His first instinct was to jump out of the truck and pursue whoever had shot at them, but he had Jena with him, and he had to get her to a safe place first.

She was tugging at her seatbelt. "Let me out."

"No! Are you insane?"

"Let me out, Caleb!" She'd unbuckled herself and was... taking off her shirt?

"What the hell are you doing?" He finally pulled over when she forced open the car door. "Jena!"

"I'm finding out who shot at us." She shucked off the rest of her clothes in seconds and before Caleb could put the car in park, Jena was gone. A loud flapping sound echoed in the truck as a wild shriek filled the air. He pulled over and ran around, but she was in the air, soaring into the night, a shadow against the moonlit clouds.

He let out a harsh breath. "What the hell?"

She was gone. Turned into a hawk and took off. What was he supposed to do with that? He kicked the truck tire and cursed, then reluctantly bent down and gathered her clothes. Belatedly, he realized there was still a gunman out there who had taken a shot at them. And Jena was in the air.

How hard was it to shoot a hawk? He had a feeling it was pretty difficult, but he had no real idea, and the thought of her in danger made him sick.

Caleb went back to the truck, throwing her clothes in and pulling his gun out from under the seat. He dug around in the torn-up uphol-stery until he pulled out the fired round. Between hitting the window and the seat, it was hard to tell, but it had to be a rifle round of some kind. Probably a 30-06. Animals couldn't fire weapons, so whoever was shooting at them was human, or had been. Caleb wondered whether Jena could tell who the shooter was if he shifted to animal form. Would the shooter stay human or shift? An animal would have a far easier time running and hiding in the desert than a human. And if he did that...

There would be a rifle sitting out in the hills all by its lonesome.

Caleb tucked his 9mm in the small of his back and headed back up the road.

chapter
nineteen

The light of the waxing moon shone down on the desert, creating stark shadows as she soared. The wind lifted her, a warm thermal pushing up from the sun-warmed sandstone along the canyon floor. Her sharp eyes roamed the ground, not looking for color or contrast. No, she was looking for movement.

A sudden cool breeze lifted the speckled white feathers of her breast, and from the corner of her sharp, golden eye, she saw it.

A figure, larger than the squirrels and rodents she usually hunted, moving nimbly over the rocks.

Bobcat!

With an instinctual shriek, she dove.

It was the greatest rush, her addicting speed, and the reason she rarely shifted to anything else but her natural form. As a red-tailed hawk, her dive could reach well over five hundred miles an hour. Her talons landing in the soft fur of her prey, clutching before she beat her wings and soared away. Jena screamed again, swooping and circling as the cat darted between the shadowed tumble of boulders on the hillside.

Not prey. She wheeled and beat her wings to watch again. This bobcat was no dumb animal, but a wily shifter in natural form. He knew she would be looking for him, so he kept away from open ground, darting in and out of the rocks, leading her farther and farther from the truck where Caleb waited.

Where was he going? She felt for the right current of air and tilted her broad wings, so the high wind lifted her, hovering as she scanned the desert landscape. The bobcat was thick, marked with the dull, spotted coloring that concealed him well in the rocks. If he had been stationary, she would have never spotted him. But he leapt and darted, zigzagging back and forth to draw her attention while still remaining infuriatingly out of reach.

Jena shrieked again, her eyes never leaving the small cat. How far could she track it? How far would he run?

Why?

Suddenly, her human consciousness took over from instinct and Jena shrieked again.

The animal was leading her away from Caleb.

She was just about to dip into the breeze and fly back to the canyon when she heard the gun shot.

chapter
twenty

Caleb jogged back down the road, then past the weedy edge before he crawled up the rocks. The road they were driving passed through a large section of canyon, but there was a jagged wash that cut through it, the kind he'd been taught to avoid since childhood. Animal tracks covered the sand in the bottom, leading away from the road and up into the rocky crevice old water had carved. With a grimace, Caleb followed them, tension thick as his feet sank into the sand.

Rain in the desert was a funny thing. Monsoons dropped vast amounts of water into the harsh landscape in short bursts, blowing away as quickly as they came. Often, that water ran over the rocks and sand, filling dry creek beds and traveling at lightning speed. A dry desert wash could fill with water from fifty miles away, tumbling and taking anything in its path as it cut through the rocky ground.

You didn't linger in a wash. Especially when there had been rain, like there had been only an hour before. If you were in a vehicle, you crossed it as quickly as possible. If you were on foot, you did the same. Caleb tried to ignore the hair that rose on the back of his neck as he moved quickly, keeping to the firmer edge and avoiding the soft sand in the middle. Red walls rose on either side of him as he jogged.

He saw the tracks end, then change, a muddled scrabbling in the dirt before new tracks emerged. Footprints—small for a man, but large for a woman—finding purchase in the sand, then disappearing up the side of the creek bed. Whoever made them must have scanned the area as an animal, followed the wash up from the road, then shifted in order to fire the weapon. Which meant if Caleb climbed those boulders that had tumbled down from the edge, he would likely find the spot the shooter had aimed from and, if he was lucky, the weapon, too.

He smelled it before he heard it, the scent of rainwater that blew past, alien in the dusty air. His heart sped up, and he ran toward the edge, scrambling up the sandstone boulders, grabbing onto the wizened roots that had been bared the last time the water rushed past. He was halfway up when his foot slipped and stuck between them.

He cried out, despite his attempts at stealth. Before a curse could cross his lips, he heard the low rumble, like distant thunder.

Just his luck, the water was coming.

Caleb shook his head. "No, dammit. I'm not dying out here."

He panted, pulling on his leg, but it wouldn't budge.

"Shit! Are you kidding me?" He was going to be swept away in the rush. For a second, he almost laughed. Thirty-five years of life, twelve years in some of the toughest law enforcement assignments he could find. Shot at, beaten up... and he was going to bite it in a flash flood like old drunk Russell Begay had when Caleb was ten. He grunted and tried to twist his leg to the side, but something had shifted beneath his foot, trapping his foot firmly in the large rocks, which were too big to lift. Too bad he wasn't old Begay, who had the skinniest damn legs Caleb could ever remember seeing on a man. The things looked like sticks. Old, twisty... sticks.

He blinked and stilled, slipping into his mind as he focused on the childhood memory. He'd never tried to force a shift when he was this panicked. He took a deep breath, trying to calm his mind and ignore the sound of the water, which was growing louder by the second.

Old. Skinny. Wizened from age and too much drink.

Caleb felt his clothes grow loose on his frame. The pressure on his leg lightened. It was the most dramatic shift he'd ever made, and he fought back the initial nausea, pulled his leg free, then scrambled up the side of the rock wall only seconds before the muddy water whipped by.

It churned past in a roar, at least six feet deep and thick with sand, rock, and the remains of a rusted old car. Caleb lay on his back, panting and looking up at the moon as he heard an owl hoot and small creatures move in the desert night. The water splashed up the rocks, soaking him, annoyed that it had lost its prey. Caleb turned and gave the dark water a smile before he lifted his hands. He stared at the wrinkled old skin, wishing he had a mirror to satisfy his curiosity. Did the picture in his memory match the face he would see? Would it be different or exact? There was no way of knowing and he still had a mission, so Caleb shifted back to his own body and held still, waiting for the twisting in his gut to pass. He stared into the dark sky.

Where was Jena? Would she be able to find him? Caleb sat up and pulled the 9 mm from the small of his back, thankful it hadn't fallen or moved when his body had. He looked around for footprints, scowling when he realized he'd made a mess of the sand at the edge. It was too dark to see much farther than a few feet in front of him, even with the bright moon. He took a few steps forward, then stilled. He closed his eyes and took a deep breath, listening.

The churning water. A scampering sound and an owl's hoot. A coyote far off in the distance. A rustling in the juniper bushes. Gravel crunched with a whisper.

More rustling... Something was in the brush behind him.

He opened his eyes and took a few steps forward. It grew quiet again. If he hadn't been paranoid, he would have missed it, mistaken it for the breeze or his imagination. But it wasn't. He slowly cut his eyes to the right. The area around the dry creek was tangled with low juniper and cottonwoods that had found some hidden moisture in the canyon floor. He continued walking, more curious to see if the animal followed or was just passing through. The grip on his gun tightened.

Jena said the claw marks looked like bobcat, but unless Cambio Springs made much bigger bobcats than he was familiar with, whatever was following him was something else. Something larger, with a soft step and a larger body that shifted the brush. From the corner of his eye, he caught more footprints. Keeping his ears open, he crouched down.

They were light, almost delicate where they had pressed into the sand. He looked around to see where they might lead and spotted it. Just over the edge of a boulder, was the barrel of a rifle, black in the silver moonlight. He crawled up the rocks until he was in the same position the shooter must have taken.

It was an old lever-action Winchester. Nothing distinctive about this one. Still, he would run the registration, if it had one. Considering how long families stayed in the area, it was entirely possible that the rifle had been passed down. He wouldn't be surprised if there was no registration on file, particularly since the old rifle had been used to take a shot at a cop. Still crouching behind the boulder, he put himself in the attitude of the shooter and imagined lifting the weapon, aiming toward the point where the road crossed the gully.

It was an easy distance for a good shot. A challenging one for an average shooter. Had the bullet been intended to scare them? Kill them? Would he have tried to kill both Caleb and Jena, or was only one of them the target? He puffed out a frustrated breath and suddenly realized that he hadn't heard any rustling in a few moments.

It was quiet. The sounds in the brush had disappeared and an ominous silence took their place. No birds chirped. No insects hummed. Something was still out there. His only consolation was that it was in animal form and he had guns.

Caleb stood, grabbing the rifle. "Want to come out and introduce yourself?"

Nothing. Or was there? He heard the shifting of a foot—or paw—to his left. A slight motion in the cottonwoods that shivered and stilled.

"You the one that shot at us? Or were you just watching?"

He tried not to look around. He was no animal and had too great a respect for their stealth to imagine he could spot it if it didn't want to be found. But did it? There was still no sound but his own rapid heartbeat and deep breaths. The longer he waited, the more tension filled the air.

"Maybe you didn't have anything to do with Alma's death." He looked, but there was nothing. "Whoever you are, at least give me an idea of what I'm dealing with here. Wolf? Bobcat? Snake?" It wasn't a snake. "There some bunny rabbit shifters that no one's told me about?" he shouted into the desert. "I'm getting bored now, so I think I'm going to just take this nice rifle here and go back to my truck. Figure I might be able to get some prints off of it if I—oof!"

He didn't even hear the attack. The massive weight slammed into his back, knocking him to the ground as two sets of claws dug into his shoulders. His mouth tasted sand as he tumbled forward, both guns flying out of his hands.

Mountain lion. It sprang away as he rolled.

"Holy—wow." The giant animal crouched in front of him. He'd never seen one up close. "So that's why they call you a lion. Not a kitty cat, are you?" It was massive, probably measuring eight feet or more from nose to tail. It snarled once as Caleb rolled toward his gun. The rifle lay in the dirt, knocked out of his hands when the animal had pounced. "Not really a lion either, are you, shifter?" It snarled again, its whiskers twitching in what might have been a laugh.

The thick golden fur shone with a dull glow in the moonlight. With one flick of its giant back paw, the lion kicked the rifle into the still-running water of the wash as Caleb came up, clutching his 9 mm. He aimed at the shifter, who hissed and sprang on him. Caleb's arms were knocked to the side when the gun went off. Then the lion pounced on him and a hawk's scream echoed in the night air. The lion lifted his head, searching the sky, then jumped off Caleb and disappeared into the night.

The breath roared back into his chest and he placed one hand over his heart, waiting for it to calm before he stood. He heard the hawk cry out again.

"Jena, where are you?" He looked around in panic. "Jena?"

Did that cry mean she was hurt? In pain? The second cry had sounded closer. That must have meant she was still flying, right?

Caleb turned in circles, wishing he could see better, but he was caught in a small sliver of ground between the canyon wall and the running wash. The water flowed on one side; sheer rock rose on the other. How the hell was he even going to get out?

Where was she?

He heard a rush of wind overhead and looked up. Silhouetted against the night sky was a raptor who wheeled around, suddenly diving with frightening speed straight toward him. He backed up, his heart racing. "Jena?"

It shrieked a high, ear-splitting noise that echoed off the rocks. Suddenly, the hawk's wings spread, tilting up as the talons reached down. As if he was watching slow motion, he saw it. The watery shimmer that enveloped the bird as its legs lengthened and its wings thinned. Feathers transformed into smooth skin and wild brown hair as she reached the ground, crouching down in a feral pose for a moment before she looked up and ran toward him.

Completely naked. Utterly wild. Foreign and magic and beautiful. Caleb's heart wasn't racing in fear anymore. Jena's eyes were still lit gold when she ran toward him.

"Are you hurt?" Her voice was hoarse and frantic. Her eyes raced over his body.

He held out his arms. "I'm fine. Are you?"

She didn't speak, running quivering hands over his shoulders, inspecting the tears in this shirt where the lion's claws had pierced. Touching. His skin came alive. His sight. His hearing. Every one of his senses careened to life. Jena was safe. He was alive. The adrenaline surged through him and he grabbed her, lifting her up. Jena wrapped her legs around his waist and clutched at his hair. A low, rough sound escaped her throat, almost like a cry.

"It's okay," he tried to sooth her. "I'm fine. Are you okay?"

Her heart raced and her breath came in frantic gasps until Caleb put a hand on her cheek. Then she stilled. He ran his fingers over her jaw, trailing through her hair, then down. "Are you okay?" She gave a slight nod. "We're safe, Jena. We're safe." His hand slid down her spine as she arched into him. Over the round swells of her hips, teasing the sensitive crease between her bottom and the back of her thigh.

The rough sound came again. It was the same sound she'd made when he'd kissed her the first time months before. Need. Desire. His hand gripped, pressing her closer. He wanted... oh, how he wanted her. In that moment, it was the only thought in his mind.

"Do you know?" he whispered. "Do you know what you do to me?"

Her wild eyes met his; Caleb was pinned beneath her stare. Jena's hands loosened their grip in his hair and slid down, digging into his shoulders, causing him to wince. She didn't notice. Her eyes were foreign and predatory. She looked as if she were still hunting.

chapter
twenty-one

Jena's head tilted to the side when she heard him hiss. He was uninjured save for the marks on his shoulders. Her fingers trailed over them in a quick swipe as he grunted and tensed. Then she leaned forward and ran her nose along his neck, from his collar, up the side of his neck, to his throat, where she took a deep breath.

He smelled like sand and rain. He was alive beneath her, and the predator in her wanted him.

She pulled at the hair at the back of Caleb's neck and tugged him toward her. Their mouths crashed together as he stumbled. Then Caleb kneeled down and she straddled his legs, pushing the torn shirt from his shoulders, desperate to feel his skin hot beneath her hands. His arms wrapped around her back and his fingers dug in possessively. She would see bruises in the morning. His hand twisted in her hair and she gasped, pulling away from his mouth as she bowed back. He licked down her chest until he latched onto the tip of one small breast and sucked. Sensation long forgotten careened through her. He released her and went after the other, interspersing kisses with teasing licks and tiny bites. She moaned and arched into him, but soon pulled his mouth back to hers, tugging at his clothes, scrambling to feel his skin.

More! Her instincts screamed. She had to have him.

Caleb pulled one arm away from her and shook off his shirt. His chest was hot against hers, burning up in the cool desert night. She fumbled with the buttons on his jeans, finally getting them loose enough to shove down his hips. He stood and turned, pressing Jena into the cool rock wall, running desperate fingers between her legs before he pulled away, poised at her center.

She stilled, meeting his eyes as he slid into her. They were open, locked on hers in a way that made her heart stutter. Then Caleb sank to the hilt and groaned, burying his face in her neck as she held him close. Their hearts beat together before he began to move. She held on, surging with him as he thrust.

It was hard and frantic. Her back scraped against the rocks, though Caleb did his best to hold her. His hands would be bloodied from it. She clung to him, her nails digging into the flesh on his shoulders, but he didn't flinch. Her pleasure began to mount. He moved faster. Harder.

Caleb pulled his head back and caught her eyes again, holding her captive with a look as he drove them toward the edge. Her breath caught. Held. Suddenly, Jena was hurtling toward climax in a swift, heart-stopping dive. Caleb fell to his knees, holding on to her as she threw her head back and cried into the black desert. Then his body tensed and she pulled him close, pressing them skin to skin as he shuddered in release.

"Jena, Jena, Jena," he whispered against her neck. She was shivering, her body racked with tremors. Caleb held her gently, stroking her bare skin while his own prickled in the cool night air. She stretched up, luxuriating in the pleasure of the fine hair on his chest brushing over her sensitive breasts. She could feel his heart pounding, his release at the juncture of her thighs...

Jena froze.

Oh shit.

"Jena?" He sounded drowsy. "Are you okay?"

She scrambled away from him, and his head jerked up. "Jena?"

"Shit!" She looked around in panic.

"Are you okay?" His voice was growing in alarm. "Did I hurt you?"

"No!" She whispered, "No, I just... Oh God, what was I thinking?"

His confusion fell away and he tried to grab for her. "Don't."

"This was... we shouldn't have—"

"Don't. Don't do this. This was not a mistake."

Jena tried to speak, but the protest was mangled in her throat. She shook her head, fingers digging into her scalp as she backed away from him. What had she done? What was she thinking? Even worse was the growing hurt on Caleb's face.

Not you, not you! She wanted to cry. Didn't he realize? He walked toward her and her eyes flew to the sky. To safety.

His eyes followed hers, then narrowed. "Don't you dare, Jena Crowe."

She took one more step back and drew in a deep breath.

"Jena..."

She whispered, "I can't." Then she closed her eyes and her hawk leapt forward, throwing itself into the night as Caleb shouted beneath her.

"Why are you running away?" he yelled. "Dammit, Jena, get back here!"

She shrieked and circled around, aching to go to him, but as frightened by the thought of leaving him as she was by staying.

"Why?" he shouted again as she wheeled away.

Because I'm in love with you.

And Jena Crowe was scared to death.

SHE WAS SOBBING WHEN SHE LANDED ON TED'S PORCH, naked and beginning to feel the effects of their frantic coupling. She ached; there would be bruises on her back. Her thighs. And she knew Caleb would have score marks on his back from her nails. Bite marks on his neck. She winced at the thought before she pounded on the door. A few moments later, Ted pulled it open, blinking.

"What are you doing here?" Then her eyes widened. "What happened to you?"

"We... we were up at Old Quinn's—"

"Did he attack you?" Ted pulled her into the house. "You had to shift? Where's Caleb? Is he okay?"

"No!" She shook her head quickly. "I mean, yes, we're both okay. We were driving back and someone shot at us. I shifted and went to look. Caleb ran into the desert. I don't know why. But a gun went off, and I came back and—and..."

"And what?" Ted's eyes were wide. "Jena, *is he okay?*"

"There was a lion on him. Not attacking, just... I don't know. Crouched. It ran off, but I was so scared. I thought it was going to kill him. I shifted back, but he wasn't hurt. He kissed me. Or I kissed him." She closed her eyes, the tears running down her face. "We... Ted, we—"

"Oh, you had sex with him." Ted pulled her into a hug. "Oh wow. Okay. Just calm down."

"And—" She hiccupped. "It was crazy. And wonderful and—I mean, it was like nothing—"

"Calm down," Ted said in a soothing voice. "This is a big deal for you. I know you have some serious feelings for this guy. Forget all the times Allie and I teased you. This is you. And you don't..." Suddenly, it was like a light switched on. "Wait, this *just* happened?"

Jena flushed and nodded.

"So, you just had crazy, wonderful sex with a man who is, if not in love with you already, well on the way, and... you flew here?"

She shrank under her friend's glare. "Kinda."

Ted shook her head, obviously confused. "What happened? Did he freak out? Say something stupid?"

"No..."

Ted's eyes bugged out. "You panicked and flew away? Jena!"

"I'm sorry!"

"I'm not the one you need to be apologizing to!"

"I know!"

They both paused until Ted started shaking her head. "Listen, I know you're Miss Cautious. I know you have trouble accepting that people are going to hang around and not die on you, but you better fly your ass back out there and—"

"I think I'm in love with him."

Ted's shoulders slumped and Jena started crying again. "Oh, Jena."

"I am. And I have no idea what's going to happen. I don't know how to do this. I'm scared to death. There was only ever Lowell. And it seemed like we had always loved each other. What if he doesn't love me back? What if he does, but he doesn't want everything that comes with me? What if the boys—?"

"Whoa!" Ted held up a hand. "You need to stop right there. You are getting way ahead of yourself and you just left the poor man out in the desert. Where, I might add, he was shot at and attacked by a cougar not long ago."

Her heart plunged. "And I left him out there alone!"

"Thank you, Captain Obvious. Will you get out of here and go find the poor man?"

She spun around right before she got to the door. "He probably won't even talk to me. Oh..." She groaned. "He's going to be pissed."

"Yeah, no kidding. Get your naked ass out of my house and go find the sexy people-shifter, please? We might actually need him."

Jena winced. "I'm an idiot."

"I'm not disagreeing." Ted slapped her bare butt and shoved her out the door. "Go. Now. Don't come back unless you're bleeding from something other than love bites."

JENA FOUND HIM STALKING BACK TO THE ROAD WEARING A stormy expression and a pair of torn up jeans. What was left of his shirt was hanging in his hand. He saw her flying above him and stuck one hand out, flipping her the bird as she landed.

"That's kind of ironic, if you think about it."

"Take off, Jena. That seems to be the easiest thing for you to do."

"I'm trying to apologize." He kept walking and she ran after him, embarrassed for the first time she could remember by her nudity. Shifters weren't modest, as a rule, and Jena was long past being self-conscious about her body. But now, she felt exposed. Weaker than her mate. It wasn't a comfortable feeling. "Will you stop?"

"Nope." He stomped down the path that ran parallel to the wash, still refusing to look at her. She heard him muttering under his breath.

Jena stopped and watched him. He wasn't hurt—not physically, anyway. He knew where he was going. His truck was just up the road. She should let him go and fly away. Let him lick his wounds in peace and forget about her overly complicated self. The thought pierced her heart with a pain that she hadn't felt in a long, long time. She barely recognized it, but it was there.

Heartache.

"I panicked, all right?" she yelled out, her voice breaking and tears coming to her eyes. "I'm sorry."

He must have heard her tears because he paused and turned. He looked like he was about to say something mean. Then he paused and scrubbed a hand over his face in frustration. "Why did you leave? Did I hurt you? Scare you?"

"No."

He stepped back toward her. "We had... I don't even know what that was. Intense. Crazy. Wonderful—"

"It was."

He took another step closer. "Then why? I mean... What the hell, Jena?"

Her heart twisted in her chest, but she forced the words to her lips. "I—I don't know how to do this."

Caleb looked her over from the tip of her toes to the top of her head, his hungry eyes bringing a flush to her skin. "I'm gonna have to beg to differ on that one."

"Not that part."

Shaking his head, he walked over and draped the scraps of his shirt over her. He buttoned the few buttons remaining, then tugged it to cover her breasts.

"You have to cover up if I'm going to have a conversation with you. This body drops my IQ about a hundred points just by existing."

"I'll have to remember that," she said with a sniff.

He smiled a little, then paused, his hands resting on her shoulders. "Why are you scared?"

"Because you could hurt me."

"I wouldn't."

"You'd hardly have to try."

He frowned. "Why do you think—?"

"Let's pretend we're going to go back to my house and spend the night. The boys are over at Allie and Joe's. We could. Say you parked your truck in my driveway instead of by your trailer. No big deal, right?"

"What—?"

"You even get up early to get ready for work. Really early. But not earlier than Betsy McCann. Nope, she's having her morning walk and she sees your truck."

He sighed. "Jena—"

"Betsy calls my mother-in-law, real casual like, to say how nice it is I've finally moved past Lowell's death. What a nice man you are. She would, too. She likes you. Then Beverly calls my mom. My mom mentions it to my dad."

Caleb gave an involuntary shudder as Jena continued.

"And within hours, the whole town knows that you and I shacked up last night. And I'm not the kind of girl who does that as a habit, so they'll pretty quickly start speculating about Jena's new boyfriend." She felt him jerk back a little. "And by the time my boys get to school, kids will be teasing them about their new stepdad."

His voice was steady, but she could feel his heart racing where his wrist touched her hand. "You're exaggerating."

"A little. But not much."

He took a step back and, just like that, there was a tiny fracture in her heart. She could hardly blame him. Who would want one bout of crazy, I'm-relieved-you're-alive sex to become a sudden lifetime commitment?

"And let's face it, you're not from here." She let the crack widen a little. "There's nothing holding you here except a weird magical quirk that you'll learn to get control of." She shook her head. "Move far enough, it'll probably go away all together."

To her surprise, he stepped back toward her. "Why the hell do you keep moving me away without my permission?"

"What? I'm not—"

"I *chose* to move here, Jena, before I even knew you existed." He moved closer and Jena tried to take a step back, but he grabbed her wrist in a firm hold. "I chose to change my life when the fights and the drinking and the stress pushed me to the edge of a place I knew I didn't want to go. I chose a fresh start. I chose this place. And I'm choosing you. I want to know you better. I want to know your life and your kids and—and what you look like first thing in the morning when your hair's all messy. What makes you happy and what makes you sad." He stopped and cleared his throat when his voice got rough. Then he leaned down and pleaded in her ear, "Stop watching me walk away, honey. I'm standing right here."

Jena blinked the tears out of her eyes. Just like that, Caleb had pulled the crack in her heart closed. Was it really that simple? Could it be that easy? She stepped close, wrapping her arms around his waist and burying her face in his chest. He still smelled like rain and sand, and she still wanted him. But not just his body; she wanted his love. For the first time in almost twenty years, Jena stopped trying to see the end of things and stood right in the middle, warm, steady, and wrapped in Caleb's arms.

After a few more minutes and a few quiet kisses, he tugged her back toward the truck. "Let's go home. And don't worry. I'll park by my trailer."

She gave him a rueful smile as they walked hand in hand. "What were you doing out here?"

"Other than worrying about you? I was looking for the rifle that shot at us."

She halted, but he tugged her forward. "Did you find it? Could there be fingerprints or something?"

"Not anymore. It's probably halfway to the river by now." He nodded at the still-running wash. "That big cat jumped on me, knocked me down, then kicked it into the water. Doubt I'll ever see it again. Certainly not with any evidence still on it."

"Did you recognize the lion?" She frowned when he burst into laughter.

"Did I—did I recognize it?" Suddenly, Caleb snickered. "Um, yeah, Jena, let me see if I could give you a description... It was a big-as-shit mountain lion."

She rolled her eyes and continued walking as he bent over, roaring with laughter.

"Let me think..." He gasped. "It had gold hair—I mean fur—and big scary paws—"

"That's not what I meant."

"And whiskers! That's right, it had whiskers."

She shook her head and kept walking as he laughed. "There are certain distinctive characteristics that—"

"And he had really big, giant claws. Know why?"

Jena tried to remind herself why she was falling in love with him. "Why did he have claws, Sherlock?"

Caleb yelled out as she kept walking. "Because he was a mountain lion!"

"Idiot," she muttered under her breath. "I'll let Ted explain." She waited by the crossing where the water met the road as Caleb hopped over and gallantly held out a hand. She took a minute to glare at him, but he was grinning and happy and just too damn cute. Plus, he didn't have a shirt and that was always a good thing. Jena held out a hand and jumped, squealing a little as Caleb caught her and threw her onto his back. Then he wrapped her long legs around his waist and kept walking down the road.

"My ass is hanging out of the back of this shirt when you carry me this way, you know."

He reached back and pinched it. "I know. That was part of the plan."

Jena bit her lip and hid her face in his shoulder. "You're shameless."

"I'm also walking out in the middle of nowhere with a gorgeous woman's legs wrapped around me. I'm gonna say shameless is working."

"Cocky."

"I believe you confirmed that earlier, Watson."

chapter
twenty-two

Caleb heard the knock at the door and jerked from sleep. He'd been taking a nap on Jena's couch. They hadn't had much sleep once they made it back to her place the night before. They'd fooled around some more, but mostly spent the night in her bed, talking, laughing, exploring each other's minds as they explored the wild attraction between them. It was sometime between kissing her as she slipped into an exhausted sleep and holding her as he watched the sky lighten at dawn that he realized he had taken the plunge from falling in love to just being in love.

It was completely right and completely terrifying all at the same time.

He scrubbed at his eyes and stood, walking to the door, which opened to a tired and irritated Ted.

"You look as exhausted as I feel."

She waved a hand and stepped into the house. "Par for the course around here. I'm either working at the clinic or making house calls. Last night, after I coached Jena through her panic attack—you're welcome—I was out at Missy and Matt's trying to figure out what's wrong with their newborn and why he's not nursing right. New moms can be a bit panicky about stuff like that. I'll admit, it's weird. This

Elizabeth Hunter

baby was full-term, but he reminds me of a preemie." She shook her head and blinked slowly. "I'm rambling. Sorry."

He nodded toward the kitchen. "Coffee?"

"Wouldn't turn it down." They walked into the empty kitchen and Ted almost collapsed in a chair. "Where's Jena?"

"Out at Allie and Joe's. She's picking up the boys, then going to the market before dinner tonight." He'd agreed with her about inviting everyone over for dinner and a meeting to update everyone on Alma's case, but he didn't have to like it. He wanted to keep her to himself. Maybe a quiet dinner with her and the boys. Watch a movie. Pack the kids off to bed early so he could fool around with their mom...

"Well, aren't you two domestic already." Ted grinned wickedly as he handed her a cup of steaming coffee.

"Is this the part where you warn me not to hurt your friend? That you'll neuter me with a fork if I step out of line?" He sat down across from the exhausted woman with dark circles under her eyes.

"I am a medical professional, Caleb. I'd use a scalpel. And maybe anesthesia," she said nobly. "But I'm not worried."

He smiled a little. "No?"

"No. I have a pretty good idea of how she feels about you, and you've made your intentions obvious. Plus, if you screw with Jena, she's more than capable of taking care of herself."

He smiled and squirmed at the same time. "My intentions, huh?"

She sipped her coffee, but didn't say more. Intentions? Sometimes this whole town seemed like it was stuck back in another century. Sure, he had intentions, but he didn't feel like nailing them to the door or anything. He figured whatever intentions he had were best shared with Jena, not the entire community.

"I'm only going to warn you. Springs people? Shifters? We're damn territorial. You can call it animal instinct if you want, but once we latch on to someone, we have a hard time letting go. The upside to that is we're loyal. Just keep it in mind."

"That's my warning, huh?"

"That's your warning, shifter."

❋ 224 ❋

For some reason, Ted calling him "shifter" warmed him. It was as if he'd passed a test of some kind. Had been accepted into the club. Maybe he wasn't exactly like them; maybe this weird collision of myth, blood, and taboo had caused some internal shift like the original families who had taken the spring water. He didn't know how it worked and he was starting not to care. For the first time in his life, Caleb felt like he was exactly where he needed to be. He felt like he belonged.

"Consider me warned," he said with a smile. "Speaking of Matt and Missy, have you had a chance to ask about Matt's alibi?"

She sipped her coffee before she spoke. "I asked my mom, who asked around. She says that since Missy couldn't shift—she was still pregnant—she can't be certain, but that her sisters verified that Matt was with them."

"Would they lie?"

"Possibly. The cats, you're going to realize, are clannish. They keep to themselves, for the most part."

"You're a lion, right?"

She nodded. "We don't play well with others, so we keep to our own family groups. There are two main cat families. Matt is from one family, Missy, the other. But cat women tend to rule the roost. So Matt is in his wife's clan now. Would his sisters-in-law lie to protect him? Yes. He's their sister's mate. The father of her kids. They could be telling the truth, but we might never know."

"Well, that narrows it down."

She shrugged. "It does and it doesn't. Alma's house is pretty far out from theirs and his mate was pregnant. I have a hard time imagining Matt would roam that far, but you never know."

"You've seen the scratches at Alma's?"

She nodded. "I think they're feline, too. You get anything from Old Quinn?"

He shook his head. "He didn't do it. He was in love with Alma. He wouldn't have it in him. Kill someone else? Maybe. But not her."

"How do you know he was in love with Alma?"

He smiled and tilted back in his chair. "Sometimes, you just know things. I tend to go with my gut."

Ted grinned. "Do you now?"

Caleb's gut was telling him that Ted knew exactly how he felt about her best friend, probably more clearly than Jena did. It was also telling him something else.

"I need to go back out to Alma's. Take a look at that scene now that I know the truth."

"That's probably a good idea. You'd pick up more on a second visit, even though the place has been cleaned."

"Oh?"

"Yeah," she said quietly. "Jena's mom hired that outfit in San Bernardino that specializes in cleaning crime scenes. I've been out there to look around. There's still a scent to it, but nothing most people would recognize."

"Good to know." And that meant he needed to talk to Jena about letting the boys go out if they wanted. He knew from his own loss as a child that not saying a proper good-bye was a wound that lingered. "I don't think she'll go back."

"Not right away. Maybe with time. She was pretty panicked that night. That's the other reason you should go look. Those scratches might not be the size she thought. And if we're dealing with a different cat, then…"

"Different suspects. Right. You saw the scratches on the body. How certain are you of the size of the animal?"

She huffed. "Not certain at all. It's almost impossible to tell since they changed as she shifted. She went from a two-foot owl to a five-foot woman in seconds. I'd say it was probably a bobcat, but it could have been a small lion, too."

He closed his eyes. "The more we find out, the more we don't know." He grunted and stood to get more coffee. "By the way, how do you tell one mountain lion from another? Jena said you could educate me."

She laughed a little. "It'd be hard for you to tell unless you've hung around with us a lot. Scars, mostly. We all play pretty rough when we first shift. One of my cousins has a nice chunk I took out of her left ear from when we were teenagers."

"Nice kitty."

"But if you look closely, there's also some difference in facial markings. The dark patches around our eyes and muzzles do vary. But the scars are more noticeable. You get a good look at the one who attacked you?"

"No." He brought the coffee pot over and refilled her cup. "It was dark and I didn't really know what to look for. But I do now, so I'll be checking ears."

She laughed as he heard Jena's car pull up. Every nerve in his body jumped at the sound and he turned to the door.

Ted said, "Whipped, I tell you. It's pretty funny."

"Shut up, Ted." He walked to the front door and opened it. Jena was handing the boys bags of groceries and loading up her arms with more as he walked off the porch. He nodded at Low and mussed Aaron's hair as he walked past. Then his eyes narrowed in on Jena and stuck. She had two bags in her hand and her keys in her front teeth.

"Can I help?" He bent down and pulled the keys from her teeth. "That can't be sanitary."

"Well, if Santa would just give me that extra arm I've been asking for—" Caleb cut her off with a kiss. It wasn't a peck, either. He hummed into her mouth as his tongue touched hers, cupping her face in his hands as he kissed her thoroughly.

"Caleb." She pulled away breathlessly. "The boys—"

"Are just gonna have to get used to me kissing you." He put one arm around her waist and pulled her close, bending down to capture her lips again. "Especially when it's been hours since I've seen you," he murmured in her ear. She gave a soft sigh and bent her head so he could lay an open-mouthed kiss on her neck. He heard the door to the house slam as someone walked out, but only pulled her closer when she tensed.

He kissed her lightly on the mouth as he saw Low from the corner of his eye.

The boy grunted, "Gross." Then he pulled a couple more bags from the trunk of the car and walked back into the house.

Caleb grinned, watching the stubborn boy who reminded him so much of his mother walk past. "See? The sky did not fall."

Her face was flaming. "Shut up and help me with the rest of these. We'll talk about this later."

"I love it when you're bossy." He gave her ass a quick pat and took the rest of the bags from her hands.

SHE WAS MAKING DINNER FOR EVERYONE WHEN HE cornered her the next time. Everyone else—Ted, Allie, Dev, Ollie, and an annoyed Alex—were out in the backyard, grilling burgers and watching the kids play. Jena was chopping up celery for a potato salad when he came up behind her and grabbed her waist.

She gasped and turned. "Oh! It's you."

"Miss me?" He bent down and kissed her cheek.

"You're not leaving me alone long enough." He could tell she was a little annoyed when she blushed.

"Aw." He gave her a mock frown. "Don't hurt my feelings, woman. I'm a sensitive man."

She muttered, "And I know exactly where."

Caleb laughed, but left his arms around her, even when the back door slammed. She tensed again when Aaron came into the kitchen.

"Hey, Mom? Where's the juice boxes?"

Caleb looked over his shoulder to see Aaron watching them with a huge grin on his face. He said, "They're probably in the blue ice chest where they always are, Bear."

The little boy giggled and ran out the door while Jena glared at him. Caleb just watched him with amusement as he saw Aaron race outside and whisper something to Low that made the older boy roll his eyes. Caleb looked back at Jena.

"What?" He blinked innocently.

"What are you doing?"

He hugged her closer, teasing one hand along her belly while the other pulled her hips against his. "I'm getting comfortable."

Caleb tried not to laugh at the catch in her throat. "I can see that."

"And showing you that the boys aren't going to freak out now that we're together."

She blushed redder. "Is that so? We're together, huh?"

He shrugged. "Well, not as much as I'd like to be right now, but—"

She slapped a hand over his mouth. It smelled like sweet onion and potatoes and his stomach growled.

"Aren't you the hungry boy?" she said in an amused voice. "Get out of here so I can finish. You're distracting me."

"I could distract you more, if you let me."

"Caleb!" He just laughed and tickled her belly until she was squirming and laughing, too. "Go away."

"Hey." He pulled back a little. "I did want to talk to you about something serious, though."

"Oh?" She went back to chopping celery.

"I need to go back out to your grandmother's," he said quietly. "Take another look at the scene." She paused in her work and he could see her knuckles turn white.

"I—I don't want to—"

"You don't need to go if you don't want. But it's been cleaned now. And I was wondering if I could take the boys if they wanted. Aaron mentioned wanting to go."

She started dumping the chopped celery in the bowl. "Um... I don't know. If you're out there working, you don't need—"

"I could ask your mom to go if she wants," he added. "I think she'd be willing. And that way, there would be more than just me if the boys needed someone. If they were upset or anything. But I think it's important for them to go if they want to. Let them say good-bye to her that way. Let them remember the good stuff."

Jena was taking deep, even breaths as he ran a soothing hand over her shoulders, squeezing the back of her neck a little. "Think about it, okay?"

She nodded. "I will." He brushed a kiss along her jaw. "I wish…"

"Hey." He nudged her face around so she was looking at him. "You'll get there when you get there."

"Okay." She managed a small smile. "Thanks."

He smiled back, feeling a hundred feet tall. "You're welcome."

THE FOLLOWING SATURDAY, HE AND CATHY PULLED UP TO Alma's house. Low opened the car door. Then he took Aaron's hand and the two boys walked together toward the back of Alma's house. Caleb frowned. "Hey guys—"

"They're going to the Cliff House," Cathy said quietly. "It's fine. They know the way."

"The Cliff House?"

She smiled and opened the door to Jena's Subaru. She'd given Caleb the keys and he'd loaned her his truck for the day, though she claimed she didn't need it since she was only working at the diner.

"It's just a little cave cut into the cliffs. The kids use it as a play-house. It's been there for years."

"That sounds cool." It did, actually. He kind of wanted to see it. Instead, he walked toward the side door and stood outside Alma's kitchen. He stared at the peeling green paint for a few minutes, trying to imagine what it had looked like to her killer that night he'd come to her home. Had he intended to kill her? Had it been an accident? Knowing it was a shifter meant that the cover-up wasn't the elaborate hoax he'd thought at first. And since Low had complained about his grandmother and mom going flying that moon night, what had been a carefully plotted murder could have turned into a crime of passion or opportunity.

"Almost anyone could have done it," he murmured. He heard Cathy open the front door and go inside as he bent down to examine the freshest scrapes at the bottom of the door. "But not everyone has claws."

They weren't as fresh as they had been the night of her death. Sand had caught in them and the color of the wood had already turned. But he could see the four claw marks. Just like what he remembered on Alma's corpse. Three deeper, then a fourth just a bit more shallow. What would cause that? A broken hand? Would a human injury transfer to a shifter's natural form? Was it a birth defect? He made a note to ask Jena or Ted the next time he saw them.

The claw marks were narrow but deep. An animal pawing at your door like that would catch your attention. It might startle you enough that you opened the door. But even without a stitch on? Had the cat wailed? Made an injured sound? It must have been something urgent if Alma hadn't even stopped to put on a robe. Then he remembered Jena disrobing before she shifted in the truck. Had Alma been trying to flee when she opened the door?

He cocked his head to the side and took a mental picture of the size, trying to match it to what he knew about large cats. It seemed big for a bobcat, but small for the mountain lion that had attacked him. How much variation was there between shifters? Mayor Matt was definitely a bobcat, but how big was he?

He pulled a small camera out of his pocket, put his phone next to the scratches for scale, then took a few snapshots. He'd show them to Ted and see what she thought. It wasn't that he didn't trust Jena's eyes, but she'd been in shock when she'd been at the scene the first time. He stood and opened the door to find Cathy sitting at Alma's kitchen table with tears in her eyes.

"I loved her more than my own mom," she said. "I'm not sure when that happened. I try not to feel guilty about it."

"Don't. Family's complicated."

She brushed at her eyes. "True."

"The ones we choose to love can be just as important as the ones we're born loving. Sometimes more so."

Cathy cupped her chin in her hand and leaned on the table as Caleb took a seat. "I like you, Chief Gilbert."

He smiled. "I think you can call me Caleb now, don't you think?"

"Because you're in love with my daughter?"

He blinked and cleared his throat. "I... well, I—"

"It's okay if you haven't told her yet. And I won't either. She's cautious."

He ignored his panicked heartbeat and said, "It's understandable."

"It is. And she and Lowell did not have the easiest relationship."

"Oh?" That was a surprise.

She shook her head. "They loved each other—crazy in love—but it was... uneven. They were so young. Jena was always the one holding the reins while Lowell tugged ahead, determined to live as much as he could. It's understandable, I guess. But exhausting. She was never easy with him. There was so much tension in their lives with that cloud hanging over them. And he hated it here. As much as Jena loved it, he hated it. Couldn't get away fast enough."

"Why are you telling me this?" he asked in a hoarse voice.

"Because she won't. And you need to know. She's happy here. Needs to be here. It's not just family. It's the Springs."

Cathy wasn't a shifter. She'd married one, raised one, but had spent her life in a town where she was always going to be just a little on the outside. "Did you like living here?"

"I liked that it was safe for my daughter. I liked that it made my husband so content. Was it always ideal?" She shrugged. "No, but no place is. And once you've lived long enough, you realize home is about people, not places. It was more important for my family to be safe and content than for me to be always happy with where we lived."

"And Jena needs to be here."

"Yes, she does. She really, really does." Cathy paused. "I think maybe you do, too."

He let out a shaky breath. "I think you may be right."

Just then, a sound came on the wind. It chilled him, despite the heat of the autumn day, and he bolted to his feet as Cathy said, "What on earth—"

"The boys!"

Fear clutched the pit of Caleb's stomach as he raced out of the house and toward the direction where he'd seen Low and Aaron walking. The cry came again. A terrified shriek from Aaron. A panicked shout from Low. He ran faster through the dry scrub, ignoring the thorns and brambles that tore at his legs.

"The Cliff House!" Cathy shouted behind him. "It's up high in the rocks. Can you climb?"

"I'll have to!" He climbed a small rise and caught his first glimpse of the scene. Low had Aaron pushed behind him and was holding a stick, jabbing at a mountain lion who had crouched on a nearby rock, snarling at them while another paced below.

"Caleb!" Aaron called out. "Watch out!"

Caleb tensed as he heard the low growl.

Not just one lion, but two. Two big, snarling beasts who were holding the boys hostage in the Cliff House. And keeping Caleb from getting to them. He tried not to panic. How was he going to get to the boys? Throw rocks? The cat on the rocks kept snarling at Low while the other began to move toward Caleb. He glanced around. His gun was back in the truck. Why hadn't he brought it? He cursed his carelessness.

"Low," he called. "Try to stay calm. I'm coming."

"Go away!" Low shouted at the lion. "I don't know who you are. Just leave us alone!" He jabbed at it again.

"Lo-ow..." Aaron sobbed behind his brother.

"Boys!" Caleb yelled. "Stay calm." Who the hell were these lions? He wanted to strangle them with his bare hands.

"Caleb, get them away!" Aaron cried harder.

He started toward the one on the ground, holding his hands up. He could see a ragged ear twitch as he walked closer, but the creature didn't attack. Neither did the one on the rocks. It snarled, causing Caleb's gut to clench in fear, but it didn't pounce when it easily could have. The animal watched him, crouching down and keeping his eyes on Caleb while its brother snarled at the boys in the Cliff House.

Elizabeth Hunter

"Who are you, you bastard?" he muttered. "What do you want?"

"Caleb!" Aaron screamed.

"Shoot them!" Low yelled.

The one near the boys whipped its head around and curled its lips at Caleb just as he heard Cathy running through the brush. He heard the distinctive sound of a pump-action shotgun a second before Cathy yelled, "Get away from my boys!"

"Low, get down!" he shouted. Low grabbed his brother and disappeared as Cathy fired the gun toward the rocks. The two lions bounded away, speeding along the canyon wall and disappearing from his sight.

"Are there any more?"

"No, just the two." He was already climbing the rocks. He could hear Low shushing his crying brother as his hands scraped along the sandstone. "Bear? Low?" he called. "It's just me. They ran off."

"Caleb?" Aaron sniffed and his head popped over the edge of the rocks. "Where's Grandma?"

"I'm right here, Bear," Cathy called from below. "Good thing Grandma Alma always kept the shotgun loaded, huh?"

Caleb could see a wooden ladder at the base of the cliffs, but it had been broken. He would have to keep climbing with his hands.

"One of the lions tried to climb the ladder, so I shoved it back," Low said in a shaky voice. "I think it broke, and the lion fell. It was pissed."

"Good boy," Caleb hissed as he pulled himself up the side of the cliffs. His hands would be torn up. He could already feel a tear in his shirt and one knee was bloody. He finally scrambled up the side of the cliff and pulled himself into the Cliff House with a grunt. Then he winced when Aaron launched himself at his chest.

"It's okay." He wrapped his arms around the little boy and patted his back. "They ran off when your grandma came. I doubt they'll be back."

Aaron sniffed. "I thought they were gonna kill us like they killed Grandma Alma."

"No way." He took deep breaths, trying to calm his heart. It ached at the fear in Aaron's voice. "Your grandma would have kicked their furry butts. And yes, you get a quarter for the swear jar for that one." He turned to look for Low. The boy was crouched a little ways away, watching Caleb holding his brother with wide, scared eyes. Caleb reached one hand out. "You okay?"

Low nodded but ignored the hand.

"You did good. Good thinking about the ladder and keeping it back with that stick, Low. Good job. You kept Bear safe."

The older boy only gave Caleb another jerk of his head. He could tell Low was moments away from breaking down and Aaron still clung to him.

"Caleb?" He heard Cathy call from outside. "Are they okay?"

"They're alright. Just shook up. Bear, can I hand you down to Grandma? Is that okay?" The little boy clutched at his neck for a moment before he pulled away and looked over the edge, wiping his eyes and nose with the back of his dirty hand.

"Hey, Grandma."

"Hi, pumpkin. Can you come down to me? Let's get you home."

"Yeah." Aaron started to climb over the edge of the cliff, but Caleb swooped him up and lowered him by his armpits, slowly lowering him into Cathy's waiting arms as the boy began to wiggle.

"I have to go to the bathroom."

"There's lot of bushes around," Cathy said as she held him. "Have at it."

The danger passed, excitement started to creep into the little boy's voice. "Did you see those lions, Grandma? They were really big and Low fought them off and Caleb was gonna wrestle one I think and then you came and he shot one! Did you see?"

Cathy said something unintelligible as Caleb turned back to Low.

"Hey," he said quietly. "You okay?"

He felt more torn up inside than out when Low started to shake. "Did Grandma get one? With the gun?"

"No, she just scared them off."

"So they're gone?"

"Yeah." He moved a little closer to the boy, worried about the still-frantic eyes he saw.

"Why didn't you shoot one? You should have had your gun and stuff."

"Sorry. I ran out here without thinking. It's locked in my truck. I was kind of panicked, but you did great."

"You're the chief of police, you know. You should carry your gun all the time." He started to sniff.

"You did good, Low." The boy was seconds from tears. "You took care of your brother."

"I have to. It's my job." His voice caught. "I yelled, but we're pretty far away. And I thought... if they got Bear—"

"But they didn't." Caleb moved closer, putting a steady hand on Low's shoulder as the boy's face crumbled. "You kept him safe."

"I was really scared," he said as the tears began to fall.

Caleb put his arm around the little man who had turned back into a boy, and he pulled him close. Low shook with silent tears as the fear began to drain out of him.

"You did great. You kept your brother safe and you called for help."

"I thought no one would hear us. And they'd kill us, too."

"Not gonna happen." Fear began to unfurl in his own chest as the adrenaline ebbed. He'd never felt more helpless in his life. "I'm gonna find out who they are, and you won't have to be scared anymore."

Low hiccuped and wiped at his eyes. "Yeah?"

"I promise."

"Okay."

"You gonna be okay?" Caleb asked cautiously, watching the boy compose himself under his arm.

"Yeah."

"You ready to get out of here yet?"

He hesitated, then glanced toward the open mouth of the small cave. He wiped his eyes again and nodded. "Yeah, I'm good."

Caleb patted his back and said, "You're great, Low. You were really brave."

The two of them slowly clambered down the rocks where Low was swept into Cathy's waiting arms and Caleb took Aaron's hand to walk back to the house. Just as the boys walked inside with Cathy, Caleb darted around the back of the house and emptied his stomach in the first bush he found.

Never in his life. Drug raids, domestic calls, even caught in an alley once with two armed gang members didn't compare. He retched again, spitting out the acid that had filled his stomach and trying to calm the shaking in his hands.

The lion crouched on the rocks, muscles bunched to spring.

The pacing animal with the sweeping tail and the deep scar on its shoulder.

Low holding them off with a stick and Aaron, crying in the rocks, sobbing Caleb's name...

The mere thought of what could have happened caused his heart to seize, and Caleb ran back to the side door where Cathy was leading the boys to Jena's car, purse in hand. She took one look at him, then stepped back as he knelt down and grabbed both boys in a fierce hug. He clutched them to his chest, wondering how, exactly, this had happened. Did Jena live with this fear all the time? That something could happen to her kids and these little people would just be gone? They were so vulnerable. It was utterly and completely terrifying in a way he'd never, ever experienced before.

"Caleb," Aaron squeaked. "You're kind of hugging really hard."

"Sorry." He cleared his throat, but didn't let go. He did loosen up a bit as he felt Low pat his shoulder awkwardly.

"It's cool, man."

Caleb pulled back and looked at them both. "Yeah?"

Low shrugged and rolled his eyes. "We're cool. Really. Just stop kissing Mom in front of me, okay? It's totally gross."

Caleb broke into a relieved smile. "I'm not sure I can do that. She's pretty cute."

Aaron giggled while Low made a disgusted sound in the back of his throat and walked to the car.

chapter
twenty-three

J ena was out the door before the car came to a stop. She was off the porch before the doors opened. She grabbed Aaron and pulled him out of the car, fighting back the tears on her face and trying to calm her racing heart. She looked around desperately, seeking Low's precious grubby face as she clutched her youngest son. Caleb was walking behind her oldest, one hand on Low's shoulder, leading him back to her.

With a choked cry, she grabbed both her sons and held them tight.

They're really all right. All right. All right.

She felt the tears in her eyes leak down her face as she remembered her mother's call from the car.

"They're fine, Jena. They're both fine. Just shaken up."

Everything was all right. Just a few scrapes and bruises. Her boys were fine. Still, she couldn't let go.

"Mom, we're okay," Low said.

She fell to her knees in the dusty driveway, holding them and rocking them, trying to banish the terror of the last ten minutes from her mind. Never in her life... She couldn't find the words. They were still caught on the lump of fear in her throat.

"Caleb and Grandma scared the lions away," Aaron said cheerfully. "And then he climbed up and got us. He's really strong, Mom."

Jena felt her father's hand on her shoulder and she tried to relax.

"Hey, guys," he said. "You just gave your mom and me a scare. Let's go in the house and get a snack. Sound good to anyone else?"

With a deep breath, Jena loosened the iron grip on her two boys and stood. They were okay. She was probably just freaking them out more with her reaction. She let her dad throw Aaron onto his back and walk up the porch while Low waited next to her.

She finally found some words. "You're really okay?" She ran her hands through his hair, sandy from climbing down from the cliffs. She could see tear marks on his dusty face, but no trace of them remained in his eyes.

"I'm cool." He sounded a little choked up. "And Caleb's going to find out who it was. So... yeah, we're cool."

She felt the tears well up again, but she tried to remain calm to match her oldest son's forced ease. She could tell he'd been shaken, but he was a tough kid. In fact, he might have stood just a little taller as he walked over to Caleb, held out a hand, and bumped knuckles with the man leaning casually against the old car, sipping a bottle of water.

"I'm going in for a snack. Caleb, you want one?"

He shrugged. "Let me talk to your mom for a sec."

"Just remember what we talked about."

"I told you, I'm not making any promises."

Low muttered something she couldn't hear before he walked in the house. Then Jena walked over to Caleb.

"Jena..." He was shaking his head. "I never in a million years would have let them go out there alone, except your mom said they were fine and knew the way, and... She said there's never been an animal attack out there in all the years she—"

"Shhh." She put a finger over his lips before she wrapped her arms around his waist and hugged him. She felt it then, the slow release of tension. The burning in her eyes. Her shoulders started shaking a second before he crushed her to his chest.

"I'm sorry!" he whispered. "I'm so sorry. I'd never put them at risk. Ever. Not if I could help it."

"It's not—" She cleared her throat and blinked back tears. "It's not your fault."

"What?"

Did he actually think she blamed him? That she would be angry? She shook her head and pulled back so she could meet his eyes. They were panicked.

"Oh," she breathed out, reaching a hand up to smooth the lines between his eyebrows. "No, baby, I'm not mad." She felt his shoulders relax, so she lifted up on her toes and kissed him gently. "How could I be mad?"

"I should've killed them," he said. "I left my gun in the car 'cause I didn't want to alarm the boys, but then they—"

"You scared them off. You protected my boys." She uncurled her arms from his waist and wrapped them around his neck, pulling his lips to hers. "Thank you." She kissed him again, ignoring the tears that ran down her cheeks, then pressed his bloody knuckles to her lips. "There are not enough 'thank yous' in the world—"

"Stop." Caleb grabbed her hands and pulled her into another embrace. "Don't thank me. Don't—don't, you know?" He paused for a moment, lost for words. Then he captured her mouth with his.

Desperate. Scared. Relieved. He said it all without saying a word. And in that moment, Jena knew the man who held her would walk through fire for her children. For her. It was exactly what she needed to know. She loved him.

He ran his hands down her shoulders, her hips, brushing his fingers along her jaw until one hand rested against her racing pulse and his other pressed into the small of her back. She held him just as close, grasping on to the sudden realization of how hard she'd fallen.

"Caleb." She finally pulled away. He was having none of it as he buried his face in her neck and scraped his teeth along her skin. "We've got to stop."

"Why?" he asked with a grunt.

"Look at the windows. We have an audience?" Caleb may have been keeping his hands PG, but what was beginning to press into her belly was definitely R-rated.

"Damn." He sighed. "Nosey kids. You're going to have to clean Aaron's nose print off that window."

"That's what I thought." She pulled his face back down to hers for one more kiss, brushing the sand from his hair and dusting off his torn shirt. "Thank you for taking care of my boys," she whispered.

He put one finger on her chin to tilt her face up to his. "Don't thank me for that, Jena. I'd do anything to keep them safe."

She felt the smile take over her face. "I know." Then she turned and walked up to the porch, pausing when she didn't hear him follow. Jena turned around to see him still leaning against the dusty car with his hands in his pockets, watching the house with a curious expression.

She put her hands on her hips and said, "Well? You coming inside, or what?"

His boyish grin made her heart flip as he walked up the steps.

SHE WAS STARING AT THE SLOW TURN OF THE CEILING FAN that night as she lay on her bed, Low curled up on the opposite side with Aaron smooshed between them. It had been Aaron's request that night because he didn't want to sleep alone, but Jena was glad for it. It reminded her of the mornings when the boys were little. She'd be exhausted from a late night at the restaurant, Lowell would be heading into work, so the boys would come and crowd on her bed, watching quiet cartoons while she slowly woke.

She didn't doze that night. Both boys had bathed and fallen into bed early, the excitement of the day finally catching up with them. She'd called Ted to let her know what had happened and her friend had called everyone else. Caleb had spoken in quietly urgent tones with his deputy before he kissed her goodnight and taken off to the station, and Tom and Cathy were sleeping in Low's room.

Jena's house felt like a miniature bunker and she couldn't have been happier. There was safety in numbers. She only wished there were one more resident sleeping in the house. Still, despite the ever-deepening ease between Caleb and her family, it would have been awkward for him to stay.

She sat bolt upright when she heard a rustling in the bushes outside her window. She looked over to the boys, who were still snoring, before she went to the closet and pulled out the shotgun on the top shelf. She cracked it and loaded two shells from the top drawer of her dresser before she snuck back to the bedroom, moving quietly toward the window.

Then, she heard the tap.

"Jena?" She rolled her eyes when she heard Caleb's whisper. She propped the shotgun on her hip and pulled back the curtain.

His grin fell when he saw her. "Hey! Whoa. Uh… probably sneaking around the house of the scared mom isn't such a great idea, huh?"

Shaking her head, she slid the window up. "Ya think? And what are you doing here? It's the middle of the night."

"Were you sleeping?"

She silently shook her head.

"Neither was I. So, I was thinking…" He held up a grocery bag with a smile. "Midnight picnic?"

"What?"

"I still haven't taken you out on a date, woman. And I feel like I need to at this point, considering… stuff. You're awake—probably pacing the house with that gun—I'm resisting the urge to stalk the perimeter of your house with mine. I say we put down the firearms and have a drink."

It was a tempting idea, but she glanced over her shoulder.

As if reading her mind, Caleb said, "I brought a blanket. We can sit right here on the grass outside the window and if they get up, you'll hear them, right?"

"I'm not sure."

"You know, I chased off mountain lions today. Two of them. Big ones. Mean."

Jena narrowed her eyes. "Are you taking advantage of my earlier gratitude for saving my children's lives by trying to guilt me into going on a date with you?"

"Yes. Yes, I am."

She burst into quiet laughter and leaned out the window. "You're really, really shameless."

"It's worked before. Date?"

"The boys…"

"Are your parents in the house?"

Jena heard a window crack open and her father's voice call out in a loud whisper. "Her parents are trying to sleep! Jena, just go have a drink with the man. We'll watch the boys."

Caleb turned back to her with a grin. "Well?"

She hesitated for only a minute before she said, "Your trailer." Then she ducked back in the window, unloaded the gun and put it high in the closet before she made her way out the front door and jogged back to the Airstream. When she arrived, Caleb was spreading an old blanket out on the front porch and unpacking a brown paper bag.

"You were serious about the picnic thing."

"I didn't have a basket, but if this is going to count for a real date, I figured I'd need a blanket. With all the sand, we can pretend we're at the beach or something."

She smothered a grin and sat on the edge while he unpacked the feast he'd brought.

"Beer." He presented the six-pack to her with a flourish. "Bottles, not cans."

"Classy."

"I try."

He pulled out a box of crackers.

"Ritz!" She smiled. "You've really gone all out."

He wiggled his eyebrows. "Hey, when I aim to impress…" He

trailed off, suddenly looking nervous. "Now, keep in mind that the Quick Stop does not have the finest cheese selection available and it's the only thing that was open at this hour."

Jena frowned. "What..." She let out a loud groan when he pulled the can from behind his back. "You're not calling that cheese."

"It's... cheese product."

She started giggling, then grabbed for the can he was clutching. "You can't call this cheese."

"It's kind of like cheese. It's cheese-ish."

Her giggles turned to snorts. "You brought a chef 'cheese in a can' for your first date?"

"Listen, Chef Snobby"—he was laughing along now—"it was this, Velveeta, or the scary-looking pimiento cheese spread that Norman had in the deli case in back."

She couldn't stop laughing. Her stomach was actually starting to ache. "It's cheese product! In an aerosol can."

"You know, if you're going to continue to mock my efforts—"

She stopped his protest with a kiss, which he enthusiastically returned. Soon, all thoughts of cheese, crackers, and beer were gone from her mind as she pulled him next to her and stretched out on the blanket, reveling in the press of his weight against her and the soft lips that claimed her own.

"Good," he muttered. "We've skipped to my favorite part of the date."

"It's going well so far. Mostly."

"I still think you're being awfully judgmental about the cheese."

"FAVORITE COLOR?"

"Guys don't have favorite colors."

"The boys do."

"Boys have favorite colors," Caleb said. "Men don't."

"You do, too. You just haven't thought about it. What's the first one that sprang to mind when I asked?"

"Red."

"See? Why red?"

"Remember that shirt you were wearing the night we met?" He grinned at her wickedly and Jena forced back a smile.

"You mean 'your special shirt?'"

He pulled her a little closer and wrapped his arm around her waist. "Yes, it is. I'm glad you recognize this now."

They had both drunk a few beers and Caleb had gone into the trailer to get a couple more blankets, which he piled up so they could lay on their backs and stare at the stars. They were curled up around each other under a blanket, talking quietly while they looked into the clear night.

"Your favorite color?"

"Green. The color of the boys' eyes. They both have Lowell's eyes." She felt Caleb tense a little. "Does it bother you when I talk about him? About Lowell?"

He paused, then let out a small sigh. "Let's just say that it kind of does, but I know it shouldn't. Don't worry about it. I'll get over it."

"I'm not..." How could she explain? "I'm not in love with him anymore, if that makes any sense. He's gone. But I did love him, and I treasure those memories, so it's hard—"

"You don't have to explain."

"I want to. I don't want you to feel like you're competing with a ghost. Because there's no competition."

With that, she felt his arms relax and she nestled her head into his shoulder again.

"You've got great kids, Jena. I'm not gonna lie. I'm a little jealous."

"You wanted kids. Your ex didn't?"

"To be fair, it's not something we talked about before we got married, which was stupid. I just assumed she did. My mistake."

"And she assumed you didn't? It goes both ways, Caleb."

He shrugged. "It's in the past. Does this resort worry you? This hotel that Alex wants to build? It'll definitely change things about the town. Expose it more, maybe expose your kids."

"It does bother me, but it's not all about me. The town needs something. Is it going to change things? Yeah, definitely. We're going to have to be more careful."

"Everyone is. But you think it's good in the long run?"

"I do." She nodded slowly. "There had to be something or the whole town would just dry up and drift away. And then where would we go?"

"You went away once."

"And it would have slowly killed me." She felt him start. "I'm exaggerating, but I do feel stronger here. When I lived away, I slept a lot. Didn't have near the energy I do here. I just always felt... off."

"But people do. Move away, I mean."

What was he thinking? She pulled away from him, feeling an ache in her middle at the thought of Caleb leaving. "Um... yeah. Sometimes. But I'm not moving again."

He put a hand at the back of her neck and tugged her toward him, pressing a kiss to her lips that slowly grew from easy to heated.

"Good," he said. "Because I like it here. And I'd like to keep you. So when the resort comes, we'll deal with it."

"We will?" She was distracted by his hands teasing under the edge of her shirt.

"Mm-hmm. I'm a good ally."

"I'm not gonna lie. You knowing everything is a big relief." She gasped when he brought his warm palm up to press against her ribs. Slow, steady strokes moving upward until she arched into his hand. He caught the cry on her lips with his kiss and pressed the length of his body into hers.

"We'll deal with it together, Jena Crowe, because I have plans. And none of them involve leaving you."

"Good." She dug her fingers into his thick hair and tugged his head to the side, licking along the rough stubble on his jaw. "I like you here."

"Right here?" He swung her leg over his hip and pressed their bodies together.

"You got it."

"Yeah." He smiled. "I do."

chapter
twenty-four

"Caleb?"

He blinked his eyes and grunted.

"Hey, why don't you go lay down on my bed? You're going to get a crick in your back from this couch."

"Mmnf. I'm okay." Her concerned face swam above him when he opened his eyes. "You need help with stuff?"

"No, Low's helping with the salad, and Allie and Ted are bringing everything else. Go sleep in my room. Aaron's taking a nap, too."

He closed his eyes, then opened them again as the warm afternoon light spilled into the living room of Jena's house. He'd slept on the couch the night before, after they'd come back from their "date," and he had to admit, his back was feeling it.

"Okay." He sat up and grabbed her arm before she could leave, pulling her into a long, lazy kiss. "Lay down with me."

"I have to finish the food. People are coming over in an hour and a half."

Caleb pulled her closer and laid his head against her hip. "Too many people."

She laughed and mussed his hair. "Go sleep. You got practically no rest last night."

And then she'd woken him up for church services that morning.

Well, Aaron had, anyway. It was impossible to sleep with the small tornado whirling around. So he'd woken up, gone to his trailer to shower, and joined them, sitting next to Jena and the boys as they listened to the priest—it was the Catholic's turn that week—offer a short homily and minister to the devout. It had been… nice. Nicer than he'd expected.

He smiled down at her. She had on a stained apron and her hair was starting to do that feathery thing around her face. The big scary "I love you" was on the tip of his tongue when Low called from the kitchen, so he bit back the words for what seemed like the hundredth time.

"I'd better go help him," she said.

"Yeah, okay."

"Go nap, sleepyhead."

It never quite seemed the right time to tell her. And he had to admit that he was a little afraid she wouldn't say it back. He bent down to give Jena another quick kiss before she disappeared and he stumbled down the hall. Looking around, he noticed the family pictures along the walls. So many pictures of Jena and her parents. Of Alma and what had to be her husband. Tons of pictures of the boys.

His house in Albuquerque had been bare. He had lived there for four years and… nothing. The few pieces of art that Leila had hung she'd taken with her. They'd never hung up pictures, not even from their small wedding.

So this was what a normal house looked like.

He opened her bedroom door and lay down on the smooth comforter, closing his eyes as he thought about the past week. Ever since they'd been shot at, had crazy desert sex—which would remain a favorite memory until he died—and had it out about her fear of him leaving, Caleb had slipped into her life a little more each day. It was just like he'd told her. He was getting comfortable. And though he'd always imagined he wanted a family and a life that didn't completely revolve around his work, he'd still worried a little that once he did, he'd be bored out of his mind.

To his surprise, he wasn't. Putting aside that he was constantly faced with some new supernatural element that he'd never even imagined, his life had become unexpectedly crowded. It was a little like Jena's house. Not just crowded with pictures, but with people, memories, traces of life, and history all over the place.

There was always someone coming or going, a friend or relative. The boys tumbling around or fighting with each other. Jena teasing them, teasing him, giving them all a hard time with that subtle humor she had. And it was nice to be bored on days like this, when the afternoon sun beamed through the windows and he was tired from a long week. Then, he could take a nap and roll around in pillows that smelled like Jena. If he'd planned it better, he might be able to roll around with Jena herself, but she'd invited people over.

Caleb sighed and closed his eyes again. Other than solving the murder that was hanging over his head, trying to figure out why he occasionally turned into different people, and when, exactly, was the right time to tell Jena he loved her, life in Cambio Springs was beginning to seem just about perfect. And Caleb, for once in his life, was trying not to predict it all going to shit. He wouldn't let it this time. He couldn't.

JEREMY KICKED AT THE PORCH RAIL A LITTLE AND NODDED. "Well, some people are suspicious. But just as many of them are more comfortable with you being here now that you're more like us."

"I guess that makes sense." They were sitting on Jena's porch while Jeremy briefed him about the latest social news.

One of his deputy's assignments, since Caleb's shapeshifting had come to light, was to gauge the mood of the town about their new chief. It had only been a few weeks since he'd suddenly discovered he could shift into other people's skin, and he was still experimenting with how it worked. He hadn't drunk the spring water again, and his abilities showed no indication of weakening or going away. If anything, he'd become stronger.

"You still gettin' that nausea?" Jeremy asked.

"A little, but just for a few minutes."

"That's good, then." Jeremy McCann had never been the most talkative of men, but since Caleb started to shift, he'd become even more silent about it. It was starting to bug Caleb.

"Spit it out, McCann."

"What?"

"Whatever you're dancing around. It's giving me motion sickness." Which was ridiculous, of course, because Jeremy didn't fidget except right before the full moon.

The younger man wrinkled his forehead. "Well, I guess… why?"

"Why what?"

"Why you?"

"Why did I change? I don't know."

Jeremy sighed. "It's not that I resent it. I don't. Hell, the thought of shifting into another person kind of creeps me out to be honest."

"Thanks."

"You're welcome. But why did the water affect you when it's never affected any others from away?"

Caleb shrugged. "I don't know. Why did it affect your ancestors in the first place? Maybe there was a witch in my background. Maybe the shit I did in New Mexico really did have some effect on my spirit like my grandmother always told me it would. Maybe there was something there that collided with all that stuff when I drank from the fresh spring. I. Don't. Know."

He tried not to be frustrated, but did Jeremy think he hadn't asked himself the same questions a million times?

"Sorry, Chief."

He patted Jeremy's back. "No big deal. I'm a freak, I know."

"Only according to about half the town." He grinned. "The other half thinks you're less weird now than you were before."

Caleb laughed and shook his head. "Does that mean the clans are going to cooperate with us about Alma's murder?"

The young officer slipped on his sunglasses. "I didn't predict miracles." He turned to go, then, right before he climbed in his truck, said, "Looking pretty at home here, Chief."

"Bye, Jeremy."

"Just saying—" The young man grinned. "I don't see any talon marks yet."

Caleb flipped him off. "Like I'd show them to you? See you tomorrow, Deputy."

"YES." TED NODDED AND TOOK OFF HER GLASSES. "I AGREE with you. These could be either a small mountain lion or a large bobcat. It's too difficult to say for certain."

"Great," Jena huffed and Caleb clasped her hand in his.

"It's just the claw marks." Ted shrugged. "If it was an actual paw print, I could tell, but just the scratches?"

Everyone had come over for dinner, feasting on the enchiladas that Allie had made, along with a huge green salad, cornbread, and beans. The youngest kids were zoned out to a movie while Low and Kevin sat with Dev, who was a decent artist. They were trying to draw the picture of the lion that had attacked the boys to see if Ted could identify the markings.

Alex said, "But we've definitely identified it as feline, right? Doesn't that leave Matt at the top of your suspect list?"

Ollie added, "And he's a bobcat."

"But," Allie said, "Missy was pregnant, which makes it unlikely he would have roamed that far."

Something struck him just then. "We're talking about a bobcat—possibly—working with two lions. Didn't Ted say the cats are solitary?"

Jena turned to him with a frown. "Unless they're mated pairs. And the cat I saw running away from us after we were shot was definitely a bobcat. But a lion attacked you and the boys."

"Two lions," Low said from across the room.

Caleb said, "So it's a bobcat who's working with lions."

Ted exchanged a significant look with Jena. "Matt's a bobcat and Missy's a lion."

Jena shook her head. "Missy was pregnant. She couldn't have shifted. And there were two lions, not just one. There's no telling—"

"Maybe she wasn't pregnant," Caleb said quietly.

"What?" Jena shrugged. "She just had the baby. Saw him in church today. Little guy is the spitting image of their other kids."

"He is a little guy," Caleb said. "A *very* little guy. Right, Ted?"

Ted gasped. "But how would they risk…? That could explain it. But would they? It'd be incredibly dangerous."

Jena looked between them. "Are you saying what I think? That Missy forced a shift when she was pregnant? That would cause miscarriage!"

"Not necessarily," Ted said. "Only if she shifted all the way. If she just let it start… You know that sensation of pins and needles we get?"

Everyone nodded except Caleb. He didn't get pins and needles. He tried not to feel left out.

"That's your body preparing itself. I can't explain it really, but you can stop at that point, if you have to. Think about it. We've all done it, when we're young. When we're just learning."

Alex's mouth gaped open. "You think she could make herself go into early labor?"

"I don't see why not. It would be incredibly dangerous for both mother and child, but it's possible. And that baby has seemed small from the beginning, even though she says he delivered after her due date. Her milk didn't come in like it did with her girls. That's part of the reason she had trouble nursing him. If she forced a shift and had the baby early—"

"At home," Allie said quietly. "She delivered at home. There's no way to verify when she delivered. Her sisters helped her."

Caleb asked, "Would her sisters lie for her?"

A resounding "Yes" echoed across the room.

"So if Missy wasn't pregnant…" Caleb let his thoughts trail off.

Alex said, "It could have been Matt and Missy working together."

Jena shook her head with tears in her eyes. "But why? Why would they—?"

Caleb clasped her hand. "Matt's ambitious, honey. Your grandmother was standing in the way of the progress he'd been hoping to put his mark on."

Alex nodded. "Matt was pushing pretty hard. Especially with the grant stuff."

Ted said, "And don't let Missy fool you with the bubbly personality and big blue eyes. She's even more ambitious than Matt. She and her sisters—"

"Hey! We finished," Low piped up. "This is it. This is the lion that was closest to us. I didn't really see the other one on the ground, but—"

"Give it here." Caleb grabbed the paper from Dev. Yep, it looked the same, down to the thick black lines that ran along the muzzle and the jagged tear in the animal's left ear. "Looks right to me." He hesitated for a moment, then handed the sketch to Ted. "Recognize him?"

"Not a him. It's a her." The doctor shook her head, a look of horror spreading across her face. "It's one of Missy's sisters. She's my cousin, Amanda."

"Are you sure?"

"I'm the one who tore her ear."

chapter twenty-five

J ena glanced back at the headlights behind them as Alex followed
Caleb's truck down the short dirt track to Missy and Matt's house.
She could see Ted's shadow sitting next to Alex. Her friend had
been enraged by the idea of her clan members attacking children,
particularly when the cats were female. Ted had called her mother and
alerted her to the problem before she'd jumped in Alex's car to tail
them.

"Why?"

"Hmm?" Caleb glanced at her before wrenching his eyes back to the
road to avoid a tumble of rocks that had spilled into their path.

"Why would Missy's sisters attack the boys?"

"I'm not sure their plan was to attack, to be honest. They never
really got close. They probably wanted to scare us. Keep us distracted."

"I still don't get it."

Caleb was quiet for a moment before he said, "Walk me through it.
What are you thinking?"

"Missy and Matt..." Jena shook her head. "I can get why Matt
would target Alma. He's ambitious. It might have even been an accident, but Missy's baby... If she really forced her body to deliver
early—"

"We're not sure what happened. That's why we're going out there, to get answers."

Jena's brain was still whirling. "It wouldn't just happen. The maternal instinct is too strong. So she would have had to *want* to do it. And it would have been dangerous for both of them."

"But if she was motivated enough—"

"I still don't get why. Why would she do that for Matt? And why were her sisters involved? None of this makes sense."

He was silent for a few moments. "What you really want to know is why they killed Alma. And I don't know if there's any good answer to that, Jena."

"She was going to vote yes for the whole crazy project," Jena said softly. "She just wanted a little time."

Caleb reached across for her hand. "Someone got impatient. And we're going to find out who."

SHE'D ALWAYS WONDERED AT MATT AND MISSY'S HOUSE. With Matt being the town mayor, Jena would have thought they would buy a house in town, close to the small city hall and the school. But they lived out on the edge of town, their house sitting among a stand of mesquite trees that were fed from a seasonal wash behind their house. Picturesque, but isolated. It was Vasquez land; Missy's parents had given them the house when they'd married and the tidy desert landscaping in front was immaculate.

"Cute house," Caleb said.

"She'd have it no other way." Jena opened the door and stood by the truck, scanning the exterior. Lights were off on one side, but the rest of the house was lit up like a Christmas tree. Glancing at her watch, Jena guessed the kids were in bed and Matt and Missy had company. She didn't see any cars, though, which made her wary.

Just as she saw a curtain flicker, Alex and Ted pulled up, Ted bolting out of the car before it was parked. The woman slammed the car door shut with no thought to attracting attention. Caleb jerked toward her. "Ted, wait for—"

She pulled him back. "No."

"I called Jeremy. Let me secure the scene. I don't want to have—"

"She's a cat, Caleb. It's better if she confronts them first."

"Stupid, hardheaded..." He ran after Ted, muttering.

Alex and Jena walked behind them. Jena may have been angry, but this was unfamiliar territory to her. Ted was the best person to approach the other cats if they wanted answers. If Caleb got involved, they would immediately clam up. She turned the corner to the side door off the kitchen just as it opened. Ted reached out with a quick swipe and slapped whoever was there before she pounced.

"Hey!" Caleb tried to pull the woman back, only to be shoved to the side by a snarling Alex. The alpha's eyes glowed a dark gold, signaling his dominance to the animals around him, and Jena could hear scuffling from inside the house.

"Chill out, boys." She shot Caleb a look before she walked inside.

"Children, Amanda?" A quick snarl and a rip came from the kitchen. "You attacked children?"

Another snarl and a high whining sound erupted from the kitchen as someone tried to escape. Jena caught them by their shirttail before they could make it down the hall. It was Missy's sister, Lisette, her body shivering in anticipation as she held back a full shift.

Jena's rage welled up when she saw the rough scar through the tear on Lisette's shoulder, exactly where it would be in her natural form. "A lion with a scar on its shoulder," Low had said. Lisette was one of the lions who had stalked her boys at the Cliff House. "You," she hissed, punching her as she tried to twist out of her hold. Jena kicked Lisette's knees out from under her as she stumbled back, scrambling like a crab into the kitchen where Missy was huddled in a corner and Ted had Amanda in a chokehold against the wall.

"Tell them, Missy," Lisette screeched, crawling to her sister. "Tell them who is responsible!"

Jena heard Caleb and Alex come in behind her.

"Where's Matt?" Caleb asked. Everyone looked at Missy.

"Gone. I don't know where." Her voice was low and hoarse, her pale face was drenched with tears, and three red scratch marks were bleeding on her cheek. She was curled in the corner as if trying to hide.

"The bastard forced her to do it," Amanda hissed around Ted's grip. "It was him. Leave her alone."

Jena stepped closer. "You forced a shift so you had the baby early?"

Missy nodded, her eyes filling with tears.

"Why?"

"He said he'd kill me. Kill me and the baby if I didn't do what he wanted. My girls, he would have hurt my girls." Missy's voice hitched. "He was obsessed. All he could talk about was the hotel. The development. He was obsessed with Alma, said she didn't respect him. Said that she was the only one standing in the way of progress. She'd vote no out of spite because she didn't like him. He—he forced me. I didn't want to go that night."

The taste of bile poisoned Jena's mouth. Caleb put a hand on her shoulder and gently nudged past her. "Why, Missy? Why did he want you there?"

Missy shuddered again and closed her eyes. "He said that he just wanted to talk, but Alma wouldn't talk to him alone. It was the middle of the night on a moon night. We're too wild. But he knew she'd be out there alone. Said she'd be willing to let me in. If she could sense I was weak, that I had just birthed—" Her voice caught. "So I did it. I was so scared. But he was right! I scratched on the door, and Alma looked out. I managed to shift back to my human form, but I was still bleeding and when she saw the blood..."

"She let you in," Jena whispered. "She took pity on you and let you in. And Matt came with you."

"Alma must have seen the blood and—"

"She was worried," Caleb said. "Didn't even think for her own safety. She was trying to help you, wasn't she? What happened?"

"She was furious with Matt. Kept accusing him of doing something to hurt me."

Lisette snarled. "She was right! That animal—"

"Shut up, Lis!" Amanda growled, still in Ted's choke. "Don't talk to them."

Jena walked over and wrenched Amanda's hair so her head jerked forward and her breath was cut off. "Don't talk to me? That's my grandmother he murdered. And *you* covered up for him. You stalked my children like animals. You attacked Caleb in the desert. Why, Amanda?" She let the woman's hair loose and Ted lightened her grip so her cousin could breathe.

"We weren't going to hurt them. We were trying to scare you away. The skinwalker needed to stop asking questions."

Lisette said, "We were just trying to protect Missy. It wasn't her fault."

Missy broke in. "They argued. I could tell Matt was starting to lose his temper. Then Alma said she was going to find my grandfather, tell him that Matt had hurt me and the baby. It would all be over. Matt's career, the hotel. It would all be gone." Jena saw Caleb's eyes narrow as he stood beside her. "Alma shifted, and Matt... He killed her. They shifted at the same time. Alma was flying toward the door, but he jumped up and killed her. There was so much blood!" Missy sobbed. "Then he took off and left me there." She closed her eyes and shuddered, gripping the gold chain she wore at her throat. "I shifted back and ran straight to my sisters' house. The baby... I knew the baby was in danger."

Not right, not right, not right. Jena's instincts screamed at her. It wasn't adding up. None of it made sense!

On the kitchen floor, Lisette crawled to Missy, pulling her sister into her arms. "I know we shouldn't have attacked Jena's boys or Caleb. But we would never have really hurt them. We were trying to scare you off. Trying to protect Missy. Alma was already dead. There was nothing we could do but help our sister."

"You bitch," Jena snarled, and Caleb held her back, keeping her from diving onto Lisette and strangling her with her bare hands. "My grandmother was dead, and you protected her murderer? The same man who hurt your sister? You crazy bitch!"

Alex said, "The rest of the clans will hear about this. I will make sure of it. You think your elders will be able to protect you? No one will trust the cats after your actions. Do you think your family will appreciate that? You've brought dishonor to them by sheltering the one who killed Alma Crowe."

"And I think our grandmother will want to hear that you cornered innocent children as if they were rabbits," Ted added.

Caleb was staring at Missy and Lisette, watching them with narrow eyes.

Lisette sniffed, a haughty look coming to her face when she saw him. "What are you looking at, skinwalker? We protect our own. I don't expect you to understand."

Caleb stepped in front of Jena and crouched down, ignoring Lisette. He stared at Missy. "Missy, where's your husband?"

She sniffed again and more tears rolled down her cheeks. "I—I'm not sure. He left earlier tonight. He didn't say where he was going."

"Did he hurt you again, Missy?" Caleb's voice was soft. Concerned. He gently reached for Missy's hand, but she tried to pull back. She was cradling one arm against her chest, her right hand hidden in the soft material of her yellow cardigan. Caleb pulled gently. "Let me see your hand, Missy. If he's hurt you again..."

Caleb reached for her right hand, and Missy resisted. She tried to turn, but Caleb's persistent fingers closed over her wrist and pulled until Missy's arm was stretched out in front of her, her right hand clenched into a fist.

"Of course your sisters were trying to protect you. Of course they were." Caleb's voice was soft and deadly as he forced Missy's hand to uncurl, revealing the crippled pinky, the finger that had been mangled in a childhood fight. It was missing the tip. No one talked about it; Missy had always been self-conscious about her scarred hand.

But Ted gasped. "Of course! The fourth claw mark."

"What?" Alex and Jena asked at once.

"There were four claw marks on Alma's body," Caleb said. "But they weren't right. I kept forgetting to ask, Jena. At first, I thought there were only three. Odd thing, isn't it? Threw me off at first. But the fourth was there, just... shallower than the others. Broken. Like your finger. And your lies. Your sisters were protecting *you*, Missy. You were the one who killed Alma Crowe."

chapter twenty-six

M issy's lip curled up in a snarl a second before she shifted. Lisette reached over and pushed Caleb back. He tumbled into Jena's legs, knocking her over.

"Go!" she shouted to her sister, who tore through the house in sleek lion form. Missy was smaller than the average mountain lion, but quick. She was out the kitchen door and down the hall before Caleb could recover. Jena quickly shot up and ran after her.

"Jena!"

"I'll track her!" She shouted, pulling off her shirt. "Just listen for me. And don't forget your gun this time."

Caleb turned to see Ted swing her arm back, knocking Amanda's head against the wall when she punched her. Amanda's eyes rolled back and she slumped to the ground before Ted rounded on Lisette, who was still crouched in a corner of the kitchen. "Stay where you are," she hissed. "You and your sister are mine."

Alex said, "I'll get help. My father will gather the clans and take them to the canyon. Caleb, try to lead her there."

Caleb rolled his eyes. "I'll see what I can do."

Alex hesitated for only a moment, then walked over and pulled Ted into a searing kiss. He stepped back and started unbuttoning his shirt.

"Really?" Ted asked. "Can't ruin your shirt, even in this situation?"

He glared at her. "I like this one. And so do you. Wouldn't want to ruin it."

Caleb glanced away for a moment and a massive grey timber wolf filled the room, letting out a low growl when Lisette hissed. It swung toward her, baring its teeth and snapping before it moved to Ted, rubbing up against her legs a moment before he galloped out of the room.

"Territorial canine," Ted muttered.

Caleb pulled Lisette up from the floor and shoved her against the counter. "Where's Matt?"

She hadn't been expecting that question. "What?"

"Matt. Where is he?"

"I think he's visiting his parents' house."

"Who clawed Missy's face? Those wounds were fresh. Was it one of you?"

Lisette looked at the ground. "Missy did. As soon as she saw your car pull up."

"You knew exactly who killed Alma Crowe the whole time." Caleb wracked his brain. If Lisette was correct, then Matt probably wasn't going to show up to complicate things. But Caleb had to go after a lion, and a 9 mm was all he had. He pulled it out, racked one in the chamber, then started out the kitchen door.

"Listen for Jena, Chief," Ted said. "She'll find Missy."

The path leading away from the house wasn't hidden. The soft dirt between the mesquite trees clearly showed the prints in the waxing moon. Still, he didn't want to rush. He worked his way through the trees, over the wash, and back farther into the scrubby hills behind the house, following the path where the lion had fled. Caleb tracked by sight, listening for a hawk's scream, but nothing broke the still night air until he heard a rustling in the brush.

He bit back a curse and darted behind a tree. He was at a distinct disadvantage, particularly hunting at night, but he was hoping those reinforcements that Alex was going for showed up early. Caleb tensed until he saw what had made the bushes shake.

It was that damn coyote again.

Letting out a grunt, he stepped back into the path. The coyote looked up at him with fearless black eyes.

"You again?"

The coyote put his nose to the ground and sniffed in a circle before he trotted down the path.

"What? I'm just supposed to follow you?"

The small animal stopped and turned, waiting for Caleb to get with the program.

He rolled his eyes. "Fine. But only because I haven't heard—"

The hawk's scream cut him off. He looked to the coyote, who lifted his head back and gave a long, high-pitched howl as if answering the bird's call. Then he ran toward the canyon and Caleb had to scramble to follow him.

"Wait up!"

Cursing under his breath, he followed the coyote, who was shivering with excitement. The animal paused at every curve, leading Caleb deeper and deeper between the dark red walls. Caleb could smell the water. It was the same canyon where the springs lay, but it turned and twisted, disappearing into dark crevices and dead ends. This was a different branch than he'd ever travelled before. Still the old scent of water and mud permeated the gust of wind and he forced himself to keep running. Just then, he heard the hawk cry directly above him, its terrified shriek the only warning he had before he heard the soft thud behind him.

Caleb turned to see a mountain lion crouched several yards away.

Missy may have not been a big lion, but she was still a lion, and as she slunk toward him, her low growl echoed off the sheer sandstone. He backed away slowly, his hand itching to pull the gun at the small of his back. If he reached, would she pounce? Would one shot even kill her? Why the hell hadn't he taken his shotgun out to Matt and Missy's house in the first place? Oh yeah, he'd been expecting a nice, civilized human arrest where the murderer confessed over coffee and a guilty conscience.

Stupid Caleb.

The coyote yipped to his right, darting into a black sliver in the wall that Caleb hadn't seen before. It was a cave. A narrow one. He'd either be cornered like a tasty, tasty lion treat, or there might just be another way out. Since outrunning the beast wasn't an option and he wasn't dealing with a dumb animal, Caleb decided to follow the weird little coyote. He faked left for a second, throwing the lion off balance, before he dove for the black sliver in the canyon wall, scraping his back and stomach as he slid into the cave.

Missy's paw swiped into the cavern, but she couldn't squeeze in. Should he just shoot her? There were still so many questions and Caleb wanted answers. The memory of Missy at the diner with her tiny blond daughter came to mind. She was a mother. A wife. There had to be another way.

His eyes swept around the dark cavern while Missy prowled the entrance. The coyote had disappeared into the black and Caleb felt along the cold sandstone, going farther and farther into the darkness.

It was pitch-black, but the air was fresh, which made Caleb think it was a passageway of some kind and not a dead end.

"Coyote?" he hissed into the darkness. "Hey!"

He squeezed his eyes shut, even though he couldn't see a thing. At least the passageway had widened. "Why am I talking to a coyote?"

Caleb heard a muffled kind of cough from the blackness. Actually, it didn't sound like a cough.

"Are you laughing at me, you mutt?" The coughing came again. The damn animal was laughing at him. He kept walking, feeling his way through the passage with both hands spread out in front of him. He stumbled a few times over rocks and bumped his forehead even more, but he kept walking. Just as he saw the sliver of midnight blue dotted with stars, an idea began to bloom. Missy would attack him as soon as she got the chance, but if Caleb wasn't himself…

He waited at the entrance to the cave. He could still hear Missy snarling and swiping at the other end of the tunnel. The sound echoed off the rock walls in between panicked screams from Jena overhead. Still Caleb waited. He crouched down near the entrance until he was almost nose-to-nose with the coyote, who sat with a patient expression on its narrow face. He looked into the animal's eyes. The coyote looked back.

Aren't you a skinwalker, cousin?

The familiar voice whispered in his mind, and Caleb blinked.

"Wh—what?" It couldn't be.

Everything happens for a reason.

Caleb was still gaping as the coyote darted out the cave and into the night.

"Everything happens for a reason," he whispered. Then he closed his eyes and focused.

SHE PACED IN FRONT OF THE CAVE, HER SLOUCHING BODY quick and powerful in the silver moonlight. He took care to remain upwind of the lion's keen nose.

"Missy." He made his voice deliberately hoarse. "What are you doing?"

She turned, startled by his appearance. The lion shifted, immediately flowing into a woman's naked form. She wouldn't be as fast now. Maybe he could reason with her, but if he had to draw...

Missy took a step toward him. "Matt?"

"What are you doing?" He did his best impression of the mayor's voice, but he knew it wasn't exactly right. He tried not to talk too loud.

"What are you doing here?" Her eyes were wide and worried. "I sent you to your parents' house! They were supposed to keep you there."

"Why?"

"You know why!"

He shook his head, letting the sorrow fill his eyes, praying she wouldn't discover his deception. He heard Jena squawk from a perch somewhere to his left. She knew it was him, but so far, it looked like Missy was in the dark.

"No, Missy… why?"

Her eyes hardened. "I told you, I'm not leaving. I'm not going to live like that again. My children aren't going to grow up like freaks, Matt. Killing the old lady may not have been your plan, but leaving wasn't mine."

"But—"

"How could you even ask me?" she cried. "You know what it was like when I lived away! You know! And you still asked me to leave with you? Are you insane?"

He didn't know about Matt, but Missy was sure as hell out of her mind. Any thoughts of reasoning with her fled when he caught her wild stare. No remorse for the woman she had murdered. Alma had only been an obstacle.

"You may be squeamish, honey, but I'm not. She had to die. You're the one who told me Thomas Crowe would be on board, and you were right." Suddenly, a desperate smile crossed her face. "You were right! The hotel plan is going to go through and everyone is going to realize how amazing you are. How much you can do for this town. And eventually, it's going to be you in that Elder's seat." She shook her head, stepping a little closer. "So don't feel guilty. You didn't do anything wrong. It was me. It had to happen; you know that."

How often had she had to give her husband this same speech? From the practiced way it rolled off her tongue, he suspected more than once.

"But, Missy—"

"Shhh." She stepped toward him, putting a soft finger across his lips. But as soon as she touched him, she knew he wasn't Matt.

Missy stepped back, her eyes widening in terror before the air around her rippled and Caleb was staring at a mountain lion again.

Elizabeth Hunter

Only this time, she was staring back into the barrel of his gun. He held the 9mm steady on her eyes.

"One shot, Missy. I don't want to, but I will."

She only curled her lip and screamed, the rasping sound filling the canyon as everything happened at once. Missy lunged toward him and Caleb fired, but the bullet only knocked up dust as her body was thrown to the side by the streak of black that hurtled through the air, talons tearing into Missy's shoulders as the bird threw herself against the lion.

It wasn't a hawk. It was an eagle.

Magnificent in its aim, the lion jerked away, twisting its body as it tried to free itself of the raptor's iron grip, but the giant golden eagle held, the long claws digging into the thick skin and its wings beating against the lion's face as Jena screamed in rage.

"Jena!" Caleb had his gun out, but was afraid to use it when Jena and Missy were so twisted up. He'd have to hit Missy's head or the thick hide of the lion would protect her from any real injury. But if he fired on the head or soft belly, he could hit Jena.

"Jena, get out of here!"

The bird was locked onto the lion, the vengeful screams filling the canyon as Caleb looked on helplessly. Missy finally twisted, baring her belly to him as her right paw reached up, claws bared, to swipe at the bird that clung to her shoulders. A final scream echoed through the night as red wells of blood burst from the eagle's underbelly.

"NO!" He fired just as the eagle fell to the ground with a soft thud. He heard a cracking sound as the mountain lion rolled on top of the eagle, bleeding from the shoulder. Then a gasping sob as Missy shifted back to reveal a twisted body beneath her.

Missy was sobbing and holding her shoulder as Caleb shoved her away to lift Jena in his arms.

"Oh shit! Oh Jena, what did you do?"

Four claw marks dug through her breasts and belly. One arm and another leg hung at awkward angles, but she was smiling, a trickle of blood leaking from her lip. She choked, trying to speak as he held her.

His body shifted back to himself and he pulled her closer, pushing back the instinctive nausea as Missy moaned and rolled in the dirt.

"Don't talk." Caleb looked around desperately as her blood soaked his shirt. "I gotta get you help. Don't talk! Just hold on."

Finally, she mumbled, "Good shot, baby." And then her eyes closed.

chapter
twenty-seven

S he probably shouldn't have closed her eyes; that just made him panic.

"Jena!" he screamed. "Wake up!" He shook her a little.

"Ow." She groaned. "Cut it out."

"You're bleeding so much. Too much." He tore off his shirt and pressed it to her belly. *Owww.* She winced and pressed her face into his chest. He smelled right. He was perfect for her. How had she been so lucky to find another good one? After Lowell had died, she'd figured that her luck had just run out. After all, you could only expect to meet one man that perfect for you in your lifetime, right? How odd to realize that you were in love with someone when your insides had just been ripped out.

"Spilled my guts," she mumbled. "Literally. But you're just right. And you feel right and you smell right. But you gotta work on the language, buddy. It's not good for the boys." What was hurting so bad? Something hurt in deep, thick waves that seemed to come and go. And the black stuff around the edge of her vision...

"Jena..." He lifted her up, choking back what sounded like a sob. "Don't try to talk. Listen to me, honey. Try to stay awake."

"Of course I'm gonna stay awake. I'm naked and you're shirtless... I think. Where are we?"

What was wrong with her eyes? Her eyes were always good. Caleb did that weird snort-sobbing thing again and lifted her up.

Owwwww.

"Caleb…" She groaned. "What the hell—?"

"Careful now." He gave her a strangled laugh. "You're gonna need your own swear jar."

"I don't think I want to go anywhere." The shock was beginning to wear off and a blistering pain radiated from her belly. She dug her fingers into his arms. "Caleb, put me down."

"Nope. Sorry."

"Where are we going?"

"Out of here. Shit," he muttered. "How many dead ends are in this damn canyon?"

"Lots. There's lots of dead ends." She winced as he turned and walked back to where she could hear Missy moaning in pain. Why was she…? Oh, that's right, that bitch had killed her grandmother. Good, she deserved to moan. She hoped it hurt. A lot. Jena knew she had liked digging her claws into the cat. It had felt great. She only wished she'd been able to dig in a little more…

Just as they were getting closer to where Missy lay, Jena shivered. The air whispered secrets. She could smell the scent of the water, and the prickling lifted the hair on her arms as she felt the magic roll through her.

"Caleb, put me down."

"Jena, I gotta get you out of here. I know it hurts, but—"

"Put me down." Her voice was strong and firm. "Lay me down, Caleb. I'll be fine."

Ted's voice came from down the canyon. "Put her down, Caleb. If she changes, you don't want to be holding her." Footsteps approached as Caleb set her on the ground, still holding her in his lap. Idiot. He'd pay with talon marks on his thighs if she shifted. But something inside her gut told her that would not be a good idea.

She felt others approaching and heard Ted call out, "Someone run down to the fresh spring and get her some water! Jena—" Ted's voice was closer now"—this is way worse than a fracture or your average cut. Do *not* shift. You hear me? I don't want your insides rolling around. Someone get some spring water. Fast!"

Water sounded good. Water would make her feel better. It always did. Who told her that? Her grandmother? Maybe... She felt herself drifting off, but her eyes cleared a little when she felt Caleb's arms tense. There was a shuffling noise in the sand. She could feel them before she heard the rattles.

Caleb said, "Jena? There are rattlesnakes. Lots of them."

"Shhh. It's okay." She tapped his mouth with a dirty finger. "The clans are gathering. The Quinns always come first."

"What do I do?"

"Just hold very still. You're not their prey. And I'm gonna try not to shift. It's hard with so many close." The more shifters gathered, the more the magic pressed on her. Her skin hummed with it. She could feel a terrible lightness in her bones.

First, one rattler slid across the dust, then another, another and another and another until the canyon filled with the echo of the snakes' ominous hum. Caleb tried not to jerk when one of the Quinns slid past, brushing his leg as it curled along the ground. They slid toward Missy, their twisted bodies circling her as their tongues flicked out to taste the terror that began to permeate the dry air.

The wolves came next. Treading close on silent paws, they danced delicately between the snakes, one brushing up and licking her face as he passed.

"Hey, Alex."

Allie, trim and alert in her fox form, came to sit at Caleb's feet, her dark nose twitching in the night air. She tensed a moment before the sound of human feet approached. Jena saw Ted bend over her.

"Heya, Teodora Vasquez. How you doing, gorgeous?" Jena smiled. "You're an awesome friend, you know?"

"You sound drunk." She kneeled next to her. "You're still conscious. That's good." Ted twitched, her movements jerky and awkward.

"Don't get all furry on me now, kitty cat."

"You know, even when you're two steps away from dying, you're still a smartass."

Caleb said, "What? Damn it, Ted—"

"Caleb, I'm joking. Now get back and let me see." Jena felt gentle hands prodding and poking. "The bleeding is slowing down. Drink this. That should help until he can get you to a hospital."

"No hospital," Jena groaned.

"You're going to the hospital. Caleb press here and hold."

"Are you okay?" Jena heard him ask.

Her vision was still cloudy, but she could feel the magic growing. It radiated around her, but still, she didn't shift.

"Is she going into shock?"

"The water should help." Ted put a bottle to her lips and forced her to drink. "Sorry, *mamá*, but you're gonna feel worse before you feel better."

She mumbled, "Is my dad coming?"

"Yes. The elders are bringing her mate. Take this blanket. Press here."

Jena blinked when she saw the circle growing. The cats surrounded the pack, hanging back from the traitor their clan offered up. Good, she thought. That was good. And there were Ollie and his bears, surrounding them all, backs to the murderer, muzzles pointed out to guard those carrying out the swift justice of the clans.

Alma's death would not go unpunished.

"Missy Marquez." Jena heard her father and other human voices. She blinked up as Ted and Caleb tried to pour more water into her mouth. She swallowed some and shook her head. It only made her feel worse. The ache in her stomach turned sharper. Her ears cleared more.

The canyon was filled with the shifters. The snakes ringed Missy's prone form, now shaking and shivering in fear.

"Please," she sobbed. "Please."

Jena sat up and croaked, "Did you let Alma beg before you killed her? Shut the hell up."

The wolves raised their hackles and snarled at the cat's weakness.

Jena could hear the smaller canines' excited yips and barks as they hung back, resigned to let their alphas strike first. She felt Caleb move under her. He was trying to sit her up. "Ted? What the hell is happening here?"

"Don't try to interfere, Caleb." Thomas's voice rang out. "This isn't your justice."

Missy sobbed and the coyotes howled in excitement. Jena blinked her eyes and tried to sit up. Her mate was young. He didn't understand...

"Tom, you can't do this!" Caleb yelled. "Let me arrest her. She has children. A family—"

"No!" Missy screamed. "Not a human jail!"

"There won't be any human jail," Jena heard Old Quinn say, his voice hard and mean. He had loved Alma. Caleb told her. Poor Quinn. Poor Caleb. He didn't understand.

"I can't stand by and watch you do this, Tom."

Jena turned and pulled his ear down to her lips. She had to make him understand.

"Caleb," she whispered. "These are my people. This is our justice."

His voice was hard. "But Jena—"

"Do you love me?"

Caleb put a hand on her cheek and met her eyes. "Of course I do."

This part was harder.

"Do you accept me?" He paused, his fingers suddenly still against her cheek when he understood what she was asking. "Do you accept all of me?"

There would be no day in court for Missy Marquez. Maybe if the offense hadn't cut so deeply. Maybe if the guilt was less certain. But not that night. That night, the judgment of the clans had been rendered. Jena heard Matt groaning as he watched his mate. He was held by two of the bear clan in human form. Missy's parents and sisters were on the other side, sobbing quietly while the cat elders guarded them. Her father towered over them with the rest of the town elders on either side.

She saw Caleb look around the moonlit canyon. He looked at her, then at the wailing woman surrounded by snakes and wolves. His shoulders sank a little, but his mouth firmed. "I will accept you." The coyotes yipped again and Caleb stood, cradling Jena in his arms as he addressed her father. "But I'm not gonna stand by while Jena bleeds."

"See to your mate, shifter." Only Jena would notice the slight wavering in her father's tone.

Ted spoke rapidly as they started out of the canyon, each step jarring her a little more. Shouldn't the water have been making her better? It just felt worse. Her head was clear and those nice sleepy waves had backed off, only to be replaced by sharp, jolting pain that radiated from her stomach to her toes.

"Caleb, it hurts. Slow down."

He ignored her. "Do I keep giving her the water? How do I get out of here?"

"Yes on the water, and take my car," Ted said. "It's the Jeep right at the mouth of the canyon. It's not the most comfortable ride, but it'll get you to the main road the fastest. Have her keep drinking as much as she can. She's gonna hurt worse, but it'll keep her awake. You need to get to Indio. And keep that shirt pressed against the wound as much as you can. She should be okay."

"*Should* be? What the hell does that mean? Aren't you coming with us?"

"She can't," Jena murmured. "She's about to shift."

Jena could hear them approaching. She bit her lip, the pain cutting through her baser instincts. "Baby, get me out of here," she said in a desperate voice.

Caleb clutched her tighter. "What's wrong with her?"

She could feel the manic energy radiating off Ted. Her friend was practically jumping out of her skin. "The crows are coming," Ted whispered. "All the clans are here now. Get her to the hospital. Jena, don't do it! You'll hurt yourself more if you shift with those injuries."

Jena groaned. The old magic rolled through her. The whispers came on the still night air. She felt the tingles in her body as Caleb started to run.

Fly, fly, fly.

The flapping sounded overhead, and she lifted her face to the sky.

Rip. Tear. Rend.

Black shadows called to her.

Fly, fly, fly.

Ravens. Crows. Vultures. The carrion eaters had come for their prey. They would pick the bones of the murderer who had killed the old one. But first, they would watch her die. Jena felt Caleb tense when he heard the first tortured scream split the night air.

He kept running.

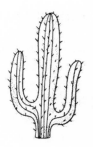

chapter
twenty-eight

Focus.

Ignore the screams of the woman.

Focus.

Ignore the howls and caws.

Focus.

Open the door. Put Jena in the car.

Focus. Focus. Focus.

"Jena." He patted her cheek and her eyes blinked open again. She was pale. Way too pale.

"I'm okay. I don't feel the urge to shift anymore."

Caleb wasn't worried about her shifting.

"She should be okay."

Should be? Should be wasn't good enough, Doctor Ted.

"Jena?" He tilted her head up and poured a little more water down her throat. "Jena, wake up."

She grunted and turned her head. "Stop it, Caleb."

He pushed her legs into the car, then pressed the bloody shirt to her stomach again. It was red with fresh blood, the wounds must have opened again as he ran. Caleb saw her wince when he pressed, but he only pushed harder, pulling the seat belt out and wadding up a jacket he found stuffed behind the seat.

"Stay awake, Jena." He used his hard voice. No cajoling for her. "You hear me? You better do what I tell you."

Any other time, she'd hit him for talking to her like that. Caleb tried not to panic.

Stay awake.

Stay alive.

Heal.

Stay with me.

Her eyelids flickered closed as he pulled the seatbelt all the way out before cinching it to her as tightly as he could. It was the best he could do and still drive.

"Jena!" He slapped her cheek. Once. Didn't work. Harder. She opened her eyes with a gasp.

"Oh, you are going to pay for that, you asshole."

There, that was better. He smiled and pressed a hard kiss to her mouth. "Promise?"

He shut the door before she could hit him back.

Focus.

Drive the car. Dodge the cactus. Climb the edge of the wash.

He was thankful Ted had sprung for the sport suspension and four-wheel drive by the time he hit the pavement. He peeled out, dust flying off the dirty Jeep, the wind whipping Jena's hair around her face. He reached over and tried to tuck it behind her ears, but it didn't do much. He kept driving.

Focus.

"Jena, drink some water."

"Don't want to."

"Don't make me pull this car over."

She snickered. "You sound like a dad."

His heart jerked in his chest. Who was watching Aaron and Low? Probably Cathy. He had to remember, as foreign as the canyon had felt only minutes before, Cambio Springs was just a little town. Half populated by ordinary people, half populated by people who turned into animals and ate murderers for sport. And those were the respectable ones.

Jena was tilting the bottle up, but most of the water was trickling down the side of her mouth.

"Try to drink a little more."

"I'm sorry you had to see that, Caleb."

He fought past the tightness in his throat. "What? I've seen you spill stuff before. I love you despite the clumsiness."

"That's not what I meant."

"I know. Don't try to change the subject."

She frowned. "There was a subject?"

Caleb forgot for a moment what had happened. Forgot where he was. Forgot she was injured. A single question burned his mind.

"You love me, Jena Crowe?"

She looked over at him and he knew the answer. He could see it shining in her eyes. "Course I do. I think it was the canned cheese that did it."

He choked out a harsh laugh, and her eyes flickered closed.

"Jena!" What the hell could he do? It was too far to Indio. The blood had soaked through the jacket that lay across her chest and belly. Caleb reached over and yanked on a chunk of her hair. "Wake up!"

"Damn," she croaked. "You're a mean one."

"Only when I need to be." He ignored the sheriff's car that passed him and swung around, flipping on his lights.

"Ooooh, you're in trouble now, Chief Not-just-passing-through. Got the po-po after you."

He tried to push back the terror at how weak her voice sounded. "The po-po?"

"Yeah, I'm down like that. I know how the kids talk these days."

Caleb watched as the cruiser's lights came closer. He reached for the phone he saw in the center console, hoping it had some charge. "I'm gonna call the sheriff's office, Jena. Just hold on."

"Do I look like I'm going anywhere?"

He punched in Dev's number and waited.

"Yeah?" Second ring. Thank God.

"Dev? This is Caleb Gilbert. I need you to call your department right now. One of your boys is following a late model green Jeep out on the highway headed to Indio. I cannot stop. I've got Jena in the car and she was attacked by a mountain lion. I'm headed to the hospital going about one-ten and I'm not going to stop. So tell them to stay out of the way."

"I'm on it." The sheriff's deputy hung up and Caleb put the phone back down. "Jena? You awake?"

"Yeah."

"Talk to me." He shook his head, willing the panic back. "Honey, please talk to me."

"If you can turn into anyone, can you try George Clooney some time? Because that would be awesome."

He blinked. "Did you... did you really just ask me if I could turn into George Clooney?"

"Brad Pitt would be cool, too."

"Hey!"

"You asked me to talk. I'm talking." She winced as he went over a bump.

"Shh." He reached over to squeeze her hand. "All this talk of George is making you lightheaded. Maybe you should be quiet."

"Make up your mind. Talk to me, Jena. Shut up, Jena..." She trailed off and her hand went limp in his.

"Jena!"

Her head jerked up and she blinked at him with owl eyes. "I want you to stay and help the boys."

He cleared his throat and ignored the panicked sound in her voice. "You know I will. I'm not going anywhere. You're gonna have to evict me at this point, and we all know that takes a long time."

"If something happens—"

"*Nothing* is going to happen! Ted said you were going to be okay."

"If Ted's wrong... Just don't leave. It might not be what you want to do, but they'll need you. And you'll need them, too."

"Jena—" He choked. "Just—just shut up, will you? Nothing's going to happen to you."

"Promise me."

"I'm not promising anything! I'm an ornery asshole and you're just gonna have to stick around to keep me in line." He winced when he went over a pothole that made her yelp and clutch her side. "See? Asshole. And you're going to marry me and make me behave in polite society."

"I am?"

He could see the lights of the city in the distance. "Bet your ass you are. We're going to get married and I'm gonna love you so much it'll annoy the shit out of you, but I'm not gonna care because you're gonna be my wife, and Bear and Low are gonna be my kids—" He tried not to choke. "And I'll be the happiest bastard on the planet, Jena Crowe. You just stay alive, okay?"

"You're cocky... even when I'm bleeding out."

"You're not bleeding out!" He rammed his foot to the floor, barely noticing that the sirens had stopped behind him and the police car had pulled ahead, turning on its lights and giving them an escort as they hit the outskirts of the city. They blasted through the first set of lights. All traffic pulled over to the side of the road as they tore into town.

"Fuck that, Jena! You better not die, you hear me? I love you too damn much. And I love those boys. And if you go and die and leave us alone, I'm gonna be so pissed off at you. So don't you dare die. Don't close your eyes..." He saw the hospital. "Don't even blink." He chanced a glance across the car, but her head was rolled to the side and her hand was limp on her stomach, stained with fresh red blood. "Jena, wake up!" He tore through the parking lot and screeched into the emergency bay to see a team of doctors and nurses waiting with a stretcher. "Jena!"

He jerked to a halt and then it was out of his hands. A man pulled open the door and two women caught Jena as she slumped out of the Jeep. Within moments, she was strapped to a board and going through the doors, doctors and nurses shouting as they walked.

No one looked at him. No one told him she was going to be okay. Caleb lowered his head to the steering wheel and screamed.

HE BLINKED AND LOOKED AROUND WHEN HIS HEAD LIFTED. Jena was in a hospital bed, out cold. But nothing was hooked up to her. There was no blood anywhere. And it wasn't night anymore. In fact, they weren't in the hospital, either. The bed was in the middle of a canyon. Red cliffs rose on either side of him and soft trees lined the edges of a creek that trickled by. He heard a laugh and looked up.

"You should see your face right now." Charlie laughed and snickered just the way Caleb remembered him. Not wasted away and sick. Healthy. His cousin was sitting across from him on the other side of Jena's bed.

"We're not dead."

"Of course not, stupid."

"So why are you here?"

Charlie nodded toward Jena. "She's a portal. One of the special ones. When she's around, I can show up like this. I just have to..." He looked around the canyon. "Alter things a bit. Do you remember this place?"

"Of course."

"Remember Dad taking us here?"

"There was a sing. I remember that part. But it was at night." Caleb looked around. It was a canyon in Arizona. A sacred place. His uncle had done a Blessing Way there for a friend.

"He loves you so much. It kills him that you left."

Caleb looked across at the cousin that he'd sacrificed. "I had to. Don't they understand?"

"Some do. Some don't. I understand why you stayed." Charlie nodded toward a sleeping Jena. "She's gorgeous, man."

"Hands off."

His cousin only laughed. "And serious magic. Serious stuff. It's in her bones and shit. Dad borrowed magic. You borrowed magic—"

"No, I didn't."

Charlie rolled his eyes. "Of course you did. You just didn't know it. It came as natural as breathing for you. He wanted you to follow him, you know? Not me. It was always you."

"I didn't want to."

"Doesn't matter. That magic clings to you, cousin. You can try running away, but it finds you. And when it found you here..." Charlie trailed off, a sly look in his eyes.

Caleb's eyes widened. "It *was* you."

His cousin tried to look innocent. "What are you talking about?"

"That fucking coyote, Charlie. That was you. I should have known. Trickster god, my ass. I knew that thing wasn't normal. Why'd you lead me to the water? Did you know what it would do?"

Charlie only smiled. "I led you where you needed to be. Maybe I knew what would happen. Maybe I didn't. But that magic following you..." His face turned grim. "It was going to poison you, cousin. You were a little darker every day. But the water... it cleaned you up. Drew the magic inside. Made it a part of you, not some shadow hanging on."

"Is it evil?" Caleb hesitated. "Like Grandma said?"

"Do you feel evil?"

"No."

Charlie's eyes looked old then, older than even his grandmother's. "Your magic is what you make it, Caleb. Just like any part of you. You can use it for right. You can use it for wrong. But you're you." He smiled. "So you'll use it for right. I'm not worried."

"Why didn't I turn into an animal like the rest of them?"

He shrugged. "Hell if I know. It's not science, dude. This shit has a mind of its own."

Charlie stood, as if he was ready to leave. "Where are you going?"

"Away." The bright day around him was starting to fade. "But don't worry. I'll visit again. Just keep hanging around her, and I'll be able to see you without the fur."

His eyes darted back to Jena's still face. "She's gonna be okay?"

Charlie just shrugged, like it was no big deal. "Of course she is. What kind of happy ending would this be if your girl bit it? That would suck."

His cousin may have been dead, but he hadn't changed much. "I miss you, brother."

Charlie stuck his hands in his pockets as he started to fade. "I'm sorry I made you do it, Caleb. I'm really sorry."

"Charlie—"

"Don't worry. I'll see you around."

CALEB WOKE TO SEE THE MONITORS HOOKED TO JENA STILL humming normally. Low had pulled up another chair and was leaning on one shoulder as Aaron curled in Caleb's lap. He wanted to stay awake. There was something important he needed to tell Jena. Something about the past...

He just couldn't quite remember.

The steady beeping of the monitors lulled him back to sleep, and Caleb drifted into a dreamless slumber.

chapter
twenty-nine

Jena blinked open her eyes. There were florescent lights above her. Where was she? She hated florescent lights. They hummed; she didn't care what Allie said. Gave her a headache. She had a hell of a headache. Why was she staring at florescent lights with a headache? And beeping. There was beeping.

She closed her eyes. Opened them again. Hospital. The last time she'd been in a hospital was when she'd had Aaron. And then with Lowell... Was Lowell here? She moved her head to the side. *Owwww.* Even the small movement made her ache. She let out a low breath and that hurt, too. From the corner of her eye, she saw someone. Turning her head farther, she saw the dark window of the hospital and Caleb.

Not Lowell. *Caleb.* Caleb, who she loved. Tears came to her eyes, but she couldn't reach up to wipe them away. He was stretched out in a crummy hospital chair with Aaron splayed on his lap. The seven-year-old's legs dangled awkwardly into his brother's chair, which was pulled up close to Caleb's so Low could rest his head on the man's shoulder. They were all sleeping. Her man. Her boys. She sniffed again and Caleb's eyes shot open.

His face split into a smile. "You're awake. Is it for real this time?"

"Did I wake up before?"

Elizabeth Hunter

He nodded. "Just for a few minutes. You owe Bear about twenty bucks for the swear jar."

She laughed a little, then winced. "Laughing's not a good idea right now. I don't remember what happened."

"You got jumped by a big-ass mountain lion. You remember that part?"

She took a shallow breath and it all came flooding back. Missy's flight. The canyon. Rage filled her when the lion had pounced on her mate. She'd shifted to the strongest thing she knew, then plunged. She could remember the feel of the thick pelt beneath her claws. The screaming. The bullet—

"Is she dead?" Her eyes flicked toward the door. "Is it safe to talk?"

"I haven't seen anyone for a bit, but..." He cleared his throat and glanced at the boys. "You were lucky. I don't think Missy made it out of the canyon. I had to race patrol cars to get you here. You... uh." His voice broke a little. "Your heart stopped once, but you're gonna be okay. You had pretty serious internal injuries and there was a nicked artery. That's why your heart..."

He looked about two seconds away from breaking, so Jena said, "But I'm gonna be okay, right?"

Caleb nodded and shifted as Aaron snuggled closer.

"I love you," Caleb said in a rough voice. "Do you remember that?"

She nodded. "I love you, too."

"I'm holding you to it."

"Good."

They were sitting quietly, just smiling at each other when Ted entered. She looked between the two of them, keeping her voice quiet, so as not to wake the boys.

"You're awake for real now, I'm guessing, or he wouldn't be smiling like that. How are you feeling?" Ted had her doctor face on and was flipping through a chart at the base of Jena's bed.

"I feel like I got clawed up by a big cat."

Ted cocked an eyebrow. "Can't imagine why. You have two fractures in your left leg and your left arm was broken. That must have been a hell of a fall. The gashes in your abdomen are healing well." She lowered her voice. "In fact, you're going to leave the hospital against medical advice by tomorrow or we're going to have a lot of curious people who want to know how you heal bones so fast. Got it?"

"Got it."

"You're also going to have a lot of scarring on your stomach. I got Dr. Perry to work on you, and he's a whiz at closing, but bikinis are probably not gonna be an option. Sorry."

Jena managed a glance at Caleb. He just winked at her. "Scars are cool. Ask the boys."

She felt herself blush, and Ted snickered. "You're so whipped, Chief."

"Shut up. Let's talk about fancy-fur kissing you the other night. That was interesting."

Ted glared at him and Jena frowned. "Fancy-fur?"

Caleb said, "Didn't you see Alex go all alpha-boy and kiss his woman the other night? Ted loved it. I could tell."

"Shut up, weirdo," Ted muttered.

"I don't remember that. Was I already gone?"

Caleb's eyes danced. "You must have already flown the coop. Metaphorically speaking, of course."

"Of course."

"You guys are too cute for words," Ted said. "You're going to be insufferable together."

They were all whispering, so as not to wake the boys, but Low shifted and mumbled something anyway.

Jena looked at Ted, turning too quickly and jerking the stitches in her stomach. "Okay, fill me in quick. Missy is gone?"

Ted nodded and Caleb said, "Matt confessed to shooting at us as we were leaving Quinn's, but he didn't have any hand in killing Alma. He didn't even mean to get that close to the truck. Killing your grandmother was all Missy. He was just like her sisters, trying to cover for her. He was terrified what would happen to him and the kids if anyone found out."

"And I talked to her sisters," Ted added. "It sounds like Matt was fed up with the Springs. He told Missy if Alma didn't approve the hotel, they were gone. He'd quit and they'd have to live away. Missy panicked. Amanda said she had a hard time in college when she lived in Phoenix. Said she went crazy at the thought of having to hide again."

Jena felt her throat tighten. "But she risked her own baby?"

"Lisette said that Missy called her the morning after she killed Alma with the same story she'd told us, blaming everything on Matt. They... didn't know what to think. Everyone covered for him because Missy asked them to. And... well, they're cats. We're stupidly loyal sometimes."

Caleb said, "Matt shot at us because he thought we'd blame Old Quinn, since we had just left his house. I guess he forgot about you tracking him. He panicked and ran. He's the bobcat you saw that night."

"But he didn't have anything to do with Alma's death?" Jena asked.

"Not that we can tell. And he's spilled his guts about pretty much everything else."

"He's leaving," Ted said quietly. "Taking the kids and leaving town. The Elders didn't want to punish him for his mate's insanity, and they didn't want to leave their kids orphans. They told him not to come back. The children can when they're older, but not him."

"He's banished," she said in a whisper. Jena had heard rumors about shifters who had been banished, but it wasn't something she'd ever seen happen. Matt was cut off from the spring, from his clan. Forever. Despite her grief for Alma, Jena's heart ached for him and his children. "And her sisters?"

"They're gone, too. But they're trying to fight it. Their clan is making restitution to your father for stalking his grandchildren."

"Good," Caleb said with a growl. His arm tightened around Aaron.

"So it's done," Jena leaned back and closed her eyes. "It's done." She could feel the tears gather at the corners, then slip down. She heard shifting around; then Caleb was next to her. She could smell him. Feel his hands on her cheeks. His lips on her forehead.

"It's okay, honey," he whispered. "It's okay now."

"She's still gone," Jena sniffed. "Alma's still gone."

"I know." He tucked her head under his chin. "But she'd be so proud of you, Jena. You were amazing back there. An eagle? What the hell? That was scary and cool at the same time."

"You were mad at me because I got in the way and you couldn't shoot her."

"Only a little. I still like you, though."

Jena's laugh broke into a quiet sob. She shoved a hand into her mouth and bit down to stop, but she couldn't. Caleb leaned down over her, embracing her as best he could in the horrible hospital bed. He was whispering in her ear.

"...and I love you so much. I'm so glad I came to this crazy town. So relieved you're okay. I was going a little nuts at first, but then you woke up the first time. Cussed me out because I started laughing. Do you remember that? I love you, Jena Crowe. I'm gonna make you so damn happy. And I love those boys. I think they like me, too. Low even stopped giving me the evil eye when I kiss you. You were unconscious, so you probably didn't notice—"

"Caleb," she whispered.

"Yeah?"

"Shut up. Kiss me and shut up."

He smiled as he wiped the tears from her cheeks, cupped her face, and gave her the sweetest kiss in the world. Her lips were cracked from the dry hospital air, his face was rough with stubble, but it was perfect.

"Were you serious about marrying me?"

"I was worried you'd forgotten about that part. You were pretty out of it. Hell yeah, I'm serious."

Ted cleared her throat. "Why don't I take the boys out of here? Cathy called a few minutes ago from their hotel. I think they're coming by to pick them up."

"No." Jena glanced at them, not wanting them out of her sight. "They're okay. I don't mind."

"No, it's a good idea," Caleb said. "They've been here almost as much as I have. Frankly, Low's starting to stink."

The boy mumbled, "I heard that, dumbass."

"Hey!" Jena barked. "Watch it, kid."

Caleb walked over and smacked him lightly on the back of the head. "Oh no, he must have been delirious, Jena. Didn't know what he was saying, right Low?"

The boy squirmed. "Right." Then his eyes turned to Jena's and all was forgiven. Wordlessly, she held out her arms and Low ran to them, a little boy again. "You're okay. Really okay?"

"I am," she soothed. "I'm not going anywhere, buddy."

"Bear said you were going to be okay, but I was still scared."

"Never bet against Bear."

She felt him laugh a little. "Right. You're really okay?" He pulled away from her.

"I'm sore and tired, but I'm gonna be fine. We found out what happened to Grandma Alma and my family is safe. I'm going to be just fine."

"Good." He glanced over his shoulder at Caleb. "He's all right, you know?"

"I like him."

Low rolled his eyes and blushed a little. "Yeah, I heard. I'm gonna go back to sleep."

"Take a shower first," Caleb said.

"Shut up—" He glanced at Jena. "I mean, thanks for the advice. And trust me, you're one to talk. Wake up, Bear."

"Mama?" Bear slowly woke up and ambled over, spending a few sleepy moments curled in bed with Jena. "I knew you'd be okay."

Tom and Cathy arrived and slowly, the room filled with loud voices, excited whispers, and the general chaos that Jena had come to associate with the people she loved. Quiet rooms made her think of death and sickness. But this... She looked around with a smile.

She was alive. Her body and—for the first time in years—her heart. Her children. Her parents. Caleb. All together, and it was just right.

Somewhere in the middle of it, he pulled up a chair next to her and sat down. Caleb held her hand, leaned his head against hers, and watched Ted and Cathy, Tom and his grandsons, and even a few of the nurses, talk about Jena's amazing recovery. She squeezed his hand and he squeezed back.

"Hey, Jena?"

"Yeah?"

"Marry me."

"That's not a question, Chief Not just-passing-through."

"Please?"

She bit her lip to hold in the grin. "Why not?"

chapter
thirty

Six months later…

I t was quiet. Caleb sat up in bed, wondering what was wrong. Why
was it so quiet?

The morning light lit up the room, turning the white blinds a pearly
grey that glowed in the darkness. He glanced around at Jena's
bedroom. Their bedroom. Then down at the woman sleeping next
to him.

It was fine. It was just quiet and he'd woken up early. The old house
creaked a little and Caleb heard a faint tapping on the roof. It was
spring in the desert and they'd been getting sporadic showers that
turned the desert to startling colors. The cactuses bloomed and yellow
flowers sprinkled the trees.

He lay back and listened to the rain, pulling Jena closer and fiddling
with the simple wedding band on his left hand. Caleb closed his eyes
and smiled.

"Why are you awake?" she whispered.

"Why are you?"

"I wake up at the drop of a hat. You know that."

"No hats here. My wife has a tempestuous relationship with
hats."

He felt her smile against his chest. His hand stroked up and down her back, teasing the strap of her nightgown.

"Caleb," she teased, "what are you doing?"

"Taking advantage of my wife."

She bit her lip to keep from laughing. "You should let me sleep. You know I need it."

"I should." His fingers slipped over her shoulder, down her back, then teased under her arm until he felt the sensitive underside of her breast. She shivered a little. "But I'm not going to. I'm shameless, remember?"

Her quiet breath picked up. "You remind me daily." She let out a satisfied sigh when he rolled her onto her back and began to kiss her neck. He slipped the nightgown farther down. The skin on her breasts was a perfect, creamy white, set off by dark pink nipples he tasted leisurely. His fingers continued to tease down her body as he licked and nipped until they were sharp, swollen peaks.

"Mmm," she moaned quietly.

"Shhh," he whispered. "Don't want to wake anyone up."

"Mmm-hmm." He grinned. She hated being quiet. It was torture for her. He kept teasing and tasting her breasts, careful to be gentle with the sensitive skin. He used soft lips to nibble at the underside before he continued down her torso, pausing to place soft kisses along the scars that still marked her belly. The memories no longer made his heart freeze. At least, not much. Sometimes, he would forget they were there when they made love. Then he would see them again and the sex would turn urgent. Fierce, as if to remind himself that she was alive. He was alive. She was his, and she was safe.

Jena twisted her fingers in his hair, holding him close as he hovered over her. He slipped his hands to the small of her back and lifted, bringing the swell of her belly to his lips. There she was, snug and safe. Their own little miracle.

"Sleep safe, baby bird," Caleb whispered against Jena's skin.

He kissed down to the juncture of her thighs, teasing Jena with soft kisses and lazy licks, forcing her to bite the heel of her hand the first time she came. Caleb only grinned and kissed the inside of her thigh. "Quiet now."

"Get up here and you try, Chief."

He crawled up, rubbing his chest along hers and sliding in with one hard stroke. He let out a soft grunt when she rocked against him. "Like that?"

"Just like that."

They made love quietly as the birds began to sing outside their window. It was sweet and hot and slow. It wasn't often she woke hungry like this. Jena was working on starting the new restaurant for the resort and most nights were late. But last night had been her night off, and it was just her and him and the boys, watching a movie on the couch until Jena had drifted off to the sound of machine gun fire and explosions. Aaron and Low hadn't even noticed.

Speaking of explosions...

She was doing that thing again. Her nails dug into his shoulders and her long legs were wrapped around his waist as she dug her heels in at just the right angle and—

"Oh, fu—" She slapped her hand over his mouth, grinning wickedly as he tried to muffle his shout.

Caleb was still panting when he rolled over and pulled her on top of him. "Holy... Woman, I'm not sure it's legal for you to be so damn good at that."

"I'm still learning what buttons to push, Chief." She leaned down and nipped at his ear. "Imagine what it'll be like with more practice."

More practice sounded like music to his ears. Caleb let her slide to his side and curl up. She was just at the point where lying on her stomach was starting to be uncomfortable with the baby. She was only about four months and seemed totally relaxed about the whole situation. He had to admit it was nice that one of them knew what they were doing. He spent most of his time trying not to feel like a giant idiot about the whole thing.

"Do you really think it's a girl?" she mumbled.

"Bear does, and I don't bet against Bear."

"We'll have to decide on a name, then."

"Catherine?" He loved his mother-in-law. She'd probably get a kick out of the baby named after her.

"No."

"Ted?"

She snickered. "Definitely not."

"Well, we've got time."

"I was thinking... Charlotte." He tilted her head up. There were tears at the corners of her eyes. "We could call her Charlie, if you want."

He'd told her, of course. And he'd seen his cousin a few more times in dreams, but never as an animal again. They would meet out in the desert for a hike or sit out on the front porch and drink a beer. The dreams didn't come often, but Caleb felt like a little bit of his soul got patched up every time he woke from one.

"I like Charlotte," he whispered. "It's a beautiful name."

"Okay."

He held her just a little closer. "Okay."

They lay quiet for a while longer and both dozed a little until a ruckus came from down the hall. It sounded like the boys had woken up.

"*Moooooom!*"

Jena groaned. "It's Saturday. Why don't children see the beauty of sleeping in?"

"They're mutants with immature brains. I think there's scientific evidence that says so."

"Ugh." She rolled to get out of bed. "Why don't they ever call for you? I thought they liked you better than me now."

"Keep telling yourself that, Mom."

She glared at him and threw on a robe. There was more commotion from down the hall. What the heck were those kids doing?

"Mom! I really think you need to come here!" It was Aaron yelling. But no Low. Caleb shot up in bed just as Jena left the bedroom. Was something wrong with Low? He swung his legs over and pulled on some sweatpants when he heard her shout.

"Oh! Oh, buddy. It's okay, just calm down." There was more commotion and... flapping? Caleb's eyes widened.

"Mom, he tried to bite me!"

Screech!

"He tried to peck you, baby. He was just feeling threatened. Stay back."

Screech!

Ho-ly shit. No way. Caleb scrambled down the hall. Aaron was peering into his brother's room with wide eyes. Caleb leaned over Jena, who was standing with her arms out as a large barn owl flapped and hooted.

"Low, stay calm. This is perfectly natural, but I know it's a little scary at first."

Screech!

"Oh wow." Caleb tried not to stare. "Is there... uh, anything I can do to help?"

"He just needs to calm down. The first shift is always a little scary. Bear, get out of here. Give him some privacy."

"This is so cool, Low!" Caleb tried to shove the excited mini-tornado back.

"Now, I want you to concentrate on your own body," Jena said soothingly. "Think about lying still in your bed when you first wake up. Can you do that?"

Screech! The owl didn't look like it was calming down at first. Then, the flapping stopped. The large white owl sat still in Low's rumpled bed. He was staring at Jena intently. Then the familiar watery shimmer covered his body as it lengthened and stretched into the recognizable boy that Caleb had grown to love.

He let out a relieved breath.

Aaron was practically vibrating. "That. Was. So. Cool! I can't wait to shift!"

"Oh my gosh, Mom!" Low pulled a sheet over himself. "I'm naked!"

Jena rolled her eyes. "Well, of course you're naked. You just shifted. It's not like I haven't seen it before."

"Caleb!" Low's panicked eyes sought his. He pulled Jena back.

"Honey, just—"

"Oh for heaven's sake," she protested. "I'm his mother!"

Low yelled, "You better not come back in here, Mom. Caleb?"

"I got this, Jena." He grinned and leaned down to kiss her. "I got this one, okay?"

"You don't shift into an animal."

"I know. But I have been a teenage boy in fear of his mother."

She let out a huff, but then Low called again, "Caleb?"

He cocked his head at her and gave her his most convincing, crooked smile. "Cook him his favorite breakfast?"

Jena shook her head and walked down the hall. "You three gang up on me now."

"But I'm your favorite, right?"

"No way," Aaron said as he chased after Jena, eager for food. "I'm her favorite."

She still hadn't looked back.

"But I'm the best kisser?"

Low shouted from his room, "Caleb, gross!"

He saw Jena's shoulders shaking. Then she turned, a laugh frozen on her face, and took his breath away when she mouthed, *I love you.*

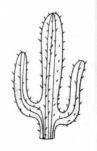

epilogue

Alex McCann pulled a rag from his back pocket and wiped the sweat from his forehead before he slipped his sunglasses back on and turned his attention back to the surveying team he'd hired. They had started at dawn, and the day was quickly growing unbearably hot. They'd have to take a break soon, or the men would pass out.

"Alex!" His foreman, Marcus Quinn, called him over.

"Be right there." He opened his car and pulled a bottle of water from the small ice chest, quickly draining it before he pulled out another.

Marcus was a good guy, one of the few members of the Quinn family who had pulled themselves up and made a real go of it in the outside world. He had a surveying company out of Barstow that did work all over the desert, and Alex was determined to employ as many people from the Springs as possible.

The town was a dying relic that needed fresh air. It wasn't going to get it without help. If he had to pull it into the modern world by determination alone, he would do it. Because the Springs was his home. No matter where he went in the world, this was the only home that mattered.

That determination had driven him for over ten years. He'd sacrificed money, opportunity, friendships—and more—in order to secure the only safe place in the world for his family and his clan. It was his responsibility, and he did it without thought.

But there had been sacrifices, some more painful than others.

From the corner of his eye, he caught the dark green gleam of her Jeep as it turned the corner from Main Street to Spring, heading to the small clinic where she worked. The window was down and she caught him watching her. From across the field, she focused her cat eyes on him.

Teodora Vasquez.

His blood hummed, and he felt every hair on his body rise in awareness. Unconsciously, he lifted his nose to try to catch her scent. She had her sunglasses on and her mouth was pursed in a disapproving pout. He'd bitten those lips, kissed them with fierce abandon, felt soft flesh turn hard when she kissed him back. That morning, she sneered a little and dangled her fingers toward him in a saucy wave.

They'd gone back and forth for years. Friends. Then lovers. Enemies. Lovers again. She was the dominating female presence in his life. The one woman that all others were compared to. He and Ted were currently trying to be friends again, according to her.

But some sacrifices had been harder than others, and Alex McCann wasn't leaving again.

Friends.

He gave her retreating vehicle a predatory smile.

Right.

For more information about the Cambio Springs series, please visit ElizabethHunterWrites.com.

acknowledgments

Many thanks to all the usual suspects.

Thanks to my amazing pre-readers, Kristine M. Todd, Nichole Chase, Sarah, Kelli, and Gen. The sheer volume of the neuroses you handle gracefully when I'm writing and editing is a wonder to behold.

Thanks to my editing team, Amy and Cassie at The Eyes for Editing, who clean up my prose, slap me over the head with proper punctuation, and send my books out into the world looking pretty.

And many thanks to my cover artist, Gene Mollica, who really captured my vision for the character and the book with his artwork. Beautifully done!

Thanks to all those who are so supportive and helpful in my career. Particularly my agent, Jane Dystel, and the whole team at Dystel and Goderich Literary Management. My writing friends (you know who you are), and most of all, my family.

about the author

ELIZABETH HUNTER is a ten-time *USA Today* and international best-selling author of romance, contemporary fantasy, and paranormal mystery. Based in Central California and Addis Ababa, Ethiopia, she travels extensively to write fantasy fiction exploring world mythologies, history, and the universal bonds of love, friendship, and family. She has published over forty works of fiction and sold over a million books worldwide. She is the author of the Glimmer Lake series, Love Stories on 7th and Main, the Elemental Legacy series, the Irin Chronicles, the Cambio Springs Mysteries, and other works of fiction.

ELIZABETHHUNTERWRITES.COM

also by elizabeth hunter

Shadows and Gold

Imitation and Alchemy

Omens and Artifacts

Obsidian's Edge (anthology)

Midnight Labyrinth

Blood Apprentice

The Devil and the Dancer

Night's Reckoning

Dawn Caravan

The Bone Scroll

Pearl Sky

The Elemental Covenant

Saint's Passage

Martyr's Promise

Paladin's Kiss

Bishop's Flight

(Summer 2023)

The Irin Chronicles

The Scribe

The Singer

The Secret

The Staff and the Blade

The Silent

The Storm

The Seeker

Glimmer Lake

Suddenly Psychic

Semi-Psychic Life

Psychic Dreams

Moonstone Cove

Runaway Fate

Fate Actually

Fate Interrupted

Vista de Lirio

Double Vision

Mirror Obscure

Trouble Play

Linx & Bogie Mysteries

A Ghost in the Glamour

A Bogie in the Boat

Contemporary Romance

The Genius and the Muse

7th and Main

Ink

Hooked

Grit

Sweet

Made in the USA
Middletown, DE
15 March 2024

51599923R00187